Pastries

Pastries

A NOVEL OF DESSERTS AND DISCOVERIES

BHARTI KIRCHNER

St. Martin's Griffin ⋈ New York

PASTRIES. Copyright © 2003 by Bharti Kirchner. All rights reserved. Printed in the United States of America. No part of this book may be reproduced in any manner whatsoever without written permission except in the case of brief quotations embodied in critical articles or reviews. For information, address St. Martin's Press, 175 Fifth Avenue, New York, N.Y. 10010.

www.stmartins.com

Library of Congress Cataloging-in-Publication Data

Kirchner, Bharti.
    Pastries / Bharti Kirchner.
        p. cm.
    ISBN 0-312-28988-X (hc)
    ISBN 0-312-33096-0 (pbk)
    EAN 978-0312-33096-5
    1. Bakers and bakeries—Fiction. 2. Americans—Japan—Fiction.
3. Seattle (Wash.)—Fiction. 4. Women cooks—Fiction. 5. Pastry—
Fiction. 6. Japan—Fiction. I. Title.

PS3561.I6835P375 2003
813'.54—dc21   2003040600

First St. Martin's Griffin Edition: August 2004

10 9 8 7 6 5 4 3 2 1

For the whole gang:

Tom, Kachi, Didi, Satyada, Rinku, Tinni,
Nivdeditamami, Dollymasi, and Apumami and her family

ACKNOWLEDGMENTS

First of all, I'd like to acknowledge my editor, Linda McFall, and literary agent, Liza Dawson, who were enthusiastic from the beginning and provided invaluable guidance in the most ambitious fiction project I'd undertaken.

For their expertise and support and for being generous with their time, I am grateful to Barbara Galvin, Diana Stadlmueller, Diane St. Marie, and Karen Bell.

Others who have helped me considerably include Jim Molnar and Laura Fine-Morrison.

For answering my questions, I'd like to give loving thanks to Leslie Mackie, Masako Seikimoto, Renee Mroczek (who also read the first few chapters), and Genjo Marinello Osho.

For their encouragement and for taking the time to read some pages, I wish to offer my gratitude to John Keegan and Alice Peppler.

Special thanks to Jim Frey and those "Freyers" who were present during the birth of the book. And to Barbara McHugh.

I have found the information in Buddhism: Japan's Cultural Identity by Stuart D. B. Picken helpful and have drawn on it frequently.

Most of all, I'd like to thank my husband, Tom Kirchner, for his love and unstinting support.

Long I thought that knowledge alone would suffice me.
WALT WHITMAN

*In the depth of winter, I finally found that within me
there lay an invincible summer.*
ALBERT CAMUS

Pastries

ONE

I, SUNYA MALHOTRA, AM A WOMAN WHO LIVES TO BAKE.

This morning I spring out of bed at five A.M., just as the sparrows are beginning to twitter, and soon drive, bleary-eyed, the ten blocks to my bakery.

Once in the airy kitchen, I go straight to the counter, caress its marble surface, and revel in the joy of its clean, cool touch. Before long I am sifting the pastry flour into a mixing bowl with a rhythmic motion—I can't resist occasionally dipping my fingers into the sensuous powder. A glance at the wall clock tells me it's time to stop dawdling and get cracking. Egg yolks slide into one bowl, whites into another. The yolks shimmer like a pool of captured sunlight; the whites repose, a limpid mass that magnifies the mosaic pattern on the bottom of the copper bowl. Finally, I set the pieces of premium chocolate in a water bath over a low flame where they melt into dark liquor with a bittersweet perfume. Whipping egg whites became a ritual for me a long time ago and I begin to make quick strokes with a handwhisk.

In the background, the notes of a Baroque melody float from the radio.

Roger, the recently departed love of my life, drifts into my mind; he adored that Baroque piece.

These solitary morning hours are still the hardest, but I'm passionate to work, to bake my signature creation, the Sunya Cake. In only a few hours, a newspaper food critic will interview me about my bestselling item; just the thought puts me on edge.

I am the sole proprietor of Pastries Café, a trendy, twenty-seat bakery in Seattle. Lately in food circles, my Sunya Cake has created quite a stir, thanks to sensational reviews and word of mouth. This success is all the more surprising because the café is tucked away in the quiet residential district of Wallingford, five miles from the glitter of downtown and its boutiques, nightspots, museums, and restaurants.

A wide variety of Seattleites flock to my establishment to sample Sunya Cake and end up coming back for other treats as well. A weight-conscious saleswoman says she takes the whole morning to finish my cumin-carrot muffin, whereas a college student, who's "addicted" to the same muffin, loads several in his backpack at each visit. My favorite city councilwoman regularly drops in and wolfs down a double order of flan, calling it her self-indulgent reward for putting up with the mayor. And the mayor has just ordered three Sunya Cakes to entertain a trade delegation from Singapore. But despite Sunya Cake's success, it's tough to be in a business where the average profit margin is in the low single digits.

A month or so ago, matronly Mrs. Cohen, a longtime patron, asked, "What kind of a name is Sunya?"

"It's Indian." I didn't tell her any more, even though I could tell she was dying for details.

Mrs. Cohen finished adjusting her glasses and continued her subtle prying. "Indian? How interesting. Always wanted to see the gardens of Delhi."

"I've never been to India myself."

Mrs. Cohen returned to her table, but the scent of her lavender perfume lingered as I went back to arranging the pastries in the showcase. Am I really Indian? For someone who grew up in Seattle, lived with a Japanese man for a while, and bakes French and American pastries for a living, India exists only in the news, Mother's spicy cooking, the Alfonso mangoes I buy at the grocery store, and, perhaps, the yoga sessions I infrequently attend.

I was born in Seattle a year after my parents emigrated from India. My father, a Buddhist, picked my name at birth. Two days later, he disappeared, leaving my unemployed mother to fend for the two of us. Mother had only a small savings account to cushion the blow. For years after he left, she maintained the hope he'd return.

I've always wondered what prompted him to choose the name Sunya when it's not a common Indian name. Part of the answer came the day I turned seventeen, but only because I asked Mother directly. We were seated on the porch of our apartment building at the time under the light of a full moon.

"Your name is a shorter form of the Buddhist word *sunyatta*," she replied at length, her voice falling a bit with each word. "It means 'emptiness.'"

Why a name that sounded so joyless? My heart aching at the implicit rejection, I searched her moonlit face for an answer. I saw myself—an unassertive nose, steep cheekbones, dark wistful eyes that seemed darker because of their intensity, and hair as black as Puget Sound at night.

A light breeze brought a snatch of music from a neighbor's open window. "What do you mean, 'empty'?" I asked Mother, unable to keep quiet.

She gave no answer. As she rose and walked back inside the

house, I caught the sorrow in her steps. Was she blaming my birth for Father's desertion? Not for the first time, such a possibility struck me. I swallowed the experience.

On the night of every full moon since, I have pondered the significance of my name and wondered about the father I never got to know. In the photo Mother kept on top of her vanity, my father looked distinguished, with a tumble of curly hair over his right eye and a crescent scar above the left. His skin was the color of chestnuts.

During my years with Roger, who was born and raised in Japan, I developed a general fondness for all things Asian though, in verity, I still have no understanding of Buddhism. I sigh today as I did then.

An acrid scorching smell fouls the air. I whirl around and find my pricey chocolate charred. How could I have been so careless? Every pastry chef learns that temperamental chocolate, highly sensitive to fluctuations of both heat and humidity, is the toughest ingredient to handle. Until this minute, I believed I'd mastered it. I find this lapse in my baker's instinct terrifying, especially now, with a deadline hanging over me. By eight-thirty, the cakes must be ready to fill advance orders. Hurriedly I scrape the scorched paste into the sink and switch on the fan.

Then I glance at the lineup of old familiar standbys on the counter—pastry flour, eggs, sugar, leavenings, chocolate, vanilla, and my secret ingredients. The flour has been freshly ground from soft winter wheat, the sexy Venezuelan chocolate obtained from a renowned purveyor in Salt Lake City, the plump fragrant vanilla beans flown in from Papantla in Mexico. I use only the highest quality raw materials to ensure the best possible product.

I hover over the second batch of chocolate mixture, breathing the buttery mist, until the correct temperature, the glossy stage, is reached. At last, I swirl the dry ingredients into the moist ones, working more quickly than usual, particles of flour rising around me. I divide the batter into several cake pans, slide them into the oven, and close the door with a bang. With a free moment on hand, I ponder the alchemy taking place inside the oven, how the high temperature is fusing a few choice ingredients into a triumphant confection—rich, delicious, unforgettable, and uniquely Sunya. As I sponge down the countertop, I declare I have begun the day anew.

An unbalanced chocolate scent wafts out of the oven. Oh, no. I have forgotten the vanilla extract. It's the fine details—the edge of Grand Marnier, the spike of a hard bit of citron, the bitter streak of espresso, and, in the case of today's baking, the jolt of vanilla—that distinguish my dessert cookery. My café would cease to exist if I lost that touch. Too late to fix the mishap now. Snatches of conversations from the café indicate my junior baker Scott has just opened for business.

In less than a minute, Scott—pale, auburn-haired, quiet, and still getting the hang of a pastry worker's job—pokes his head through the door. "How's it going?"

We discuss the day's schedule. As he turns to go back to the bakery counter, he says, "I was taking the garbage out just now. I saw a guy loitering in the parking lot. I think I've seen him a couple of times before."

"Must be the garbage collector or the meter reader," I reply absentmindedly, still thinking about the missing ingredient in the cakes baking in the oven.

"I don't think he's either—no uniform and garbage pickup is on Tuesdays," he says as he withdraws. "You might want to be careful."

Scott's appearance provokes a question I've been asked frequently: Why do I slave in the kitchen when I have three cross-trained assistants laboring round the clock?

The answer is simple: I let them handle other cakes, pies, tarts, and puddings but not the Sunya Cake. It's a secret recipe I carry in my genes. I'm the one who created it. This very thought affords me a fleeting feeling of power. Today I badly need that.

A while later, Scott peeks in again to announce the arrival of food critic Donald J. Smith. It's a jittery moment, even though as a restaurateur seeking exposure, I should welcome Donald. He writes for the city's most prestigious newspaper, the *Seattle Daily News*. Two years ago, Donald cited me in his weekly column "Fine Dining with Donald." Though he allotted just a small paragraph, it was a significant event around here, mentioned by patrons for months. The column, now a browned custard shade, hangs on the refrigerator, the lettering still dark and legible. Donald declared:

> Sunya Cake is tasty, beautiful, hypnotic, and lyrical. It's an accomplishment perhaps only my mother could match. But my mother doesn't have the secret recipe. Only Sunya Malhotra has it—and she isn't telling.

Since then, Donald has made prodigious attempts to acquire the "secret recipe," which he believes will give him cachet with his readers. The last time he came to visit, I let him sample the cake to his stomach's capacity (which is ample) and allowed his photographer to shoot all the photos he wanted (as many as thirty), but refused to part with the recipe. Donald is nothing if not persistent, and so any encounter with him leaves me a touch rattled.

Now Donald waddles into the kitchen, all two hundred forty pounds of him packed into a checkered sport jacket and dark trousers, his hair the color of wheat toast. As usual, he has a scarf draped around his neck. At sixty, he has had a lengthy career with the *News*. He was raised on beef, spuds, and frozen apple pie, and has a definite bias in favor of the regionally based big business. In short, he represents old Seattle. Many readers believe his retirement is long overdue and his taste buds no longer conform to the city's current preferences for an infusion of international flavors, but he's stubborn and refuses to let go of his territory.

Donald's eyes sweep the kitchen as he sniffs. "Must be heaven to work here."

"Yes." I shake myself out of the trance, force a smile, and pull up two chairs. Donald takes his seat, while throwing a glance at the kitchen counter strewn with a fifty-pound sack of flour, a thirty-pound box of pecans, an industrial-size KitchenAid, a high-heat spatula, and a massive beechwood rolling pin.

"These are all part of the baker's arsenal," I say, as I serve him a mug of coffee and a wedge of a cherry-almond scone from a heaping platter. I had intended to dish up Sunya Cake and find myself hoping he won't notice the omission.

"Definitely the right metaphor, Sunya." Donald's voice gathers more strength as he goes. "As a matter of fact, I'm planning to write about the impending Bakery War."

"Bakery War?"

He looks away, though I spot a smirk playing on his lips. "Cakes Plus is opening a branch just four blocks from here," he says. "At the corner of Meridian and Fifty-sixth, what used to be the site of M and R Produce Market. It'll be more than double the size of your bakery. Their new management is very aggressive, as I'm sure you're aware."

Hands in my lap, I sit in absolute stillness. This is the first time I've heard of this development. My café, though it barely ekes out a profit, has become an informal social center, a pied-à-terre to the patrons. Surely, they wouldn't desert their second home for some franchise.

"I don't think we serve the same clientele." I play with my coffee mug, feigning a lack of concern. "People come here because of the quality of our goods, the ambience, and the fact we're small. They like small, Donald."

"You wouldn't be the first small business that Cakes Plus steam-rolled." He pulls the scone apart and examines its fruit-flecked interior. "Just between you and me—their new scones taste very similar. Almond-spiked dough studded with sweet bits of dried cherry. They didn't somehow get hold of your recipe, did they?"

I lean back in my chair. "That would be highly unlikely."

He polishes off his scone, except for a tiny piece that eludes his grasping fingers. After several attempts, he finally manages to pick it up. "If you don't mind my saying so, yours is better. But they do make a great hot cross bun. Those are making a comeback, did you know that?"

"Another scone?"

He shakes his head, while stealing a wistful glance at the platter. "The Bakery War will be great for those of us who have a sweet tooth, Sunya. Pardon the pun, but I'm sure the cream will rise to the top."

By now, I'm only half listening, as my mind tries to assess the implications of the unwelcome news. How, as a small business owner, will I compete with a long-established bakery financed by the region's preeminent bread company that has enough money to buy a full-page advertisement in the *News*? Donald will, most likely, not be on my side.

"And what's that wonderful smell coming from the oven?"

"Sunya Cake. It's not ready yet."

"And the recipe . . ."

"Is still a secret . . ."

"I'd be willing to give the recipe half a page. Think how many new pairs of feet that'd rush to your door."

"Sorry, Donald. Secrecy is still the most alluring spice."

It's just past nine when Donald finally departs, leaving me feeling even more off-center than when he arrived. As it is, espresso wagons and drive-in coffee bars are cutting into my business. And now a new competitor? It is then that the Sunya Cakes come out of the oven; they are flabbier than usual. My spirit dampens further; I'm used to flawlessness and the praise that comes with a perfectly executed product. I frost the top. As I shave frilly curls from a block of chocolate for a final garnish, Scott rushes in to wheel the cakes away to the sales floor.

"We missed our eight-thirty deadline," he says.

I turn away. How could I have done that? This is the first time.

"By the way, Mrs. Hawthorn would like you to autograph her cake, if that's not too much of a bother. It's for her young granddaughter, who loves just about everything from this shop."

Despite the compliment, I'm in such a funk that it takes me a few minutes to collect the tools—a pastry bag oozing with whipped cream and a star tip. Soon I am signing my name on the cake surface with a flourish.

Minutes later, I'm taking inventory—rotating the oldest flour bucket to the front—when I hear an insistent knocking at the back door. I turn around. Roger is standing stiffly, well put together in his crisp blue-striped shirt and houndstooth pants, holding a cardboard box under one arm. I wipe my hands on my bib apron—even now, I'm impressed by Roger Yahura—and invite him in. We stare at each other for a long instant. I take in the solemn expression, the determined jaw, trademark well-pressed short-sleeved shirt, and muscular arms that had once held me close in a secure embrace. A glimmer of hope flickers within me, as it has all too often these past four weeks.

"Hope I didn't catch you at a bad time."

"No, no. Come in."

He hesitates a moment, then steps inside and hands me the box. Voice empty of joy, "I found some of your things . . ."

I open it: old droopy socks, threadbare T-shirts, a broken watch, and *Surfing: A Book of Morning Poems*, a slim volume he'd given me on my last birthday. I look up from the box and experience an up-welling of desire for the lips I used to nibble, the hair my fingers so gently twirled, the temples I massaged when he was stressed. Massage was the surest way to his heart. *Oh, Roger* . . . The sentiment I feel, but don't express.

He touches the back of his knuckles to my cheek, as he's done so often in the past. The brief contact unhinges me until I catch the expression in his eyes.

"I'm moving to a bigger apartment," he says. "I wanted to tell you before you heard it from someone else . . . Kimiko is moving in with me."

The planet stops rotating at this unexpected news. I squeeze my eyes shut and recall my first meeting with Kimiko Iwata that took place a year ago at the annual Fuchsia Show in the Seattle Center. She—a thin creature, not devilishly pretty, but with tofu-smooth skin—had pushed aside a lock of stretched-silk hair and regarded me with intense obsidian eyes.

"Fuchsias," she said, "remind me of teardrops in fancy skirts."

I was amused. We talked some more and stopped for green tea at a nearby tea parlor. For the next several months, we kept in touch off and on about our mutual interest. And so, last summer when the two huge fuchsia bushes in my front yard, Foxtrot and Fully Double varieties, were blooming profusely in their lavish red-and-purple skirts, it seemed only natural to invite her to a party at my house. I was disappointed when she gave the fuchsias a cursory once-over, turned to Roger, and spent the rest of the evening in a shadowy corner of the living room chatting eye to eye with him. Several times, as I caught the expression on his face, it seemed he'd been struck by sudden summer lightning. Still, I was in denial and thought nothing of it. After all, Roger seldom had the opportunity to speak Japanese in Seattle, much less catch up on news from Tokyo. Conversing in their mother tongue, they both appeared free and happy and instantly intimate.

How foolish of me to trust them.

"How could you do this?" I ask Roger, though I'm not sure I want to hear the answer.

"You should know," he says. "You worked too many hours. All you cared about was this bakery."

"I didn't have much choice. I'm up to my chin in debt. The bakery could go under any day."

"What have you got to show for all your work, your obsession, if you can't even pay your bills?"

"And what have you got to show for all your meetings and demonstrations?" I snap. "Have you saved the planet?"

He blinks at the dig, but at least we're back on a common theme. The passion in our relationship began to subside about a year ago when Roger, bored with his job as a fashion salesman, joined People's Trade Campaign, a coalition of consumer and environmental groups, as a volunteer. I still remember what their brochure said, the gist of it: Transnational corporations—"world elites," "parasites," or "Mafia families"—were taking over the planet.

This autumn the social activists planned to demonstrate against the Third World Trade Conference, also known as the Seattle Ministerial, which was slated to launch a new round of global trade talks. Overnight, artistic Roger lost his inhibitions along with his Japanese accent, and began giving inspired speeches in church basements and neighborhood council meetings. With the zeal nouveau converts often demonstrate, he denounced the evils of globalization, which he said exploited the developing countries, threatened the environment, and undermined regulations protecting consumers and the workforce.

It all sounded like standard radical boilerplate to me. Worse, Roger would come home late and, if I complained, would ask a counterquestion such as, "Does it ever concern you that a farmer in the less developed countries is forced to buy seeds from a multinational corporation when he should be allowed to save them himself?" The cause, which might have been too overwhelming for him, sucked up his time, energy, and libido. When we were together, he assumed a distracted expression I didn't understand. Though his pet phrase on the topic was "Focus on the human face," he hardly focused on mine. We fought, then made up, then fought some more. If he was worried about the cause, I was worried about his safety. These demonstrations could turn ugly.

"Back to criticizing my social involvement again?" Roger's voice breaks into my thoughts.

There comes a faint thud of the newspaper being delivered at the front door and, for a heartbeat, we both fall silent. Neither of us is willing to give ground. I still care, though my voice has a sharp edge. "You just make sure you don't get your head caved in."

He pinches his sparse eyebrows together, starts to draw away, and that hurts. He didn't have to come back and remind me of what we once were. I shove the box under the workbench, saying, "This is all junk. You've wasted a trip."

"So it seems."

The words, cold and brittle, snap the air, as he slips out the door into semidarkness. I hear quick steps, then the noise of a car pulling out of the driveway. The silence and empty door convey a bleak finality. How a man leaves tells a lot about him.

Dazed, I lean back against the kitchen counter. In my head, I go back over the history of our relationship—to my apprenticeship days in Paris five years ago, when Roger encouraged me to follow my dreams. Later, when I tried to secure a start-up loan from banks in Seattle and was without exception shown the exit, he consoled me. "My little apricot, you'll bounce back, even stronger, because of this . . . " (Apricots were the rarest of fruits to him as a child in Japan.)

I'd go back to the kitchen to create new recipes. He'd inscribe advice, comments, insights, and amorous phrases on the back of my recipe cards. After tasting my cherry-plum tart, he scribbled in ecstasy, "Only Sunya's kisses are more inviting." Finally, when I founded this bakery, he became an integral part of it. He came here every morning. He knew where I stored the yeast packets, how many pounds of sugar I ordered each month, the qualities I looked for in a job applicant. The breakup has left me feeling like my river has been cut off at its source.

Just when I am faced with the prospect of a bakery war.

TWO

AT SIX A.M., THE GRAY LIGHT OF DAWN CREEPS IN THROUGH MY BED-room window. Listening to the lilting cadence of the chickadees, I throw the warm wool blanket off and rise. As I shower, my mind still reels from yesterday's news about Cakes Plus moving into the neighborhood. I shuffle over to the closet and choose a well-pressed V-necked cotton-blend dress, black geometric print on a blue back-ground, a Nordstrom markdown. Fashionable it isn't; but no matter, this longish dress and a pair of sensible calfskin flats will see me comfortably through the day and show no stains in the bargain. It will also keep my sexuality hidden, as Mother taught me. I sweep back my shoulder-length black hair into a gold barrette and take one last glance at my slim neat figure. People tell me I am pleasant-looking. As usual, I don't fuss with makeup—not even mascara—or take time to fix coffee. But today is Tuesday and I must take the recycling bin out before I leave the house. I am meticulous about recycling.

I roll the huge bin out onto the pavement and, as I stoop to pick up the morning newspaper, spot a man lounging against the lamppost across the street. He—medium height, early thirties, with blond hair that resembles a wind-lashed wheat field—is wearing a deep brown goatskin jacket. His face is turned toward my house; his eyes are concealed behind purple sunglasses.

Sunglasses so early in the morning?

As I pull the newspaper out of its plastic wrapper, I notice that someone has stuck a white business card under the rubber band. To my amazement, it is inscribed in black with elegant Japanese-style characters. Immediately Roger pops into my mind.

The back of the card is covered with handwriting, also in Japanese. I recognize the curvilinear style of hiragana script, though under the circumstances I'm not able to appreciate its beauty. For now, I stuff the card into my purse. Roger can translate it for me.

Then I remember: There's no longer a Roger in my life.

When I come out again bundled in a quilted coat, car keys in hand and ready to confront whoever is there, the man has disappeared. Out of habit, I take a moment to glance around, feeling at one with the same quiet scenery I experience every morning: the purple berberis hedges that border my property, the red oak that stands resolute on its ground across the street, the sloped roofs of a two-story stucco that peek out of the still-remaining darkness half a block away. For a city dweller like me, this is nature.

Mrs. Petrocelli, an early riser who lives three houses down, is approaching with her poodle. She, our block-watch captain, is a neighbor I stay in touch with. A one-time weather woman at a small-town television station, the widow and empty-nester is now in her seventies and lives alone. On a rainy weekend, when she doesn't like to venture out, I bring her a Danish claw or a wedge of blueberry buckle and we sit down to chat. "Every woman is entitled to just desserts," she quips. She prefers colors that "birth the dawn," which today is a vermilion windbreaker, and "weighty" jewelry, which today is a pair of handcufflike silver bracelets. When I bump into her in the morning, she never fails to give me the weather report. She'd say, "Rain, no Rainier." Or, "The mountain is out." Or, "Thirty-five! Forty! Forty-five!" Coming from her musical throat, the predicted temperatures for the various times of the day would sound like the body measurements of an aging actor.

As I stop to greet her, her dog busies itself sniffing a dandelion bud on the parking strip and, for once, she doesn't fling any Fahrenheit at me. Instead, she asks, "Did you see the blond man?"

"Yes. He was leaning against that lamppost over there. Is he a new neighbor?"

"No, at least I don't think so. I saw him dropping something at your door. From the way he was looking around, he seemed awfully interested in your house." She announces this with a certainty that comes across as a crisp warning, the kind I don't need. Might the blond be the same person Scott mentioned yesterday? Folks around here don't hang out on the sidewalk so early in the morning. He must also be the one who put the Japanese business card at my door. My stomach does a little flip.

"It's probably nothing." I make a half-turn toward the garage.

"He's cute. Do let me know if you see him again. Let's go, Timbuktu." Mrs. Petrocelli tugs at the leash and the dog, a red nylon collar around its neck, follows after her. Even though I don't particularly care for dogs in general, I like Timbuktu.

Once again, I am back to fidgeting about the Cakes Plus move. How can I, who have been raised by a single parent who worries constantly, take such warnings lightly? As I drive through the cherry-tree-lined streets under a hopeful dawning sky, ideas, a wink of a solution, begin to pop up. I can start a catering line, usher in a new pastry a month, take on orders for custom wedding cakes, advertise in select local magazines. Another side of my mind kicks in a duel:

How will I get the extra funds? And manage the additional time and legwork necessary for promotion?

And what to do about that loiterer?

Well, this one's easy. I'll talk to Detective Colby, who's a regular at the bakery for breakfast.

Within minutes, I enter the bakery kitchen to be greeted by the rhythmic thunk-thunk-thunk sound of metal striking wood. I smell the sweet-tart fruit even before I view it. Today is caramel apple pie day. Pierre, my number one baker, is slicing shiny green Granny Smith apples into crescent-shaped pieces, as to be expected. The knife is scoring grooves on the cutting board. Something is amiss.

Pierre doesn't like to be disturbed while he works, so I stand unobtrusively in the doorway. In chef's whites, wearing wire-rim glasses and gazing down intensely, the thirty-two-year-old looks more like a doctor than a baker. Once when I mentioned that to him, he replied that he'd begun a study of medicine in France, but never made it past the second year. This didn't come as a surprise as Pierre is more of an artist than a scientist. He will reduce the amount of sugar in a pie if the fruit is overripe, forgo the egg wash on the top crust at intuition's call, or open the oven door before the timer signals simply because his nose warns him the dessert is done.

The only quarrel I have with Pierre is his hours. I contracted with him four eight-hour days a week, and all was well for the first two years. But in the last month or so, he's fallen into the habit of three ten-hour days, Tuesday through Thursday, and that's not the same thing—I need him here for four full days. This morning I am going to insist.

Today's recipe, hand-scribed on a gilt-edged index card and signed (as I always do), has been taped onto the overhead dark cherry cabinet. Pierre has no need of it. He pours sugar into a pan, measuring by instinct, and sprinkles in cinnamon and cardamom from jars with a flourish. Once finished, his gorgeous presentations, served on their own without ice cream or whipped cream topping, will be gone within two hours. Tasty and pretty, they evoke nostalgia as well. A regular customer, who happens to be a two-hundred-pound longshoreman crane operator, grew misty-eyed at his first taste of one just out of the oven. You never know who has a well-tuned palate or a tender spot buried deep in the heart.

Inhaling the sweet warm fragrance of spices, I watch Pierre dart back and forth between the cabinet and stove. For an instant, I fantasize being out with him on a dance floor, feet nimble in high-heeled pumps, legs twirling about his. But no, he works for me and already has a life mate. I banish the wayward thought, chalking it up to my current loneliness.

With a flick of his wrist, Pierre tosses a handful of the apple slices into the saucepan, the slices that aren't uniformly shaped. Now, finally, he notices me. He calls a *bonjour*, adds, his cheeks turning mauve from the heat, "Must be my thousandth batch of pies."

I nod uneasily at the implication that baking is wearing him down. Not only has Pierre turned out to be an excellent baker, but he's also brought a carefree air, an esprit into my bakery. His sentences are seasoned with *donc, c'est vrai?*, or *de toute façon*, just often enough to convey a sense of Old World chic without alienating the Gore-Tex parka set in this environmentally correct Seattle district. Every morning when he opens the bakery door, a flurry of *"bonjours"* converges on him. Once, when he was serving at the counter, a woman gave him a hundred-dollar bill for paltry dollar's worth of peppermint tea. Jill would have gone hunting for change. Pierre raised his eyebrows, gave an expressive shrug, and delivered a "But, *madame* . . ." The chas-

tened woman rummaged around in her purse and produced four quarters paired with an apologetic smile. I'll never know if it was the
shrug or the accent or just Pierre.

Now he stirs the pan. A wayward stroke of the spatula causes
several apple slices to tumble out onto the stovetop. He picks them
up and throws them into the sink. *"Merde,"* he mutters, as he thrusts
his burning fingers under the faucet. A moment later, he turns the
water off and heaves a sigh.

A concern rises in my mind until I notice that a piecrust on the
counter is weeping tiny beads of liquid. "Do you think there's too
much heat, Pierre?" The crust has to be chilled in the refrigerator or
it won't flake in the oven, and he ought to know that.

Pierre grimaces and switches on the fan on top of the stove. The
cool air and steady noise seem to calm him. He slides a bottom crust
onto each of ten Pyrex pie plates, his face a mask of concentration.
That done, he looks up. "Lately I've been wondering what I want out
of life."

Such philosophizing is hardly an optimistic sign. People don't venture the great questions of life when they're bubbling with happiness.
"What do you mean?" I ask.

"Does fulfillment mean buying another antique vase? Stephan
seems to think so. The other day he went to an estate sale and bought
an expensive copper urn, which he put on our mantel. All evening
he kept staring at it. Sure enough, it had some beautiful, intricate
designs carved on it and I didn't have to get a bouquet of lilies to
make it stand out, but it did nothing for me. *Rien.* There's a missing
element in my life, one that screams at me every so often and tells
me to get off my *derrière* and do something about it."

In the past he has confided to me that, like most couples, he and
Stephan have had their share of disagreements: Where to settle
down? Whom to invite to dinner? How to spend the bonus? And

always, who'll take the garbage out? Pierre, by nature affable, has a tendency to become overwrought at the slightest sign of conflict in matters of the heart. I have seen that happen before. Still, just to have a partner is nice, even one who disagrees with you. I find myself wishing I still had Roger around to fight with. The stab of a dreaded question follows that wistfulness: Will I ever meet a suitable man again? To hold hands, share meals and a common bed, and face our days and dreams together; to have someone whose universe intersects mine. Mother reminds me she was married at twenty-four, an age I passed five autumns ago. It has never been easy for me to relate to the opposite sex. Because I'm an only child and grew up without a father, I find men perplexing. Their language and code of behavior are incomprehensible to me. However confident I appear at the bakery, socially I am reserved; I don't make small talk easily, at least until I know the man well.

"Lately I haven't been sleeping well," Pierre adds.

His uncharacteristic introspection prompts me to further examine my own situation. I peck away at life, like a bird on a tree trunk that never quite breaks into the sap stored inside. I can handle individual days, but not "life." I have collected a long list of "shoulds" and "wants," but they don't rise out of any grand strategy.

"To tell you the truth, I'm perturbed, myself," I confide. "It's been a whole month since Roger and I broke up. I kept thinking we might get back together, but yesterday I found out he's moving in with a new girlfriend."

Eyes brimming with compassion, Pierre looks over at me. "*Désolé*. But if you don't mind my saying so, he wasn't good enough for you. His ego drives him. He carries on about global trade like it's some evil conspiracy. I happen to like the idea of globalization. Doesn't it make the world a single marketplace and give the developing countries a chance? *Mais*, what's worse, he seems to think he can actually stop the Seattle Ministerial. Was he always arrogant like that?"

"Believe me, he wasn't. When I first met him, he was fascinating, and sweet. Coming to America, fulfilling his dream, thinking he has no boundaries, has changed him. He's become cocky. But you're right. It's time to let go. Get thinking about other things. Especially now, with Cakes Plus moving into the neighborhood . . ."

"You really think Cakes Plus can make a go of it here?" Pierre snorts. "We have conscientious customers. Why, they even bring their own coffee mugs and cloth napkins to save trees. For them, personal is preferable to the commercial. I doubt they'll pay much attention to our corporate competitor."

Pierre is not considering the facts that Cakes Plus is open till midnight, offers two-for-one coupons in its newspaper ads, gives free coffee to seniors on Tuesdays, and has lower prices. "I'm afraid, Pierre, in the end our customers might choose Cakes Plus because it's cheaper to go there."

With the gaze of a loving father sending kids to school, Pierre steps back and gives his pies a final once-over, a proud pink suffusing his face. "Why sweat the competition? Worse comes to worse you can sell this bakery and run away with a tidy profit. You know you can get a job at the drop of your chef's toque."

"It's not so easy for me to let go of this spot, *mon ami*. In fact, it's impossible. My mother would never forgive me. You should have seen the expression on her face when I mentioned that I'd dedicate my bakery to her."

Pierre puts the pies in the oven, his steady hands cupping the baking pans as though he's making an offering. I flash back to those early years when Mother, a single parent, hung on to her tiny dough-nut shop to support us. Once, when I was young, five or six years old, she only had enough money to buy milk for the two of us and none to pay for tea bags. So, she served herself a thin blend of milk and hot water and called it "white tea." "If you don't think about it too much," she insisted, "it tastes like weak tea." As soon as I was considered employable, I took part-time jobs after school to help Mother out. On weekends, I worked in her doughnut shop.

Now I shake my head at Pierre, a tiny but strong shake.

He washes his fingers with hand-milled French soap and dries them on a linen tea towel, both personal requirements. *"En vérité,"* he says, "I am perturbed that Cakes Plus will steal some of our customers. Tell you what, Sunya. Give me Thursday off and I'll go visit their main store and check it out."

"No, Pierre, you're too recognizable. I'll send Jill."

Pierre beams at my diplomatic refusal. *"C'est possible.* Somebody did recognize me last night when I went to the Truffaut retrospective over at the Grand Illusion. During intermission a man approached me and said, 'Aren't you Pierre from Pastries?' " A slight pause and he asks, "May I have Thursday off?"

"You may. But in return, I want you to work Monday next week on top of your usual three days. We have a big order from the Women's Funding Alliance for their annual fund-raising dinner."

Pierre's expression is intense with dismay. "Monday is not possible. Stephan and I have plans. We haven't spent much time together lately and he's been complaining—"

"Oh, please, Pierre, it's not just for me. Francine Cole is one of your devoted customers. Remember how she gushed about your sugar poppy garnish on the Mother's Day cake? How she used the cake as the centerpiece?"

Pierre remains resolutely silent. He has a way of closing his lips tight and looking downward to indicate the subject is closed.

"Look, a couple of years ago you didn't even know how to whip the cream. Now you get the biggest bonus and the first choice of vacation days."

How different was the day he came for a job interview. As I showed him around this sizable kitchen boasting three colossal shelves, two huge windows, and a central island—our workbench—covered with an extra large balloon whisk, an electronic scale, and a heavy-duty mixer, I observed a bewildered look alight on his round face. "And where did you bake before?" I asked.

He replied sheepishly, "Actually, madame, I have not worked in pastry at all."

Imagine his nerve, interviewing for a baker's job when he had zero baking experience. I reminded him that my ad in the *Weekly* had clearly specified my need for "An experienced and imaginative baker." I wasn't looking for a baker's helper.

Eyebrows arching up thick and black, he cocked his head to the side and challenged me. "Experience, alas, no. Imagination? *Mais oui.* And you must remember, madame, that I'm French. The cooking, it is in our blood and in our hands."

With the guttural certainty in his voice and his Gallic accent, he reminded me of the culinary stature of his native land. But what made me decide to take a chance were his sturdy capable hands and dazzling attitude. As we say in the pastry business, "The attitude, the spirit, is half the skill required."

I hired him on probation for a month. He failed in puff pastry at his first try (it was leathery), his sponge cake collapsed, and his melted chocolate "seized" (stiffened into an unusable lump), but learn he did by observation and persistence. Before long, in his hands, the components came together harmoniously. He became a master at baking apple pie American style. That came as a surprise since the bountiful indulgence is so at odds with its cousin—the open-face, scantily layered, rectangular *tarte aux pommes* found all over France.

Roger and I first met in Paris over just such a minimalist *tarte*, though right now, I refuse to let myself relive that afternoon.

Apple pie isn't all. For Pierre, the perfectionist, nectarine tarts must have the reddish-yellow blush nature intends but seldom delivers. The plum slices he uses to garnish his famously tall pound cake (baked in an angel food cake pan) must be soaked in cognac overnight to bring out their full flavor. Even an uncomplicated number like shortbread cookies, which Pierre makes on Bastille Day, gets fussed over. He adds rice flour, nothing less, to his dough to make the result crumbly and tender-textured. Last month he bought some bitter honey to play with in his recipe for raspberry linzertorte. His *trucs*, or techniques, are important to him and they clearly elevate his craft to the sublime. Right now, I'd like to shake him out of his black misery. With a Bakery War looming on the horizon, I can't afford a prima donna, even if he's charmingly French.

I resume speaking. "You've got to understand the situation I'm in. I need your help."

"But Stephan . . ."

Suddenly I remember the opera tickets I bought in advance and hid in my jewelry box to keep them away from Roger's eyes. They were meant to have been a present on his upcoming birthday. Every so often, I'd glance at them, get a charge, and rehearse the evening: I'd take the afternoon off, head for downtown, indulge in a facial and a massage at the Spa Club, then get back home in time to don my halter-top evening gown, a chain silver necklace, a lace-appliquéd stole, and stiletto sandals. Soon, I'd glide down the carpeted hall of the Opera House arm in arm with Roger. After the performance, we'd drop in at the trendy Flying Fish in Belltown for a late supper. With a satisfied belly and a heart "as full as the autumn moon"—a Japanese expression Roger often uttered late at night—we'd go dancing.

Now the tickets are lying there, as unsightly as a cracked gemstone. I need to get them out.

"How would you like to go to the opera on Wednesday night with Stephan?" I ask, hoping my voice doesn't sound fractured.

"The opera?" Pierre turns with obvious interest. "Perhaps I *could* work this Monday. But the week after—"

"Let's take one week at a time."

"Stephan will be up by now." Pierre zips over to the wall phone and, with a jerky motion, snatches the receiver from its cradle. He murmurs some endearing French words into the mouthpiece.

Turning away, I allow myself a faint smile. One cake layer stacked on top of another, one tiny goal achieved at a time—this is how I glide through my bakery day.

On my way out the door I peer through the western window of the kitchen. Pearl sunlight burnishes the metal shingles of a Craftsman bungalow. The street is deserted but for a parked white truck with the words "Rent a Son-in-Law: Handyman Supplier" stenciled in black on its side. I venture into the rock garden, only to find the rays are fading. In Seattle, the autumn sun is a fickle guest.

When I arrive home, twilight by then, I find a bouquet of yellow lilies wrapped in crinkly green paper by my front door. What a joy. I pick it up and stare at it from many angles. The blossoms are so bright they seem illuminated from inside. A few buds hold themselves tight, like a magician's fist about to unclench.

Inside the arrangement, there floats a card, and it reads: "A sunbreak for Sunya." Signed, "Pierre and Stephan."

It's their way of softening the blow of my breakup with Roger.

I try not to grip the bouquet too tightly. I must not crush the petals.

THREE

THIS EVENING'S NEWS ON TV GIVES ME A CHILL, EVEN IF THE SHORT segment lasts only for a minute or two. An activist, who reminds me a lot of Ralph Nader, is being interviewed. He delivers an indictment of giant agricultural corporations for seeking to patent basic food crop seeds, thereby forcing third world peasants to buy them at inflated costs.

I turn the set off, recalling the evening a year ago when I heard Roger coming in from work, his steps halting, almost dragging on the carpet. For a change, I'd worked a shorter day at the bakery. Sitting at the kitchen table, I put down the *News*, where I'd been browsing a report about the upcoming global trade conference scheduled to be held in Seattle in November 1999. Outside, the evening shadows were beginning to lengthen, but when Roger greeted me I detected a hint of late-night weariness in his voice. His lips, normally full and warm, were pinched and cold as I kissed them. What could be the matter? In my typically direct manner, I began to probe.

"You look a little weary . . ."

"I'm totally beat," he replied, "and I haven't even done all that much."

"Are you bored with your job?"

"Bored and disgusted."

No surprise there. He'd complained before about the shoppers who walked into the trendy little shop where he worked. Shoppers who thought their fat wallets bought them the right to treat him condescendingly while they looked for yet another new "thing" to fill the hole in their lives. They'd feel better about themselves if only . . . He hated waiting on them.

Aware of my well-worn turtleneck and pants, acceptable though not fashionable, I grew uncomfortable and replied, "What's the purpose of fashion then if not to bring out the frivolous side of a person?"

He crossed to the refrigerator and stood there. He wasn't small but, for once, the Frigidaire dwarfed him. "Fashion—I went into that field, thinking it'd be more than just fun." He'd believed in the twenty-first century, fashion would harmonize us with social, political, and environmental realities. How naïve he had been. Fashion catered to the fetishes of the decadent, fattened the bank accounts of rich investors, and manipulated the great masses into buying cheap knockoffs, which they thought would elevate their social status. "It's sickening," he added.

I could sense the frustration raging within him, hinted at by his vacant gaze and the way he tightened his lips. He'd taken the trouble to immigrate to a new country and, in the end, found himself unfulfilled and tormented by fears about what his family in Japan would think.

My bakery had had a satisfactory, if not profitable, first couple of years. It was my turn to help him now.

"Maybe the floor sales job isn't right for you. Maybe if you did something more original and creative . . . Weren't you thinking about sending your fashion sketches to a New York designer?"

"Yeah, what I had in mind was military chic. Army fatigues, boots, helmets, that sort of thing. It's going to catch on one of these days, but I doubt Seattle's the place for it. I get my ideas from watching people, but they're so gray and brown and loose-fitted and low-key here . . ."

"Maybe not much longer. Check this." I pointed to a column with the heading "Trade First, People Last." "Did you know citizen's groups are already forming in the city to protest against global trade? The newspaper is saying it may not be such a peaceful confrontation. Perhaps that could provide you with some inspiration?"

He turned, opened the refrigerator door, and grabbed a can of milk-coffee covered with unfathomable Japanese writing. I wished he had offered me one, too, but that wouldn't have occurred to him. Eyes shut, he took a sip. "Save the article for me, will you?"

A week later, Roger blew in through the door, several hours later than usual. It had been raining all evening and I had not relished being home alone. Damp weather makes me grouchy, impatient, and prone to imagine the worst. Especially when I'd come home earlier than usual to spend the evening with him.

"Where were you?" I asked, not bothering to hide the petulance in my voice. "It's ten o'clock. I was worried . . ."

His face fairly glowed with excitement, which the lightweight olive blazer he had on and the hint of gold at his throat only magnified. As usual, his hair was uncombed—he liked it that way. "I went to an antiglobalization meeting." He remained standing.

When we were dating, he'd enjoyed sitting around and chitchatting for hours. Now that we were living together, he'd grown remote. It was up to me to ask questions if I wanted to know his opinions about anything. "What happened there?"

He began to recount the evening's events. At first, he checked out the scene and thought it'd be boring: soft eyes, friendly stares, polite exchanges, and weak tea. Then they brought in Vandana

Shiva, India's biodiversity guru, as their featured speaker. As she talked, she painted a bleak future of absolute control where even seeds were monopolized by greedy international biotech corporations. "What a frightening prospect," he concluded.

"Sounds like she planted a seed of a different sort in your mind, beyond fashion . . ."

"It's like my eyes were closed before and now they're open. I came away with a lot to think about. And I have much reading to do." He began to turn.

"That's commendable, dear . . . But did you forget that we were going to have dinner at the Ichiban restaurant? You read a review somewhere and wanted to try it out, remember?"

"Oh, no. I totally forgot. I'm so sorry." There came the ritual rubbing of forehead and a fountain of apologies. "Can we do it next Wednesday?"

As it turned out, we never made it to that restaurant and a tiny regret, a twinkle of an itch, would always stay with me. I could have insisted, but that wasn't my nature, I held back a little. Once I asked him playfully if he realized that forgetfulness killed passion. He only blinked and looked guilty.

But then, in this relationship, I had no one to fault but myself.

FOUR

IT IS WEDNESDAY MORNING AT THE BAKERY AND I'VE JUST TURNED OFF THE oven. The Sunya Cakes, a successful batch, albeit on the second try, are cooling on wire racks. I drift out of the kitchen to the front of the store.

The morning rush is over. My assistant baker, Jill, twenty-one and fresh-faced with truffle-brown hair pulled back into a ponytail, is occupying a table near the entrance with a customer in his mid-twenties. From the lively way she is yakking with him, I can assume he's a friend. I am about to walk away when I confront the emblem on the man's corn-colored T-shirt: a three-layered white cake. Below it bold letters proclaim, CAKES PLUS.

I stop and stare at the logo. Jill follows my gaze and turns on a reserved smile. "Sunya, this is Earl. He used to bake for . . . I met him at a party last night. I invited him to come here."

I stiffen, but a second look reveals sandals, bright eyes, an open face, a ponytail, and a well-worn backpack. How can I possibly hate him? The motto "Know your enemy before you select the sword" comes to mind. I have good reasons to want to speak with him. "More coffee, Earl?" I ask in a friendly tone.

"No, thanks. I don't want to wash away the taste of your poppy seed bundt. I must say it's first class, if a bit fancy for my taste."

I ignore the backhanded compliment and am about to turn when Jill asks, "Care to join us?"

I plunk myself down in the nearest chair. A college student with a laptop looks in our direction, then goes back to typing. "You still wear that T-shirt?" I ask Earl.

"My brother plays in a jazz quartet and Mr. Cartdale has hired him for opening day on Meridian Street. I'm going to help them set up. Mr. Cartdale expects the whole neighborhood to turn out."

Though jolted once again, I put on a pleasant expression and relate to Earl my dream of enlarging the size of this café someday, extending the hours into the evening, and providing live music. He listens with sympathy to the woes an entrepreneur faces in coming up with financing. I conclude by asking, "So, what was it like to work at . . . ?"

"The pay was good, better than the industry standard. Otherwise, pretty unpleasant."

"Unpleasant, why?"

Earl hesitates. Both Jill and I stare at him. "Oh, the things we were asked to do to cut costs," he says eventually. "Like using second-grade flour, and sneaking in margarine with the butter. Like garnishing our Valentine cakes with plastic hearts, even though my specialty was making decorative roses. Once we were told to take day-old cakes, crush them, then reshape and bake them again into a bunch of minimuffins. Only the hot cross buns were made fresh daily."

I can hardly believe my ears. Recycling leftovers is a most unsanitary practice. Shaken but excited at the same time, I turn to Earl with eager eyes.

"We were so rushed. The pork for the humbow buns was often left out on the countertop at room temperature."

This is far worse. In fact, it borders on being dangerous to the public's health. "Food inspector Irene Brown who works for the city health department would like to know this," I tell Earl. "What about the customers? Didn't they smell spoiled meat in their buns?"

"How could they? We spiced the meat so heavily. Besides, customers like freebies. Mr. Cartdale, who owns the operation, hands out free coupons for humbows all the time. The seniors especially fall for that. Mr. Cartdale says the old fogies have no taste buds—serve them whatever. Profit is all that matters to him. 'Rush the idiots,' he would admonish the waiters. Twenty minutes per customer per table was his limit. And he's very competitive. We've all heard the story at his staff meeting. When he was managing a Laundromat, he dropped his prices way low and offered special deals until all the other Laundromats in the vicinity had to close their doors. Then he immediately jacked up the prices. His motto is 'Push the competition to the wall, the way you push a pin into a pincushion.' "

"Sounds like he doesn't lose any sleep over ethics."

"That's an understatement, but it's not my problem anymore. I'm back in school now, studying modern philosophy. What's ethics in business anyway? Whatever makes money is it for most folks. And why not? Customers have no loyalty, really." Earl's eyes travel the room. "They just go for the newest fad. They are goners."

Gazing out the window, I examine the interplay of light and shade in the pathway under the black walnut tree. When I established this bakery three and a half years ago, I didn't anticipate a life of ease. Still the occupation has turned out tougher than I expected. Eight weeks is all I have to drum up a strategy, or my business will be another victim of that predator Cartdale. Tough as the battle may appear, I can't afford to lose it. It's not just my bank account hanging in the balance but also my profession, and along with it my sense of self-worth.

"Listen for my brother's band a couple of months from now," Earl says.

"My customers like it quiet."

In the itchy silence, Jill points out that we have installed the cash register at the other end of the counter to keep the noise down and that our background music, Bach at the moment, is "drowsily low."

Earl rises from his seat, mumbling that he'll be late for a class if he doesn't get moving, and shoves back his chair.

Jill says, "Do you think you can call the health department?"

"I don't have the time. But you can always entice me to come over here, Sunya." Earl winks. "Just make sure you have the poppy seed bundt."

"Not too fresh for you?"

Then, without giving him a chance to reply, I thank him. He straightens the collar of his jacket as Jill marches him to the door, a murmur of conversation trailing them. She gives him a quick hug and he's out the door.

She half turns toward me. "Break time."

With Scott off on jury duty, I am short-staffed as it is. I could call her on break time with Earl, but decide not to make an issue of it. "Okay. I'll take over."

"By the way, we're completely out of raw-sugar packets, Sunya."

"Couldn't you have reminded me yesterday?"

"I thought it was Scott's responsibility."

She is lying, not for the first time. I think of her as a half-grown kid and exercise a measure of forbearance when dealing with her, even though when I was her age I considered myself a full-grown adult. "You know better than that, Jill. Put some regular sugar cubes out, and be back in twenty."

I set about transferring the Sunya Cakes from the rolling racks in the kitchen to the retail section. A glance confirms that all the cus-

tomers have been served. Standing at the counter, I survey the scene
and relish what I see: a brick fireplace, fresh biscuit-colored roses
gracing the tables, recessed ambient lighting between the wooden
beams, ivy trailing down from pots suspended over a brass-trimmed
service counter; and a long glass showcase attractively displaying a
flotilla of pastries in red, beige, and deep brown shades. Mellow notes
of violin caress the air. It has been my intention to create a space
for the clientele to cozy up with a friend, lover, or relative, take on
a novel, or relax in solitude. Mostly, I suppose, I have succeeded.
Right now, I spy Mrs. Cohen sinking deep into the rust-colored up-
holstered chair off in a corner, only her jaws working; fast-talking
Dennis Butler conferring with his mustachioed dot-com partner, oversize breakfast cups before them; Mrs. Chong, a henna artist who's said
to be proud of her full-size fashions, lost in a dream and peach turnover. Sam Khan, graduate student at the University of Washington,
has most of his face buried in a textbook, with only his eyebrow ring
showing; there are several others I don't recognize but who seem to
have blended with the atmosphere. A few hardy souls have chosen
to kick back outside in the serene rock garden that borders the northern edge of the bakery. A headphone, perched on a Little League
father's head, peeks out through the window.

I hear someone enter. A thin man of medium height, clutching
a black binder, sweeps into the bakery. He pauses to sniff, while
taking in the whole room with inquisitive brown eyes. I guess him to
be a good five to six years older than I, probably pushing thirty-five.
His hair is a nondescript shade of brown and his face is on the ordinary side, but there's an imperious air about him, like he's used to
having assistants flutter about. His gleaming white shirt, fitted chalk-
stripe pants, and well-shined shoes afford an overall impression of
class, wealth, education, as well as taste. His kind intimidated me
when I was a struggling student at the University of Washington,

when I did my shopping at thrift stores. But now that I'm a successful businesswoman, I am less impressed. Still, for some reason, I find myself staring at him.

"Good morning." I use my cheery customer voice.

He responds with a nod. Without losing any time, he bends over the pastry case and takes in the offerings, his eyes large, opalescent, and tea-tinted behind thick glasses. He returns to the Sunya Cake sitting on gilded foil in its spot of honor on the top shelf. He regards the cake with evident appreciation. I suspect that it is his intelligence rather than his looks that gets him what he wants.

As if rising out of a yogic pose, he brings his stooped frame erect, and presents an enthusiastic face to me. "Would you like to try a piece of that cake?" I ask, knowing from experience that male customers often appreciate a little nudge when they're having difficulty selecting.

"Yes, and an iced chai."

I slide a cherry-rimmed chocolate wedge onto a white plate and, as a final flourish, top it with a fresh rosemary sprig. His gaze seems transfixed by the spasm of color and form. Where our eyes go, our hearts will follow. I pour chilled chai into a tall glass, set it on a saucer, and accompany it with a tiny silver antique spoon. The clear glass saucer shows off the spoon's silvery luster as well as the filigree work on its handle. Mother gave me the spoon as a gift. I only have it out here so I can polish it in my spare minutes. It'll go back to the kitchen later in the day. Staying in a retail business requires constant analysis of people and situations and a certain nimbleness of mind. This man, I sense intuitively, appreciates the finer aspects of life.

"I heard about this bakery from my brother who lives here." His gaze is intent on my face, his tone complimentary. "He said I should try it."

"I don't think you'll be disappointed. I'm Sunya, the owner."

"Andrew."

Only his eyes light up. Perhaps he comes from a place where smiling openly is considered suggestive or menacing. "Where are you from?" I ask.

"L.A."

To me Los Angeles is farther away and harder to comprehend than Japan. I can't fathom living in a city that size, where one's neighbors are strangers, and where the sun shines every day.

He takes his cake and chai to a window table and sits facing me (though he could have taken the opposite chair and garnered a better view of the street), casually opens the binder and begins to scan it. I take a soft cloth and polish the brass trim of the showcase, all the while studying him. After a minute, still focused on his reading, he reaches out for the cake and steals a nibble. Then he lifts his disbelieving gaze from the papers and focuses on what he is consuming. I smile to myself. A short time later, he examines the pattern of crumbs on his plate as though he were reading tea leaves. Mostly, I think, he's sorry that the cake is gone.

From the periphery of my vision, I watch how his neck arches and how his knuckles jut out from his rawboned hands. I am beginning to get an inkling of his robust spirit and an equally robust appetite. Somewhere a pager beeps.

Does he want more Sunya Cake? I refrain from breaking through his silence to ask.

There's a bustle at the entrance. Five jeans-clad men, bantering among themselves, amble in. One of them marches up to the counter and places a rather large order, while the others cluster around Andrew. They're his subordinates, I assume. He holds court, querying each in turn about the status of their assignments. From this distance, I can't hear much of their conversation. The crew seems to be on a tight schedule, for they pick up their coffees and biscottis and rush toward the door. Andrew gets up, pushes the chair back to its place, nods in my direction. Our eyes lock momentarily. I experience a tingling inside me, delicate and tentative as the first flicker of a candle flame.

Then I put the antique spoon away and chide myself for paying so much attention to a customer. Am I that desperate?

I resume polishing the brass.

FIVE

LATE MORNING ON THURSDAY I INSPECT THE PASTRY CASE, LURED BY THE tantalizing smell of nuts melding with white chocolate. Jill has just brought in an almond torte, a new offering on my menu. I've decided to introduce a new pastry every month to hold the interest of my customers and this attractive, two-inch-high beige ring, with fluted sides and a white chocolate finish, is my opening salvo in the Bakery War. I am also soliciting special orders from businesses, again in an effort to combat Cakes Plus. Now it comes to my attention that Jill, in her haste, hasn't allowed the flavors to ripen. The cake should have sat on the kitchen counter for at least an hour.

Jill's halfhearted effort should come as no surprise. With Pierre calling in sick, Jill has grudgingly taken on the additional responsibility of cakes and pies. Better known around here as the "Custard Queen," she has a knack for making creamy desserts of all types. Give her eggs, milk, sugar, and a few flavoring agents such as rum, kirsch, Kahlúa, or orange liqueur, and she creates—paints would be a more appropriate word—voluptuous desserts that slip off the spoon as if of their own accord. Last year, I taught her how to make crème anglaise and she mastered that on the first try. Sadly, she lacks Pierre's obsession with perfection, as is evident from the spotty dusting of confectioner's sugar on the cake's imperfect surface.

I am about to take the cake back and hunt for the sugar shaker when I spot an Asian woman sauntering through the door. Attired in a tailored black suit, double string of pearls, and medium heels, she is perfectly proportioned, neatly put together, and oh so composed. I give her a welcoming glance—each new customer is a small victory. Then I recognize her and stop mid-stride. As our eyes lock, she musters a gracious smile. "Sunya-san!"

Kimiko Iwata, my erstwhile friend and, now, Roger's girlfriend. She never forgets the honorific "san."

Her grip tightens on the chic alligator purse hanging from her shoulder, though she continues to smile. "Just happened to be in the vicinity. I hope you don't mind my dropping by."

"Of course not." I walk toward the cash register at the other end of the counter, hoping she'll turn around and find herself a seat.

Instead, she trails after me. "Roger doesn't know I'm here. I came strictly on my own."

Roger. How do I obliterate memories rooted as deeply as the source of my breath? As I turn, my gaze pauses on the rustic-framed, nine-inch-square print of a half-split apricot hanging on the opposite wall. Roger helped me acquire the sketch earlier this year in my effort to lighten a dark corner. He had a good sense of what kind of art fit in where. When I stood on a stool and hung the print, he steadied the edge of the frame. My fingers brushed the top of his silken hair.

Maybe Kimiko can read my mental state. She hovers there a few seconds, rustling and folding a newspaper and asks, "Do you have time to talk?"

I am about to say no when Mother's image floats into my consciousness, bringing with it an incident from my childhood. On a Sunday afternoon, Aunt Madhu, the cumin-breathed community gossip, had come over for a surprise visit. My mother, though frazzled from a hard week at the doughnut shop, smiled, fixed dinner, chatted, and stifled yawns till ten, and I kept wishing she spoke her mind a little more. Afterward when I asked why she put up with that woman, Mother replied, "She was a guest. Guests are Narayan." Then she used a Bengali phrase, *Jano na?*—"Don't you understand?" She followed that with a lecture on how in ancient India, lacking Holiday Inns and Denny's, the masses were obligated by custom to take care of anyone who knocked at the door, even strangers. It could be the god Narayan in disguise, testing you, people reasoned. No one took a chance. Certainly Mother didn't.

I find myself replying to Kimiko, "Let's go to the garden."

In the tiny garden, where every rock is perfectly in place, we settle ourselves on a bench by the petunia patch. I let my eyes wander over the late-season explosion of soothing pinks and purples. Some plants don't give up their lust to flower even in cool autumn weather.

Kimiko breaks the trance, "I read about the Bakery War this morning."

Is it a sense of pity then that has brought Kimiko here? Pity that a larger business will overwhelm me? My impulse is to grab the folded newspaper from her hand and scan for the offending news item, but she's clutching the paper tightly. "The columnist is gossiping about you."

Immediately I'm on alert. Seattle may have turned into a major metropolis but it takes little for it to revert to small-town behavior. Here, traditionally, news spread by word of mouth and could make or break an eating establishment in short order.

Scott, who has been hovering in the background with an expression of barely concealed curiosity, walks up to us and interrupts Kimiko with, "May I get you something?"

"Demitasse coffee with cream. What's fresh in the showcase?"

"Everything we serve is fresh, ma'am, but the almond torte is still warm from the oven."

Inwardly I smile. Scott's been well coached. He's laconic and private, but in times of need, he delivers. He times his appearance perfectly, speaks with conviction and nonchalance, and he's protective of me, which is evident from the private look we just exchanged.

"I'll try a slice."

"And you, Sunya?"

"The same."

Kimiko turns her head toward me. "Oh, what a lovely garden. First time for me to sit here."

I come back with, "Roger designed it."

Silence hangs between us, both of us contemplating the phenomenon of Roger, until Scott returns with a tray hoisted in his hand. Like a good hostess, I wait until Kimiko picks up her fork and breaks off a piece of her cake. This she does hesitantly, as if reluctant to damage the cake's delicate interior. As I dig into my piece, I discover that the taste is slightly off. Jill hasn't toasted the almonds before grinding and, as a result, the cake hasn't reached its potential. Could Kimiko possibly have enough of a palate to discern this shortcoming? The next instant I chide myself for having this malicious tendency to underestimate her.

Kimiko frowns, takes another nibble, reflects on it for a brief second, sets the plate aside, and picks up her cup. "Last night Roger's cousin Bob Nomura brought us his chocolate cheesecake. Did you ever meet him?"

I shake my head a tiny no. Roger mentioned his cousin, that's all I can remember.

"Bob came from Kyoto to study at the California Culinary Academy and recently graduated at the top of his class. Now he's here to work. It was absolutely the best cheesecake I've ever had, Sunya-san. Roger went wild over the hazelnut crust."

A new baker in town is making a great cheesecake without my knowledge? The Seattle food scene has so expanded that I can no longer stay in intimate touch with all the new talent.

The question must have revealed itself to Kimiko. "Bob's not known around here," she plunges on. "Not yet. He's so new, but so very talented. He buys the best ingredients he can find in the market and does everything from scratch. As Roger says, the Greeks invented the cheesecake, but the Japanese perfected it."

"And just where might I find this perfect cheesecake?"

"At the Georgian. Bob is substituting for the regular pastry chef, who's on vacation. You must try it in the next few days, Sunya-san. This is his last week there."

Ah, the gracious Georgian, the top restaurant in the Four Seasons Hotel, with its exalted ceiling, well-spaced tables, and impeccable service imparting the feeling of a more genial era. Roger took me there on my last birthday. We spent a splendid evening over artfully presented, contemporary Northwest dishes. Right now, my respect for the unseen baker goes up a notch. But . . . Kimiko is yet to make her point. Her eyes on the swelling moss on a rock, she seems to be in no haste.

I gaze down at my empty plate. "Well, Kimiko, it was nice of you to stop by."

She looks down at the *News*—her eyes zeroing in on Donald J. Smith's column—and begins to read out loud. " 'But Malhotra will have to double her business to survive.' " Abruptly she raises her smooth forehead above the newspaper. "How will you double your business, Sunya-san?"

"My bakers will be working longer hours."

"Starting next week," she persists, "Bob will have a couple of days a week free."

"I'm not planning to hire another baker, if that's what you're getting at. And since you're here, why don't you take a piece of Sunya Cake home for Roger? He likes it with a large glass of milk." With that I make a motion to rise.

"You misunderstand me." Kimiko tenses her voice slightly, probably as tense as she ever makes it. "I liked you, Sunya-san, the very first time I met you. And I have great respect for bakers. You might find it hard to believe, but I want to help you. I'm sorry it didn't work out between you and Roger."

I don't need her pity. And as for her gesture of friendliness . . . Well, I have to see if it's for real. "Have Bob call the Sorrento Hotel. They're expanding their tea service and might need a pastry chef."

As if by magic, a pen and a notepad appear in her hand. In neat slender strokes, she scribbles a reminder in flowing Japanese characters, puts the notepad back in her purse, and the cap back on her pen. She reminds me of a well-organized dressing table drawer.

Then she rises on her feet, thrusts the *News* into my hand, bows slightly, thanks me, and backs out, taking tiny steps, as though her legs are struggling through the folds of an invisible kimono.

I stay seated on the garden bench for a while longer.

SIX

IT TAKES AT LEAST AN HOUR TO DISMISS THE KIMIKO INCIDENT FROM MY mind. Around noon, with a few minutes to kill, I call the party planner at the Washington Athletic Club. Their yearly Father-and-Daughter Dance should be imminent. In the last two years, my bakery has catered desserts for that special affair. Now the party planner informs me that Cakes Plus has offered them a better deal and henceforth will be their vendor of choice.

"Sorry, Sunya," the woman concludes. "Your cakes are yummy, but I've been told to cut costs by my management. Dessert is one place where I can be a little cheap. After a full dinner, dessert is not such a big deal."

I tell her that diners do pay attention to the dessert; that a meal ought to close with something sweet and lovely for the final taste and a sight to linger on the memory; that a bad dessert annihilates the effect of a fine meal.

"We'll consider you again next year. Thanks for calling."

Painfully, I put the receiver down.

———

Around four o'clock, while I'm on the phone with Northwest Food Bank arranging a pickup for the unsold "day-olds," Pierre glides into the kitchen and makes a beeline for the shelves.

I finish the phone conversation, then ask, "You're here on your afternoon off?"

"Just came to see if I left my cell phone somewhere." Clothed in a light-colored corduroy shirt and cotton flannel pants, he appears cheerful. As he combs the shelves, he remarks, "I wonder if I lost it over where they were filming. We were watching and I got distracted."

"They were filming what?"

He sneaks a wary glance at me. "Ah, a story built around the upcoming trade conference."

"A documentary?"

"No, according to the newspaper it's a feature film, a love story. Stephan and I watched the filming over by the Wells Fargo Bank. There was a crew of about twenty and they had traffic backed up for at least half a mile."

The news of the movie shoot exhilarates me. I can't wait to tell Mother. The Indian in her worships movies. She tells me in India people consider movies—"fillim" as they pronounce it—glorified Technicolor dreams, a means of uplifting themselves. In a land where politicians have been found to lie and steal and sadhus turn out to be fake, movies deliver a comforting escape from the everyday routine. In the anonymous darkness of a cinema house, young and old stay glued to chairs for three long hours. They come away feeling goofier; they conjure themselves taller, richer, and brighter. It could be due to the genes Mother has passed on to me, but in my mind, film folks wield magical power. But all magic, I remind myself, is temporary.

"We even saw Andrew Johnson," Pierre adds. "Do you know who he is?"

"No."

"He's an indie director from L.A. who directed *Storm Country*, which was a big hit at Sundance some years back. I thought he'd be some wild guy in a black T-shirt and long tangled hair down past his shoulders. Funny, but he was decked out in a Brooks Brothers shirt and dress trousers. He has a nice *derrière*."

Why did my heart skid? Do I even want to concede that it did? With a casual air I ask, "What does he look like?"

"Medium height, terribly thin. Mid-thirties."

"Does he wear glasses?"

"I believe Monsieur does. Why?"

"I'll bet it's the same guy who was in here yesterday. He had some of my Sunya Cake."

"Really? He was here?"

"Yes. I talked to him briefly. Jill was on a break."

"If he had the Sunya Cake, he'll probably be back." Pierre's blue eyes twinkle in merriment. "Perhaps I can get his autograph next time. If I'm not here, will you get it for me?"

I look down at my thick, three-pocket waist apron with its silly print of oversize habanero chiles, the same one I wore on Wednesday. I need a lighter, prettier apron; I do think Andrew will return. Maybe I'll have a film director for a regular customer, at least for the duration of the shooting.

"Jill stood and watched him too," Pierre says teasingly. "She'd like to get to know him better, I'm sure."

Silently I make up my mind to give Jill Wednesdays off from now on, just in case Wednesday does become a habit for Mr. Johnson. Jill often bitches she can't get up on Wednesday mornings after spending Monday and Tuesday with her boyfriend, a flight attendant who flies most weekends.

Pierre gives up his search, frustration painting a frown on his forehead, helps himself to a leftover pear turnover from the refrigerator, and grabs a stool. He doesn't usually nibble much during working hours but now, as he stabs his fork into the gooey, caramelized pear slices, he succumbs to the pleasures of his own creation. We like to spend time this way—talking and arguing together in the kitchen. For a few passing seconds, we both lapse into silence. The phrase "instant gratification" is thrown around in baking circles as the reason why we bake, but I think that a baker's gratification comes slow and late, from the pieces left over at the end of the day. Bite after bite, we determine if all the ingredients worked together in harmony, which is what Pierre is doing right now with the discerning palate of a professional.

He must be satisfied, for now he asks, "Do you know the blond fellow with sunglasses who loiters around the building?"

This is the third time someone has pointed that man out. Unwilling to reveal the funny feeling I have about him, I ask casually, "You noticed him too?"

"*Oui*. It's rather curious. He just hangs around, watching who's coming and going. Actually, he's quite nice-looking."

"Robbers do that sort of a thing when casing a bank."

"He's probably okay. And besides, this neighborhood has all kinds." Pierre recites his list—gardeners, slackers, elderly ladies, novelists, cats, and even a transvestite flamenco dancer, but he doesn't stop there. He describes the dancer. All decked out in slim-heeled dancing shoes, bouffant skirt, and skyscraper hairdo, she got out of a truck the other day, sashayed over to the corner postbox, and slipped a letter into it with a theatrical flourish. "It was a sight."

"That blond man isn't a recent addition to your roster of neigh-borhood characters, is he, Pierre?"

"*Mais non*. But what makes you think that he's up to no good? Perhaps Madame has been reading too many mysteries?"

"No. I just read mysterious people." I step out of the kitchen with a disquieting feeling.

SEVEN

THE HEADLINE ALONE IN DONALD J. SMITH'S LATEST COLUMN UNNERVES me. With a little trepidation, I reread what he says.

BAKERY WAR HEATS UP

When asked about the war, Sunya Malhotra calmly reminds me that her bakery has been in existence for three and a half years and has turned into a retreat for the neighborhood. She believes premium products and loyal customers will save her. But, in my opinion, Malhotra will have to at least double her business to survive. If I guess correctly, her kitchen is getting hotter these days. Will she be able to stand the heat?

I do hope we haven't seen the last of her sublime Sunya Cake, though.

They sure haven't!

These last few days have not been the best, what with the constant interruption from people, well-meaning and otherwise, asking me about the Bakery War. The reaction to Donald's column has been widespread and vocal. One overimaginative patron, a stringy-haired retired historian, says he visualizes me sword in hand like Joan of Arc. Another asks me why I don't stay open till eleven P.M. like Cakes Plus does, as if that were so easy to do. A sweet elderly lady has volunteered to copy and distribute a leaflet about my bakery at the bus stop, but so far hasn't followed through.

This afternoon as I'm whipping up a batch of lime curd, tinkering with it to achieve just the right balance between acidity and sweetness, Mother rings me to say she's in the city and will drop by. She must be coming over to see for herself how I am doing after the publication of the article. And rightfully so, I remind myself, since she's partly the power behind the start of this bakeshop.

As I strain the shiny lime seeds out through a sieve, I travel back to the time six years ago—a time of innocence—when hope murmured its amorous words to me.

It was the day I finally quit my job as a customer service representative at Mayberry Department Store. I hated my intrusive boss, a late forties man with sleep disorder, who once went so far as to phone me at home on a sick day just to see if I was there. And despite the fancy job title, the salary barely covered my basic expenses.

Later that morning, I stood in my apartment kitchen, my eyes caressing the oven where a pan of date diamonds was baking. A warm fruity aroma rose up, first to my nose, then to my forehead and cheeks, and I started to hum in pleasure tinged with uncertainty. This was what gave me a charge, chopping, mixing, and kneading in the kitchen, turning out pies, scones, cobblers, and puddings for friends and neighbors. Over a period of a year or so, I'd refined this bar-cookie recipe, tweaking it till it was perfect.

Waiting for the timer to go off, I considered my career options. A year out of college, I'd tried working for a corporation and hadn't liked the job, the boss, or the pay. So often at night, I'd have a recurring dream: I'd enter a bakery, giddy with hopefulness. The glass-front case before me would be stocked with glamorous confections of all sizes, shapes, smells, and colors. Just as I started to reach out with my hand, mouth salivating, I'd wake up, and wonder what the dream implied. What did I really hunger for? Do those pastries represent fulfillment I craved but never really got? Would a career in the pastry industry be the right choice for me?

The timer rang. With gloved hands, I popped the date diamonds out of the oven. The crumbly oat top was toasted just so and the rich soft fruit pieces underneath bubbled merrily. A cloud of homey fragrant vapor settled over me as I allowed the pan to return to room temperature. Once, out of impatience, I touched the heated rim of the pan and winced.

A self-taught home baker, I was sorely lacking in the professional training requisite for operating a commercial bakery. How would I acquire that skill?

In the afternoon, toting a few foil-enclosed pieces of date dia-monds, I went to visit my mother in Mount Vernon, a town north of Seattle. It's a modest brick house, Mother's, with an entrance to the north. (Mother had attested before buying this fixer-upper that vatsushastra, India's version of feng shui, recommends north or east facing entrances.) We took our seats in her living room just as the fog lifted to reveal a luminous vista of the Cascade Mountains through a bank of windows. But I was in no mood to appreciate the snowy grandeur of the peaks.

Mother unwrapped the date diamonds, poked at one, and praised its gentle perfection. In silence, I listened. My limeade glass remained untouched.

"What's the matter, Sunya?"

Head down to the jewel neckline of my sweater, I explained my

latest job catastrophe, knowing that repeated failure is not the pre-
rogative of an immigrant's daughter.

"I love you so much, Sunya, I feel even your tiniest pain like it's
my own. I have never tried to run your life, truly, not even once—
you've grown up so independent." She hesitated in her motherly affection and bit her lower lip, but ultimately asked, *"Ki korbe?"* But
what are you going to do? It wasn't so much a question as an expectation.

I had the answer and it came from visiting a French bakery, Le
Délice, in San Francisco on a recent weekend: the gentle nudge of
puff pastry, seduction of pastry cream, fillings and toppings that required one to pause and reflect after each bite, loads of ambience.

"I'd like to study baking in France." I finished the sentence barely
above a whisper and examined Mother's face for reaction.

The large umber eyes widened even more. "France? Why so far?"

I gave details about how American cooking schools focused on
fish and meat cooking, which didn't interest me, whereas in France
baking was highly respected. I could have gone on: French pastry
chefs learned their craft so well that if they ever migrated over here,
they were at the top of their profession. I'd like to have that kind of
expertise. Quick learner that I was, a short course would do. Besides,
I'd done my homework. Seattle had plenty of room for gourmet bakeries, especially those that served French-inspired American pastries—
a growth area.

Mother's mouth twisted in a smile of nostalgic pain. "That was
my dream, too, to have a full bakery."

She never articulated what she really wanted, which might have
had to do with her upbringing, which dictated a "girls must keep
silent" code of behavior. While I was growing up, she rose at two
A.M. every morning and worked at her shop till four P.M., rarely ever
complaining. She dressed in the efficient attire of trousers and a top,

though she hated trousers, which she considered manly. We lived much of our day inside a confining little cubbyhole where the air was thick with the scent of cinnamon from Vietnam, nutmeg from the West Indies, and saffron from India, what we called our "kitchen kingdom." She let me stir the sugar syrup, while she sifted the flour and crooned a song from India, whose words I didn't understand. As customers appeared, I'd hustle across the hard cement floor bearing their orders from a creaky window that served as a counter to Mother in the back. I did that so often during the day that my tender feet ached all night.

"Why did you run that doughnut shop for so long?" I now asked. "From what you've told me, you had never even tasted a doughnut before you left India."

"*Taito.*" That's true. "I took to doughnuts right away." Her dark complexion still retained a reddish cast from being so close to the stove for so many years. Her lips had always been pale, rough, cracked. She never remembered to use a lip balm. Yet her face flushed as she recalled those days. "I practiced and practiced until I came up with the best method of preparing them. What I made, I made with great care. I even cut my precious silk saris to make window curtains for my shop."

Red-orange curtains shot with gold, on an alley spot. The woman was particular about her doughnuts and the upkeep of her shop, that I'll vouch for. She used yeast to raise the dough, so the finished product would be light tasting and textural, even though that committed her to a more elaborate, time-consuming process. When deep-frying the fritters—always in small batches—she kept the oil temperature as close to 375 degrees as possible. A deluxe candy thermometer helped her achieve that goal. As she worked, she made me sweep the shop floor constantly to keep it spotless, despite my childish whining.

To keep my young mind occupied, Mother spun stories: How the Pennsylvania Dutch settlers brought doughnuts, at the time no more than fried balls of dough, to America. Then an inventive cook gave his imagination free rein and punched a hole in the middle of the dough, thereby shortening the frying time. "Now, why didn't I think of that?" other cooks no doubt have lamented, Mother would say laughingly. The story amused me; at the same time, it planted in my young mind a kernel of inspiration that someday I ought to let my imagination run free. Mother's doughnut shop was an incubator for dreams I cherished, those I hold even today.

"I like your confidence, Mother." Now I tell her, "It's a pity that you didn't have an opportunity to do more."

She stared at her gnarled, ringless, arthritic fingers. (She'd sold all her jewelry to start her business.) "I couldn't take the risk. And I never will. But you, my daughter, you can. You have the limber fingers of a pâtissière."

I sat in silence, recalling what my neighbor, Mrs. Uspensky, said when I took her a batch of date diamonds earlier that day. When are you going to open a bakery, Sunya?

"When will you open a bakery?" Mother asked.

"It takes a major investment, Mother."

"My life's savings are not much to speak of."

I looked away to hide my embarrassment. How could I ask her for more than what she'd already given me? I felt fortunate just to have her time and affection. But another side of me, stuck like a fly behind a closed window and desperate to free itself, came up with a reply: "I'll pay you back with interest . . . And I'll always take care of you. You know that."

Mother turned to gaze at the mountain, a pattern of behavior she displayed whenever she needed time to analyze a situation with ramifications. "I know you will," she said after a while. "It's competition that worries me. Big business. They let me take the risk of starting a doughnut shop. Then when I became successful, they gobbled me up. I'd have liked to hold on to my shop a few more years . . ." Lines of sorrow creased her face. "I know you mean well, but what happens if . . ."

"If I, too, am forced out of business . . . ?"

"Yes. How will you pay me back? How will you take care of me? I barely have enough to live on. Even though your intentions are good, *ami jani.*" I know that.

"I have to take a chance, Mother. I'll find a way to take care of you . . ."

Eyes to the Cascades, Mother grew silent. I bet she was weighing the risks. She must have decided I had a chance to succeed, for at length she smiled. Her face relaxed, became lit. It was as though she'd made a key decision and, somehow, set her dreams free.

"I couldn't win out," she said, "but you would. *Ami jani.*"

She rose, a carefree expression setting her cheekbones agleam, and breezed out to the bedroom. It was as though she were already living vicariously and gaining some satisfaction out of that. I glanced at my untouched limeade glass, picked it up, and took a long sip. As usual, she had given it an extra kick with fresh-pressed ginger juice. Then I raised my eyes and marveled at the sheer ramparts of the Cascades, wondering at the same time what extraordinary stamina and courage it must take to scale them.

Mother returned, her eyes still glittering, her eyelashes damp by now, and produced a bank check. A flutter of excitement, the promise of a great future, surged through me, even as the uncertainty of the venture did its best to show its daunting face. Again, I gazed at what promised to be my ticket to a better future. Mother's signature was larger than usual and she'd scripted the amount with a careful hand. I swallowed around the lump in my throat, as I accepted the check from her.

Mother extended her hand and touched my head in a blessing and full support. I felt humble and, at the same time, exhilarated.

"Go study baking in Paris, my child," she said in a clear, happy voice.

Now Mother bustles into the kitchen. She moves quite nimbly for someone whose thickened waistline is discernible through the mandarin-collared, well-fitted sweater jacket she has on. Even after decades in this northern climate, she wears her outer garment as though it's an inconvenience to be endured temporarily until she returns to her hot humid native land. Her hair is bound up in a little nest at the nape of her neck. I drag a chair over for her and help her out of the jacket.

The spirited smile confirms that she likes this little courtesy extended to her but, as usual, she protests, "You don't have to stop working just because I came. *Elam ektoo.*" I'll stay just a short time.

Her makeup, which she has started applying only recently, has caked like parched earth on her chin. Still, I am fond of Mother's kind, composed face. That face tightens in the lower forehead region only when she gives voice to her concern about the Bakery War.

"Don't worry, Mother," I put in at one point. "You know I don't give up easily."

I pick up the citrus zester and begin to zest a lime, my gaze focused on the transparent green ribbons as they slip into a bowl, mind awhirl with thoughts. I don't want to give Mother even the slightest reason for concern if I can help it. Her blood pressure has a way of rising at the first sign of stress, sometimes going past 180 over 100. And, even though we squabble often, we're very close, a natural consequence of taking care of each other for years.

"It's such a huge challenge." Mother stares out the window, though I'm sure she's not contemplating the deep maroon of the laceleaf maple tree. "I wish Roger was around to help you."

That's a switch. During my early courtship days with Roger, Mother had misgivings about him and Japan. She'd read a myriad of samurai novels and distrusted the warlike tradition they portrayed. Over time, as Roger taught her about modern Japan, she became a convert to taiko drums, *sumi-e* brush paintings, ikebana, anime films, and origami.

I grab a hand towel from a drawer. "Don't mention that name again, Mother. I don't need him around. I'll make it on my own."

"You won't close this bakery like the newspaper says, will you?"

"Not a chance."

Mother sits quietly for a few seconds; her quietness scares me. "Dushan said he'd like to talk to you," she says.

I cut away the bitter white pith of the lime and discard it. I loathe Mother's fiancé, Dushan Bashich. Though younger than her by a decade, he orders her around constantly. A recent arrival from one of the perennially unsettled Balkan countries, he is prone to arguing on the slightest pretext no matter what the topic. Why does he still have to be that way? As I grip the severed lime, I also try to establish why the man wants to see me.

As if sensing my reluctance, Mother adds, "He has a *bhalo matha* for financial matters." A good head.

Apparently, Mother thinks that Dushan, loan officer for the Home Street Bank, can help me out. In my past attempts to raise capital for the bakery, I have encountered more than my share of bankers.

Most turned out to be visionless nervous watchers of the bottom line. Perhaps this also unveils in part why I am not particularly fond of Dushan.

"I'm having trouble paying the loan I've got, Mother. In fact, I may be late in paying you this month. I've got a few extra bills that I wasn't expecting."

"*Deri? Koto deri?*" Late? How late? Mother looks up at me, her eyes bulging with alarm. "Did I tell you I have to put in a new roof? My roof is twenty years old and starting to leak. I've been holding off on the repairs until you pay me, so I'll have enough to cover the down payment."

Imagining a cracked roof, rainwater seeping through and drenching Mother's hair, her catching a mean cold, I shiver. "It'll only be a couple of weeks."

"All the more reason to talk to Dushan, my dear." Mother craned her head toward the stove. "What are you making over there anyway?"

"Would you like a taste?" Receiving a prompt nod, I spoon some lime curd into a miniature tart shell, top the ensemble with whipped cream and toasted coconut, and serve it to her with a flourish. Hopefully she won't pursue the topic of Dushan.

Mother takes a tiny exploratory bite. Years ago she taught me how to analyze the components of a dish with small initial tastes before the mouth becomes overwhelmed. Her lips puckering, she asks, "What's in this besides fresh lime?"

She listens carefully to my explanation of how I've tempered fresh-squeezed lime essence with bottled Persian lime juice and frozen blood orange nectar for that extra dimension of fruity tartness. Her motto has always been: "The end could be found in the beginning." In dessertese, this means the final result depends on the quality of the raw materials one starts out with.

Just when I think we've moved on to a more congenial topic, Mother says, "I believe Dushan would like this lime curd. Yes, he would." She gives an emphatic nod.

I turn my face away. At the edge of my peripheral vision, I sense Mother is watching me.

"I know he can be overbearing at times, but he cares about me a lot . . ."

I am about to inject a "but" of my own, when Mother plunges on. "It's been so long since I've felt this way. I've finally let myself trust a man again and I can even talk about it. I was never able to express what it was like to be without a partner for thirty years. O baba." Mother used a Bengali exclamation to indicate a difficult situation. "Your father was supposed to have been the gentlest soul on earth, a wise being, an honorable man, and look what he did to us . . ."

I've heard Mother articulate the same sentiment many times, but I am still terribly affected. There's that whole unsolved mystery of Father disappearing though, secretly, I still haven't given up hope of finding him. Whenever I pick up a newspaper, I scan it for the name Prabhu Malhotra, half expecting it to appear somewhere in connection with a chemistry research project. Since he was a highly regarded academician, I've even used the Internet to search for his name in the departments of elite universities. So far, nothing has turned up.

Mother now shoves her empty plate away, peeks at her new engagement ring—solitaire in platinum—and her eyes take on a long-missing luster. She hadn't been able to afford jewelry or frivolity of any kind till she met Dushan. Why couldn't I be more understanding of him? I scan Mother's face. She radiates happiness in a way we want our mothers to do.

"Dushan is very eager to speak with you. Don't be surprised if he stops by in the next few days."

"Shouldn't he check with me first?"

"I've already told him it's okay."

The lime curd should immediately go into the refrigerator—any disturbance will liquefy it—yet I stand, bowl in hand, unable to move, furious at how Mother exercises her power over me.

"I know what's good for you." She stands up, her chair making an irritating scraping sound, then slips out the door in her usual delicate way, turning once to utter a benign "Thank you, see you later, *accha choli*," and rendering me speechless.

EIGHT

AFTER MOTHER'S DEPARTURE, FINDING IT IMPOSSIBLE TO CONCENTRATE on the tasks at hand, I migrate to the retail section of the bakery. Jill, wearing a turquoise cotton crinkle shirt and standing at the counter, scrutinizes my face.

"Would you like a cup of tea?" she asks.

Of all my staff, I have the least rapport with Jill. She says little; has a cold front that I haven't been able to warm. Her kind gesture dumbfounds me. "Sounds marvelous."

"Why don't you sit down? I'll bring it over."

A window table is where I settle myself. Soon Jill leans over me with a mug of chamomile tea and murmurs a word of thanks for the next Wednesday off.

"I ran into Earl," she adds in a whisper. "He still hasn't called the health inspector. He said he forgot." Then, her turquoise bead bracelet clicking softly, she saunters back to the counter.

I wish someone would call the health department about unsanitary conditions at Cakes Plus's kitchen. I drink from my mug. Though the sun outside is weak, this tisane, with its deep herbal aroma so redolent of the earth, is comforting. (We use loose dried herbs, not tea pouches, never.) A pleasant embracing sensation radiates through my belly. I slow down my thoughts.

Images from the past, Mother's stories, come flying to me. How Father disappeared with just a few of his belongings—a suitcase, two shirts, two pairs of pants, some books, and his toilet kit—leaving a terse note on the vanity of our Seattle apartment. When I turned nine, Mother handed me the note and shook her head. Written with fine pen and India ink, in a script even and well controlled, with no indication of a mind in turmoil, the note didn't include a salutation. As though inscribing her name would have lured him back. He didn't bother to sign his name either.

I raised my eyes from the notepaper, not at all confounded to find Mother seething, giving out a small hissing sound through closed lips. She must have touched, scrutinized, and mulled over that piece of paper a thousand times. Ma Durga! She called out to her goddess. Forgive a man who renounces *samsara*? Though a more scholarly meaning of the Indian word was the "painful cycle of birth, death, and rebirth," for common folks it simply meant the duties of a house-holder. Forgive a man who drops the sole responsibility for raising a newborn on his wife's shoulders and takes off? In the months that had followed Father's disappearance, Mother suffered the opprobrium of her Indian acquaintances. They squinted at her darkly like she was a bad omen. The final straw was when she overheard Mrs. Tewari, a self-appointed community leader, remark to her cronies, "When a good man leaves, the reason can be found in the kitchen or the bedroom. In her case, it's not the kitchen." Mother never attended another community function. She even stopped visiting her relatives in India, fearful they, too, would lay the entire blame for the misfor-tune on her.

As she finished speaking, Mother would wipe her eyes and a flame of anger would rise inside me. My young hand would stiffen in protest. Father must be a bad person, a disgusting creature with shifty eyes. If ever I were face to face with him, I'd have a few strong words for him. But secretly (I could never tell Mother), I yearned to meet him, just once, so I could see for myself how disgusting he really was.

Another sip of tea. I picture Mother two years ago as she went out the door on her first date with Dushan. She was so nervous that she forgot to take her purse. At the restaurant, she dropped her salad plate on Dushan's lap. She would not let him hold her hand. These days she laughs about that incident. I'm proud of her. The once-bashful woman has overcome her inhibitions, thumbed her cute nose at the norms of her staid Indian acquaintances, and pursued romance late in life, with more than just a few awkward moments. In contrast to lonely elderly women, like the now-spouseless Mrs. Tewari, who languishes before the television and munches on high-fat gulab ja-mons with friends, Mother attends the symphony in Benaroya Hall with Dushan, hikes up the hills in Discovery Park, indulges in make-over lessons at Nordstrom's Erno Laszlo counter, and generously do-nates her time to the cause of People for Progress in India. Her acquaintances, at the start so disapproving, have begun to regard her with admiration. "A strong woman," Mrs. Tewari is believed to have recently admitted in reference to my mother. "And gentle too." She's planning a bridal shower, a bachelorette party, for Mother. She's promised to invite me.

I snap back to the present when from a nearby table a white-shirted figure nods at me. I return the nod absentmindedly, then re-alize it is Andrew Johnson.

The film director is back so soon? Perhaps he's hoping to see me? I look away so as not to betray my reaction.

Beyond the window, autumn leaves flutter red and gold. I marvel at the endearing sight of a harassed-looking mother chasing after her toddler on the sidewalk, and register the meowing of a cat; a peek at this neighborhood. At the same time, I am vaguely aware of Jill's presence at the counter, her keen eyes casting an inhibiting shadow on me.

In one clean move, Andrew picks up his iced chai and slides over to a chair across from me. A smooth white collar proudly underscores his rough-skinned face. I never thought I'd find bad skin in a man attractive, but those little cuts and blemishes seem to show themselves on him as character trademarks.

"I managed to get a few minutes off and came over here for the Sunya Cake, but was told there isn't any today." His tone seems to demand an explanation. When none is forthcoming he continues. "Actually the apple pie is not a bad consolation prize." He speaks with the self-assurance and authority of an Ivy League graduate.

"One of these days," I slowly let out, "I'll make a Sunya Cake just for you."

His face taking on a bright sheen, he gazes at me with deep brown eyes—a reservoir after a rainfall. The pull we feel toward each other has gotten stronger—the symbiotic bond between the pastry practitioner and the consumer.

"I certainly could use some Sunya Cakes for a party I'm throwing in a few weeks," he says. "It's for my crew. I'm shooting a feature film."

"So I've heard. I have to admit I haven't seen your earlier film, but I won't miss this one . . ."

"I think it'll be worth seeing. It's the best work I've done so far. We're taking some risks and going to use some innovative techniques that aren't often employed in feature films, like actual footage of the trade conference." He talks about having a good staff and crew, and a pool of talent to cast from. "But I need local color and atmosphere."

"What do you need?"

"I have a scene in which two people who meet for the first time show up together at a place. It could be a bar, café, or pastry shop."

"You haven't found one yet?"

"My scout has been on the lookout—no luck so far. I'm rather particular. Actually I've been thinking about this bakery."

"Here?" The question mark is mere politeness. I am flattered. Besides, with competition about to land on my cake plate, any publicity, short or long term, is most welcome.

His gaze sweeps the room, then thaws. "I fell in love with your bakery the moment I walked in. I like the texture of this place and I thought about asking you." He pauses, hesitates, lets out, "But it'll be disruptive. And I don't have a huge budget to pay for it."

I consider the consequences. I can't afford to shut the bakery down for a day and lose income. How would my clientele react if they encountered the Closed sign? Would they ever return? Or would they be excited to visit a place made famous as the site of a movie shoot? I come up with what appears to be an acceptable solution. "Can you shoot early?"

"I guess I could." He ponders a moment. "I'll need to shoot the exterior of your bakery. Would you mind if we brought our own sign?"

"I won't allow that." The rectangular board, hand-painted in yellow and green and nailed just above the entrance, pops into my mind. Mother chose the dramatic shades and stylish lettering. She never forgets to look at the board whenever she enters.

"In that case, we'll use your sign. Also, would you mind if I take a few shots of the inside? The ceiling is high enough for our camera. The ceramic planter you have by the door makes a good foreground."

The safety of my bakery concerns me, but then this is a unique opportunity. "I guess that'd be okay."

"We'll be careful and put things back in their places. We'll start at midnight and be done by six A.M."

"How soon would you want to do this?"

We discuss dates, eventually deciding on next Tuesday, and negotiate suitable payment. "Will there be anyone around to let us in at that hour?" he asks.

"Yes, Pierre, my baker. He's here by midnight. Please try not to disturb him too much. He's a brilliant pastry chef, but easily distracted and more than a bit temperamental. Keep the noise down as much as you can. I'll show up around five."

"Can we use your parking lot? We'll be bringing at least one truck." He looks pointedly out the window to the new condominium construction that is taking place directly across from the bakery. Part of the street has been barricaded, making street parking illegal. "The less distance we have to walk with the equipment, the better."

I nod yes. Of course I'll let him use our lot. At that time, it's empty except for Pierre's Volvo. He can park, bring his equipment through the back door, and then walk on through the kitchen. I'll make it easy for him.

While he scribbles the details in his pocket notebook, I lean back, imagining Mother's reaction. Once a week she drives alone from Mount Vernon to Renton, two hours each way. Her destination is Renton's Roxy Theater, which screens Hindi box-office hits on weekends. Pierre, the cineaste, will also be ecstatic. He goes to movies at least twice a week. And Jill, who's standing at the counter and eyeing Andrew surreptitiously in between ringing up sales, might not mind the filming either. Finally and most importantly, my customers: I envision no trouble there. Many of them are movie buffs.

Now finished writing, Andrew shakes my hand, the grip pleasantly firm. Suddenly I become aware of my body—the tightness of the bra, the sweaty heat of the sleeves around my armpits, the slithery feel of the skirt hem as it brushes my knees.

"Come on, let me show you around."

In the kitchen, Andrew looks around and sniffs. Nostalgia smolders in his eyes as we take our seats. "This smell takes me back a ways," he launches in. "When I was fourteen, I came out here with my dad for a couple of weeks. He was a television reporter doing a piece on the Pacific Northwest and he let me follow him around. I loved the mountains, lakes, and lush green landscape, but unlike New York, where I grew up, there weren't many bakeries here back then. Fortunately, after much walking around, I stumbled on a doughnut shop with the most beautiful silk curtains on the windows. It was hidden in an alley and didn't look like much from the outside, but served the most wonderful cinnamon doughnuts. I've never tasted anything like it, not even in New York. Every morning I used to run up there and order a couple of doughnuts at a time. I'll never forget how the white frosting stuck to my fingers, how I licked it all off. I considered it my biggest discovery on that trip. I wonder if the shop's still there."

My expression must have betrayed my shock. Andrew thrusts his neck forward, a look of concern on his face. "Oh, my, I hope you don't think I was putting your bakery down."

"No, no, it's just all so strange. You see, that was my mother's doughnut shop! The shop's been closed for many years. She sold it and retired."

Andrew sits up. "Such a coincidence. I can hardly believe it."

Doughnut—circular shape—he had to return. That's what Mother, in her folkloric wisdom, would say. I hear Andrew asking, "Were you there? You must have been a young girl."

"I helped Mother after school. Looking back I'd have to say it was good training, even though I didn't know it at the time."

"From the taste of your pastries, especially the Sunya Cake," he says, "I can see that you've obviously inherited your mother's talents. The bakery was a good career choice."

That's what Roger used to say. That is, until I became thoroughly absorbed in my trade and he found himself hating his job. Roger.

Memory. Like caressing a favorite old dress that hasn't been worn in a while. I get hold of myself and answer Andrew by saying, "Fresh out of college I didn't believe that at all. My last job, after I'd completed my studies in Paris, was working for a mortuary. You can imagine what that's like . . ."

Andrew gives out a zestful laugh, one that rumbles up his chest and tilts his head backward. He appears far more accessible in the relaxed placement of his hand on the table. The leader in him has dropped away.

Before I know it, I am telling him about my school days, how other kids taunted me as I passed them in the hallway. They weren't the only ones. Many of Mother's Indian friends owned restaurants in the city, the kind with tablecloths, candlelight, batik work, two-for-one coupons, and stereotypical names like India Pavilion, The Taj, or most popularly Bengal Tiger (regardless of the fact that those tigers were nearly extinct). They considered owning such businesses a prestigious occupation, but deemed running a doughnut shop "low class" work. Socialite Mrs. Tewari, obese even then, stopped inviting us to the autumnal Diwali observances at her home. "You already have some commitments, I've heard," she'd remark to Mother if they met in the supermarket, then bid her a dismissive "good day," and move on without waiting for a reply. And Dr. Hussain, that insufferable self-important cardiologist, could never resist pointing out that in India only the illiterate worked as cooks. Behind his back Mother called him "food illiterate," a man who cleaned his plate in two minutes, then looked bored, one who couldn't tell the difference between a naan and a kulcha. What did he know about the important role food played in Indian culture? Worse yet, what did he really know about the human heart? One day his minimally supervised seven-year-old son tugged on the train of Mother's sari and giggled. "My dad says you can't read or write. That's why you have no choice but to make doughnuts." Unable to endure the humiliation, I slapped him, the only time in my life I'd ever done such a thing. I was twelve years old then. I slapped him with such ferocity that my palm burned. The boy screamed and ran away, crying, "Mommy! Daddy! She hit me!" To my knowledge, he never again harassed Mother. I got a big scolding from her on this, but I didn't care. Besides, I detected a gleam in her eyes even as she berated me.

Aunt Madhu (who wasn't related to us) and a few others remained our allies. Mother would lament that so many otherwise bright people didn't fathom that she made doughnuts by choice; that her fritters brought cheer to the textureless mornings of so many souls.

Andrew listens, really listens, a quality I appreciate in a man. As he leans forward, I get a whiff of his soap, cologne, hair cream, or a fusion thereof—refreshing, whatever it might be. Is his interest genuine, I can't help but wonder, or does he only care about the deal he made with me?

He asks, in a mock-serious manner, "Where's Mrs. Tewari these days?"

"Oh, she's still in the area, comes in every Saturday. She still likes her sweets. You can hardly recognize her. She's put on so much weight that she practically has to enter the bakery sideways."

Another explosive laugh from Andrew. Listening to it, enchanted by it, I raise my eyes to the wall clock and decide to get down to business. I've lost track of the time and so has he. The notebook and the call sheet spread out before him, he asks pertinent questions and jots down the details, pausing to glance up at Jill when she comes by to pick up some silverware. I notice it, yes. It takes another half hour to hammer out the plan, whereupon he snaps his notebook shut, slips it into his back pocket, gathers up the call sheet, and murmurs some words about the pleasure of doing business with me. Then he drags himself out of his chair. Our time is up, I recognize with a touch of regret.

A restrained smile playing on his lips, he bids me a short cordial farewell. I hope our parting handshake has not revealed my tremendous excitement.

Alone in the kitchen, I slump happily into a chair and reflect on the turn of events. My bakery will live forever in a well-known director's feature film.

Eat your plastic heart out, Cakes Plus.

NINE

A T THE INSISTENT RINGING OF THE DOORBELL, I QUICKLY GO OVER TO the front door of my house and open it a crack. It's Dushan, Mother's fiancé, head hunched down between his shoulders, hands jammed in the pockets of a heavy woolen jacquard sweater.

"Hello, Dushan, I wasn't expecting you for another ten minutes. Come on in out of the cold." My energetic voice belies my inner tension. As I open the door, it sticks for an instant. I fumble with it and finally it grudgingly swings open.

Dushan scuffs his feet on the welcome mat and breezes in, ducking his head to avoid some obstruction only he can see. Tall and bulky, with an overfed look, he towers over me, though I don't allow myself to be intimidated.

"I took some time off this afternoon to come see you," he announces, as though delivering the news of an auspicious event. Then he draws out a handkerchief and coughs into it.

"You sound terrible."

"Yes, this cold has got me down."

I motion him to the living room. Though Dushan has neglected to mention the purpose of his visit, I vow to myself not to cross him, whatever the topic is. This time, for Mother's sake, I will simply hear him out and avoid getting lured into an argument. The haunting aroma from a pot of hot cocoa (to which I've mixed in my secret component of a stroke of espresso coffee powder) simmering on the stove bears witness to my good intentions.

I indicate a couch in the cozy sitting area, where a south-facing window coaxes in a few rays of the feeble autumn sunlight. Dushan sinks down onto the couch and the cushion groans in protest. I take the opportunity to steal another look at him. The blotchier-than-usual complexion, sorrowful rheumy eyes, blushing nose, and puffy face all conspire to make him seem less feisty than usual. Mentally I sigh in relief.

I pay him full attention as he talks about a crisis at the bank, where a new check-numbering system has caused mass confusion, even though the topic holds little interest for me. "A lot of earaches for me," he concludes. I suppress an urge to smile at his mangled idiom, as I remember Mother mentioning that Dushan is prone to earaches. Then he tells me about a box of 150 tulip bulbs that he purchased for Mother on sale from Chubby and Tubby's, and how spiffy the blooms would make her lawn appear in spring. "But she'll have to hurry to get them in the ground before freezing weather sets in."

I rearrange the coasters on the coffee table, as I imagine my poor mother digging eight-inch holes for each one of the 150 bulbs. "Of course, you're going to help her, aren't you?"

Dushan looks positively incredulous. His unruly eyebrows rise up on his forehead, as though they want to escape. "Me? I'm a banker, young lady. Bankers don't dig holes in the ground." He sniffs.

Already I'm wound up, which is nothing new. All our past conversations, every single one, have ended on a sour note. Last time was at Mother's a couple of weeks ago. Sitting in wicker lounge chairs on her patio, the three of us were idling away an afternoon over my brown butter nectarine layer cake. In answer to Mother's query as to what made the cake so moist and silky, I'd given away my secret—superfine sugar. Sugar was an uncontroversial subject, I had assumed, that is until Dushan interrupted me. "*Zucker?* Let me tell you about *Zucker.*" His mother, apparently, stocked her pantry with little white pillows of vanilla sugar, a refined sweetener of possible German origin that American pastry chefs, provincial as they were, had never heard of. Pity, he lamented, as vanilla sugar would add an element of European refinement to my already commendable effort. Not that my cake was bad, he allowed. His voice trailed off. That statement was like having the lawn sprinkler spray right into my eyes. Naturally, it drew a reaction from me. Politely I countered that the flavor or the brand of sugar didn't matter as much as the texture. The finer the sugar, the better it absorbed moisture. Dushan, however, stuck to his guns or, more accurately, to his *Zucker* tooth, and on we went for another half hour, the conversation growing increasingly heated, until Mother finally intervened with a cluck of her tongue.

"Would you play a little piano for us, dear?" she interjected, looking at Dushan sweetly. I sat there staring in silence, while Dushan butchered a Chopin waltz. Barely had the off-key note faded away when he rose, gave a bow, and marched over to the table where he appropriated the last piece of cake without offering to share it. That incident made me wonder about his family and childhood.

He appears to have forgotten all about it and is at ease as he tells me about the wonders of an auto show he recently attended. (He, of course, dragged Mother to it.) He reels off a stream of unfamiliar terms such as V6, standard AWD, four-wheel ABS, and off-road capability. I shift in the chair.

"I'm glad you took time from your busy schedule to visit me, Dushan. There must be something important on your mind..." I keep my sentence open-ended to allow him some latitude to reveal his intentions.

In response, he looks toward the kitchen and sniffs once again.

I rise and make a half-turn. "Oh! I was so absorbed in what you were saying that I forgot to bring you some hot cocoa." I dart to the kitchen where, for a beat, the rich cacao fragrance, now at its peak, overcomes me. The caramel-colored brew streams into a cup and froths. I sprinkle cocoa powder on top.

Dushan accepts his cup with a nod and takes a gulp of the scalding liquid. He grimaces, then exhales, a tiny gurgle of satisfaction escaping his lips. The man must have a tongue of steel.

"When I was growing up," he proclaims, "hot cocoa was a luxury. My mother made it only during Christmas. We weren't royalty, she'd say if I asked for it any other time. Come Christmas morning, my older brother would toss down his cup first then, when my mother wasn't looking, take mine away, drink most of it, set the cup back down in front of me, and sneak out of the room. He was such a bully, so I learned to drink fast. He's now in jail in Texas."

A spurt of sympathy, for a little boy crying over his lost cup, wells up inside me. Not for the first time, I wonder about his past.

"Where did you buy this cocoa?" he asks.

"I order it specially from an importer in France. It's deluxe, made from heirloom beans grown in Venezuela. But sorry, Dushan, no vanilla sugar."

Dushan seems to absorb the jab well. "It's the best cocoa I've had in a while. Nothing but the best from Sunya's kitchen, eh?"

I accept this uncharacteristic compliment cautiously.

Dushan clears his throat and leans forward, his craggy features softening. "You have put so much into that bakery of yours, and it has become quite popular. People say the nicest things about you. But lately . . ."

"Lately what, Dushan?"

He shifts his bulk on the couch to better settle his body. "You're a small bakery. You don't really think you can go head-to-head with a giant like Cakes Plus, do you?"

"Head-to-head?" I smile. "Or should we say 'cake-to-cake'? Now that I have had a chance to think about it, I don't see it as going head-to-head. They're a large industrial bakery lacking imagination and atmosphere. All they have to offer is cheap goods in bulk. You get what you pay for. I may be a small neighborhood place, but I provide quality pastries and a spot for people to gather. We're not really in competition. Still I'm making some adjustments in how I run the business. I'll be fine. It's going to be a piece of cake, pun intended."

Dushan takes a long swallow of the hot cocoa, accompanied by a slurping sound. "Like it or not, my dear, you *are* in a competition. And it's a war you are most unlikely to win."

I struggle to keep my hands from forming into fists. "You seem to know a lot about our war."

"Cartdale happens to be one of my clients at the bank, though I'd acknowledge that to only a few people like yourself. And let me warn you, he's formidable."

My angry throat is constricted. "Are you here on his behalf?"

Dushan starts at my direct question, spilling a splash of cocoa on his lap. He makes a face as he reaches for a paper napkin. I ask, "Would you like me to bring you a damp towel?"

His head shakes a big no. Even after he's made several rubbing attempts, a muddy stain clings to his khakis. Finally, he gives up. "I never seem to be able to have a good talk with you, Sunya. Never."

Given our conversational history, it's asking a lot to expect this one to be our first success.

"Cartdale thinks you're a tremendously talented baker." Dushan licks his lips, searching in vain, I guess, for a nonexistent drop of cocoa. "Over dinner the other day he admitted how much he adored Sunya Cake. Why, he even had his cousin order a whole cake for him. He couldn't bring himself to order it in person." Dushan smiles mischievously. "He ate it all by himself."

"I'm waiting for the 'but' part."

Dushan makes a show of wiping his nose with a handkerchief. He slurps the dregs of his cocoa and pointedly looks down at his empty cup, though I refuse to take the hint. He says, "Cartdale would like to buy you out."

The grave tone rings in my ears and makes it plain that he's serious. "I didn't know I'd put my business up for sale."

"You haven't, not so far, but the man is shrewd. He's bought other businesses in the past. He can see the day coming when you'll fold. He'd like to spare you the embarrassment. Here is his vision, as he defines it. He'll keep your bakery just the way it is, with you at the helm, and pay off your bank loans with very reasonable salary deductions. If, in the years ahead, you decide to quit, then and then only, will he change your café to convert it into another Cakes Plus. In the meantime you'll have your bakery, your employees will retain their jobs, and Cartdale will have eliminated his competition."

I am so stunned that nothing, not even the second hand on the wall clock, seems to move. "He's nuts if he thinks I'll go for that. The bottom line is I'll lose control. It won't be my bakery anymore."

"You're so unreasonable, Sunya. Why can't you be more like your mother? She is sweet and gentle and always happy to take my suggestions, which are always in her best interest, I might add."

"Leave my character out of this for now. I'll sell pastries from a cart on the street before I sell my business to Cartdale."

"Can't you see, my dear girl, he's saving you? As things stand, you will soon go bankrupt. What will you do then? How will you pay your mother and your investors back? Cartdale is willing to give you a week or so to think it over. Don't be so hotheaded, for a change, okay?"

"Does Mother know about this?"

"If I were you, I wouldn't bring this up in her presence. Lately her blood pressure has gotten higher, even with the increased dosage of medication she's taking."

"I'm sure Mother's health is uppermost in your mind."

"What do you mean by that?" Dushan glares at me, shakes his head. "Think about it, Sunya. This is the least disruptive solution for all concerned. Nothing really changes."

"Everything changes. All that I stand for vanishes. I may not have inherited my mother's sweet disposition, Dushan, but I've got her tenacity and independence. She fought and fought to keep her doughnut shop against bigger outfits. I'll fight Cartdale the same way. No, Dushan, I will not sell my bakery."

"What you may not know is that the food reporter—Donald J. Smith—is on Cartdale's side. Donald has an offer of an executive position with Northwest Bread, the regional company that partly owns Cakes Plus, when he retires. Donald will not make a single negative remark about Cakes Plus in his column. As you can see, Cartdale has all his bases covered."

My fingers are ice-cold. Like I am standing in the midst of a devastated land in a scary dream. "I'm puzzled, Dushan. Why are you taking such an interest in this? What are you getting out of it, if I may ask?"

"My only interest is your happiness, which is ultimately Dee's happiness."

Dushan is staring at me full in the face. Their wedding date is set for June next year. I visualize my mother. She, a blushing bride, has squeezed herself into a crystal- and pearl-beaded antique-white wedding gown. A tiara on her head, she walks gently toward Dushan, searching my eyes with her soft glance for affirmation that she deserves bliss in her new life. It saddens me that Mother doesn't automatically feel entitled to happiness even now, though, in my opinion, she has long earned it. If I let the rift between Dushan and me degenerate into open conflict, it'll destroy whatever chance Mother has for happiness. A cloud of gloomy frustration descends over me as I contemplate my dilemma.

Dushan seems to interpret my silence as indecision as he continues in a fatherly tone. "Though you may not believe it, Sunya, I truly like you and am trying to help you. You're family to me."

I smile tightly. "I'm honored, Dushan, but my decision is to stay and fight."

We stare at each other. Dushan's eyes bore into mine as if to change my mind by force of will; then abruptly he heaves a sigh. "Hopefully you won't live to regret it."

"That's my problem, isn't it, Dushan? Now, if you'll kindly excuse me, I have to get back to my work."

Silently, through the miasma of the tension that has enveloped the room, I walk Dushan to the door. We each mumble an awkward farewell. He departs with a pained expression on his face, handkerchief out once again, coughing worse now than when he arrived.

I shut the door behind him. Relieved by the quietness of the house, I put on some flamenco guitar music and curl up on the sofa. But I fail to lose myself in the melody.

Any minute now the phone will ring. It'll be Mother, in her rare, frying-temperature voice. What's the matter with you, Sunya? Dushan was only trying to be better friends with you, but you twisted everything he said. And you didn't even offer him any cake. No cake in a baker's house? He was sick and you lashed out at him. Couldn't you have been a little more considerate? Freshen his cocoa? *Ki meye*. What kind of a daughter have I raised?

In the midst of these imaginings, an idea kicks in and inspires me to reach over to the phone. Too bad it has to be me making this phone call. There seems to be no other way to stop a businessman who endangers public health while pursuing relentless expansion. Mentally crossing my stiff fingers, I punch in health inspector Irene Brown's number, even as I imagine her cheerful quip: What's up, Sunya? This is a switch.

Irene has a right to be puzzled. Usually it's the health inspector who initiates contact with a food establishment.

The phone keeps ringing at the other end, the sounds switching eventually to a voice mail message that blares at my ear: I'm on vacation till . . .

What an inopportune time for her to be away. My tone urgent, I leave her a message to call me when she returns. Then I subside into the chair again.

TEN

IT'S TUESDAY MORNING A FEW DAYS LATER. WHEN I PULL INTO THE BAKERY parking lot a little after five-thirty A.M., I observe that several cars and trucks are parked there. Sure enough, Andrew is filming in the bakery, exactly as scheduled. Judging by the blinding light in the windows, some action is taking place.

Already I'm worried. Today is both Sunya Cake and cherry-plum tart day; the latter, fortunately, is Pierre's responsibility. Will I be able to put together my cake in the allotted time? Lately I seem to have acquired a severe case of baker's block. I've lost my touch and it takes me twice as long to complete the preparatory steps.

I snap my purse open, extract the key, and automatically poke it toward the lock, pausing when I discover that the door is already open a crack. Then I remember: Andrew and I had previously agreed that the door should be left open. Stepping into the well-lit kitchen, I sniff in a current of humid air drifting toward the open door. It is bound with the scent of burned, scorched fruit, a true sign that something is amiss. Then I notice Pierre standing in front of a smoldering pot, staring at the floor, a spoon dangling from one hand. Usually he is a bundle of frenetic energy, tempered, just barely, by fierce concentration. The recipe card, its gold borders flashing, is posted as usual on the wooden cabinet at eye level. I struggle with a rush of panic as I wonder what has happened to reduce my master baker to this sorry state.

"*Bonjour*, Pierre. What happened?"

He looks up with a start. "Ah, Sunya! Where have you been? It's impossible to work with all this confusion. I cannot concentrate. Why, just a little while ago the cameraman and another crew member almost got into a fistfight. What is going on here?" Growing more agitated, he begins to wave his hand, sending the spoon flying across the kitchen.

I pat his shoulder. "I'm so sorry. I should have gotten in earlier."

"The sound man complained the fridge was making too much noise. I didn't let him turn it off."

I rush to put my purse down, take off my jacket, hang it on the wall coat hanger, then pour him a glass of water; my fingers are cold. I know from past experience this usually settles him down. He accepts the glass, drinks from it, and clutches it to his chest. "Actually, I could use a glass of wine right now."

"*Désolée*," I console him. "Later."

Pierre sets his water glass down in the sink, hitches a chair, and slouches down into it.

Only twenty minutes left before the bakery opens.

"I'll speak with Andrew right away." I march into the retail section, which is barely recognizable, crowded as it is with cameras, screens, stands, microphone, a tripod, and paraphernalia. A bearded man is yelling at someone. The rest of the entourage is chattering and laughing as they return tables and chairs to their places. Andrew, who is in the midst of shouting instructions, notices me. Hair disheveled, eyes glazed, cheeks hollow, and garbed in a striped shirt and black pants, he stops in mid-sentence and steps closer.

"Is everything okay, Sunya?" The voice is fuzzy from lack of rest. "May I have a word with you in private?"

I lead him to the quietest part of the kitchen under an oak-framed photo of Mother and me standing below the Pastries Café sign on opening day.

"Pierre hasn't been able to bake at all. The noise has disturbed him."

If I'm not mistaken, Andrew reddens a little. "I apologize, Sunya. It's been one of those days. But we're wrapping. If it'd help, we'll go out through the front door. Fortunately, I got what I wanted on the first try, so I won't be causing you any more trouble."

As if an apology were enough to cure today's baking fiasco. I walk with Andrew to the front entrance. Soon about ten people stream out with their equipment, taking the long way to the parking lot. Andrew follows, spinning around to say apologetically, "Talk to you later, Sunya."

As I close the door, I listen to the sound of car doors slamming and eventually the rumble of trucks driving away. I am alone in this. Back to the working section of the bakery. A ball of dough sits forlornly on the counter. Pierre, leaning over the phone, is intent on a conversation. The fruit sauce, still burning on the stove, has overflowed to the stove surface, the smell not exactly sweet. Just below, the floor is freckled with red blotches. With a flick of my wrist, I turn the stove off, and check the clock, a drowning sensation in the pit of my stomach. The time is five forty-eight A.M. and there's no finished tart to deliver to the bakery showcase. Fortunately, Scott had worked late last night and prepared enough rolls, muffins, and scones to get us started.

My train of thought is interrupted by a sharp banging sound, as Pierre slams the wall phone down. He approaches me, his eyebrows rushing into a frown. "I've been trying to reach Stephan all night, but he's not answering."

With a gaze toward the stove, I come in with, "Maybe he's asleep. It's still early."

"Hassles all the time. We ran out of vitamin C tablets, it was his turn to go to the store, but he forgot. He said if I needed vitamins so badly, I should have bought them myself. We seem to be fighting over the smallest things. It's getting worse every day."

It's nakedly obvious that baking is far from Pierre's mind. I cross to the sink. "Are you going to give the tart another try? I'll lend you a hand cleaning up."

"Tart? *Mais* it's your recipe, Sunya. You know best how to do it. I've completely lost my rhythm. My heart is not in place."

"But, Pierre—"

The phone trills, Pierre leaps up, dashes toward it, scoops the receiver off its cradle, and speaks in a low tone. I dump the cherry-plum sauce into the sink and busy myself scrubbing the pot. My arm muscles stiffen from the effort—part of the sauce has scorched at the bottom and doesn't come off easily. The blood red rinsing water stains the sink; the odor burns in my nose.

I turn. Pierre is coming toward me, looking so traumatized that my upper body goes numb.

"Stephan's in the hospital." Pierre's voice cracks, forcing him to catch a gulp of air. "He tried to commit suicide."

Suicide? My grip on the pan loosens; it clatters to the floor. "Oh, my God!"

"Sleeping pills. Fortunately a friend of ours found him in time."

It is as though all the air has been squeezed out of me. "Is he all right?"

"*Oui*, they've pumped his stomach. But I have to go to the hos-

pital right away." Pierre, looking pale and upset, seizes his jacket from
the hanger on the wall. "I hate to leave you with this mess but I
won't be any good in the kitchen today."

Stephan comes to mind, curly-haired, the same height as Pierre,
quieter and less flamboyant. I've seen him a few times, though I hardly know him. He's precious to Pierre, hence precious to me. Now
picturing him in a hospital bed draped with stark white sheets, plastic
tubes dangling nearby, I am struck by a sense of loss and that "anything can happen anytime anywhere" fear. "Is there anything I can
do?"

"No, Sunya. You have enough to handle right here."

"Be sure to call me and let me know how Stephan is doing. Take
tomorrow off if you need to."

Pierre murmurs a *merci* as he zips his jacket, then slips out the
door with a barely audible *au revoir*. I hear his quick steps trotting
across the parking lot. I'll have to manage without him.

In the next several minutes, scrubbing the pot until it is immac-
ulate helps me to return to a more poised frame of mind. As my
employees straggle in, I explain the situation as calmly as possible
and declare with as much confidence as I can muster, "Everything is
under control." Jill's younger than the rest of them but has been
working here the longest. She knows most of the patrons by name,
so I entrust her to open the bakery door and let in the regulars. Her
low "Good morning"—which I peek in to hear—isn't as effusively
welcoming as Pierre's hearty *"Bonjour, bonjour,"* but there's really no
alternative. Shortly the faithful stream in; most head for their usual
seats. Some look a trifle peeved at having had to wait.

I retreat to the quiet of the kitchen and try to formulate a con-
tingency plan. Following a habit, I jot down my tasks for the day in
a notepad and prioritize them. My temples throb from lack of morn-

ing coffee, but I don't want to take the time to pour a cup. Jill informs me through the open door that the film crew has broken a porcelain sugar holder. I instruct her, even as I grit my teeth, to go to the pantry and hunt for a spare bowl. I wonder if Andrew realizes the trouble he's stirred up.

My immediate concern is the tart prep. I suppose I could summon Scott but decide to do it myself, hoping to construct something glorious out of this day. The dough for the crust has been sitting around for a while and has assumed a brownish cast. Out it goes into the trash can. I begin from scratch. With anticipation, I dip my hand into the mélange of unbleached flour, ground cashews, and sugar. My stiff fingers have difficulty crumbling the chilled hardness of the ultracreamy butter.

It's seven-fifteen A.M. when Detective Jack Colby shuffles into the kitchen. He has a sallow complexion; looks perennially fifty-five and disgruntled, the type of man you might find eating alone in a fast food outlet. Despite an air of friendliness, he'll be invisible in a room full of people. As usual, his body is huddled in a rumpled raincoat with collar turned up. The effect lends a comic touch to his otherwise slovenly appearance.

"Got your message, Sunya. Someone loitering? Do you keep cash around here?"

"No cash overnight . . . but I have recipes."

A snicker squiggles out of Colby's nicotine-stained lips. "That's a new one. Why would anyone want to steal a recipe?"

His mocking is offensive. "Because Sunya Cake is so famous, and so far I've kept its recipe a secret. Every business has its treasured possessions. My 'company jewels' happen to be recipes."

"I've often wondered what's in it myself. It's so incredibly rich and tasty." His eyes are on me; his smile is a polite inquiry.

I stare at Colby to make him aware of my indignant reaction.

He wipes the smile off his lips and fixes his stare to the floor. "Well, Sunya, you have to catch the guy doing something . . ."

Just as I get ready to tell him about the Japanese business card, Colby receives a radio call about a bank robbery. "Try to get a good look at him," Colby says on finishing his call.

"Please don't talk to the press," I implore as Colby whips around to leave. His brother is an accountant for the *News*.

"Rest assured no one will find out about this from me." Colby departs.

I turn my attention to the next step in the construction of the cherry-plum tart: the eggs. Out come a large glass bowl and a hand mixer. In the next few minutes, even though the kitchen's temperature is an ideal sixty degrees, I am unable to whip the extra large eggs up to their usual frothy lightness. The arms and the fingers are the first to go in baking, the industry insiders tell you. Such a possibility gives me the jitters.

Four frustrating hours pass before the tarts are done. The cashew crust, which normally has the delicacy of a thin crisp cookie, turns out rigid and brittle. The cream cheese filling, the "soul" of this dessert, splits in the middle, the result of an overly hot oven. The cherry-plum sauce blackens from simmering beyond the allotted time. These tarts are not even close to my usual standard, and still they have worn me out.

My next task is Sunya Cake. I arrange flour, eggs, chocolate, and the rest of the ingredients on the counter in place in the order of use. Then, realizing the futility of even trying to create the cake in my present state, I set the foodstuffs aside. My heart is not in it. The customers will just have to do without Sunya Cake. I ask Jill to prepare a speedy blueberry crumb cake.

For the remainder of the afternoon I busy myself with myriad other chores—reviewing accounts payable and cash flow, tracking food costs, and updating my Web site, even though I don't care for such administrative tasks. I concentrate harder the moment a distracting thought about the bakery buyout springs up in my mind.

The day illuminates for me a little when a local importer of Middle Eastern delicacies drops by to hand-deliver several sheets of mango leather. The intriguing aroma speaks of tree-ripened fruits and women working hard in the field under a blazing sun somewhere far away. I store the purchase on the backside of the refrigerator. The merchant has barely left when Pierre calls to inform me that Stephan is resting well at home and that the crisis is over, but doesn't mention when he'll return to work. Still concerned about Stephan, I don't press.

It's almost five-thirty P.M. before I take a break. A glimpse at my reflection in the bathroom mirror shows a drained face with parched lips. My hair swinging just above my shoulders is limp and sheenless, and the ends are not trimmed. A headache is coming on. As I search my purse—a genuine leather bag with a gold-plated lock, my one luxury—for a lip balm and an aspirin packet, my fingers brush first against the dental floss, then the card the loiterer left behind. Who is he? Is this his calling card? A spot he frequents? Why did he drop it at my door? What message does this contain? These questions grip me, wrestle with me, as I gloss my lips with the honey tangerine lip balm.

Battle-weary but more presentable now, I step from the kitchen into the bakery. Casually I glance out through the entrance, half expecting to catch a glimpse of the loiterer. But the street corner is deserted. There's a doll's house quality to the symmetry of houses and trees in this neighborhood when viewed from afar.

The report from my staff isn't cheery: sales have been low all day. I swallow the gloom and squeeze past a few departing customers to reach the table near the door. My longtime patrons, Mr. and Mrs. Cohen—thank God they've shown up for their afternoon pick-me-up—greet me. The aroma of Assam extra fancy tea teasing the air, Mr. Cohen, a pensioner with a receding hairline, points to the construction work across the street. Another single-family dwelling—in this case a 1930s bungalow—is being demolished to make room for a condominium and shopping complex.

"It'll only bring transient people to this neighborhood," he says.

"Brick by brick our life is changing," chimes Mrs. Cohen, holding a brandy truffle. My mood still down, I listen, and make appropriate noises.

Just then—I blink to make sure—Andrew glides into the bakery. He's freshly shaven and white-shirted. The dark smudges rimming his eyes disprove his eager, even jerky steps. As he draws closer, I confess to a stirring inside, but manage only a small hello. Like I am used to him, like he's no big deal. With all that has happened today, I am benumbed. I ache to go home and cocoon there the rest of the evening.

We stand at a corner. "I'd like to invite you out for dinner," he says.

My mind picks up and discards one excuse after another. Then I spy Jill. Standing sideways to exhibit her nubile curves to best advantage, the peachy-checked server is eyeing Andrew. Isn't one boyfriend enough for her?

Andrew keeps his gaze steady on me, his face conveying a zest and friendly openness. "I had to come up with a really good excuse," he claims, "or my team wouldn't let me go. This is an extremely busy time for us. I just was hoping that you'd be free."

My heart thumps. The fringed scarf beneath my chin is the only stylish accessory I have on. Can I lose this opportunity? If I were to face the truth rumbling around inside, I'd have to admit I have more than a smidgen of curiosity about him. And hunger is flickering through me. "Dinner sounds lovely."

"You name the place. I'm parked two blocks away."

"Let's just walk over to Forty-fifth Street. There are plenty of restaurants there to choose from."

He gives me an enthusiastic nod. My mood soars as I collect my leather handbag and jacket. I haven't been out to dinner since my breakup with Roger. To me food is order, sanity, and, as Pierre would call it, *intimité*. Nothing beats the conviviality and graciousness of a shared table, especially when someone else is at the stove. As a culinary professional, I dream of such an opportunity—to be a "civilian," to be pampered. Because I am inside a bakery all day, I doubly appreciate the atmospherics and scents of a full-service restaurant. To steal a glance at the next table's order. To taste and judge what my peers are concocting. To be inspired. To kick back and just be.

At the door, I smile and give a small wave to Jill. She whips away, but not in time to conceal her disappointment.

What do I care? After all, it's just a business dinner, I try to remind myself, but I fail to be convinced.

ELEVEN

AS ANDREW AND I AMBLE ALONG FORTY-FIFTH STREET'S RESTAURANT district, a mélange of aromas beckons us to sample the cuisines of Cuba, Mexico, India, and other lands, too far from here physically and psychologically. The evening is warming up. The noise of a leaf blower from across the street reminds me this is autumn.

As we pass Ichiban restaurant, I pause to consider. Roger and I planned on trying out this venue at one time, though we never got around to it. Perhaps that unfulfilled wish has driven me here tonight. Then, too, the calling card left by the loiterer may have insinuated Japan to my consciousness. I look up at Andrew and silently wonder: Does he care for Japanese?

From the sidewalk, he sniffs the fragrance in the air. "Smells great. Just like my neighborhood in L.A. Typical of the Osaka region, I'd say."

An eastward tilt. The man is full of surprises.

We step inside, his head jostling a rice-paper lantern, and are seated in a shiny wooden booth. It's still early, we're the first customers, the atmosphere is laid-back, and the cushioned seat easy on the back. The manager is cordial, but perfunctory, as he bows to us and then walks away.

Now comes the uneasiness part. Two single people in an empty room with all the implied social pressures. The space is so clean and tidy that only the babble of multiple conversations could make it seem less sterile. It's one thing to be attracted to a man from a distance; it's quite another matter to be staring at the pores of his face. He's not terribly handsome, which is a relief, and still my cheeks are a hidden fire. I take refuge in the salty tamari smell escaping the kitchen.

His hair sticks up like a new straw broom. The men I like never seem to have a grasp of the hairstyling basics. But somehow, he's all the more endearing because of that.

"I want to apologize again, Sunya, for the upset I caused you."

The tone is personal and the wide-open eyes darkly express genuine regret. I suddenly realize how upset I've been all day. Already, without my chief baker, the shop hasn't functioned too well. "As long as Pierre shows up for work tomorrow," I allow, "I'll be fine."

"I'm so glad you agreed to come to dinner with me. I thought you might still be angry."

I toy with the brown bottle of shoyu. "Angry? Oh, no."

A smile of relief. Then his eyes sink deeper into their sockets. "I'd be disappointed if I never saw you again."

How to get across to him that I've broken up with a boyfriend recently? There's the old pain, whose source I'm slowly forgetting, but whose aching sensation still cripples. As if that's not enough, a discomforting vision of Cakes Plus and their new Meridian branch location flits across my mind. This is no time to even fantasize starting a new romance.

But then Andrew and his underlings already hang out over pastries and coffee at my bakery on their way to and from filming—delicious detour, as they call it. My fingers caress the wooden chopsticks. "Well, you know where to find me in the daytime."

"I'm always happy to see you." Andrew raises the water glass ceremoniously. "To our friendship."

I clink my glass with his. The sound reverberations are still hanging in the air prolonging the moment when the waitress appears. Tranquil in a blue print kimono, hair piled on top of her head in a bagellike bun, she bows to us as though we're special. Andrew's face so softens that the shadowy lines on his forehead disappear. Why do men, who've reached adulthood, fall for abundant hair, long dresses, and tiny subservient women?

With one hand, I take the long stiff menu the waitress offers me, with the other I hold up the calling card. "Do you read Japanese?"

The waitress bows again, this time with a proud smile that shows her pinkish-black gums.

"Would you mind interpreting this for me?"

Bending over slightly, she takes the card with both hands, with ritual respect. Just then, a throng of loud diners makes its way toward a large round table in the back. One woman in the group jokingly asks her companion as she barges past our booth if he can stomach raw fish and seaweed salad. He puffs out his cheeks comically in a mock vomiting expression and lumbers after her.

The waitress, seemingly oblivious to the buffooning or too used to it, scans the card. Her voice is like a breeze wafting from behind a hand-fan as she lifts her head and announces, "It's from a bakery in Kyoto, the Apsara Bakery."

Apsara. Celestial maidens. I turn the word over in my mind. During my girlhood, Mother taught me the word, saying that it originated in India centuries ago in a mythical tale. It came half-way across Asia, meaning intact, to eventually land in Japan. Ancient Buddhist paintings often show *apsaras* in the background. What a fascinating name for a bakery; it implies pleasures of heavenly proportions in the form of baked goodies. But there's more information on the card than just that name, including the handwriting on the back. I'm holding my breath. The waitress lifts her gaze to the new arrivals and her innate sense of duty reasserts itself. She sets the card down on the table with a bow and floats over to greet them. I'm disappointed.

From across the table Andrew casts a curious glance at the card and then a warm one at me, whereupon I give him an account of the loiterer.

"A blond man with a Japanese business card?" he asks.

"This is a Pacific Rim city after all. Sushi is our everyday lunch fare. We celebrate the Bon festival in a big way. Even blond Caucasians study the hiragana script."

Andrew assumes an amused expression.

"Please don't talk about the incident with anyone. It's not good publicity for my bakery and I don't want word of it getting out. Cakes Plus might use the information to their advantage. They're so greedy, you know, they want everything. I won't let them have my bakery. It's my niche, my vision, my pride."

"That's one of the many things I like about you. You stand up for what you want."

Roger would have considered this fierce protectiveness toward my business endeavor a negative trait. I am still savoring Andrew's sweet little approval when the waitress reappears. She rummages around her kimono pocket and comes up with a pencil and a small notepad. It disheartens me that she's forgotten all about the card now that she's rushed. I'll have to hunt for another interpreter.

"Are you ready to order?"

"*Hai.*" I reply yes, the way the Japanese do, with a stress at the end.

Andrew reads out our selections. He watches the waitress as she retreats behind the set of bird-motif curtains, then turns his face toward me and says that he lives at the edge of Japantown in Los Angeles, where he shops and dines and browses the community publications. "I adore Japanese cuisine and couldn't be happier that you chose this place."

Silently I review my own Japan connections: Roger, the loiterer, and now Andrew. What is really going on here?

The waitress returns with our dinners: hijiki salad, pickled cherry blossoms, broiled mackerel, and gleaming rice. Being a nibbler, this is the way I like to dine—with exquisitely prepared fare served in small portions and accompanied by large helpings of good conversation. "Just these few bites and I already feel full."

"The Japanese have a saying," Andrew says. " 'Let little seem like much, so long as it is fresh, natural, and pretty.' Who knows how many haikus, how many paintings, have been inspired by a tiny ball of vinegared rice?"

"Someday I'd like to visit Japan."

Later, when dessert arrives, Andrew picks his up—a sesame-seed-encrusted nugget—and eyes it for a fraction of a second. "This is where I part company with Japan. I don't care for their desserts. No dessert can compare with the Sunya Cake."

"Why, thank you."

"What a lovely name, Sunya. I like the sound of it."

"It's Sanskrit. Means 'empty.' "

"But there's more to it, isn't that so? Buddhists clear their minds to make it *sunya*, so they don't stay stuck. *Sunya* is an emptiness that's full—that has the potential to open up to all of life. It's the beginning of peace."

His interpretation of my name embarrasses me a trifle. I drop my gaze to the teacup and stare at the shy leaves of sencha expanding to their fullness in the pale green liquid. A floodgate of curiosity has burst open in my mind, all the more unusual because I am not at all religious. Only on rare occasions do I attend service at the Hindu temple, where Mother kneels before a gold statue with a flower offering, and where the priest speaks of *puja, bhakti,* and *dana.* The waitress reappears and sets a lighted candle between us. The six-inch candle casts a golden net over Andrew's face.

"How do you know all this?" I ask.

"There was an article in a Japanese community paper not long ago about a Sunya Tradition of Buddhism in Japan."

"Is it some kind of a cult?" Asking so makes me realize how swiftly my mind has jumped to this bizarre conclusion, where I picture nerve gas and passengers trapped in the Tokyo subway. I laugh tautly at the absurdity of the image, though an icy feel runs down my spine. Perhaps it's not a mere coincidence that the loiterer left an address of a Kyoto bakery. In the next instant, I chalk this all up to a case of nerves on a bad baking day.

"Not a cult, but rather a Buddhist tradition." Andrew's voice takes on a teasing tone. "You'll have to excuse me but I always think in terms of film possibilities. If this were a movie, practitioners of that order would be after your Sunya Cake recipe because it's their namesake. In effect, they'd be after you."

The plaintive background notes of a samisen seem somehow familiar, reminding me of a place I've never been. I let go of all my puzzling and adopt a lighter tone of voice. "Speaking of films, is yours based on a novel? What's the title?"

"I wrote the script myself. Some years earlier, I did a film based on Neil Duncan's novel *Storm Country,* but this one's all mine. I wrote it, I'm producing and directing it. It's my baby, and as yet untitled."

"Are you keeping the story a secret?"

"From the press, yes. Would you like to hear it?"

"Usually, I don't like to be told the storyline of a film ahead of time, but since you've written it, yes, I'd like to hear it in your own voice. That'd make it special. I promise not to repeat it to anyone."

"More tea?" The waitress pours. I listen to the exuberant burbling sound. By now, all the tables have filled up; the atmosphere has a richer feel.

Andrew takes a sip of tea in a ritual manner, then fastens his gaze on me, conferring the sense that I've come into his privileged inner circle. His voice is low, for my ears only, even a trifle conspiratorial.

"Picture our guy getting off a plane at Sea-Tac," he begins. "Werner is thirtyish, handsome, medium height, and wearing black jeans and a flannel shirt. He checks into a motel, sets down his wallet, and removes his service handgun from its holster. He's a cop back in Atlanta. Here in Seattle, he's a demonstrator.

"Seven P.M. Werner walks into a meeting of Citizens Against Global Trade, CAGT for short, takes a seat in the last row. A big green banner with bright white lettering on one wall stands out. It reads: 'Peace, Not Guns, Is the Lasting Solution.'

"It's obvious this assembly of about eighty or so people believes in holding hands, silent walks, and singing and beating on drums, not what cops consider 'actions.' Does he, a seasoned cop, really belong here?

"The group leader—tall, bald, glasses, and good posture—announces that the police have cordoned off the area surrounding the Convention Center, the 'no-go' zone, and will arrest anybody who tries to get in. He needs fifteen or so folks to break down the police barriers. 'But think before you do. The cops will be playing hardball this time.'

"One guy jumps up and says he'll come in a turtle suit. No one will touch him. His bravado is greeted with whistles and loud applause.

"Werner is thinking: romantic fools. He listens to a man going on and on about the 'big boys' of transnational corporations. When he finishes, Werner stands up. 'Let me tell you what this is all about—for me.'

"He was raised on his dad's small farm in Wisconsin. Then, as the family operation came under increasing pressure from large industrial farms, his dad was forced to sell at fire-sale prices. The old man, his will to live destroyed, died within five years. Ever since that time, Werner has nursed a hatred for large corporations. 'We love the land,' his father used to say. 'These guys just see it as resource to be used and cast aside.'

" 'Not many farmers will be there,' Werner now cries. 'There aren't many left.'

"Again, everyone applauds. As the sounds die down, a shiver ripples across Werner's back. He's just crossed an invisible line and landed on the 'other' side. These peaceful citizens scare him. Naturally, he doesn't reveal his true identity. He's more comfortable traveling incognito. In any case, these people wouldn't believe that a cop could share their compulsion to oppose immorality.

"The meeting adjourns. Someone calls out to him. It's the quiet Asian woman who sat in the front row and recorded the minutes for the meeting. She's tall, unusually so, and pretty, with a sheer red scarf wrapped around her neck. The usual cop thing, always noticing details, nothing more.

" 'Hi, I'm Emily Takahashi. Could you give me your last name? I didn't get it.'

" 'Noble.' He checks her face to see if she has caught the lie. 'Noble,' he repeats.

"A group has formed around them. 'Coming with us for coffee, Emily?'

"She nods, turns toward Werner, asks him, 'Care to join us? We're going to Pastries Café.'

" 'Let's hope there's more than one piece of chocolate cake left,' a second adds. 'Otherwise there'll be a fight.'

" 'Definitely the best, west of the Mississippi,' a third chimes in.

" 'Well, I guess that settles it.' Werner grins. 'Count me in.'

"They all pile into a Honda. Werner is torn. As a married man, separated from his wife for the first time in their eight-year marriage, should he have accepted this invitation? This is not what he's come here for."

A tinkling brings me back to the restaurant booth, where the waitress has returned and started to clear the table. Andrew stops speaking and glances at her, then takes up his cup, and gazes into it.

I take a sip from my cup and swirl the flavor of the fragrant liquid in my mouth. It is sinking in, this whole issue of cross-border trade; the way Andrew, or, rather Werner, presented it. I grew up working, my mother worked, and I still identify with people who work. People like us value democracy. It's our only chance to have a say in matters that affect our lives.

In an odd disconnect, I find myself replaying Roger's heated lectures on the same issue, words that tumbled out of his mouth. I experience a momentary pang that I didn't understand him at the time. I used to tear my gaze away from his intensity—a sign of my insecurity, I now realize. I took his outpouring of passion for anti-globalization activities as a threat to our relationship, instead of a genuine sense of outrage on his part at corporate greed.

I look into Andrew's eyes. "Your film has given me a lot to think about. How did you come to choose the subject?"

"Mostly from talking with immigrants and small farmers. They told me how the government gives huge agricultural corporations subsidies that enable them to undercut small farmers, especially in developing countries. It has driven most of them out of business and caused major social disruption."

"Are you making the film for political reasons then?"

"In part. I think someone needs to expose the dark side of globalization." A smile. "It's sure better than getting my head broken in some street demonstration."

In other words, the issue is not an obsession for him. When the film's over, he will have done his part and move on. I feel a sense of relief—no Roger, this guy.

"So your characters are going to Pastries." My voice is as whimsical as the scarf around my throat. "No tear gas on the way, I hope."

"Not this time." He falls silent for a second, looks down at the table, then up at me. "I can't tell you the whole story tonight . . ."

"But you have to . . . now that you got me hooked."

"It's not that simple . . . you see. I don't have everything worked out yet."

"You mean to say what you've told me so far is all you've got?"

"No, I've got the overall strategies figured out, and a rough script—but there are details missing. Some scenes in the middle I only have a vague idea about. And I'm still having trouble figuring out how the ending goes."

"Can't you at least tell me the rest of the story as far as you've gotten?"

"Well, okay, but only if you promise to have dinner with me again."

I am seeing the director side of him, a smooth blend of control and manipulation. Though I smilingly say, "Promise," a disconcerting thought creeps into my mind. Have I gotten myself ensnared in his web?

"Where were we?"

"Werner goes to Pastries Café with Emily and the gang."

"In the next few days, he begins to spend more and more time with Emily, though he never tells her who he really is. She fascinates him, this single woman, so dedicated to the organization, so passionate about the issues. She makes him understand that the cause is much bigger than his own narrow concern about farmers' welfare. He's inspired. He's ready to give more of himself. He's also falling in love with her. This is about as happy as he's ever been."

Ah, a romance is in the atmosphere. I sink deeper into my chair.

"Now comes the opening day of the trade conference, the climax of the movie. As he wakes up in the morning, Werner remembers he has to catch a flight back to Atlanta that evening to return to his family. He's torn. Later, standing on the frontline, Emily right next to him, he looks at the line of cops in riot gear and realizes what a huge challenge he's facing."

Andrew pauses; his face is drawn with fatigue from a hectic day, but his eyes still glow. Men often assume a contemplative expression when they don't want you to know them too well.

"That's about as far as I've got. As I said, I'm still not quite sure how it'll end . . . but it'll have to be a tragedy of some sort, I suppose. And there are scenes in the middle I mentioned earlier that need work. Actually, we'll probably have to get together more than once. Maybe you can give me some fresh ideas."

I smile as I glimpse the future. Fireplace and wine, a quiet cozy atmosphere, the allure of Andrew's voice, the charm of his script, and perhaps an answer to the question, What's the story really about? How much of himself has he put into it?

I glance at the watch on my wrist, as I adjust the band. "Oh, my gosh! It's nine. I have to be at the bakery at five A.M." Bending down, I scoop up my handbag from the floor. With the spell of the story fading, reality has kicked in. "Let's get together again for the conclusion. Maybe next week? I have to go now, or I'll be supertired at four A.M."

"You're right, Sunya, I'm beat."

We both rise from the booth. He pays at the cash register, while I wait on one side. Snatches of conversation peppered with laughter hit my ears, but I'm not listening. Rather in these few unguarded minutes, I am watching Andrew—how he pulls the wallet out from his back pocket, then squeezes it back into its place; the grace in his nod to the cashier, the smoothness of his motions.

At the exit, he scribbles his home phone number on a piece of paper and says I can call him anytime. Few people have this number.

Casually I accept it, though my hold on it is tight.

TWELVE

WHO WOULD BELIEVE THAT ON THIS MORNING I'D CHANCE UPON Roger at Tweedy & Popp's Hardware down on Forty-fifth Street? The moment I spot him at the back of the store, he looks in my direction, and our eyes slide past each other. Before I can clamp down on my emotion, the old hurt starts to burn, so I turn away and begin to examine the screwdrivers, soon locating one that looks just the right size. At the cash register, as I present my Visa card, Roger sidles up behind me—that's just his way—a paintbrush in hand. Realizing I am being rude, I turn around. Good manners are essential to him and rank not too far below air, water, food, and the Emperor. His eyes betray a brief flicker of regret, but he manages a weak "hi" and I return his greeting. Minutes later, I step outside the store with him right on my heels, just as the traffic light changes. I cross the street and pause at the opposite curb. Hair blowing about his forehead, he comes up beside me and stammers out an apology about our last encounter in a low voice. Face flushed with embarrassment and anguish, he adds belatedly, "I didn't mean to hurt you, Sunya . . ."

"I guess I owe you an apology too . . ."

"Sometimes you get overwhelmed by people and situations and say and do the wrong things . . ." He shuffles his feet in a heavy way, but doesn't elaborate, then says abruptly, "Do you think we could be friends?"

Quite frankly, I feel as though I've been demoted. In that state of mind, it's not easy to be chirpy or generous. However, given that I am unwilling to analyze the countless shades and nuances of the word "friend" right now, I seize the easy way out. "Sure," I reply, whereupon he confesses how much he's been missing my bakery—his daily fix of pies, tortes, muffins, or crumbles, as well as the sane restorative atmosphere. He confesses he's even tried patronizing Cakes Plus as a substitute, but to no avail. "Their scones are like bullets, Sunya."

I relent. "By all means, come to the bakery."

"I'll be there on Friday at opening time."

Does he mean . . . ? "We have many new items. This week I'm offering a cream scone. It's rich."

"Just hearing about it makes me salivate . . ."

I am about to turn. The conversation has gone as well as could be expected. Then I remember the business card sitting on my coffee table at home. . . . "By the way, I wonder if you could do me a favor," I ask, a tad hesitantly. "Would you mind interpreting some Japanese writing for me?"

"Not ancient literature, I hope. I had trouble with it in school."

I shake my head, laughing.

"I'll stop by your house tomorrow night, say eightish?"

I nod and he takes off.

Roger is half an hour late, which is not unusual. He has a way of entering with such sure steps and aplomb as to make lateness seem stylish. Tingling with an uneasy premonition, I wonder if asking him to come over was such a smart idea. I can't really be friendly with him—there's too much raw hurt still. An image of Andrew sneaks into my head. I'd rather not indulge in that.

For the third time, I check the clock on the living room wall, then peek through a gap in the pinch-pleated window draperies for any sign of a gray Nissan approaching. With darkness cloaking the street, all I see is a blurred reflection of myself in the glass: the center part of my hair, straight line of my nose, wink of the golden studs on my earlobes, and cheeks burning with anticipation.

I flop into a chair. There was a time when I wouldn't let Roger see me in the same clothes—like this ancient flip-tie print blouse and a knit skirt in eggshell—that I'd been wearing all day. There was a time when I'd spruce up the living room just before he came home, hiding extra magazines under a sofa cushion (once they fell out during lovemaking, causing some hilarious laughter), and shoving the sewing machine into a file cabinet.

Shortly after we decided to live together, I purchased this bungalow, the biggest investment I'd ever made. Then came the task of decorating the interior. At the Bon's furniture department, I got to see Roger, the ace couturier in action for the first time. He caressed each fabric to get its feel. "A chair isn't a lifeless object," he insisted. He checked its color, line, and shape, placed it against a wall, examined how it stood out against a solid background, and asked me to sit in it. "A chair can create a whole mood." At first, I was amused that it took a whole day to procure three bowback wood frame chairs, then noticed that he arrogated the final decision regarding the purchase.

"Couldn't you have asked my opinion?" I inquired later.

"It slipped my mind."

"Is that how things were done at your home? Your mother bowing to your father's wishes?"

He looked away. "I thought you liked the chairs."

"That's hardly the point. You've traveled so much, studied in France, and still . . ."

"Young American women are so hard to please . . ."

"Is that it, or do you think young women, in general, are there only to please men?"

He looked disgruntled. The pattern continued and expanded into every aspect of our common life. However worldly he seemed in public—he could talk about baseball, the Brazilian film industry, and skiing from hut to hut in the Alps in the same breath—at home, the "new modern man" expected to be the sovereign. He repainted the inside walls of this room to a seashell color, inviting in more light and animation, again without consulting me. He updated the arrangement of the furniture from the usual square to a diagonal for a touch of the "unexpected," and replaced my tiny stone-top coffee table to which I had a sentimental attachment with a larger glass-top one for "balance and flow." His attention extended even to the way a magazine protruded from a basket. All this was too formal for me, but I went along with it, telling myself that if I reigned in the kitchen, it was only fair that he should reign in the living room.

The fastidious man sorted his pencils in separate holders according to their fineness. Once I tried to figure out the difference between number 2 and number 2½ pencils, but gave up the effort as hopelessly trivial.

Thank God, I don't need to please him anymore. A relaxing sigh escapes me as I glance at the loose pile of magazines: *Pastry Art and Design*, *Shape*, *The Sun*. Sometimes, loss can be a relief. And a regaining of self. Then the doorbell rings, the usual two short buzzes, and immediately the tranquility vanishes.

Roger stands on the porch. Snuggled in a lamb's wool sweater in faded blue-pewter (the typical Seattle sky color) and pleated cotton pants, he seems different, somehow more L.L. Bean and less Saint

Laurent. Vivid images of happier times tumble in my head: Roger crossing the threshold; a passionate embrace and long kisses punctuated by nibbles and murmuring; trying to annihilate the distance that had grown between us during the working hours. Soon a trail of discarded clothing would point us to the sites of a joyous reunion: bed, couch, the rug by the fireplace; it didn't matter. Nothing mattered beyond our appetite for each other.

With a steely resolve, I suppress the memories. I can't afford to brood over those times now.

"Sorry, I got delayed at a meeting, Sunya. Hope I'm not keeping you from something."

"No, no. Come in. Have a seat. Trade conference business, I suppose?"

Roger nods, sits himself on the sofa, and places his feet neatly under the coffee table, perhaps already forgetting that he called this place home. His boots appear new and ominously heavyweight. A glance at the overflowing magazine basket; his eyes dart to the bowl of bananas, also overflowing. "This is a crazy and exciting time to be in Seattle," he says, the appraising expression on his face morphing into warm enthusiasm.

I can almost feel the sense of fulfillment that he's getting from his volunteer work, one that his career didn't deliver. He seems relaxed enough to allow silence to flow in. Curiously enough, I can understand his inner needs much better now that there is some emotional distance between us.

"By the way," he adds, "in case you didn't know. Those bananas are sold by an operation that is driving the Central American peasants from their lands in village after village."

"Would you like a cup of tea? Or does tea also harm some indigenous population?"

"Have you considered volunteering some of your time, Sunya?"

"I don't have any time to spare. I spend every free second figuring out how to save my business . . ."

"Sorry, Sunya . . . Is it still . . . ?"

"As rough-going as it can get." I allow an appropriate pause, then hand him the loiterer's business card. "What can you tell me about the Apsara Bakery in Kyoto? I doubt it's owned by a multinational institution," I can't help adding.

He squints his eyes at the card, as if he hadn't heard me, and I chide myself for being so petty. "It's both a bakery and a school," he says, "with the motto 'Becoming whole through baking.' Sounds like nonsense to me."

Baking has been a passion, a challenge, a living, and, lately, a torture for me, but I've never considered, at least not consciously, its potential for healing. I refuse to dismiss the idea as easily as Roger does. "What does it say on the back?"

"The handwriting is pathetic. Whoever wrote it must either be a kid or just learning to write Japanese. It's the directions to find the bakery." He reads them aloud, while I quickly grab a notepad and jot them down with a stubby pencil.

"Who gave you this card?"

"A loiterer."

"A loiterer with a calling card?" He sets the card down on the coffee table. "What else is new?"

I give him an abbreviated version of the filming incident, playing down the Andrew part.

"How's the old Pie-erre doing?" Roger asks.

I ignore the jibe. "Pierre is resting at home for a couple of days. He has had some personal problems lately."

"Poor baby. I bet the film shoot and all the confusion that went with it really freaked him out. One more incident like this and he'll probably go running back to his *maman*."

"Don't say that! I can't afford to lose him."

"Well, Sunya, if that loiterer shows up again and causes problems for you, let me know. Here's my new address and phone number."

I know he means what he says. It's his nature to help. For an instant, I hold the card, symbol of his new life, then set it down on the coffee table. "Have you heard of the Sunya Tradition of Buddhism?"

"Sunya Tradition? No, I haven't. But Kimiko might have." His face grows animated in a way I don't care for. "I'm sure she'll be glad to help you. She still stays in touch with her colleagues at *Japan Times.*"

"Thanks, Roger, but I've got plenty of help."

He gets to his feet. "You're cutting off your nose . . . Kimiko can help you if anyone can."

I walk him to the door. With my hand on the doorknob, I ask casually, "Do you know what *sunya* means?"

He ponders a moment. "It means 'emptiness.' "

"That's just the literal translation, isn't it?"

"What's gotten into you, Sunya? You're asking the oddest questions tonight. Okay, there's also a meaning behind that meaning . . . 'fertile void' . . . 'fullness.' "

"Why didn't you tell me this before?"

"You weren't ready for the truth."

He whirls and bounds down the steps, two at a time, his boots squeaking, as if protesting this unaccustomed exercise. Feeling confused and more than a little irritated, I close the door behind him.

Returning to the kitchen, I hunch down at the table with a cup of wu wei tea, which pacifies my mouth with its sweet herbal taste. Who's Roger to decide whether or not I'm ready for the truth?

It is unlike me to sit and brood in the evening hours, what with dishes stacked in the sink and the hibiscus plant crying for its nightly misting, but that's exactly what I do.

THIRTEEN

Five autumns ago, I flew alone to Paris to attend a short culinary program on classic French pastry techniques at the Bon Ton, a baking-arts school. Only a month earlier, I'd broken up with Jeff, my first serious boyfriend after college. As I disembarked at Charles de Gaulle Airport, the pouty low clouds and sharp air greeted me and reminded me of my recent loss. The next few days, touring the gardens, museums, and boulevards, I found that the Paris sky was often overcast like Seattle's and equally prone to sodden drizzles. No matter. Here couples stole kisses anywhere, in any weather. A damp bridge, a dark street corner, even a crowded metro was considered a suitable setting. Alone and homesick, I'd return to my room at the family-run Hotel Port Royal and grow even more miserable. I missed Jeff, the paramedic, even if his sirenlike snoring did keep me awake half the night.

In between learning the fundamentals of folding, icing, creaming, and rolling, I sought solace in the city's pâtisseries (my "street research"), which became a sort of home away from home for me. Pastry salons could be found on most street corners, their showcases glittering with row upon row of jewel-colored pastries. Part of my fascination was figuring them out—madeleine, tuile, palmier, savarin. "They're an art form for the common folk," a Parisian taxi driver confided to me. Often a baking master who operated such a salon placed his signature card next to his specialty, much like a visual artist would. Yet, these pâtisseries also had a kind of approachable informality I grew to cherish. Walking into one was less burdensome than going to some overpriced two-star restaurant and weighing myself down with a big meal. I began to intuit why Parisians began their day with croissants and ended their evening with pear tarts, and why a pretty little *gâteau* frosted their relationships in between.

One afternoon, as I wove my way along a rather ordinary block in the Fourteenth Arrondissement, I happened upon a posh pâtisserie with an ancient oak façade, somewhat of an oddity in this pocket of the city. Nestled among the usual items in its window case was a Normandy apple tart, which consisted of glistening layers of paper-thin apple slices burrowed in a browned rectangle of puff pastry. Back home, I had acquired a reputation for my overstuffed, opulent pie made with Washington State Granny Smith apples. But this thin, understated apple tart captured me. I had to go inside.

A waitress in a black dress and white ruffled apron seated me. While waiting for my coffee, I took in the ceiling mural of maidens dancing in a lush garden, then the rest of the room: mosaic floor, burnished brass accents, black marble-top table, cream linen. Space was at a premium in this salon, as in most Paris eateries, and so I took little notice of the Asian man at the adjoining table, even though he was sitting so close (at least for my American sense of space) that his shirtsleeve nudged my shoulder. A tantalizing buttery scent caused me to glance discreetly at his plate, which contained a slice of the apple tart I'd just ordered.

Soon I was looking around for a spoon to stir my coffee, but the waitress was nowhere to be seen. The man turned and handed me his spoon. He had a freckled face (unusual for an Asian man but not unknown), full with an applelike shine, and the ease of someone adored by family and peers. His hair wasn't typically Asian smooth and flat; rather it was tousled. He was swathed in expensive wool gabardine (Italian yarn, hand-finished buttonholes).

"*Merci, monsieur,*" I responded.

He must have caught my appreciative glance at him and his plate, for he began to extol the qualities of the tart and the bakery in accented English. This nagged at me. Clearly, my French had been neither charming nor convincing. His English had a pleasant lilt, with the emphasis falling on the word endings, the accent only reinforcing that air of worldly sophistication. The sounds were oddly soothing after a day of mostly futile attempts to fathom the rapid-fire Parisian *français*.

My flat but frivolous tart arrived. I breathed in its cozy aroma and tucked into it with gusto. Three generous bites later, the tart was gone. Only the mild fruity aftertaste lingered on. I flashed back on my own dome-shaped, luxuriant apple pie. No way would a piece of that pie vanish in three bites.

"How was it?" the man asked.

"It's rather insubstantial really, but it has an interesting flavor and it's pretty to look at. I'd like to know the baker's secrets."

"I'm not a cook, but I can tell you."

I cocked a skeptical eyebrow. That's a new line.

"I lived in Normandy for a month. That region is known for its apples and pears and they make the best fruit tarts I've ever tasted. I boarded there with a French family to improve my conversational French. My hostess would quiz me on vocabulary while she prepared the evening meal. Apple tarts were her specialty and so I had plenty of opportunities to watch them being made."

I waited patiently, as he cut a small portion off his tart, silently willing him to reveal the technique. Just then, the waitress bustled past and he ordered more coffee for both of us in perfect French. It was as though our taste buds had bonded us in a camaraderie of sorts. But since I was in Paris for only a short time, I wondered if I should risk getting overly familiar.

"I was first introduced to fruit tarts in Japan." He began talking about how European pastries were the latest fad there. I was always interested in hearing about pastries, no matter what corner of the world they came from. As I had missed his last few words, I leaned toward him in an effort to understand.

"Sorry for my atrocious accent. My English teachers were all Japanese and none of them could speak it very well. I picked up some bad speech habits from them. I wonder if I think with an accent as well."

I laughed and took a closer look at this bon vivant. Speaking multiple languages, and acting casual and accessible, he represented the new generation of "global" citizens, able to function in any society. Perhaps I should prolong my stay a few more minutes.

"Where are you from, mademoiselle, if I may ask?"

"Seattle. I was born and raised there."

"Ah, the crown jewel of the Pacific Rim, famous for coffee, apples, flannel, software, and drizzly weather. Do you really get that much rain?" Then stealing a sly glance at me, "I'd have thought you're from South Asia. You have an aura about you that is distinctly Asian."

"I'm an American." I tried to hide my annoyance at this probing of my ancestry. "My parents were born in India, but I've never been there. I don't really know much about Asia. I have no Asian identity, religious affiliation, or aura, whatever that might be."

He smiled faintly, accepting the rebuke with equanimity. "Asia is a huge continent. Who can really define an Asian with any precision?

As for your aura, it's your destiny—that's what my oldest uncle would say."

I found his manner patronizing and was about to excuse myself when he began to talk about himself. Roger Yahura was raised in both Tokyo and Kobe. His mother was Christian, hence his English given name. (His traditional first name was Ishiko.) Tacos were his preferred lunch in college. In the daytime, he frequented his favorite *kissatten* for darkly roasted, smoky coffee; only in the evening did he drink the delicate green tea the Japanese love. His family went to a Shinto shrine to celebrate the birth of a child, conducted family weddings in Western style, and funerals according to Buddhist tradition. "So it's not too surprising that I didn't follow any one religion." However, growing up surrounded by uncles and aunts who pursued Shinto, Buddhism, and had even adapted some Hindu rituals, he'd picked up, or skimmed, as he put it, a few concepts such as "aura" and "destiny."

As I peered out the window at the darkening street, some lights winked on. I heard him saying, "But you grew up in America . . . I like everything American. It's the place where one is allowed to dream big."

I turned to look at him again, the man who lived beyond national and religious boundaries, and felt myself guilty of a little stereotyping. Good manners would dictate that now I make a favorable comment about his country. But what did I know about that island nation? The names of four cities popped into my head: Tokyo, Kyoto, Kobe, and Osaka, one of which was the sister city to Seattle, but which one?

Instead I settled for, "What brings you to Paris?"

"I came here to study fashion design." It turns out that he'd graduated from an art college in Japan. His specialty, as he clarified, was women's clothing, "*la mode japonaise.*" He preferred irreverent shapes and monochromatic colors, mostly blacks and whites. His inspiration came from everywhere, like the delicate curve of the chair he was sitting on, the hand-painted roses on the umbrella stand over by the door, and from watching people. He had one more year of study and wasn't sure if he'd go back to Tokyo after that. "As you've probably noticed," he added, "the latest style rage in Paris is the ethnic look . . . Could you kindly describe the Seattle fashion scene to me?"

I shifted in my chair, wondering if he was making fun of me. In denim shirtwaist, clunky silver bracelet, and Birkenstocks I felt flat-footed and heavy despite my five feet four inches and 112 pounds. Alas, my whole wardrobe was completely obsolete here and my franc-pinching budget allowed nothing more frivolous than a lipstick from Printemps. My hair was hanging loose down my back in a less than artful manner. I was definitely not *au courant*. And yet, I was being invited to expound on fashion.

"Our style is 'rugged outdoors.' " I forged ahead and went on to bring up REI, Nordstrom, and a high-end new downtown boutique named Giselle's, Of Course, which I'd seen only through a plate-glass window. I omitted the fact that the store mannequins wore either impossibly long and elaborate dresses or skimpy, bare-shouldered tubes in shocking colors that almost hurt my eyes to look at. I couldn't possibly wear those outfits.

He'd stopped listening. In fact, he was fighting an urge to look over at the table to his right, which a photographer's model, very *soignée*, was now occupying. A bone-colored lacy scarf around her alabaster neck, she was nibbling daintily at a baba au rhum cake. It made me wonder if he didn't have a French girlfriend tucked away somewhere.

I made up an excuse about a prior engagement, pushed my chair back, and rose, remembering belatedly that Kobe was Seattle's sister city. He scrambled to his feet and walked me to the door, forgetting the model for now. "I've enjoyed speaking with you. Perhaps I'll see you again?"

I shuffled my feet on the doormat. How could I accept this offer? My long class hours left me exhausted. But then that baking secret . . . It was obvious he would not give away the secret too easily. Besides, I was beginning to relish our little game and admitted to myself that I sort of liked him.

"Would you have dinner with me some evening? I know lots of nice places." When I accepted his invitation with feigned reluctance, he said, "Next Tuesday, then?"

In the following weeks, as we dined on bouillabaisse at three bistros on three different nights for purposes of comparison, I discovered the warmth of Roger's personality. He accepted me into his life the way a tree solicits raindrops. I did Versailles with him (his fifth time, my first), read *manga* or Japanese comic art books together (he interpreted, I laughed), and branched out to "invitation only" prêt-à-porter fashion shows. The names of Paris designer houses—Dior, Givenchy, Yves Saint Laurent—were soon rolling easily off my tongue. Once, in between activities, we discussed the significance of my name, which Roger, confident of the Buddhist influences in his life, emphasized had the meaning "emptiness." As if I needed to hear that a second time. I hated him at the moment but, for the most part, I liked his company. He turned out to be better traveled and far more knowledgeable about food, pop culture, and global affairs than I, yet he spent all his free time with me. If he did have a French girlfriend, he must have abandoned her. During lovemaking, unlike my muscular ex-boyfriend Jeff, Roger touched me gently, preparing me emotionally and bodily. On a dank day, after making love, I would walk down a cobblestoned street with him and feel energized by the mere sight of *Paris Match* selling on the sidewalk. I got used to his "ees" for "is," his stumbling on *l*'s, his tender *t*'s. He had a grasp of the English language, though he lacked practice in speaking. Once when he couldn't pronounce a particular word, he simply held my hand and I knew exactly what he meant. Sweetheart that he was, he translated for me whenever necessary. When I told him that my grandest wish was to open a bakery, he replied, "You'll be a well-known baker someday. I know that."

But he still hadn't revealed the secret recipe for that apple tart.

My courses were over in a few months. I gained a diploma and, not long after that, ran out of money, so had no choice but to book a return flight to Seattle. On my last day in Paris, we went back to the same pastry salon and, once again, both of us ordered Normandy apple tart.

The moment I poised my fork over the apples, without any prodding on my part, he turned to the topic I'd been waiting for. He lit an image before me—the baking hour at his French host family's home. A middle-aged woman, Madame Cardin, stood at a counter in a narrow kitchen. A creaky old stove and a blackened rectangular tart pan were her companions. The yellowed book on the shelf, a thousand-recipe collection entitled *Tante Marie* was there for comfort, not consultation. Despite a busy day teaching French conversation to her boarders, she found chopping, sifting, blending, and finally pulling the tart out of the oven a most soothing occupation. She brushed a blend of apricot jam, unflavored gelatin, and kirsch on top of the finished tart for glazing then, with hand enclosed in an oven mitt, popped it under the broiler. Just as the sugar caramelized to the right shade of brown and the air became redolent with a winey sweetness, she extracted the tart pan from the oven, held it up with a grin, and exclaimed, *"Voilà!"*

When I looked down, the plates before us were empty.

Overjoyed, I illustrated to Roger how, with these new tips, I would modify what I had believed the perfect two-crust apple pie recipe.

From now on, my apple pies would be open-faced, with a glazed top, a trick I hadn't learned in my pastry school.

Noticing a perplexed expression on Roger's face, I asked, "Have you ever had an American apple pie?"

He shook his head. It was my turn then to portray a voluptuous pie that contained two pounds of apples, filled the room with a tart-sweet twinkle, and left a nostalgic aftertaste. The words and images popped out with more enthusiasm than was usual for me and I ended up feeling rather foolish.

His smile dissipated my embarrassment. "*Chérie*, you've convinced me there's a whole universe of apple desserts beyond what I've experienced so far. I *would* like to taste an American apple pie, Sunya-style."

"Come visit me in America then."

How absurd that sentence sounded to my own ears. We both grew silent, knowing it'd be difficult for Roger, who was still a student on scholarship, to make such a costly trip. In the silence that encroached, an emotion for him gained power. A realization chimed inside me that I'd gotten far more out of Paris than just a baking course.

The next day he came to the airport to see me off, bearing a bone-colored lacy scarf. Again a cloudy day. Again drizzles. "I'll never forget you, Sunya. I'll visit you, I promise. And . . . keep dreaming your big dream."

Back in Seattle, I missed Roger. My sphere had expanded only to be showered with more emptiness.

Roger's letters frequently showed up in my mailbox.

> *I went to Fauchon by myself and, though I got elbowed a few times, the place seemed deserted without you. I walked out without ordering.*

Another time:

> The cosmos patch you liked in the Luxembourg Garden is
> even more prolific this year. Only no one to admire it.

Yet another time:

> The man who sold galette des rois by the George V metro
> station has an assistant now. You don't have to wait as long.
> I remember you didn't like waiting.

No new man came into my life. Seattle, though beautiful, acted as
indifferent to my well-being as the craggy Cascade Mountains to the
east, especially so during the sunless winter months when people
kept their chins down to avoid the driving rain. I took long prome-
nades through the arboretum, with trees, birds, and squirrels as my
company.

Spring and summer floated by, then autumn came. My favorite
time of the year became even more so when Roger called from Paris,
his voice intense with enthusiasm. "I've just graduated and a job offer
has come along." I had barely congratulated him when he cut in to
say, "From Giselle's, Of Course in Seattle. It's a sales position, not a
designer job, but I'll give it a try."

In that moment of celebrating Roger's good fortune, I became so
ecstatic that all I could fumble out as a response was a squeak. When
I regained my equilibrium, I had congratulatory words flowing from
my lips. That upscale boutique with its glossy catalog—for me the
only affordable item—was garnering national attention. At the same
time, a painful reminder flooded through me that I was stuck in a
dead-end clerical job at a mortuary. It paid well (much better than

baking jobs), but that was about all. I had been desperately trying to save up enough funds to start my own bakery, though I realized that it'd take more than that. Lately I'd been scouting for private investors. So far, not one soul seemed interested in backing me in such a big-risk proposition.

Would Roger see me as a failure?

But . . . I had created a robust apple pie, basing it on a tart described lovingly by him on a memorable evening. I had fussed over the recipe till it was perfect.

"A Japanese family in Bellevue will put me up temporarily," Roger said before hanging up, preempting any fears I might have had. My boxlike studio apartment couldn't accommodate him.

He called the minute he arrived at the airport. "I'm here, Sunya. I'm here. I'll come see you tomorrow."

The following morning I went shopping at the Pike Place Market and bought firm, tart Granny Smith apples from a local orchardist whose motto was "Only the perfect." Roger burst in, just as I was taking my kilometer-high pie with deeply fluted edges out of the oven. Tendrils of sweet fragrant vapor rose from the pie top and encircled us. He put his hands on my shoulders, drawing me as close as the pie in my hand would permit. That intimate gesture transported me back to the time of our first meeting, to that magical tart we shared. When I came back to the room I understood that happiness is when one's past and future converge in the present.

After taking his first bite, Roger commented, "Not as subtle as a French tart, but it has the New World 'oomph.'" (He'd picked up the word "oomph" from an American war hero living in France, he explained.) Staring down at his plate he added, "But I can't tell what all is in it."

I smiled mysteriously.

We kept eating and talking. At one point, he confided he'd had a job offer in Paris as a designer's assistant, but he'd refused that in order to be near me; that added to my ecstasy.

In the months that passed, Roger became a connoisseur of American desserts, from pear crisp to blueberry cobbler to plum upside-down cake. We conducted many discussions on how desserts—sweet, sensual, and inviting—coax the embers of desire into a roaring fire. And we both shared a love of Washington apple pies and the intimate interludes that followed.

My baking skills improved apace until one inspired afternoon I became intent on creating a new, really innovative, chocolate cake.

"Hasn't that already been done to death?" Roger asked.

I ignored his skepticism and persevered, convinced I could surpass even the best chocolate creations in town, if I only gave free rein to my imagination. I orchestrated the usual items along with a few unexpected ones and flew into a creative frenzy. Thus was born what would soon become my signature creation: tender, multitiered, a subtle melding of complementary flavors and chile heat, graced with a silken bittersweet chocolate skin, more delicate than a regular chocolate cake but taller. Roger, intoxicated by chocolate et al., pronounced it a "transcendental" experience.

"I'll name it Sunya Cake," he added.

After several prospective investors tasted the cake and crooned its praise, it finally became possible to obtain financing for my long-planned retail bakeshop. Then, too, the time was fortuitously ripe for investment in restaurants in Seattle, which had become a nexus for artists, Zen seekers, outdoor sports enthusiasts, and software entrepreneurs. Food was the lingua franca of this diverse population.

Finally, conditions were favorable for me to realize my dream.

In the early days of operation, Roger and I would sit at a table in my bakeshop and reminisce over pastry and cappuccino about our time in Paris though, peculiarly enough, never once did my Asian identity, or lack thereof, became a topic of discussion. Flush with the excitement of a new venture, I was more concerned about such earthly objects as cash registers, French ovens, and walk-in refrigerators. Yet, there remained in me a latent curiosity about my Asian aura, why I projected it, and why I had to go all the way to Paris to learn about it.

FOURTEEN

A HEAVY THUMP AT THE FRONT DOOR ANNOUNCES THE ARRIVAL OF THE morning newspaper. It interrupts my train of thought about the Japanese business card, which has been very much on my mind since Roger translated it last night. What am I supposed to do with it, if anything? I reflect, as I lounge in bed in my cheetah-patterned pajamas, nursing a toothache that has forced me to take the morning off.

In a minute, sliding my feet into a pair of house slippers, the clunk and whine of a truck grating my ears, I shuffle to the door, retrieve the rubber-banded newspaper, and return to my bed where I open the paper to food critic Donald J. Smith's weekly column.

The top half of today's column is devoted to yet another glowing report on the downtown steak house scene followed by a gossipy little lecture on the pitfalls of a husband-and-wife team owning a restaurant. Donald cites the example of Joseph and Shirley Smith. Less than a month ago, they announced their divorce, followed by the news that they're closing the doors of their stylish Lakeside Grill. Rumors have been circulating that Shirley and the sommelier . . . I skip the details.

It seems to have escaped Donald that Seattle, with its abundance of creative new chefs and quality regional ingredients, has in recent years developed a sophisticated, vibrant food scene comparable to New York and San Francisco. He remains stuck in the bygone years with his nostalgic fondness for staid Seattle fixtures (like the Gasworks Steakhouse) more often than not owned by one of his cronies, which he touts as Seattle's signature fare. Only occasionally does he include snippets of gossip about innovative young chefs, like today's sorry piece, in a lame attempt to liven up his column. It is common knowledge that the new breed of Seattle culinary cognoscenti consider him dated; but poor Donald seems unaware of their derisive snickers.

As I fast-forward to the last paragraph, my heart jumps:

AN EMPTY PASTRY CASE?

Not such cheery news this week from Pastries Café either. Pierre Talon, the head baker, has been conspicuously absent of late. The pundit of pies is rumored to be recovering from a mysterious "illness" at home but, whatever the reason, his absence means a shorter line at Sunya Malhotra's cash register. His apple pies and cherry-plum tarts have become so popular they have to be ordered days in advance. During last year's holiday season, a lottery system was put in place to select the lucky buyers. These days Malhotra's pastry case is annoyingly empty.

Perhaps not coincidentally, an unsavory character has been seen hanging around her café. There has been a certain amount of speculation as to whether that has anything to do with Monsieur Talon's sudden "illness." Apparently, Ms. Malhotra was concerned enough to hire a private investigator.

Unsavory character? Pierre? That's ridiculous. Donald has concocted a lie to create a sensational narrative. What is he implying? I can ill afford this kind of innuendo at such a critical time. I wonder who informed that fool about the loiterer. It could be anyone who's noticed him and the list is long.

I throw the paper to the floor. Then I get up, go over to the phone, grasp the receiver, and hesitate. What good will a call do? Donald won't listen. I might end up giving him fodder for another lowbrow column. And besides, what can I prove?

Instead, I ring Detective Colby and leave a message to call me. I'd like Colby's brother to report this misinformation to his management at the *News*. It's unsubstantiated, goes beyond personal distaste, and provides an example of unprofessional journalism.

Then I check the time. I have made my emergency dental appointment for nine. I can't wait to have the tooth checked. As it is, I am cavity-prone, which I chalk up to occupational hazard. An ache is a reminder that we inhabit a physical self, my wise mother often says.

The dentist's office on Ravenna Boulevard is a mere seven-minute drive from home. En route, I pass by the storefront location on Meridian Avenue and Fifty-sixth that Cartdale has leased for his Cakes Plus branch and is in the process of remodeling. A workman is painting the outside walls an anemic lettuce-green. It comes as a shocker when I read the name of the realtor on a large signboard: Paradise Properties. I am well acquainted with Jim Paradise—I lease my bakery space through him and have, so far, enjoyed doing business with his outfit. He's leasing to Cakes Plus as well? This adds to my distress.

In minutes, I arrive at the destination and park my car up a block from the dentist's office. Walking past George's Green Lake Cycle Shop, I get distracted by the window display, so appropriate for this city: a cardboard man on a real bicycle, with these words printed below: "I share the road with cars." Our bike-friendly city boasts a large system of urban trails. Just then, an athletic man in tricolor spandex shorts, coming out of the cycle shop, sweeps by me. I turn, our eyes lock briefly, and he jogs off down the street. The unkempt blond hair is somehow familiar.

As the green and yellow number 16 downtown bus roars by, I am jolted by the realization that this is the man who has had my house and pastry shop under surveillance. I whirl and run back, ignoring the red light and the squeal of brakes, as I dodge a blue SUV, provoking a stream of profanity from the driver who swerves to avoid me. Before I can catch up, the loiterer is halfway up the block. He climbs into a silvery Honda and speeds off. I try to read his license plate number, but can only decipher the first three numerals, 108, before he turns onto Sixty-fifth Street and disappears.

Not much of a clue, but a start. Though I am spooked, it dawns on me that George, bicycle guru and shop manager, holds a monthly breakfast meeting with his staff at my bakery. One of the staff members might be able to clue me in about the blond man. I walk inside.

Annie, the flame-haired, twenty-something cashier, stands behind the counter. Her petite form and white chiffon "ladies who lunch" type blouse seem out of place in this warehouse strewn with rugged bicycle gear, skateboards, and backpacks. She greets me in her usual bubbly manner. "I read about you in this morning's paper."

"Don't necessarily believe everything you read, Annie. By the way, who's that gorgeous guy walking out of here just as I was coming in?"

"Jordan Jorgen. You noticed him, huh?"

"Oh, definitely. How can I get in touch with him? He left his umbrella at my bakery." Too late I remember it hasn't rained in a week.

She smiles sweetly. "Oh, I'll be happy to return it to him."

"Oh, no, that'd be way too much trouble. I can take it to his house. I've seen him often enough on the street—he must live around here somewhere."

"Not really."

"No? Where does he live?"

"He lives in Kyoto. He's just visiting his parents in Kirkland."

"Didn't I also see him by the kung fu school down the block? Does he study kung fu?"

"I don't think so. He's a Buddhist. They're not really into that type of thing. Actually he does aikido."

"He doesn't seem the Buddhist type to me."

"He's really into it. He's even trying to get me interested. But it's not straight Buddhism—some offshoot."

"How often does he get back here?"

"Not often enough." Annie smiles meaningfully, then turns to deal with an impatient customer, assuring him that she's run out of aero helmets, but expects a shipment soon.

While waiting for Annie to free up, I go over the possibilities in my mind: Jordan Jorgen, erstwhile loiterer, may somehow be connected with Apsara Bakery in Kyoto (according to his calling card) and possibly with the Sunya Tradition (Andrew's conjecture). But what is Jordan really after? And does any of this have to do with my Asian "aura," which Roger mentioned years ago? I've done some research. So far, all I've gathered is this: Auras are seven or so fields of energy that surround the human body, reflect a person's spirit, and reveal who she really is; I can't seem to tie all this together.

George—robust man, curly hair, baritone voice—materializes. He greets me with a "Hi, Sunya," amplified by his broad smile. Outdoorsy people always act cheerful, as though the sun never sets on them. "Signing autographs today?"

"Sorry, George, it'll have to wait." Belatedly I realize I am due at the dentist in five minutes. "I'm late for an appointment."

"Come back soon."

I wave good-bye and set off for the dentist's office.

When I return home, despite the dull ache of two new fillings, I am imbued with a feeling of expectancy. Annie has unwittingly turned out to be a terrific source, a direct pipeline to the loiterer. And then I call up the memory of Roger's offer to help. What if I got in touch with Kimiko as he suggested? As a former *Japan Times* reporter, she might be able to dig up some information about the Sunya Tradition. I've surfed the Net, but many of the relevant sites are in Japanese. Then I recall our last meeting. Bitterness on my tongue, I muse: What alternatives do I have? My bakery is in peril.

I step to the phone. Weren't Kimiko and I pals once? I try to reassure myself.

"Kimiko, this is Sunya."

She greets me with her usual questions concerning my well-being, as well as that of my mother and the bakery. I ask her how she is and she reports that she and Roger are painting their new apartment, "So it'll look like us."

I bear the words in silence. As if that's not enough, she pauses, following which I hear her calling her cat: "Come here, Gulzar. Come here, baby."

"I have a problem, Kimiko. Roger thinks you might be able to help me."

"Oh, no." She screams. "Gulzar . . . Gulzar just fell into the paint bucket. So sorry, I can't talk right now. I have to get her out. Will you please call back a little later?"

"Of course. Sorry to have called you at an inconvenient time." I place the receiver back and lean against the phone table, both amused and humiliated.

It takes a few minutes to restore my composure, but I console myself by saying this was still a good try. If Kimiko continues to be unavailable, I'll figure out how to get the lowdown on the Sunya Tradition without her assistance.

FIFTEEN

IT IS MORNING AND DETECTIVE COLBY CALLS ME AT THE BAKERY. HE'S DONE a check on his department's database and other undisclosed sources. Here's what he's found: Jordan's father Clyde Jorgen was an attorney in Seattle and his mother Moira Jorgen, a schoolteacher. Both are now retired and living in Kirkland. Jordan went to school at Roosevelt High, then attended Washington State University. After graduation, he took off for Japan. Apparently, he likes it there. He's boringly normal and there's no criminal record on him. He might be a prankster. Colby says all this in a monotone.

A prankster?

I hate it when Donald J. Smith turns out to be right. Strolling through the café section of the bakery I note that the place isn't humming. The cash register indeed has been ringing less often in Pierre's absence. My patrons have begun to complain.

"I miss the crunch of Pierre's streusel and his rich buttery caramel." Janet Porter bought just a cup of coffee the other day.

"I miss Pierre." Keith Mueller, a likable piano teacher.

"Where's your delightful Frenchman?" Chris Hussey, just back from a tour of Western Europe.

It's been two weeks since the filming at the bakery and Pierre hasn't shown up for work even once, the place he used to call his *maison*.

Did I press him too hard to work extra hours? As I enter the kitchen, his fleur-de-lis pan seems to stare at me accusingly from the shelf. Yesterday his favorite spoon slipped out of my hand when I stirred with it.

I walk over to the phone and key in his number, using my free hand to organize the oversize pots on the bottom shelf. Pierre sounds delighted to hear my voice. After we get past our *"Bonjour"* and *"Comment ça va"* he says, "You're in the kitchen. I can hear the pots and pans. I can almost smell the browned butter."

"How's Stephan?"

"I'm spending as much time with him as I possibly can while he recovers," Pierre confides. *"Quinze jours."*

Heavens! Two more weeks? At the same time, I sense the guilt that is gnawing at Pierre—he once considered leaving Stephan. Am I not equally guilty, I ask myself? Did I not place the bakery before Roger at least some of the time?

"It hurts the business a bit, Pierre, but I'll support you in this. I'll wait. Do come back. This is your home."

He takes a moment to answer. "I can't tell you how much I appreciate your checking in with me, Sunya. *Oui*, I miss the bakery very much. Since I left France, I haven't really felt at home anywhere. When you grow up, home is where you invest the best hours of your day, *n'est-ce pas*? Pastries has come closest to being my home in my adult life."

———

Later in the day, I step into the kitchen only to be revolted by an odor of overbaked cakes emanating from the oven. Jill bangs the oven door, as she removes a tray of mostly botched bourbon cakes. She's working extra hours to cover for Pierre and lately has begun to complain of exhaustion. "I'm getting shin splints from standing on my feet so much," she says, tiredness puffing her eyelids.

Had Pierre made these cakes, he'd have finished the tops with a hazelnut-chocolate glaze. Jill does a quick cleanup job, drops the two unburned ones unceremoniously on a rolling rack, and scampers off to the bakery. I should call her to task, but I know she's overextended, and I'm afraid she might quit. Right now, I can't afford any more employee turnover. I bite my tongue.

In a minute, Jill trudges back, her indigo apron sporting brown smudges. "Still haven't found anyone to take Pierre's place?" she asks irritably.

"Pierre told me he'd come back."

"You believe that, Sunya?" Jill gives it a couple of beats. "I absolutely must have a week off from these damn cakes. Working with flour is getting to me. I'd like to go back to flan."

"Sorry, Jill. Flan is new around here. Customers just don't order it as much."

"How could you expect customers who have been weaned on doughnuts to appreciate something as elegant as flan?"

In my current frame of mind, I'm in no mood for cheap shots. "Look, my mother made a honest living selling doughnuts. There's more to them than you think. And even though we don't make them here, I have a lot of respect for anyone who can turn out a good doughnut."

Jill takes her apron off and throws it into the laundry basket. "You're the expert on cakes and pies."

"Meaning why don't I take them over? Believe me, there's nothing

I'd like better than to get back to baking full-time, but there aren't enough hours in the day."

Jill riffles through the drawer, locates a clean white apron, and stalks out of the room, tying it around her waist as she goes. I run my eyes over the neat shelves, the large windows luminous with light and the uncluttered workbench. This is a room where every object is in its place, inviting me to create, and I have the desire, but the truth is I've misplaced my talent, my focus. I forget to strain the scalded milk. I hasten the cooling process of a cake. I find sifting the flour a messy job. Being in this kitchen used to enrich my senses, now it aggravates me. Yesterday, most unusual for me, I kicked the refrigerator in frustration. Fortunately, my staff wasn't around.

What happened to my skills, my *tour de main*, as Pierre would call it? Have I been driving myself too hard? Agonizing too much about the business end of things? Is it the estrangement from Roger? Or could it be that the war with Cakes Plus is getting to me?

What does a person do when her heretofore-reliable talent vanishes?

I believe we're given certain blessings at birth. For me, the gift consisted of an ability to dream up confectioneries. I awakened fully at the smell of pastries in the oven. The kitchen is where I functioned in a state of heightened awareness, every sense attuned to the subtle changes in hue, aroma, taste, or texture. The act of baking defined me; the designation "pastry chef" became my identity. Now, stripped of that sense of self, I stand helpless and frustrated, a spiritual amputee, a fistful of formless sand.

A small noise causes me to look out the window. The walnut tree stirs in the wind, indicating that rough weather is coming. Only four weeks before Cakes Plus opens in this neighborhood and I am in worse shape than ever. At this rate, the Bakery War will be over before it even begins.

SIXTEEN

IN THE COZY BACK ROOM OF TULLY'S COFFEE SHOP, ANCHORED AT THE intersection of Forty-fifth Street and Meridian Avenue, I wait for a tête-à-tête with food inspector Irene Brown. She doesn't yet know that I'm going to hint at numerous health violations taking place at Cakes Plus. That's why I've chosen a place away from my bakery, where we're both anonymous and have the luxury of talking in private.

At this late morning hour, the windowless Internet chamber, complete with electrical outlets, a gas fireplace, chairs, and tables, is empty save for a well-known local poet who is ensconced in a comfy easy chair by the opposite wall. He pecks away at his keyboard, occasionally raising his eyes to the blank space before him, as though it is sprinkled with invisible words. He applies the same care in choosing and mixing his words, I imagine, that I once did with my ingredients.

A glance at my wristwatch and I see with a start that it's almost ten. Time to put aside idle ruminations. I've met Irene several times before, mostly during the annual surprise inspections she's conducted at my bakery. The first time she came across a minor violation, called bare hand contact, when she caught Jill, then a new hire, lifting a tuile cone without the aid of transparent bakery paper. Later I had a private talk with Jill and, to my knowledge, she has never repeated that sin. These last two years, during Irene's subsequent inspections, I've received a clean bill of health. Afterward we sit down and talk shop over coffee and cookies. Irene, who likes to connect with people, takes satisfaction in our little network. And I feel comfortable enough with her to go out on a limb a bit.

Despite her sunny personality, Irene Brown is the toughest health inspector the city has ever employed. Rumors abound about "what she'll nail you for." Restaurant owners dread her visits. In a recent issue of *Restaurant Trade* magazine, an anonymous letter writer called her a "fussy and neurotic sanitorian to whom hand washing is akin to a religious sacrament."

Good hand hygiene isn't all, however. Irene's other major concern is food safety. On her inquiry whether I used colored cutting boards— one color for meat, another for vegetables—I replied, "Mine is a meat-free operation."

"No meat, no problem." She beamed.

In a recent newspaper interview, she asserted that preventing food-borne illnesses is her mission. "I see bacteria everywhere," she remarked half-jokingly. No matter where she goes, she carries a properly calibrated probe thermometer (her "little helper," as she called it) that she pokes into comestibles. "I swear she makes the beets in my salad bar bleed," a restaurant owner, who'd also been interviewed for the same article, complained.

Now I see Irene's tall, avocado-shaped figure entering Tully's. With her huge purse, oversize briefcase, and weighty laptop, she seems like a mobile office. She plops down at a chair across from me, dumps all her paraphernalia on the floor, and expels a breath of relief. The red lipstick, accentuated by a smile, stands out on a lightly made-up face.

"What a pleasant surprise to get your call, Sunya." She scrutinizes my hands, which I chalk up to an occupational habit. Fortunately, my fingernails are cropped short in half-moon shapes and have a natural sheen. I do my own manicuring.

"It's been a while, Irene. It was time to get together."

"What a week!" She announces that she's just been promoted to a supervisory position with responsibility for forty employees. I smile and flash her a congratulatory thumbs-up. She's paid her dues. Seeing my gaze float over her gold-and-silver necklace, she veers into the subject of her new partner, a real estate developer, who has given it to her as a gift. Her face shining, she says, "So nice to have Marvin in my life." I have barely finished congratulating her again when her smile fades, replaced by a frown of concern. "But, Sunya, you look frazzled. And I hear you aren't making Sunya Cake anymore. That's a loss."

"I'm doing fine. Just needed to take a break from baking. And besides, there are so many luscious items in my display case—"

"But not Pierre's apple pie. Is he taking a 'break' too? Not very good timing, I'd say."

"He's on vacation." I try not to look away and reveal my lie. "Would you like some coffee?"

"Sure."

"How about a muffin?"

"They won't be fresh this late in the morning."

That's a perfect setup for what I have to say. Happily, I fetch a tray containing two filled mugs to the table and settle myself. I stir my coffee for a few seconds while I gather my thoughts, then look up at Irene who is regarding me with mild curiosity.

"I heard about this on very good authority, Irene . . . I wasn't sure I should tell you or not, then I realized that there was a potential health problem I'd be derelict not to report."

"Really? What is it?"

"It's the pork humbows at Cakes Plus."

"What do you mean?"

I inform her about the unhygienic conditions at Cakes Plus's kitchen. When I mention how leftover meat is being kept on the kitchen counter for long stretches of time, then put back in the refrigerator and reused days later, she leans so far back in her wicker chair that I worry it might topple over.

"This may sound funny given that I'm a competitor, but that's not where I'm coming from. As you can see, somebody could get sick eating those humbows."

She returns her chair to a neutral position and smacks her lips. "Cakes Plus's humbow, eh? That just happens to be my favorite."

Belatedly I realize that I have broached a sensitive topic. A person's food preferences are sacred, no arguing there. What I hadn't expected is that even a health inspector has food weaknesses. I make a mental note to check out where to find the finest humbows in the city. The next time I should be able to give Irene some alternative sources. Her tone has alerted the poet, who grunts. Perhaps he fancies humbows too?

"You haven't actually seen any of it," Irene counters. "You've only heard about it secondhand. And you said yourself that you're a competitor."

If she assessed my temperature right now, it surely would register well above 98.6 degrees Fahrenheit. Still I persist. "When did you last inspect Cakes Plus?"

Staring at the space above my head, Irene searches a mental bank. "Oh, a year or so ago. I suppose it's about time for another on-site inspection, but I'm short on manpower. Several staff members are on vacation."

"What if a customer gets an E. coli attack after eating there in the meantime?"

The poet, now making no attempt to hide his eavesdropping, winces at the unpretty E. coli word.

"I have bigger headaches this week, like mice in the pantry of a popular restaurant on The Ave." She holds her nose against some imagined odor, then begins to speak about gnawed boxes and mouse droppings in a low, urgent tone as though a murder conspiracy is unfolding. "That's where I'm going next. With my flashlight."

"Why don't you stop by Cakes Plus on your way back from The Ave and try a pork humbow?"

She considers this for a moment, then nods, but warns me with, "Maybe I will, at that, but you'd better be right, my dear."

Or what? She doesn't clarify.

No point elaborating any further. I ask about her vacation in Peru, and she's back in a buoyant mood. She natters on about how much sunscreen she used (three tubes), how many rolls of film she shot (twenty), and the souvenirs she brought back (woolens for Marvin, which didn't fit him but, fortunately, fit her). After another ten minutes, we both rise from our seats. She thanks me for the pleasant time.

I step out of Tully's into the dazzling blue-silver light of midday. To someone born and raised in Seattle, intense bright light is a slap on the skin. Reflexively, I don my shades.

SEVENTEEN

THE AUTUMN LIGHT HANGS FRAGILE AND MISTY BLUE OVER MY BAKERY following a postnoon sprinkle. Clouds curling on the southwest horizon are a harbinger of more rain to come. I have just returned from a meeting with a purveyor of glazed fruits on the east side and parked the car. A gust of damp chilly wind whips through the parking lot and penetrates my wool-and-cotton-blend suit as I hurry toward the back door. Just as I am ready to slip back into the toasty kitchen, I see a black Toyota SUV pulling into the lot.

I frown in disbelief as I recognize the person scrambling out of the car. Dushan strides toward me, smoothly negotiating the rain-slicked surface with a sliding gait that I attribute to his years of cross-country skiing.

He has a lot of nerve showing up here even if he is my mother's fiancé. We haven't spoken since the day he proposed I sell out to Cartdale. That argument still gnaws at me. I position myself at the back door and turn, trying to think of an appropriately chilly greeting to discourage him from coming inside. To my dismay, images of flashing ambulance lights and Mother strapped on a gurney soak my mind instead.

As Dushan approaches me, I notice that his characteristic scowl is missing. His soft mohair sweater, a gift from Mother, contrasts with the rugged planes of his face. He regards me, exclaiming, "Sunya!" The look is not unkind. "I have to pick up Dee from the ophthalmologist in fifteen minutes. She can't find parking in the University District, so I drove her. I thought I'd stop by and see you."

Thank God, his visit will be brief. And it's gratifying to know that he takes good care of my mother. With a gesture of my hand, I motion Dushan into the kitchen.

The air is heavy with the fragrance of citrus bread pudding Scott has prepared a little earlier. Flecks of coconut are scattered confetti-fashion on the counter. Oblivious to this comfy ambience, Dushan drops into a chair. I slide onto a stool. As usual, he talks about his work, the enhanced Web site of the bank and how much pizzazz it has added to the organization's public image. Perhaps he dreads the topic he wants to bring up. I bide my time by mentally reviewing the day's shopping list and phone calls I have to return. Finally, unable to bear it any longer, I prompt him with, "So, Dushan, to what do I owe the honor of this visit?"

"Ah." He pauses, pats his breast pocket unconsciously for a cigarette. He smokes, though never in front of Mother or me. I visualize twin tendrils of smoke drifting from his nostrils as he regards me with hooded eyes.

"My cousin Paul recently moved here from New York. He's a nice guy, lives in Bothell. You might enjoy meeting him. He's a trucker, but a sensitive one. He even reads books."

I almost laugh, but rein in the impulse at the last moment. For a spell, I am trapped by the familiar sounds of someone placing an order at the bakery counter (*a piece of that pear cobbler and a cardamom-pecan star, please*) and hope my staff is not listening in on this conversation (*that'll be three ninety-five*).

I can almost taste the crispness of cardamom-pecan star in my mouth. "I'm seeing someone, Dushan." But then . . . I haven't seen Andrew in a few days. Last time he came to the bakery for a few minutes he looked at me longingly and said that he was a half-day behind schedule in his movie shoot.

"What if my cousin came over and you two went fishing together?" Dushan continues unfazed. "He's off on Tuesdays. He finds fishing relaxing. You could certainly use a little relaxation these days."

"Thanks, but I think I'll pass. One man at a time is enough for me."

"I've already told him—"

"No."

"Young lady, how much longer do you intend to stay single?"

I get up and shove a cake pan from its precarious position at the edge of the shelf to the back. What Dushan is insinuating is that my mother is happily ensconced in a secure relationship, whereas I haven't found anyone to settle down with yet. That it's true only magnifies the pain.

"One more thing. Have you renewed your bakery lease?"

At once amused and relieved at the change of subject, I settle myself on the stool again. "Why should you be concerned about my lease? I'll renew it this December and it should be a routine matter."

Dushan shakes his head. I examine his face to make sure it's not a joke; he holds a stern expression. My lower back is tightening and not just from sitting on the hard stool. I have always trusted Jim Paradise, the owner-manager of Paradise Properties, but now I'm bewildered at the implication that he's going to refuse me a new lease. I remember how I sank eighty thousand dollars' worth of repairs and upgrades in this shop when I first moved in and how impressed Jim was at the time, as well he should have been. Since then, I've always paid my rent regularly. Well, maybe I was a bit late last month, but the clerk at Paradise Properties didn't even notice. I was within the grace period. That is no reason to terminate my lease.

"And how do you know so much about Paradise Properties, Dushan?"

He crosses his arms, squeezes his lips. "I'm a banker. It's second nature for me to know people's financial circumstances."

"Meaning Cartdale?" A peek through the window shows a furious downpour lashing the side of the bakery. "You really should be more careful about your reputation, Dushan. But I guess business is business."

"I'm actually trying to help you, Sunya. Not you per se, because you mistrust me, argue with me, and show me no respect. No, I'm here for Dee's sake."

The situation, I now realize, is more complicated. Jim Paradise owns the building where Cakes Plus is opening a branch. In fact, Paradise owns practically half the commercial buildings in the Wallingford District. Cartdale must have convinced Paradise that I am a financial risk. As a result, Paradise has decided not to renew my lease.

Dushan looks straight at me. "Cartdale'll give you another opportunity to consider his offer. He'd still like to buy you out. If I were you, I'd consider that seriously."

"How about some hot cocoa, Dushan? It'll only take a minute." The truth is I could use a cup myself.

"You baffle me, Sunya. You completely disregard my good advice. Do you realize the situation you're in?"

"I understand you have my best interest at heart and I'll certainly bear your advice in mind."

Dushan regards me with a mixture of disgust and pity as he uproots himself from the chair with a sigh. At the door, he fumbles with the brass doorknob, which disappears in his huge paw.

"It's a relief that I don't have children of my own," he grumbles, finally managing to open the door.

"We're so much trouble, aren't we?"

Dushan's shoes clatter on the steps. He lopes into the rain at an angle, trying to deflect it. By the time he shoehorns his ample frame into the car seat, he's soaked. Wheels spinning, he backs out of the parking lot. As I inhale the cool air, the even chillier consequence of what Dushan has suggested seeps into me. I see a stray dog pause to shake itself before continuing its sodden excursion through the downpour. A wet dog is a sorry sight.

A gust of wind shoos some fallen leaves across the parking lot. As I reflect on the last part of the conversation with Dushan, my eyes grow moist. Yes, parents, too, can cause anguish, some by their presence, others by their absence. If my father hadn't disappeared, Mother's days would likely have been more fulfilling. She'd have had the free time in her younger years to lounge on the lawn and flip the pages of a novel. And my days would have been painted in brighter shades. I wouldn't be taunted by the shadowy images of a missing parent.

What kind of a man was he? Suppose he was kind and genial, not argumentative like Dushan, supportive of my independent spirit. Suppose he had an affectionate heart that reached out when I needed tenderness. I'd really have liked that.

EIGHTEEN

As I CONSTRUCT A WORK SCHEDULE FOR NEXT WEEK, MY GAZE FALLS on the calendar on the pastry kitchen wall. Today is October 18, a significant date for me, as it marks my parents' wedding anniversary. As the years floated by, Mother appeared to have forgotten the date, or she pretends to; but I have been unable to let it go. I think it represents a last, tenuous link to a father I never knew. This being Saturday, Mother is probably off somewhere with Dushan to watch a boat race, attend a home show, or prowl the antique shops. He's always the one to decide where they stop for a bite afterward, even though he's incapable of distinguishing between fine food and mediocre fare. Still, he's given her a lot to look forward to in her leisure time and I'm grateful for that. She'll call me later in the day and talk about her excursions, her tone as happy as the floral brushed-satin lounging pajamas she'll be wearing. In a way, I rejoice that she's gotten over my father, at least on the surface.

Now I look out the window and watch a blue Hyundai cruise by. I've never met the illustrious Prabhu Malhotra. The name does not pass my lips easily. On our entry into this planet, we're supposed to be loved, nourished, and sheltered by our father, but that was not to be in my case. Many times I've asked myself what would cause a man to abandon an infant. Did he want a different type of life? I might never have the answer, but that doesn't stop me from wondering where he's living now and why he didn't ever return or get in touch. Couldn't he at least have contacted us once in a while? These gloomy unanswerable questions have eaten away at me ever since kindergarten. I'm as baffled and shamed today as I was then.

Now that I've checked every item off the to-do list for the day, I sit down at the kitchen table to sample our latest offering—mango kulfi. I've taught Scott to prepare this Indian-style ice cream fragrant with the essences of rose and mango. We serve it with plain madeleines. Pastry aficionados order the ensemble even in cool damp Pacific Northwest autumn weather. Now the dense solid kulfi sits before me in a lotus bowl with delicate wavy porcelain edges. The kulfi's top, flecked with pistachios, glistens under the light. The bakery business being fattening enough as it is, I allow myself such a treat only on rare occasions. My palate anticipates the cool creamy resistance and intense fruity sweetness as it slides down my throat. In the next moment, I lose all desire to pick up the spoon, as Mother's story about how she met my father replays in my head.

It was thirty years ago in the unglamorous *para* of Behala in Calcutta. Only a couple of weeks ago, a marriage broker had delivered a marriage proposal for Dee, known as Deepika then, to her parents. The broker, who had been working on Dee's father's behalf, had boasted that this was a "good" family. He'd been unable to unearth any instances of lunacy, sex scandal, or drug addiction in the last few generations. In addition, the young man was gifted, having perennially finished first in his class.

Dee had also learned that Prabhu was twenty-six, two years older than she, and that this was going to be the preliminary "arranged meeting" with the parents acting as chaperons. So now on this Sunday afternoon, Dee and her parents waited in the drawing room of their flat for Prabhu and his family to arrive. A loud Bangla *adhunik* song was blaring out from the music store below when Prabhu, his parents, and his younger brother entered. Prabhu, dressed in a white shirt and natural-color pants, stood out in the darkish room cut off from the sun by the shadow of the adjoining apartment complex.

Dee lowered her eyes to conceal the fact that she was shaken with terror. She had had two such "arranged meetings" previously with other prospective grooms, but they had not panned out. The last time she'd detected rejection in the narrowing eyes of the visiting family even as they took their seats. They stayed a perfunctory half hour, then offered an excuse about a relative arriving on the Toofan Express in less than an hour, and departed. Dee knew the train didn't run at that time of the day. It particularly devastated her when they left without even touching her specialty, the delicately sweet white rounds called kachagollas, which now sat on a shallow silver bowl on the rickety coffee table in the center of the room.

Today, she'd once again labored the entire morning in the kitchen, preparing her beloved kachagollas, using only homemade cheese and raw cane sugar, leavened with a generous measure of digital dexterity. Only this time, fearing yet another rejection, she'd prepared half a recipe, thirteen such rounds, two per person, and one extra to placate the goddess Durga.

Dee raised her eyes and glanced in Prabhu's direction. At first sight, what stood out was a square face that reminded her of the shape of a children's playground she once used to frequent. The finger with which he was pointing at a scroll hanging on the wall was stubby and misshapen like a neglected tree branch in the same playground. She wouldn't call him good-looking even if she had been blessed with Ma Sarada's benevolence. He seemed uncomfortable as well.

The overhead electric light, filtered through a dust-encrusted lightbulb, flickered in response to a power dip. That launched a pigeon, its wings flapping violently, from its perch on an exposed-brick wall outside the window. Dee took note of the humbleness of her surroundings and reconsidered her evaluation of Prabhu. On a second look, she noticed his robust figure, twinkling eyes, the healthy glow on his face, and the kindness with which he held a chair for his mother.

Dee took her seat, noticing that in her nervousness she'd forgotten to change the old sandals she wore around the house. She hid her feet under the chair. Nobody really noticed anyway, as by this time, the initial stiff formality had given way to a relaxed conversation in Bengali between the parents. The senior Malhotra announced that his eldest son Prabhu, the family's brightest light and already a highly regarded research chemist, had been awarded a doctoral fellowship in chemistry by the University of Washington in Seattle. The parents were eager to see him get married before he embarked on his long journey to the United States in a few months' time. "He must not go there alone," the senior Malhotra intoned. "We'd be worried sick."

Did she qualify? Dee considered herself neither a brilliant student, nor a dashing beauty, at best medium in every respect. She was of medium height, had a medium complexion (neither dusky, nor fair), the middle daughter in a family of all daughters. Not that she lacked good points, had anyone bothered to probe beneath the surface. She taught geography at Beltala Girls' School, an institution of solid repute. She prepared all the meals for a family of seven finicky eaters, always respectful of their individual preferences and dislikes, even the unreasonable ones. She fixed barley water for her sisters when they were feeling under the weather. In the eyes of her mother, she was a model girl, obedient, respectful, and willing to please. But then just yesterday, she'd overheard her father lamenting to a relative: "Our family has a reputation which is my duty to maintain. But this is a most difficult situation. You see, the girl is basically unmarriageable . . ."

Now as her father signaled, Dee poured tea for everyone, the heavy teapot burdening her hand. There was only enough left to partially fill her own cup, though no one paid attention. This was the way it had always been. During her childhood, Dee had watched while her two older sisters were given new clothes and dolls more often, because they were "older and, therefore, more deserving." Long since wedded into respectable families, the two sisters produced children every couple of years and had thus acquired even higher esteem in their parents' eyes. Likewise, her two younger sisters were fed the ripest yellow mangoes, because they were "so young and tender." Dee always ended up with either the greenish or the overripe fruit or a partially filled teacup and, as a result, a poor opinion of herself. All her life she had had to make do with hand-me-downs and leftovers, as if she were an afterthought. Early on, she had come to know the meaning of the word "deprivation" in a personal way, confronting it on a daily basis, and accepting its crude physical manifestation (such as having to choose between bus fare and lunch), as well as the more insidious forms that weakened the underpinnings of her self-worth. In spite of these daunting obstacles, she'd resolved to make the most of her circumstances. Now, at age twenty-four, she dreamed about being married and living elsewhere, anywhere on earth, with whoever her husband turned out to be. She had long since grown weary of being a burden to her parents.

So, now, seeing Prabhu sitting back in a more relaxed posture and stealing a smile at her, Dee felt an inflation of hope. It was a sensation akin to that which she experienced when approaching the ceremonial stage during the yearly festival of Durga Puja, just as the musicians began to beat on their *dholoks*.

Dee observed that her mother was watching with dismay the rapid disappearance of the kachagollas, as several hands reached out for the platter simultaneously; they were her mother's favorite sweets, especially Dee's ethereal version. Dee could tell that only the ingrained self-denial instilled in Indian women from childhood kept her mother from plucking one of the delicacies from the bowl while there was still time.

A pigeon cooed. Prabhu now engaged Dee's father in a conversation, relating how just that very morning, he'd persuaded his reluctant teenage brother to accompany him to a Buddhist temple. "It's not enough to understand calculus or memorize the dates of various Maurya emperors' reigns in ancient India," Prabhu said. His Bengali was refined and elegant; his speech bespoke unusual linguistic ability polished by years of study. "Children ought to have an understanding of our deep spiritual roots. Only then will they behave properly. Don't you think so?"

"Most unusual," Dee's father replied, "to hear a scientist speak this way."

"There comes a time during my experiments, when I bump against the limits of my understanding, when a sense of wonder takes over. At that point I know there is a higher intelligence."

"Well said."

The name Prabhu, Dee recalled now, aptly meant "lord." She promised to herself that if this proposal were to come to fruition, she would visit a Buddhist temple, even though that was not her faith, and place a wad of rupee notes on the donation platter.

To everyone's hilarity Prabhu now delivered an equation: medi-

tation plus temple visits equaled teenage discipline. The two families
were surely coming together, all due to Prabhu's sense of humor and
his ability to feel at ease with new acquaintances.

At this point, the embarrassed teenage boy, who had been until
now pouting in the background, could contain himself no longer.
Looking straight at Prabhu, he interrupted with, "Listen to Prabhu-
babu speaking *ong, bong, chong* Sanskrit words. One would think he
is the family sadhu, no less." It horrified Dee that the boy would
make fun of his older sibling and attribute the term "sadhu," or holy
man, so disparagingly. "Myself, I like to play with computers," the
boy added. "I speak Fortran." He concluded with a formula of his
own. "Meditation plus temple visits equal computer illiteracy."

Stung by the remark, Prabhu sat there in silence. His mother,
who'd only made small, restrained remarks so far, came burningly
alive. She turned toward the boy, her nostrils flaring like a cave on
fire. "Don't forget your brother is going to America. When he was
your age he was first in his class. Your grades are nothing much to
speak of. And you failed in geography. I'd be surprised if you even
knew where Seattle is."

The boy looked away and swallowed the kachagolla in his hand
in one gulp. The sweet tender taste must have mesmerized him, for
he extended his hand for another. His mother reached over and
snatched the kachagolla away from her son's hand. The boy grimaced,
then squirmed in his seat. His father fixed him with a glare that
promised dire consequences in the event of further transgression. Dee
found this amusing, but hid her laugh.

"It's refreshing to see our young people getting excited about computers," Dee's mother, always the diplomat, interjected. Dee knew her
mother was being charitable, for the boy was ill-tempered and undis-
ciplined. Her own sisters never behaved so badly at home, much less

in front of guests. But Dee's mother must not have wanted any un-pleasantness in her home, regardless of whether the marriage mate-rialized or not.

"You're lucky not to have a teenage son," Prabhu's mother said. The initial polish in her voice had begun to wear thin. She finished her errant son's half-eaten sweetmeat, then snaked out an arm half-covered with gold bangles to claim her own pieces, which she de-voured with a blissful expression on her face. Her cooking had at least won the woman's approval, Dee thought hopefully.

Prabhu's father cast an angry glance at his wife, then smiled at Dee's parents. "When I was growing up, there was no such thing as teenage. We were children till we were fourteen or fifteen, then just like that we became adults. Teenage seems like a fun period to have. You take no responsibility whatsoever, speak your mind, and don't have to listen to anyone if you don't want to. I'd relive my own youth now if I could."

"I'd flunk teenage," Prabhu replied. A few squeals of welcome laughter followed. He lifted his teacup and tilted to catch the last drop, adding, "And I would not have appreciated this fine cup of tea in my teenage." With the upraised cup partly shielding his face, he glanced at Dee, who returned the fleeting look.

By the time Prabhu's parents were ready to depart—they'd risen from their chairs and were repeating some pleasantries—a time had been set for the fathers to contact each other by phone. As Prabhu rose to take his leave, he shared another glance with Dee and, in that cherished moment, she comprehended there would be a future.

Bursting with excitement, she collected some cups, then drifted away. While her parents shut the door of the drawing room for con-sultation, she hid herself in an adjoining room on the pretext of ironing a blouse. Her parents didn't suspect she would be listening in on their conversation, even though the walls of this cheaply constructed building were known to be thin.

"Prabhu is obviously a boy of fine character," Dee's father began. He was in the habit of calling every man under the age of forty a boy. "He's gentle and so modest. And he's going to the United States on a fellowship. I must say it's beyond my expectation to have such a candidate for Dee. The boy definitely has a future."

"That's well and good," Dee's mother, no longer the diplomat, replied, concern evident in her voice. "But what about the present? How will he support my daughter? It'll take him years to finish his research and get a good job. Until then, he won't make enough money to live on. Dee will have to scramble for a job right away in a strange country. You hear stories about how they exploit immigrant laborers there, especially women."

"You're the one who always insists your middle daughter is a *kajer meye*." The Bengali expression denoted "a woman who toiled ceaselessly."

From the next room Dee shook her head in anger. Just last night she'd served her father a five-course dinner, including his favorite muger dahl, exactly at eight P.M., as he required. He ate silently, without ever looking up at her. She felt the sting of his inattention.

"She's done enough work. It's time she had children and a home of her own." Dee's mother threw in more objections to the proposed marriage at her husband, such as her daughter's lack of fluency in English and the difficulty a girl of average intelligence would have in keeping up with an academically brilliant man.

Dee ground her teeth in frustration. As always, her parents underestimated her. She had a certain quiet faith in herself. Growing up in a lower-middle-class household, she'd learned to make use of every *paise*, even secondhand objects that came her way. How can language stand in the way when she had so many feelings, so much eagerness inside? She would take classes in chemistry, particle physics, botany—whatever was necessary to keep Prabhu interested in her.

"He's a holy guy—a Buddhist for that matter," Dee's mother said. "We're Hindu."

"All religions have the same destination," Dee's father replied. "They just pursue different paths. Have you forgotten that Buddhism has its roots in Hinduism? The two beliefs align in so many ways." He lectured to his wife that Buddha was a Hindu prince who gave up his indulgent palace life to find the truth, adding, "Look, we have a wonderful opportunity here. They're desperate to get their boy married."

"The boy doesn't care who he marries," Dee's mother said. "He's going through the motion just to please his parents. Not a good sign. Let's keep looking some more."

"How much time do I have left?" Dee's father pressed, and Dee knew that he was reminding his wife subtly that he was in poor health. He had a cabinet full of medicine bottles. What if his heart suddenly failed? How would the family manage?

Dee's mother fell silent, possibly because she still had two daughters to marry off before she would arrive at what a common Bengali expression described as *"jhara haat paa,"* hands and feet shaken loose. Only then would she be free from parental and financial concerns. She was willing to let go of her industrious daughter and her terrific meals for the sake of that goal. She must have looked up at her husband and acquiesced.

Dee pirouetted away from the wall in exultation. Imagine getting married and relocating to the States. Her condescending friends and neighbors would be so envious. "The girl who doesn't know how to wrap a sari properly is getting married?" they'd whisper. "And going to the States with her husband? *Bhaba jai na.*" Hard to believe.

In that moment of frail joy, as all joys had been for her, toned with a measure of vindication, Dee did a little dance around the room. Simultaneously, with a flick of her wrist, she tossed the blouse she'd been ironing in the air. As she stretched out and captured the blouse with one hand, the train of her sari got tangled with her feet and she nearly stumbled. She smiled to herself. Just wait. She would have a fine life with this religious intellectual who couldn't quite conceal the twinkle in his eyes.

How long have I been sitting in the kitchen like this? Sounds of scraping chairs, rattle of coffee mugs, mutterings of good-byes, and shuffling of feet issuing from the front indicate that Scott is closing the retail area.

The mango kulfi has dissolved in a creamy orange puddle. The solid texture I crave has vanished.

Lost in thought, I slide the bowl into the sink, unemptied.

NINETEEN

ON WEDNESDAY, I RETURN HOME AFTER WORK, STEP INTO MY LIVING room, and find a week's worth of newspapers stacked on the floor. Too tired to hang my sweater jacket, I toss it at a recliner, but miss. The jacket lands on the newspaper stack and topples it. I don't straighten the mess. Instead I flop down on a chair and prop my feet on the coffee table without bothering to remove my loafers. The cut-glass vase by my feet still holds the long-stemmed orchids with a spicy scent that Andrew recently sent. They still retain their violet hue even though a few petals are strewn about on the coffee table in an effect reminiscent of a Japanese painting. The flowers were a surprise. The card simply said, "Thinking of you."

I begin skimming the classified section of today's *News* that my assistant Scott handed to me as I left the bakery. And there it is . . . circled . . .

> For sale. Two-bedroom rambler. Excellent
> location. Minutes from Green Lake. Only
> one block from the popular Pastries Café.

Bless Scott. All is not lost. People still consider my bakery a destination.

Green Lake. I think about walking on the trails around the lake, beneath giant pines and through grassy meadows, in the company of ducks, Canada geese, squirrels, and silver-sided trout.

Should I call Andrew? After I mailed him a card, thanking him for the orchids, he called and left a message. Scott mentioned that Andrew had also stopped by the bakery while I was at the dentist. "Still no Sunya Cake?" He ordered an iced chai, and sat and waited for me. Eventually his crew arrived to pick up their carryout orders and, as usual, he departed with them.

I have put off calling him, telling myself I need to go slow. Still, I can't help checking out every person who wanders into the bakery, searching for that familiar bespectacled figure with intelligent eyes and an air of brisk efficiency.

And I await another discussion of his film story, partly because it has to do with the trade conference. These days when I peruse the newspaper, I search for any article related to the matter. Big business could crush me, just as it did my mother. The same process seems to be at work throughout the world. I am beginning to see why Roger maintained that the tactics employed by large companies deceive workers and pose a threat to democracy.

Andrew has pulled me into the lives of Werner and Emily in other ways as well. Fictional characters? Perhaps. Certainly, he's created each from his wishes, imaginings, and dreams, but his thought processes interest me, nonetheless. It's not just a simple love story, I've gathered that much, and am curious about the film's day-to-day development.

Fortifying myself with these excuses, I walk over to the phone. Andrew answers so cheerily that I suspect he's waiting for someone else's call. Jazz pulses in the background. My mood, precisely.

"I just looked outside—it's rare to get this much sunshine this late in the year. I feel like a walk around Green Lake. Do you want to . . . ?"

"I'd love to. I'd like to see you. My brain's foggy from the day's shooting."

I take it as an auspicious sign when I slip into the last spot in the parking lot behind the Aqua Theater. As I hop out of the car, the sharp edge of the breeze asserts that it's going to be a chilly night. Fortunately, my fleece-lined jacket has hand-warmer pockets. An agile soccer player sprints the length of the playfield across the drive that winds along the south side of Green Lake, nudging the ball before him. Strolling a short distance, I spot Andrew, in jeans and an ash-colored parka, standing by a telephone booth just a few feet away. Shyness stirs inside me; my feet drag. He saunters toward me, sunlight sparking on his eyeglasses and a smile flooding his face, we shake hands, and a tingle travels up my arm.

"Shall we just stick to the trail?" I ask and he nods.

We head north along the east periphery of the lake. I am aware that this is only the second time we've met outside the bakery. To mask any lingering self-consciousness, I point out familiar landmarks: a white birch grove, an imported eucalyptus, a katsura tree with brass-coin leaves. Looking out over water, I notice ducks emerging from their hidden nooks by the shore. Andrew must have glimpsed them too, for we both stop and turn at the same instant. Mama duck followed by a flock of fluffy babies waddle ashore. One duckling nibbles at my feet, quacking gently to snare my attention. I catch a tender, almost beatific, expression on Andrew's face. He'd like to pet and hold it, but wouldn't allow himself to do so.

My gaze follows his to the red-, gold-, and orange-streaked sky glowing like molten metal behind the lattice of vine maple branches.

"Like Dutch masters' paintings," he says. "Is this lake natural or man-made?"

"Care to make a guess?" I'm trying to size him up.

A light breeze ripples the sleeves of his parka. I wonder what his deltoids might look like underneath. He asks, "How far is it all the way around?"

"Two point eight five miles."

"If it's that exact, then it's probably man-made. Let's forget you said that. I'd like to think it was natural."

Oh, he's a romantic. I glance sideways at him. "Well, the fact is, it was actually formed by a glacier and then remodeled in the early twenties by a landscape architect who thought he could improve on nature."

This elicits a tiny smile from him. "So when can we expect Sunya Cake again?" he asks.

His abrupt switch to a sensitive subject throws me off balance, but then I realize that he has every right to inquire, since we practically met over the cake. "Good question . . . I'm having trouble baking lately."

"You've probably just hit a blah period. I have gone through several periods like that myself. I hope for everyone's sake you get it back soon."

But how? Hearing a rolling noise, I focus on an in-line skater who is passing by us, playing a harmonica while gliding backward nonchalantly, acting as if he does this every day. Once my baking skills were equally sharp. I could handle icing, folding, and kneading blindfolded. These days I'm not short on techniques. What I lack is an inner focus that harmonizes techniques, processes, and materials to create perfection. How do I get it back?

We're walking along a curve of the lake. Just ahead of us, a young man and a woman on bikes whiz toward each other from opposite directions, almost colliding before braking hard and sliding to a stop. Standing astride their bikes, leaning on their handlebars, they exchange an adoring look and an eager kiss, then adjust their helmets and start pedaling again in opposite directions. Just like in the movies. I take the opportunity to ask Andrew about his film.

He glances at the line of trees on the west side of the lake, then at me. "Today wasn't my best day. I got through about half of what I'd planned to accomplish. I shot a scene in which Werner remembers how he rummaged around in his grandmother's attic when he was a twelve-year-old. Mostly it was junk—broken coasters, a frayed table-cloth, a bunch of plastic carnations and the like—but eventually he found a pair of genuine, early-twentieth-century champagne glasses wrapped in tissue paper. He held the glasses to his chest and was overcome by nostalgia. In the film, you see the emotion in his eyes. I had a feel for the scene and wanted the glasses to be authentic, but my prop master got some plastic champagne glasses from Costco. They were so cheesy. Can you believe it?"

Despite the note of complaint in his voice, I register how he comes alive as he discusses his occupation. The face becomes sunny; the voice sparkles, the walk is more energetic. His work is where he fully invests himself.

"While we're on the subject, I'd like to know how the filming is going."

He leaves me hanging without an answer. The dull, hollow roar of heavy traffic intrudes as we approach the Aurora Avenue side of the lake. "That's where I'm staying." He points to the upper window of a three-story, stylish condominium building across the street, as he slows his walk. "Would you like to stop in for a drink? There's a nice view of the sunset from the living room. And I can fill you in on some of the scenes that I've worked out since we had dinner."

We pass by a birder with binoculars and a fisherman baiting his hook. As a single woman, I have some well-founded reservations about going to the house of a man I've just met. Perhaps sensing my hesitation, Andrew changes the topic and asks about the types of fish in the lake. I tell him about trout, carp, and bass, the insects, and hatching.

"It's my brother's place, in case you're unsure . . . I'm using his spare bedroom. You'll probably meet him sometime this evening."

I allow a small pause. "Well, yes, I'd like to see the view and hear more about Werner and Emily. That's what you're talking about, isn't it?"

At Andrew's charming condominium, the sunset light shimmers on the wall outside the window. To my pleasant surprise, the din from Aurora Avenue is quite acceptable. A fire crackles in a corner fireplace across from a home theater system; the air is flush with a gingery fragrance emanating from a pot on the stove. With a glass of sherry, I sit on a stool in the living room, my feet on the Aubusson rug, and flip through an issue of *Filmmaker* magazine, though I'm actually watching Andrew move about the open kitchen, with strong and decisive strides accented by his chic jeans. I only wish he talked more. Our time together is precious, but his mind appears to be somewhere else.

His brother is out. There is a brother: I have checked out the toothbrushes in the bathroom. Actually, I'm glad for his sibling's absence. Our intimacy is still too fragile to flourish in the presence of others.

He puts on a CD: a Brahms concerto. My attention veers to the side table, to a black-and-white snapshot of a couple in a pewter frame. The man, who bears an unmistakable resemblance to Andrew both in facial features and body type, smiles a cocky, television-anchorman smile. The woman, about forty and plain, is self-conscious in a busy polka-dot dress that makes her appear overweight. Her smile seems rigid and forced against the natural background of a line of trees.

"My parents." He takes a few steps closer to the photo, but doesn't pick it up. "That's Central Park."

"So, how did you like living in New York?"

"I was born in Manhattan, even went to school there." He drops into a chair, pushes his hair back, and reminisces about the Park Avenue apartment building where he was raised, the kind with a dozy doorman and maids in uniform. His parents were invited to parties where guest lists were tightly controlled secrets. His father was out most nights and his mother didn't fit in the social circles, but they gave Andrew and his brother the best education a sizable bank account could purchase. Eventually his mother left her husband and two children.

Now that he's given me his authorized bio, he moves his gaze away for a good five seconds. It'll require a bit of prodding on my part for him to open up enough to show me the place where he truly resides. "Do you ever go back to Manhattan?" I ask.

"I go visit my father once in a while, but not my mother." The tone of voice is heavier. "When she divorced my father, she divorced Evan and me too. I was fourteen at the time and I'm afraid I didn't handle it very well. I did a few things I'm not proud of." He moves over and switches on a parchment-shaded wrought-iron wall lamp, which casts a lemony light on him. "And your parents?"

"Well, Mother always gives me good advice no matter what the subject, but my father . . ." My voice falters and I can't finish the sentence, though I must have trusted Andrew more than most to reveal this much emotion.

He changes the music to a waltz. "Would you like to dance?" His bow is as proper as the British accent he affects; he's smiling. Yet I sense something is bothering him. I am sensitive to people's fears and discomforts, partly because I have so many of my own. Deep in one's fears lies the clues to a personality, or so I believe. In the midst of a well-executed ballroom step, I raise my head, noticing the impression I've left on his shirt's shoulder, and ask, "Is there anything in life you're uneasy about, afraid of, paralyzed by?"

"A tight shooting schedule, nuclear war, a delayed flight . . . abandonment."

And then suddenly he leads me into a whirling step. We bump into a rack of dishes that rattles but fortunately doesn't break. We turn over a basket of Gala apples. By now, we're laughing wildly, our steps dreamy on the floor. Such is the spell of the hour that, finally, I can leave the thousand back-straining details of the bakery day behind and respond to an altogether new sensation coursing through my veins.

The telephone jingles irritatingly from one of the bedrooms. "Excuse me," Andrew says in a far-off voice and lets go of me, causing a brief spell of dizziness. In this unfinished moment, I watch as he jogs up the hallway and vanishes into his bedroom, though a kitchen phone is within easy reach. I reclaim my seat by the window and peer out. In the ferocity of darkness, city lights glitter like fallen stars. By this time, the music has stopped and the discordant sound of traffic from Aurora Avenue has returned, causing me to twitch.

Andrew comes back in a few minutes—but with a distracted expression, our dance forgotten—and drops down in a chair beside me.

"Anything the matter?"

"Just some . . ."

A moment lost, a moment that could have brought us closer. I am wondering how to gracefully take my leave when I hear him saying, "It feels good to get off my feet for a change. I have to stand all day."

"And yet you would still go for a walk?"

"Yes, I like to explore. This city is scenic and I am enjoying it tremendously, though I must admit I miss the *Los Angeles Times*. I'm having it delivered starting next week."

"Not much to recommend the *News*, is there?"

"Except Donald's food column. He's a friend of my dad. I had dinner at his house the other day. Networking. It's part of a director's life."

"Did you see what he wrote about my bakery?" I speak to Andrew's back as he rises and steps into the kitchen. "I still don't know who gave him the scoop."

An off-the-wall inkling of suspicion pops into my head and is as quickly dismissed for lack of motive. He returns to his seat, reaches over for the wine bottle and, without asking, refills my wineglass. I notice how the fingers of our free hands are slowly entwining.

"Were you an imaginative child?" I ask. "Did you like to tell stories even when you were growing up?"

"Yes, to my brother and baby-sitters. Storytelling was my way of making sense of what was going on around me. It may sound funny, but making up stories put me in a secure spot. The world's more manageable when you get to put your own spin on it."

Story time, I assume.

He takes an instant, contemplates his wineglass, then looks up, his expression open, giving, deeply absorbed, and alert all at once. "Now . . . the scene I've just finished. You remember Werner, Emily, and her friends were heading for Pastries Café? When they get there, it's closing time, so Emily invites everybody to come over to her place. Off they go. Werner is reluctant, uneasy about what he's getting into."

I visualize the scene as though it's being reenacted for me: Emily's two-room apartment in a boxy new building. Its only furnishings are an ancient couch, several mismatched chairs, a battered dhurrie rug, and an acrylic coffee table bought at an estate sale. Only the sheer, bright white window curtains are new. She looks out the window often. Over coffee, they discuss the trade conference. Emily mostly nods and keeps the coffee flowing, turning her dainty head often to follow the conversation. Eventually, one by one, they begin to drift out . . . all except Werner, who fidgets with an empty mug on his lap.

"What do you do?" he asks.

"To pay the rent?" She laughs softly through even white teeth. "I teach school. You know about schoolteachers in Washington State, don't you? Long commute, little pay, even less respect."

"Then what gets you up in the morning?"

"My work as an anticorporate activist. Before I got involved with CAGT, I used to wake up depressed. When I brushed my teeth, the water would taste slightly off. I'd wonder how I'd get through yet another day at school, bear another evening alone in this apartment. To tell you the truth, I was almost suicidal. Then I started to volunteer. It brought me back to life."

"It's not just any volunteer work for you then?"

"No. I see us giving our freedom away little by little to the government and big corporations. They hand us lollipops—salaries, material goods, physical safety—to keep us quiet. We've become such pleasure seekers as a nation that we don't notice when someone has yanked the dhurrie out from under us."

She's caught his attention so completely that he has to check the floor below his feet to make sure the rug is still there.

"What do you do?" she asks.

He blinks. "I manage a nonprofit organization." That's a lie and he hates himself for the deception. He flashes on a recent talk with his wife about his desire to get into another field. She reminded him, with a sharp cold look, that the pay and benefits were excellent.

Werner suddenly feels drained. He excuses himself, gives Emily a long look, and is soon on his way to his motel. He always leaves quicker than he enters.

Andrew is quiet. I gaze at his introspective face, and think: Werner is searching for fire, the fire that warms one instead of burning.

"Has Werner been burned in some relationship?" I ask.

"Maybe."

He slides his empty glass to the end table, touching the bottle and making a clinking sound, then takes my hand and holds it. "You know, a sentence just came to me, a feeling that comes over Werner as he's having coffee with Emily. 'When I am with her, I forget the mess of this world.' "

"Good line. You should write it down."

"You're right," he says, our hands parting. He fetches pen and paper from the kitchen, sits down, and hunches over the lined yellow pad with the dedicated expression I've observed before. Words fly off his pen; he seems totally oblivious to his surroundings, and me.

I scan the room—the reclining chair, chamois ottoman, PC desk, colossal television with a blank dark screen—and wonder if imaginary characters and situations, rather than the ambiguities of a loose sloppy real life, better satisfy his inner needs. The top of the reclining chair is covered with a patina of dust. He finishes writing, sets the notepad down on the side table.

"How long will you be in Seattle?" I ask.

"Till the middle of December. I hope we can wrap it up by the sixteenth."

Not to despair, I tell myself. When these two months have passed, the storytelling will be over and he'll be gone. But what if I start to get serious? What's that little tug in my chest right now? Why can't I take my eyes off him?

"I'm hungry. How about you?" He rises and motions me toward the kitchen.

Sitting at the kitchen counter, I watch him. Standing on the other side, he slices a baguette into rounds, arranges them on a platter around a tub of commercial red bell pepper dip, and sets it down between us. As I start to munch, he asks, "How's the bread? I actually made it myself."

"It's great. So, you cook?"

"Yeah, but I especially like to bake. I'm glad my brother has fully furnished this kitchen."

How unexpected. Earlier I felt a tad intimidated by the fact that he was a writer and filmmaker. Now I experience a new feeling of kinship. Baking is hands-on and people oriented, as much as it is detailed and exacting. Bakers know where each other's juice comes from. I'll be able to relate better to him on ground we mutually occupy.

"What else do you bake?" I ask.

"Last Saturday I whipped up a chocolate cake for my brother's birthday. He liked it. I took what was left to the set the next day. It was a hit. I thought it was okay, though it certainly wasn't in the same league as Sunya Cake. But then, what is?"

I examine the piece of bread in my hand, hard crust with a soft porous interior. He has aggravated my sore spot. I mumble my appreciation for the bread, only that.

"I love your Sunya Cake," he continues. "Just a couple of weeks ago when I was having my first taste of that cake . . . and I still can't believe it myself . . . a terrific idea about the script came to me. Plato said, 'Do not seek pleasure, but go toward knowledge.' I have to disagree with him. Inspiration can spring from pleasure, from leisure, from a grand view of a mountain, or from a piece of fine cake."

"I agree with Plato in the sense that knowledge—for a baker—is precious," I reply. "Without that, you go nowhere. But is that alone enough? That's the question that haunts me these days."

He brings his glass of water to his thin lips, drinks from it, then looks at me. Immediately I'm brought back down from the Plato-sphere to the hard chair. Could he be after the recipe? Sunya Cake, my holy of holies?

I glance at my wristwatch. Eight-thirty P.M. Much as I like the finely tapered, elegant fingers that are now stroking mine, I need to go now. I stand up, walk over to the sofa, bend down, and collect my jacket, saying, "Just what I needed after a rough day."

If he's disappointed, it doesn't show. At the door, we linger a few more minutes. When he asks where I live, I reply that I'm just across the lake.

"I need a boat, sailing lessons, and eyes that see in the dark."

Now that we know each other better—and the film script is help-ing—our good-byes are getting longer. As he leans toward me, I turn my face up, and he kisses me. Shy and edged with pain, it's an en-ticing kiss, a practiced kiss, an attempt to link, an overture is what it is, and I feel myself weakening. His lean chest is harder, more solid than I expected. In the end, a sensor inside tells me to clear out of here. I manage to pull away.

"Much as I like spending time with you," my voice dissolves into a soft whisper, "I'm not quite ready for this." I read another kiss in his eyes and witness an instant of vulnerability at my reticence. He has obviously failed to listen to Plato once again. Our lips meld briefly, feverishly one more time, then separate.

As I walk out, a single line of a poem flashes in my head: *Come dusk they danced their dream.*

Only wish I could remember the rest of it.

TWENTY

AT HOME THIS MORNING AND STILL PONDERING LAST NIGHT'S RENDEZ-vous with Andrew, I open the mailbox with keener than usual anticipation. I've always delighted in the surprises the mailbox holds in store for me; notes, letters, loud-colored junk mail, all elicit a shiver of excitement. But now, as I sift through the pile and turn up an apricot-hued envelope with Kimiko's name and return address inscribed on the upper left-hand corner, my curiosity is inflamed. Kimiko wouldn't even speak to me on the phone the other day, so why has she gone to the trouble of communicating with such fine stationery? I tear the letter open and read her enclosed message inscribed in tight graceful script, as I go back inside the house.

> *Dear Sunya-san,*
> *I must apologize for hanging up on you the other day. That*
> *was rude of me. I could not call you back right away, as*
> *our cat, Gulzar, got paint all over her. She was wet and*
> *angry and tore around the rooms until I finally caught her.*
> *Then Roger and I got into an argument about who should*
> *clean her. Guess who did the job?*

Roger tells me you are having problems with some religious
group in Japan and could use my help. Will you be free in
the next couple of weeks? If so, I will come by your bakery.
I would like to help you in any way I can.

By the way, thanks to you, Roger's cousin, Bob Nomura,
has started working two days a week at the Sorrento Hotel.
He only wishes his hours were more convenient.

I must apologize again.

Yours,
Kimiko

I stash the letter in my untidy to-do basket. Roger's family would
have shown me the same formal courtesy. A casual verbal "sorry"
wouldn't have been enough for them, just as it wouldn't for Kimiko.
Following an old Japanese tradition, she is offering me a sincere apology through the more permanent medium of paper and ink.

Clever girl. While offering to lend a hand, Kimiko lets me know
that Roger's cousin is still available for employment. I have to admit
I could use the help. In fact, I'm desperate. I've put several ads in
the *Weekly*, but gotten few responses. It seems that most job-seekers
are flocking to the area's countless software companies, which offer
far bigger paychecks as well as stock options. Though I can't wait
much beyond today, the mere thought of hiring Roger's cousin fills
me with despair. What choice do I have? And, now that I think of
it, Roger did want to be friends with me.

Another potential quandary: How would Pierre feel about the
move? The last I heard Stephan was doing well, but Pierre's got laryngitis. In other words, he needs more time off. He might see the
new hire as a threat. Or, maybe that'd hurry his recovery and return
to work.

I picture Bob Nomura as small and frail, with eyeglasses, rounded shoulders, and a shy, formal bearing that doesn't match his Western first name. Can a man who grew up in Japan, where stovetop cooking is the norm, really take to Western-style baking? Will his pastry-making philosophy match mine? Can he adapt to the informal atmosphere around here? Can he embrace the pressure?

Perhaps I can try him out for a day—a standard hiring practice in bakeries—and see how things work out.

A few evenings later, I've just finished my solitary dinner of tossed salad and soba noodles and plated the dessert when there's a knock at the door. Inwardly I frown—I wasn't expecting anyone—then hurry over to the door and open it. Much to my surprise, it is Andrew, still and solid in a tightly knit, port-colored pullover.

"Andrew!"

He shuffles his moccasined feet hesitantly, though his eyes sparkle as they gaze at me. "Just stopping by to say hello on my way to a meeting. I haven't seen you in a few days. I was thinking about you. Am I disturbing anything?"

"No, not at all, come in." I lead him into the kitchen, where we sit at the table with a view of a fig tree. We're just so happy to see each other that words tumble out in a sweet and cozy manner. "We're back on schedule," he says about his filming. "Our dailies look good."

Noticing that he's staring at the cheesecake on the counter, a treat I carried out from the Sorrento Hotel a couple of hours ago, I ask, "Would you like a bite?"

"I never refuse anything from Sunya's kitchen."

It is with delight I cut the cake slice in half and offer him the bigger portion. He digs into it with gusto, pausing just long enough to murmur, "Lust at first bite." In no time, he's scraping up every last crumb on his plate with the tines of his fork. "You've come up with something almost as luscious as Sunya Cake."

Firm and dense, the cake's more delicious than I expected, both in flavor and texture; it's manifestly the work of a genius. With a delicate flowing nuance of vanilla lingering on my palate, I confess in a small voice: "It's not my recipe."

He ignores my reply, exclaiming, "It's incredible." He chats amiably for a few more minutes, then casts his eyes at his watch and says that he must be on his way if he's to make his meeting on time. So soon. As I watch him leave, my hope and joy in these difficult times, I taste disappointment in the back of my mouth.

Alone in the kitchen, I wash the dishes. Andrew has added a spark to my evening, but also reminded me of my recent string of baking disasters: tough piecrusts, burnt chocolate, beaten egg whites whose peaks droop. My shoulders sag at the recollection.

Next morning at the bakery, I receive a call from the party planner at the mayor's office. "You don't happen to make cheesecakes, do you?" the man asks.

"As a matter of fact, I do."

"I'd like to place an order for three of them."

As I put the receiver back in its cradle, I wonder who will bake the darn cakes. In my current predicament, I can't botch this order. Neither Scott nor Jill has cheesecake in their repertoire, and I haven't baked one in several years.

A day later precisely at eleven forty-five A.M., an athletic-looking Japanese man in his early twenties arrives at the bakery kitchen door and greets me with a small polite smile. He's about six feet tall, with zero body fat, and has the springy step of a college basketball player. His hair is combed up in a pompadour, with a patch above the forehead dyed an electric-purple hue. A Husky sweatshirt, bearing the logo of the University of Washington Athletic Department, hangs on his muscled frame.

So, this is Bob Nomura. I shake his shy, tai chi–graceful hand, then lead the way to a vacant kitchen; Jill is on break. I watch the applicant closely, as I give him a rundown on tools and materials and inform him of the working hours. He listens and looks around in a pleasant manner.

At length we sit down for the actual interview. The man can turn out cheesecakes—my palate vouches for that—but how well does he know the basics of baking? His intense gaze seems to anticipate my concern. I feel a bit silly as I ask the cheesecake master, "How closely do you measure your ingredients, Bob?"

"To the nearest gram."

"How long do you mix cream cheese and chocolate?"

"Only till they make a liaison."

"How long do you cream butter and sugar?"

"Till the mixture is like silk. The butter can't be too cold."

"What kind of butter?"

"Always unsalted."

Prompt, correct answers, but I need to find out more, so begin to chat informally about baking. He reveals that he adds fresh fruits to his cakes and pies whenever he can, on the premise that fresh flavor is the critical element in a fine pastry. That's an answer I appreciate.

"Yesterday I perfected a marionberry coulis," he confides. "It was exquisite on top of a crumb cake."

Berry coulis happens to be my favorite fruit sauce and the marionberry version sounds like a real winner but, in the present situation, I can't afford too many new ingredients. Bob carries on to say he opts for minimal, varied toppings, rather than devoting hours to whimsical decorations that only detract from the natural elegance of a pastry. Perfect. I have no use for a baker who lives to create an extravagant blown-sugar sculpture. *Décoratifs*, such as gold and silver dusting, chocolate leaves, and lacy lemon zests, are okay.

"I've tried your cheesecake, by the way."

"You have? Well, a lot of people find it hard to believe that I can make cheesecakes—being Japanese and all."

Before I can think of a diplomatic reply, he adds, "My teacher at the Culinary Academy in California liked to yell across the kitchen— 'Don't put too much wasabi in your cake batter, Bob.' Everybody seemed to think that was hilarious for some reason."

"Did you ever put wasabi in your cake?"

"Yes, just once, on the topping, when no one was looking," he replies innocently. "I bought a jar of wasabi powder and mixed in a dab to a combination of whipped cream and crème fraîche to make the topping. It had lovely specks of green, and the bite of the horseradish contrasted with the velvety texture of the cream. The cake was gone in minutes. After that my classmates stopped making fun of me."

I allow a brief pause. "What made you go into cooking?"

"The standard cooking school answer is money, women, and power. But actually, my family ran a noodle house in Kyoto. We lived above the shop. When I was a baby, my mother kept me in a crib in the kitchen while she cooked. After a while, I couldn't fall asleep unless I heard kitchen noises and smelled the soba. So, I guess you might say cooking is in my soul. Still I didn't think I'd get into cooking, especially baking. It's through some unusual circumstances that I became a baker." His cheekbones glisten. "Baking gets me high."

The young applicant displays a good attitude, an eagerness to learn, a mastery of the basics, and a zeal for this line of work. He grew up in a similar environment to mine. But he's Roger's cousin. I still have trouble with that fact. How smug Roger would feel if I hired a relative of his. All's well between us, he'd assume, and forget the fact that he deceived and deserted me.

"Roger . . ." I check for Bob's reaction and he fidgets. "Were you close to him when you were growing up?" I ask.

"We grew up in different cities and he's a few years older . . ."

Bob sits back. Even after all this questioning, he doesn't seem flustered. Best to disregard the Roger factor. Bob meets my criteria. A trial period will not be necessary. I experience the exhilaration an employer feels on those rare occasions when she comes across an exceptional talent.

"I'm ready to offer you a part-time position, Bob." His gaze expresses gratitude. We discuss hours, salary, and benefits, and complete some paperwork. "I want you to know about a loiterer," I remark at one point. "You'll have to work alone in the early morning hours."

"I already know about him—Roger told me. I can take care of myself. I study martial arts four times a week, a practice I'd started back in Kyoto."

"What kind?"

"Aikido. It's great fun and ties right into baking—moving your ki or energy source through your entire system so you function better."

If asked, I could offer a few facts about that ancient Japanese martial art. It's based on centering oneself spiritually; and using an assailant's energy to immobilize him without inflicting permanent harm. I only wish I could apply the same technique to Roger.

"Just tell me how many cheesecakes you want," Bob says, "and I'll have them ready by six."

We trade thoughts about the size, quantity, and types of cheesecake we should offer. It's going to be a bit of work, but he takes the final decision so calmly. "The kitchen is yours tonight," I conclude. "You'll find all the ingredients on the shelves. But you'll have to do without wasabi until my next shopping trip."

He breaks into a grin, the smile dimpling his cheeks, and transforming him from a suave, self-assured adult to a gangly, self-conscious adolescent.

The hiring part was straightforward. My next task is to integrate him into my workforce—which might not be so easy—and see if he can tolerate the pressure.

TWENTY-ONE

THE AIR IS HECTIC WITH THE TART-SWEET NOTE OF AN OVEN FULL OF lemon bars. But the background scent reminiscent of movie pop-corn has me wondering if Jill measured the butter correctly. Oh, well, I'll just have to tolerate it. Huddled with my assistants around the workbench in the kitchen, I'm now in the midst of one of my twice-a-month staff meetings. In Pierre's absence, there is no one to crack jokes, serve us crumbles of cake, and mutter, *"D'accord, d'accord."* The meeting has been rather dull, as evidenced by glazed eyes staring off into space. The time is ripe for my announcement.

"Oh, by the way, I'm sure you'll all be happy to know that help is on the way . . . I've hired a part-time baker, Bob Nomura. He's an up-and-coming pastry chef. He should make your jobs a bit easier."

Heads snap up and eyes refocus as the news dives in.

"Nomura? Isn't that a Japanese name? I suppose we'll have to learn Japanese now?"

"No, just the accent," someone answers.

"What did you say the guy makes? Chocolate-covered sushi? Tofu vanilla pudding? I thought the only dessert the Japanese made were those icky, sticky, pounded-rice mochi balls that glue your mouth shut."

"Aw, come on, gang. Aren't you at least glad to have an extra pair of hands?" I ask, somewhat taken aback by the negative feedback.

Mumbles around the table indicate that I haven't overcome their reservations about my new hire. "Can he really bake?" one of them asks.

"Look, anyone who's good enough to work at the Georgian and the Sorrento Hotel can bake," is my answer. "But don't just take my word for it. Wait till you try his chocolate cheesecake. I bought a slice from Sorrento and shared it with a friend. He was impressed . . ."

From the collective murmurs I register, it appears that cheesecake is a personal favorite of several staff members as well. "Cheesecake, huh?" Scott says. "Well, if he can do cheesecake, he'll probably work out okay." Then, with a lingering trace of sarcasm, "So, when do we get to meet this maestro-san?"

"Tomorrow morning when you come in. He'll work from midnight to six."

"You're giving him Pierre's slot?" they gasp in unison.

"One night a week only. Pierre can still come back to his three nights."

On that note, the meeting breaks up. Jill jumps up and scurries over to the oven to remove a sheet of wimpy lemon bars. Crestfallen, she admits that she mistakenly doubled the butter and promises she'll be more careful the next time. Though wasting food gets on my nerves, I instruct her to throw the batch away and start all over; it's still early in the day.

Bob Nomura's cheesecake has become a hit. It is generally gone by eleven, despite the fact that its tariff is double that of other cakes—

except the Sunya Cake, which I don't bake these days. I just don't bake period. I lack concentration. Bob's cheesecake provides a welcome boost to my anemic bottom line, even though he uses some pricey materials. He orders Belgian chocolate from a food broker in the East. He goes berrying; he visits the Pike Place Market to select the freshest Oregon hazelnuts and, in both cases, I pay for his commute time. But beyond these privileged ingredients, the cakes are pure Bob Nomura: his slow baking in a hot water bath, the chemistry of a dash of strong coffee, his garnish of poached apricots, his crust of nuts and almond wafers. A litany of praise from my patrons reaffirm that I made the right decision when I hired him:

"Well worth a couple of extra hours on the treadmill."

"Better than sex. Well, maybe not better, but . . ."

"Orgasm."

Everyone's abuzz with enthusiasm about this new concoction, everyone except Donald J. Smith. Sitting at a bakery table this morning, a faint sunlight misting the window, I brace myself and open the *News* to his column. Here's what he says:

CHOKED BY CHEESECAKE!

The Bakery War gets stickier as Sunya Malhotra tries to reinvent cheesecake. Her recent hire, Bob Nomura, does his best to add pizzazz to a tired old calorific dessert by drizzling a caramel sauce on the surface, or swirling in a cloying mango puree. Some of you old-timers might recall that cheesecake was wildly popular in the seventies, then vanished for good reasons. A slice of that cake may appear light and airy to the uninitiated, but in truth is solid as a brick, sticks to the roof of the mouth, clogs the throat, and coats the taste buds with a layer of high-cholesterol fat for hours.

So, in this latest battle of the Bakery War, will the classic

lightly spiced hot cross buns, with a cross of white icing on
top, from Cakes Plus be able to hold its own against this
overpriced, high-fat holdover from the seventies? My guess
would be yes, folks would opt for simple old-fashioned goodness in the end. We'll have to wait till Cakes Plus opens its
branch in Wallingford and that, I've been promised, will be
before Christmas.

I snap the newspaper shut and dump it in the trash can. Is this Donald's revenge because he didn't get the Sunya Cake recipe? Or is
Donald just repaying Cartdale in advance?

Yesterday the cheesecakes were gone practically the moment they
hit the pastry case. They've become a gift alternative to a dozen roses,
a bottle of chardonnay, or a handcrafted greeting card. We book more
advance orders than we can fill. Baking only one day or sometimes
two days a week, Bob doesn't turn out enough of them to fully com-
pensate for the loss of the Sunya Cake sales. As a result, I am barely
staying ahead of the bills.

There's another issue here. As I'd feared, though Jill sets aside a
wedge of cheesecake for herself, Scott won't touch it. It's always "too"
something in his opinion—too rich, too soggy, too Kyoto, too much
of a production. Yesterday he snapped at Bob for filling up the refrigerator. Fortunately, Bob and Scott work different shifts.

This morning I catch Bob just as he's wiping off the kitchen
counter, his last act of the day. Dressed casually in fleece-cotton knit
V-neck pullover and utility pants, a headband around his forehead,
he's holding the sponge like an artist's brush and scrubbing at a stain,
his fingernails creamy against the pink of the sponge. The assertively
sweet scent of anise overhead is a tip-off that Bob has tried out yet
another new flavoring. The experimentation must have gone well.

His sleep-deprived eyes still hold a sparkle—he never shows any sign of tension—and that provokes a twinge of envy in me.

"What a wonderful smell," I throw in casually. "I'd like to have more smells like this in here throughout the week. What are you going to do the rest of the day?"

"I'm learning to ski. I go up to Crystal Mountain on Mondays and Thursdays."

I suppress the worry in my voice and ask, "And the days you're not skiing?"

"I play the guitar. Sometimes I take my watercolors, brushes, and paper over to the arboretum and paint flowers."

Optimism crisps up within me. Skiing takes money. Best to take a different tack: "Roger worked sixty hours a week at the fashion boutique when he was first getting started."

"With the trade conference only two weeks away," Bob says, "Roger's on three-quarter time this month. He took last weekend off with Kimiko."

It is as though the very air of the room is trying to suffocate me. Another little development that I'd just as soon not have heard about.

Bob is saying, "As for me, I like to enjoy life. A man does not live by cheesecake alone."

Straightening my posture, I gulp down my pride. "Could you work more hours, Bob? Things are pretty tight these days. I could really use your help."

"I couldn't work any more hours. It'll cut into my . . ."

"I just wish I knew what to do about cash flow . . ."

Bob starts, his eyes registering shock and concern, and faces me. "I do care, Sunya . . . You take care of your employees. You don't micro-manage me like my last boss did. He was always on my case, right down to telling me how many walnuts to use in the muffins."

"Then help me out. I need more cheesecakes. They're the hottest item on our menu, not to mention the difference between a profit and a loss."

Bob says nothing for a long second. Then he fishes out a three-by-five white index card from his pants pocket and hands it to me. "Here's the master recipe. Keep it to yourself, will you?"

I stand there mutely, cradling the prized recipe card in both hands, as he walks out the door, whistling.

In a jiffy, I feel a reassuring glow within me as it sinks in that Bob trusts me enough to share his signature recipe. Even though he's been here a short time we've managed to form a bond of mutual trust and respect, and that means a lot to me.

But then what use is this recipe to someone who's lost her ability to bake?

TWENTY-TWO

A FEW DAYS LATER, I AM STANDING AT THE BAKERY COUNTER, WHEN Eric Lawson, a retired naval officer in his eighties, comes by. I welcome my friendly long-term customer and ask him how he is doing.

"Old age is terrible, Sunya... I've forgotten my car keys twice this week." He looks wistfully at the display case. "But I never forget the tang of Pierre's apple pie."

As I serve Lawson an oatmeal bar and a glass of hot apple cider, I recall how much I miss Pierre's presence in the kitchen, his soft French mutterings and curses, the confidences we exchanged. Lawson walks back to his table. As I restack the napkins on one end of the counter, I go over the situation in my mind. It's been several weeks, more than enough time for Pierre to get over his "laryngitis."

The food service industry has an unusually high employee turnover rate and, consequently, the loss of an employee is not considered anything out of the ordinary. With all the bending, stooping, lifting, and pushing, commercial baking, as any insider will confirm, is hard on the body. Burnout is common. It's the under-thirty-five crowd who enter the profession then over time move on to other establishments for a chance to learn new skills. But Pierre, a rare combination of talent and personality, is different.

With Cakes Plus making its grand opening in the neighborhood in a few weeks—if the official date still holds—I cling to the hope that he'll return and help me save my business. Also, in my mind, a tray of boring hot cross buns and half-spoiled humbows are a poor match for Pierre's apple pie and Bob's cheesecake.

It's a day later and I'm waiting for the light at the busy intersection of Fiftieth Street and Sunnyside to change. On my way home from work, I have decided to drop in on Pierre to talk with him face to face, to see what's really holding him back. The light glows green. Within minutes, I arrive at the southern edge of the Wallingford District, the section bordering Lake Union, jokingly referred to by its residents as "Baja Wallingford." I park the car in front of Pierre's turn-of-the-century Dutch Colonial and hop out, struggling with a festive white bakery box trimmed in pistachio green. I've filled it with several choice items from the pastry case. The rest of my team has joined me in adorning the top flap with handwritten personal notes.

Knowing Pierre's afternoon habits, I open a small side gate and peek into his backyard. A jungle of fast-spreading wild blackberry, meant to provide a natural fence on the western side of his property, is strangling his normally well-tended yard. Somehow, Pierre has let the assertive brambles get the upper hand. The graceful Japanese plum tree, Pierre's pride, is covered with unsightly water shoots. It hasn't been pruned in a long time.

I let my eyes wander around the garden. Ah! There he is at the other end of the yard, attired in loose sweats, curled up in a chair, a glass of wine in his hand, a magazine on his lap. Even on a perfectly lazy autumn afternoon, he looks morose. With quick steps, I go up to him.

"Sunya?" His arms stiff by his sides, Pierre stands up, but doesn't hug me. "What a surprise! You smell of chocolate and honey, as usual."

"And you smell of cabernet sauvignon."

He shrugs and half-smiles. With a mock flourish, I offer him the box. "Here's something to perk up your afternoon."

He sets the box down on a side table. It is obvious he's not quite ready to reconnect with the bakery. As I take the extra chair, he returns to his seat, heaves an elaborate sigh, and scans the sky. A ray of intermittent sunlight streaks his forehead.

"I'm feeling much better now." He doesn't quite look at me. "I finally got rid of the laryngitis."

"Pierre, it's been almost a month. We miss you. We really need you at the bakery."

"Does Lawson still show up?"

"Yes. He asked about you."

"And that director friend of yours?"

"Oh, yes, he shows up with his crew quite often." I grin, trying not to show my impatience. "When we both have free time, we get together."

"I didn't like him when I met him, if you don't mind my saying so. You're too trusting, you know that?"

Pierre's grave tone hasn't escaped me. I give out a laugh to make light of the situation, though it comes out a trifle forced. "You sound just like my mother."

"Speaking of that, my *maman* wants me to go visit her in France."

Oh, no, not at this critical time. "And what does Stephan think about that?"

Pierre casts his eyes downward and falls silent. So, he and Stephan are still having problems. The bleak reality of the situation rattles in my head like ancient metal pots. I know how losing one's mate chews away at the foundation of one's life, sapping the body of its energy. And now, Seattle's changeable autumn weather must be making the situation worse for Pierre. Lately, with the sun slinking low across the southern horizon, we get only about eight hours of weak watery daylight. "Don't have your heart broken in autumn," goes a saying around here. "You'll have the eternity of cold damp dark Northwest winter to live through." I feel for Pierre, even as my wound resurfaces, just when I thought I'd gotten over it.

"There's something else, Sunya . . . You've given my shift to someone else."

A jet thunders overhead. Every four minutes an airplane blares over this part of the city, I'm told. As the noise subsides, I tell Pierre, "I had no choice."

His attention veers toward the cake box on the side table. I join him in giving the lid a fresh glance; it doesn't look bad at all.

Jill has drawn a cartoonlike crying child and scribbled underneath in small, neat letters (with the help of a tattered volume of *French for Dummies*): "*Tu nous manques.*" Bob had spared a few minutes to stop by on his way home from his aikido practice, bringing his special pen with him. He's inscribed some elegant Japanese calligraphy, which, I believe, translates into "We miss you, return soon." Scott has managed to disguise his hostility toward Bob long enough to scrawl a good wish and sign his name. As for me—in reference to the apple season that is fast passing by—I've sketched an apple tree with nearly bare branches and a bird pecking at a single lush fruit.

Pierre's face softens at this *salut* from his colleagues. With a small flick of his wrist, he lifts the lid to reveal the items. I expect his eyebrows to shoot up any moment in response to the unanticipated treats. Instead, he stares at them and stares at them. I can't quite see which piece he's focusing on.

I shift my chair to get a better view. The items peek out: an apple strudel and a hazelnut disc, both of which are Pierre's favorites; and, I can't believe my eyes, a wedge of chocolate cheesecake, its wavy top crowned by roasted piñons. A shudder runs through me. How did the cheesecake get in there? Pierre is stunned into silence. A crow circles overhead lured, I'm sure, by the dual scents of chocolate and pine nuts.

"Cheesecake, cheesecake, cheesecake, that's all I hear these days." He bends forward and slaps the box shut. The top flap caves in, smearing his palm with chocolate. He seems not to notice it.

I twist in my chair. Why couldn't I have checked the contents of the box before leaving the bakery?

"And as if that's not enough, that wretched Donald J. Smith slandered me in his column. What will people think? I, Pierre Talon, connected with some 'unsavory' character. A drug dealer, perhaps? Or a bookie?"

"Have you noticed lately that—"

"That Donald has it in for cheesecakes? Yes, I have. He seems to have forgotten me. Have you also forgotten I was your number one baker?"

I take a much-needed deep breath. "You're still my number one. Bob works only one day a week. Besides, you can't compare apple pie and cheesecake. Apples and cheese, you might say." My weak attempt to lighten the mood falls flat.

"There can't be two number ones in a kitchen, Sunya."

I pause to bask in the brief flash of sunlight pouring through a break in the clouds, my eyes roaming the thorny blackberries and tattered rhododendrons. With cheesecake outshining apple pie, it's Pierre's pride, his confidence, that has been hurt. He always had an innate ability when it came to baking, an instinctive sense that advised him when to reduce the sugar and lengthen the simmering period because the apples were juicier, to turn the pie pan in the oven for even baking at just the right moment, to glaze the top only so much. Perhaps he fears losing that precious gift, just as I do.

"You'll be working different days, Pierre."

"Fire him."

"I can't. The mayor and the first lady, among others, have taken a liking to Bob's cheesecake."

"Then I must give you my resignation, Sunya."

I leap to my feet and raise my voice. "No, I refuse to accept it."

Pierre sweeps to his feet. I scrutinize his defiant expression as he says, "Nonetheless, Mademoiselle Malhotra, I resign. Perhaps there are others who might appreciate my talents better."

My worst fear obliterates everything else in my mind, cuts out all city noise, and extinguishes the heat of the sun. I hear myself saying in the distance, "You're going to Cakes Plus, aren't you?"

Pierre's mouth goes tight. "You give me no choice."

"You're *not* taking my apple pie recipe with you."

Doesn't he hear me? He shuts his eyes for an instant, totes the cake box, and heads for the supersize garden trash bin in what he'd describe in his native tongue as *"une huffe."* I watch with horror as he throws the box into the bin. It topples the garbage pile inside, setting off a cascade of rattling breaking noises. I want to sob as I visualize a pure work of edible art, hours of fussing, now mangled and left for insects to devour.

"Thanks so much for stopping by, Sunya." Pierre makes a turn toward the house. "And, now, if you'll excuse me, I'd like to go back to bed. *Fatigué.*"

"Think you've had a hard life at my bakery," I call after him. "Wait till you work for a scumbag like Cartdale. You'll have to make do with canned apple fillings and margarine. You'll stand on a street corner and hand out coupons. Is that what you want to do?"

He jerks open the door. I notice the frisson in his body as he flees inside without looking back, and hear the sharp click of the latch snapping shut. Standing there in empty silence, I shake my head in shocked disbelief. Then I plod back to my car.

TWENTY-THREE

A T HOME THIS MORNING, STILL ANESTHETIZED FROM THE PIERRE INCI-
dent, I'm giving baking a try by attempting to make a carrot
torte. Just now, when I reach for the eggs, they're not there. I haven't
brought them to room temperature, which means they'll require more
beating. I chop the walnuts, which look kind of coarse, and pour the
overmixed batter in a springform pan only to notice that the lemon
juice is still sitting on the counter.

The torte goes into the oven and soon a sugary smell wafts out
of the oven. Not a complete loss, I assure myself. Then I open the
News to Donald J. Smith's weekly column. Masochistic, one might
say.

APPLE PIE VS. CHEESECAKE?

The latest intelligence from the front lines of the Bakery War
has it that Cakes Plus has scored a major coup by hiring
former Pastries Café star Pierre Talon. His fantastic open-
face apple pies, a Gallic rendition of the traditional American
favorite, will be standard fare at every Cakes Plus store in
the near future.

I stop reading for a minute and stare out across the room at the photograph of Seattle's skyline hanging on the wall. I imagine that the jagged profile, captured from a vantage point on Queen Anne Hill, could resemble a computerized printout of my swinging mood over the past several weeks.

Donald concludes:

> Anyone out there still up for cheesecake? Better get it while you can, because the sentiment in most quarters is that it won't be around much longer.

My head pounding, I let the paper drop to my lap. The stunning deception by my former baker and personal confidant slices to the core.

The sound of footsteps on the front porch interrupts my dismal train of thought. It's probably Mother. She's supposed to drop in on the way home from running some errands. I spring to my feet, fold the paper neatly, open the door, and put on a congenial face. Sure enough, Mother is standing there, shopping bag in hand. Her tiny frame is at odds with the glint of determination in her eyes. Though I'm taller than she, we have the same fine bone structure. Her fond gaze wipes away my hurt and I can't help but smile. Once inside, she wiggles out of a pair of buckled red patent pumps and nudges them over by the door with her foot. It's an Indian custom that years in this country have failed to erase.

"Oh, you must see what I bought." She shoves a crinkly shopping bag with the Wallingford Center logo into my hand. "It reminded me of you."

A pair of burgundy taffeta throw pillows with beaded (better known as "modified hippie") fringes are nestled inside the bag. "These would look well in your living room, Mother."

She tugs at her jacket to alleviate some unseen constriction and grimaces; her shell buttons glitter. The boxy two-piece ensemble is absolutely wrong for her; it makes her look stocky. And the moss-green fabric lends a somewhat muddy cast to her olive-brown skin. Still, she appears so maternal, so approachable, and her presence so illuminates my living room that I willingly overlook her fashion fault.

"You know, this is the first time I've ever seen you in a suit . . ."

She giggles. "I know, my dear, I could never have worn a suit, except that Dushan has asked me to have lunch with him. I thought I'd try to dress like a professional."

That name chafes my ears.

With quick precise steps that come from years of moving within the confines of a sari, Mother crosses the room. Standing at the kitchen door, she surveys the area with an appraising glance. I gesture her toward the table. Since she comes to the city only occasionally, I have spread a lace cloth on the table, which I have further adorned with bamboo place mats and a bouquet of cream-tinted roses. I've made sure the milk pitcher and the sugar bowl match.

Mother takes her accustomed seat by the wall, leaving me the chair by the window with a view. She still considers me her little girl who must be given the best choice. My murmur of protest, as always, goes unheeded.

We settle down with our late morning tea and fat slabs of still-hot carrot torte. Donald J. Smith's column so tipped me off balance that I left my usually superb torte in the oven five minutes too long. As a result, the rich carrot-orange hue has turned a poor cook's burnt brown that even a hasty application of orange glaze has failed to conceal. My feeling of chagrin is compounded by the awareness that I've lectured my assistants over and over again—the biggest sin of a baker is to overbake.

Mother mutters an introspective "Mmmm" as her teeth crunch

on a piece of nut. She smells of the Clearasil soap that she's used for twenty-five years. Glancing toward the living room, she says, "I love those violet orchids. *Sundar.*" Lovely. "Are those the same ones I saw the last time I was here?"

"No mother, its a fresh batch." Mother hasn't, so far, met Andrew. Curiously, she hasn't shown any interest. So, now, I cautiously add: "Andrew sent them."

"This torte isn't the same without your maple cream cheese frosting."

No response to Andrew's name. Worse yet, I can tell from the tone of disapproval in her voice that she has an issue to get off her chest. We're treading on sensitive ground. Because of her own sad marital experience, Mother is critical of my boyfriends. Roger charmed her by escorting her to the Cherry Blossom Festival, giving her a series of ikebana lessons as a birthday gift, and buying her bags of sweet rice from Uwajimaya. Best not to get into the topic. "I was just trying to cut down the calories for you."

"Dushan doesn't think I need to lose weight. He calls me his little bird. Isn't that nice?"

She beams to herself, wipes her lips with the napkin, folds it into a neat square, and sits back. Just when I begin to think she's forgotten her agenda, whatever that might have been, she says, "This Andrew sounds a little mysterious."

Normally Mother is so black-and-white about everything that I'm glad just this once she seems less than totally sure. Too, at the mention of Andrew's name, something resembling a quiver ripples through my chest. I lower my head to the plate. Andrew appreciates me; he has welcomed me into his exclusive club—food, wine, Plato, and his film. I, rarely a joiner, am enjoying the membership. But I'm not at all sure I understand him.

"From what you've told me," Mother says, "I can't seem to put it all together . . . like there are some missing parts . . . like you can never know the guy completely . . . How does he get along with his mother?"

I straighten a crease on the tablecloth. A question I'd rather not answer.

"Is he going to stick around for a while?"

"For at least another month. He talks about moving here."

"How do you know he doesn't have a wife down in L.A.?"

The carrot torte I'm nibbling feels like sand in my mouth. On so many occasions in the past, Mother "smelled this," "observed that," or "felt weird about something," and she's often turned out to be right. To her I reply, "How do I know? Well, he doesn't wear a—"

"Lots of married men don't." Mother looks down at her lap, plucks a crumb from her skirt, and deposits it on the place mat. "I don't like mystery in a man. Now on a woman mystery can be wrapped around like a fancy scarf and have it become her. For a man, mystery is a warning sign he is concealing some major flaw."

"I like being with him. Isn't that enough?" Still, both she and I know a seed has been planted.

"I have no doubt he enjoys being with you too. Lots of men these days want a trophy Asian woman in their arms, encounter of the exotic kind—"

"You haven't even met him. How can you make such a judgment?"

"Surely I've heard of fickle movie types. He's here to shoot his scenes, and cliché or not, my dear, you might just be a part of one."

"He's different, Mother. He has an education and good taste and a sophisticated view of the world—"

"Have you heard of many long, happy marriages in Hollywood? *Bolte parbee?*" Can you tell me?

I have to give Mother credit; I can't come up with even one happily married show biz couple. "Well, anyway, he's been good for me. I have gotten over my breakup with Roger, wouldn't you say? I'm just enjoying getting to know Andrew. That's all I can handle right now."

"You're the serious type."

"I'm not looking for romance and marriage."

"You're my daughter. And you're like me. You don't get involved with someone just for a couple of dates, then forget him, and start flirting with another. You take it seriously, *amar priya meye*." Beloved daughter.

"My generation doesn't consider marriage as the only outcome of a relationship."

"Stop twisting your hair."

I let the strand of hair around my index finger unwind and stir my tea.

"Oh, he's too good to be true, isn't he?" Mother sticks one elbow on the table, caresses her temple with her fingers, and wipes out an imaginary headache. "Just like my good husband was."

"Andrew is *not* like my father. He would never expect me to sacrifice my life for him . . ."

A frown has scrunched up on Mother's forehead, destroying the pleasing balance of that face. In her first year of marriage, Mother poured all of herself into her married life. She cooked, polished the floors, shopped, and held a part-time job, even found time to study the *News* so she could converse with her husband. He stole that first year of their marriage.

Reaching for the platter, I cut a second helping of solace from the torte. From the way she leans forward in anticipation, I can tell she's ready for a change of topic. She doesn't handle conflict well. It gives her motion sickness. She *is* like a little bird, as Dushan calls her.

Eyes on the brownish-orange slice on her plate, Mother asks, "Organic carrots, aren't they." It's really not a question. "Even in winter you go hunting for them in the stores."

And I'm relieved that at least for now we're back to our tradition of small talk, sharing little pleasures as we always have, harmony returned between us.

TWENTY-FOUR

STANDING AT THE THRESHOLD OF ANDREW'S LIVING ROOM, HOLDING two boxes filled with chocolate cheesecakes, I search through the crowd to the farthest corner of the room. He left a message a few nights ago, reminding me of the party. "A get-together for my team and a few friends," he said. "Hope you can make it."

I'm dressed in dagger-heeled pumps and a short-sleeved black chemise. To complete my outfit, I have spritzed a light mist of Red Door perfume on my wrist and behind my earlobes, and clipped on half-moon-shaped silver earrings that practically slice my jawline. I only wish it was easier to breathe. Parties are miserable for me and have been since I was a child, always the outsider, the last to be invited, the first to leave.

This particular affair—music pulsing to a snarly drumbeat, satin floor-lengths, boutique jeans, and caterers in navy uniforms—is bigger than I expected. Exalted food scribe Donald J. Smith stands in a far corner in his usual checkered sport jacket and with a matching scarf wound around his neck, playing the debonair raconteur to a rapt circle of nymphets. He holds his wineglass between his thumb and forefingers like it's a trophy he's about to present. Even at a distance,

I can see that his puffy cheeks are glistening with a thin sheen of perspiration—he must have gained a couple of pounds recently. He spots me and grins.

Andrew threads his way through the crowd. Excitement sweeps through me as we eye each other. A peck on my cheek and he lifts the cake boxes out of my hands. "So glad you made it," he whispers. This private greeting I love. In a jacquard shirt, all blues and yellows, the kind a sales clerk carefully lays between the folds of tissue paper at an upscale boutique, this is the most dressed I've seen him. He eases me into a clutch of people, introduces his brother, Evan (a look-alike, though a bit shorter and stockier), then Wayne, Mac, and Peter. "Friends from L.A." Andrew nods to each in turn. "We work together."

"Sunya Cake?" Wayne, the bearded Angelino, inquires. "Delish is the word."

"The cheesecake's a national treasure," interjects Peter, emerald studs in his ears.

"That chick at the counter—Jill—is a real treat for the eye," Mac, easily six six, chimes in.

As the friendly banter continues, I notice that a fourth person whose face carries an attitude has insinuated herself into the group. She's about my age, this tall vine of an Asian woman with a boy-cut hairstyle and ominous purplish lipstick that reminds me of those campy vampire movies I watched as a teenager. Draped in ankle-length, magisterial violet, she appears to be someone who subsists on a banana a day. She looks me over coolly, contemptuously, then before I can blink, herds Andrew over to a corner. Soon they are engaged in a conversation punctuated with laughs, hand gestures, and knowing smiles.

I shrug inwardly at the feeling of being unloved and am about to turn away when a bearded man with a candid, friendly face positions himself before me.

"Hi, I'm Chuck. I love your bakery. I'm the DP, the director of photography," he explains.

"I saw you during the filming at the bakery. Weren't you the one yelling at the actors?"

"Oh, yes, I confess I've done that upon occasion." Chuck treats me to an impromptu rundown of his entire trade. The words "cut," "zoom," "composition," "front lighting," and "cross-fading" pepper his talk. My gaze keeps drifting to Andrew, but I'm grateful for the cover Chuck's talk provides. "All the actors kiss up to me on the set," he concludes. "If they want to look good in the film, that is. Until I show up on the set, they're all just killing time. Not bad for a boy from Moline, Illinois, eh?"

He laughs expansively, the sound is pleasant, and I smile, not wanting him to leave quite yet. A caterer comes by with tiny lavosh triangles that some misguided cook has slathered with at least five unrecognizable toppings. I take one and nibble tentatively as if it were some mysterious delicacy to be savored in small bites. Unfortunately, it's salty to the point of being inedible. Chuck takes two, makes a sandwich, and swallows the whole thing. Wild laughter and lively exchanges animate a space so crammed that it feels as claustrophobic as being way down in a cave. Moving through the crowd, wine goblets in hand and exchanging greetings, we pass a young man gesticulating wildly. "Exposure equals Intensity multiplied by Time."

"Film school students." Chuck grins. Then we find ourselves face to face with Donald J. Smith.

"Well, we just keep running into each other, don't we, Donald? This is Chuck, one of my 'unsavory characters.' "

Chuck laughs out loud—ribald proof that he approaches Donald's columns with the proper disposition—then asks if we want refills, a transparent excuse for a trip to the food table.

Now we're alone. Donald's face has turned the color of mashed yam. I didn't know he was capable of suffering this much embarrassment.

"Well, well . . ." He fumbles for words as he stares at the floor.

"Why, Donald, I don't think I've ever seen you at such a loss for words. By the way, I've been thinking about asking you who gave you the scoop on the loiterer?"

"You know I can't reveal my sources."

"What gave you the idea that the man was up to something unsavory? Do you have a clue how your innuendo may have affected my struggling business? I believe there is a term for that in the legal profession—slander, or something like that."

"I suppose it's possible all the facts haven't been checked. Some inferences may have been made that could prove unfounded at a later date."

Chuck returns with a plate and glances at both of us. We turn and gaze at the wedge of chocolate cheesecake capped with sour cream and mandarin orange slices.

"Since you haven't been to my bakery lately"—I hold out the plate to Donald—"you probably haven't had an opportunity to try our new chocolate-orange variation."

Donald turns the plate around, examines it from all angles, sniffs in a manner that is obviously a ritual for him, pops a forkful into his mouth, and shuts his eyes. "Mmm, I might get used to cheesecakes, after all."

"No unsavory character baked this, Donald."

Donald keeps his gaze riveted on the plate. "It'd be nice to have a peek at the recipe . . ."

Purposely I stay silent. In about six more bites, Donald finishes the cake and sets the plate on a side table. "I really must go now," he says. "My column's due tomorrow, then I'm off on vacation to New Zealand." Glancing at me, then at the door, he starts to turn away.

I practically hold him by the hem of his jacket. "About that retraction, Donald?"

"I'll take it under consideration." Donald's breathing is a trifle labored, and not just from eating too fast.

"How badly do you want the recipe, Donald? That's also under consideration."

Barely have I turned when amid blown kisses and a sudden drop in the level of conversation the woman in the violet dress crosses the room. Someone shouts, "Have a safe flight."

At last, I can breathe again. Head down, Andrew walks over and joins Chuck and me, but avoids my eyes. In a minute, he gathers himself and offers me a restrained smile. As a cluster forms around us and the talk gravitates to film, he includes me in the conversation, explaining terms and taking pride in introducing me to newcomers who drift into the group. At some point, his fingers wander to mine and lace them. His moist grasp tells me that he's come back to me, that he's mine, never mind the violet dress, never mind Mother's warning. With a newfound sense of well-being, I stroll easily with Andrew among the guests. My silver dazzling, my black dress giving me polish, I don't let it worry me that I'm straightforward, that I don't have the allure of an actress. Every so often, Andrew turns and gives me a warm glance. I squeeze his hand, finding strength and delight in that. On second thought, I really don't hate parties.

By now, it's late, the room is quiet, the temperature has dropped, and Andrew and I are alone with soiled plates, spilled cups, crushed napkins, and cigarette butts. Through the thin walls, I can hear his brother Evan snoring in the adjoining room. I begin putting away the food items, asking Andrew, "Where does the sugar go?" and, "Should I save the bread?" As he answers me, he collects empty bottles and beer cans and pitches them into a garbage can. A lone sliver of chocolate cheesecake, still holding its shape, beckons from the coffee table.

"Want to split this?" I call out to Andrew.

He spins around, spots the cheesecake, and hustles theatrically. "All that cheesecake and I thought I wasn't going to get any. There's cosmic justice, after all."

There is not a single clean spoon or fork in sight, so we wash our hands in the kitchen sink, return to the living room, sink down into the sofa, and dig our fingers into the mousselike top. Andrew seems lost in the delirium of chocolate. "The amaretto-laced sour cream lavished on top is not entirely necessary," he says after a few moments, "but it prepares the mouth. A small pleasure to precede big pleasures, that sort of thing."

Each luscious bite calls for an encore and soon the frivolity disappears. Once again, as I look around the room, I wonder, Who was that woman? It pains me to be reminded of her. And this very room, this very corner where they stood together, reminds me of her. Just as I turn, Andrew looks at me fondly.

"Want to hear what we've been shooting this week?"

"Yes, oh, yes."

He dims the lights. It doesn't take long for the sharp corners of the room and furniture to fade into the shadows, imparting a sense of warm and fuzzy intimacy. When one sees less, one feels more and, at the moment, I'm softer, newly receptive, and less questioning.

He says, in a voice that seems to originate from somewhere off in the darkness, "This is what we've got in the can . . . Werner has been seeing Emily every day for a week. This evening they leave another CAGT meeting together and go to her place. Emily asks if he'd give her a hand making some flyers. Werner says yes. They huddle at the computer keyboard. Somewhat of a whiz at computer graphics, Werner draws a huge fist. The bold slogan below it in green reads: 'Smash Global Trade!' Clutching the printed page, she dances around the room, alternately miming a volunteer handing out leaflets, and a demonstrator thrusting her fist in the air. 'The obese cats are in for a surprise tomorrow,' she chortles. 'We're ahead of the game. We've been given some inside intelligence about how many cops will be called in.'

"The way she spits out the word 'cop' makes him cringe. Still he can't get up and leave. This is what has brought them together, their personal dedication to the cause. He draws her close and begins kissing her. At first, they are tentative and gentle kisses, then they become the deep probing passionate kind. She pushes away, saying, 'I've taken a vow of celibacy.'

"He can't quite believe the word: celibacy. His watch reminds him it's getting late. But then he takes a look at that lovely face. He draws her head to him and a longer kiss seals her surrender.

"In the morning, Werner awakens to unfamiliar surroundings. He's sprawled out naked, Emily next to him, in her bedroom. He rubs his eyes, yawns, and wonders how he could have let himself get this far. An image of his wife, Alexandra, comes into his head. Werner stretches his legs out, as though pushing away Alexandra's accusing face. Emily is not his first dalliance . . . but he'd rather not dwell on that now.

"They spend the day together, doing ordinary tasks that couples do. In the evening, with her hand in his, he sits in her living room and lapses into depression. 'Tomorrow's the day,' he says.

" 'You're not going to go all out, are you?'

" 'Afraid so. It's the only way I know. Now, you mentioned some inside information a little while back. Perhaps you could share it with me? It could make all the difference.'

"She hesitates a moment, stands up, and fetches a large diagram of the Convention Center and the peripheral area. 'The cops will be here and here and here.' She points to several places with a pencil.

"He pores over the chart. She's hiding a smile. She has deliberately misled him to keep him away from the danger zones. She doesn't quite understand this mysterious man or what he's up to. She flashes back to last night—that hidden revolver among his clothing, the snatches of conversation with his children in his sleep.

"She reviews her own plan inside her head. She'll be there on the sidelines outside the Convention Center and follow Werner's movements closely. If per chance he's getting too close to the police barricades, she'll jump in and steer him away. She'll distract him before he gets the gun out of its holster, with a passionate kiss.

"She gazes at his frowning appearance and offers to serve him a dessert, chocolate cake from Pastries Café. He says he'll pass. It's time for him to go back to his motel and get a good night's sleep. He promises to get together with her the next day after the demonstrations are over.

"A lie. He flashes on the return ticket to Atlanta in his billfold. The flight departs right after the demonstration is over. He takes her face in his hands, tastes her lips one last time, then he's out the door."

I've been so deep in the story that I can almost believe these characters exist, that maybe they're even carrying on with their lives someplace nearby: Werner talking, laughing, seducing, and hiding his guilt. Emily working, shopping, driving, putting money in parking meters, and dreaming: She can't aspire to long stretches of happiness. She can only grab a few moments here and there, as circumstances permit.

Andrew is sitting so close that it's as though we share a common skin. While he gathers himself, my imagination goes to work again. How much of Andrew has gone into Werner? True, Werner is less cerebral than his creator, but do they have similar fears, desires, and vulnerability? Put rather bluntly, how well do I really know this man who has so thoroughly captivated me these past few hours?

I don't dwell on that for very long, or rather Andrew doesn't let me. He pulls me toward him, my bare arm brushing the fine fabric of his shirtsleeves, his fingers gently pressing the ridge of my spinal column. He pours soft sweet kisses on my lips. Instantly I'm wide-awake, with a sense of how a bud opens its petals at night, the struggle involved. A few more kisses flood away the last vestige of resistance on my part, drawing me away from the mental realm. Then I hear some stirrings from the next room. We separate, our common dream interrupted. The softness, the melting I experienced in my body disappears, though I'm glad our hands are still joined.

Evan pokes his head out from his room into the dark hallway. "You guys still up?" he mumbles. Wrapped in a bathrobe he steers toward the kitchen sink. "What time is it, anyway?"

Both of us breathe deeply. Andrew chokes out some incoherent words, while Evan turns on the tap and pours himself a glass of water. The sudden noise thunders in my ears.

"Oh, my." I collect my purse from the corner of the room and feel for the car keys inside. "I didn't realize it was this late."

Andrew walks with me to the door and helps me with my coat.

"Call me soon," he whispers and opens the door. Darkness is all around us, though that doesn't inhibit the deep look we bestow on each other.

I answer with a smile, touch his lips with mine, and hurry down the steps into the crisp dark November night.

TWENTY-FIVE

THIS LATE IN THE MORNING, THERE'S A LULL BEFORE THE LUNCHTIME crowd begins to arrive. The bakery is nearly empty; vacant, but not hopeless, I think as I walk in from the kitchen. Then my eyes hit two men, both in their early forties, bending over the display case. They're studying the pastries and exchanging comments in hushed whispers. Their detectivelike manner captures my attention. Comments and suggestions from my patrons are always welcome, so I sidle up behind them as unobtrusively as I can, and listen in. Jill is at the other end of the counter boxing some items for them.

"That gigantic daisy bun looks good," one man whispers to his companion, "but I doubt it tastes half as good as my hot cross buns."

"After all that negative publicity in the *News*," his companion says, "I wanted to try a slice of cheesecake it, but it looks like they've run out."

"She obviously can't afford to have too many." The first man snickers. Upon finishing each sentence, he pauses to make sure his audience is suitably impressed before he continues. "I have it from a reliable source that she's in a deep financial hole."

I stifle a gasp as the realization crashes on me that this is Willy Cartdale!

And this is the moment I've been both anticipating and dreading, an actual face-to-face encounter.

How dare he sneak into my shop at an off-hour to check it out? I take a step back and assess the man: calculating gaze, smooth gestures, lips that spew honey and poison at the same time. All in all a formidable foe, but I must rise to the challenge.

I take a deep breath, pull a smile on my lips, and turn to him. "Good morning, Mr. Cartdale. It is Mr. Cartdale, isn't it? I'm Sunya Malhotra."

He nods, forces a smile, and regards me with a peculiar squint.

"I tried serving hot cross buns, by the way, when I first opened this bakery. Customers said they just couldn't compare to the daisy buns, so I discontinued them."

His eyes rove over the room, to the mostly unoccupied chairs, then he turns to me with a secret smile in his eyes. "Customers?"

"Oh, you're lucky. You arrived after the rush. You wouldn't have been able to get in."

"Well, yes, I missed it, didn't I? Would you care to sit down for a minute?" he asks.

"Sure."

"I'll join you in a few," his companion, now chatting with Jill, calls out.

Cartdale follows me over to a table by the window; a bit too closely, which I suspect is a tactic designed to discomfort me. I wrinkle my nose at the stale cigar smoke on his breath. He sits down, clasps and unclasps his hands.

"And what brings you to my shop?"

"Take it as a compliment. Dushan and I are buddies. We go fly-fishing together. I've been teaching him, and he's getting quite good,

I must say." A prickly pause. "Naturally the bakery business comes up from time to time. It's a very competitive industry, as I'm sure you're beginning to see."

"Oh, Mr. Cartdale, I'm not an industry. I'm running a small neighborhood operation that caters to a limited local clientele. I'm no threat to you. You're the one who's worried. You're the one who doesn't have a 'bake and let bake' philosophy."

"Afraid of you? Hardly. That's not how Cakes Plus works. We're growth oriented. Our shareholders want us to perform at the highest possible level, with the bottom line always in view. Our earnings have been excellent since I took over, but I'm not done yet. I can envision a prominent place for Sunya Cake in my pastry case. Sunya Cake, the crown jewel of cakes. That's my dream. By the way, I didn't see any in your display case today."

"You can shop here anytime you want on a retail basis, just like my other customers . . . but—"

"I'd like to take Sunya Cake to the top, make it even more famous—"

"I'd like to maintain my small separate identity."

"Your debt is so high, Ms. Malhotra, and your equity so low. Think seriously. Cakes Plus may be the only place people will be able to get Sunya Cake in a month or so. Your charming café will be empty, even emptier than now, but you'll see lots of activity over our way." He leans back, his white-shirted chest expanding, and doles out a smile that I rather hadn't seen.

"So kind of you, Mr. Cartdale. I can't tell you how much I appreciate it, but—"

"You won't get an offer from Cakes Plus once you've lost—"

He goes silent, though his eyes put across a warning that he doesn't take no for an answer, so best to take what's on the golden table now. I sit strong and upright before him, my stare conveying once again my decision with clarity. His companion, holding four boxes, approaches our table, flicks glances at both of us, perhaps wondering what has transpired to generate such a tense silence between two new acquaintances.

Cartdale rises, making a huge scraping noise as he pushes the chair back. "Well, it was interesting to have met you, Ms. Malhotra. You're exactly what Dushan said you'd be."

"You're full of compliments today, Mr. Cartdale."

I'd like to have added that he's just like the pastries he sells, but he would not have heard me, busy as he is stalking toward the door. Wound up as I am, in the battle of wills, I've held my own, and I smile at the thought.

Then again, I haven't seen the last of him.

TWENTY-SIX

MOTHER HAS INVITED ME FOR DINNER AT HER HOME IN MOUNT VERNON to celebrate my twenty-ninth birthday. Twenty-nine years seem like a lot, but thirty, a major intersection, is not too far away, I remind myself. We're seated at the dining table arranged beautifully with linen, silver, and sprigs from a red-berried mountain ash tree that form a cheery contrast to the grayish-green walls. I've just polished off the last of the peanut rice and spicy roasted eggplant, two of my favorite homey dishes though, as always, birthdays leave me disquieted.

While Mother is preoccupied with cleaning the table, I take the time to admire the Burmese jade ring on my finger that she's given me as a birthday gift. Set in gold, the lavender jade lends a lambent cast to my finger. "Oh, Mother, it's just beautiful."

"A while back you described a ring you saw on a customer," Mother confesses, "and how much you liked it. So I made a trip to the International District and went from one jewelry store to another until I found this one."

She walks over to the sideboard, picks up a book, and holds it out before me. It's a copy of *In a Baking Mood* by Elizabeth Dorchester, a well-worn, mass-market paperback recipe collection from a bygone era. Perhaps this gift is a monument to the time when I used to pore through volumes of ancient cookbooks for inspiration. Right now, still puzzling over the encounter with Cartdale, I am not particularly disposed to read about baking but, for Mother's sake, I feign interest as I leaf through the pages.

"I found this at a flea market in Bellingham," she announces above the rattling sound of dishes.

I watch her as she flutters about the living room, chatting about this and that, while waiting for the tea to finish steeping. When it's ready, she serves it in china with a flying-bird motif. Lifting the cup to my nose, I breathe in the pungent aroma, and sip. She has prepared the tea just the way I like it—leaves brewed extra strength with milk and an inch stalk of lemon grass (her big secret). Still I wonder whether beneath the enchanting ambience of this special day, she nurses a seething resentment at the misfortune that befell her right after my birth. Does this day somehow remind her of her husband's disloyalty?

She may have sensed my discomfort, for she goes to the drop-leaf desk, fetches a vinyl family photo album, takes a seat beside me. Proudly she flips through the pages and points to pictures of my child-hood. She's trying to distract me, to show how much she cares. And it works. I bend over the album and am immediately engaged. One shot goes back to the time when I was six years old and wore a hand-embroidered dress; my front teeth were missing. In another, camera-shy little imp as I was then (a trait I've never overcome), I seemed to be staggering away with both hands in front of me. "I had to offer you English toffee to make you stand still for pictures." Watching my expression, Mother laughs with pleasure. Then she opens her album page to a nine-by-twelve black-and-white portrait of my paternal grandmother. The woman sits in a chair and looks away from the camera. She's in her early adulthood then, possibly right after her marriage when dreams were aplenty. From behind a diaphaneous veil, her eyes glow with a bright expectant light.

I look away, but not before something catches Mother's eye. "When you were looking at her photo just now," she muses, "it was like you were looking in a mirror. She was a graceful woman, you know."

"No, I don't know." It's a sore point for me that Father's family has ignored Mother and me. "I've never met her."

There's a lull, as though a blind man has just walked in. Perhaps it's the picture, or the indirect connection with Father, but the atmosphere of the room has subtly changed and Mother's expression has turned somber. I drain my cup, engage in small talk for a few more minutes, then excuse myself, pleading the long drive to Seattle and a busy schedule tomorrow. The pain in Mother's eyes is unmistakable as we embrace at the door and I walk down the steps with the guilty feeling that I haven't spent enough time with her.

On the way home, my mind wanders back to the circumstances of my birth, gleaned from stories that Dee, my mother, has let slip over the years.

Carrying her two-day-old daughter in a crimson and white quilt, Dee slipped in through the door of her apartment in Seattle's Ravenna District. She thanked the kind neighbor who'd given her a lift from Virginia Mason Hospital, and cheerily refused any further help. "I can manage," she said untruthfully. "Prabhu will be back soon."

Closing the door behind her, she recalled Prabhu's routine. Every day he started out from the house promptly at eight A.M., with a bulging briefcase in hand, walked across the street to the store at the entrance to the alley, left with a couple of doughnuts and coffee, and drove to the University of Washington campus, where he researched and lectured in chemistry as a teaching assistant. He returned late, never before the clock on the bookshelf read eight P.M. Generous and dedicated, he carried more than the normal workload for his department.

During the day, whenever she called him, he dropped his reserved workplace manner. "How are you, Dee? What did you do today? Anything I should pick up on my way home?"

"No, no, just wanted to say hello."

"*Accha, accha.*" Very well, very well. "I'll be home the usual time."

"I'll be waiting."

Even that brief contact seemed to soothe him and he'd express his appreciation for her call before he disconnected.

In the evening, she would be weary of sitting in the living room, sipping a cup of fennel tea (a natural systemic cleanser, she believed), and sewing baby clothes. He'd slip in with the same bulging briefcase, his face drained of its deep brown color. He would manifest his apology with a flicker in his gaze. It took a few minutes before he articulated the words. "So sorry that you're sitting and waiting for me again. And you haven't eaten yet." As they sat down to a dinner of flat bread, mango pickles, and a vegetable *ghonto*—his eating habits were remarkably simple—he'd talk about his day. He held nothing back, not even the most intricate research problem he'd encountered, and with no overtone of condescension, he presented his findings to her, as though she were a peer, or an old classmate. She loved him because underneath his academic success, he was a decent man with ordinary desires. At times, his gaze held blankness, as though what he looked for wasn't there. She didn't bother to probe. She understood that, as a new immigrant, his job options were few. He toiled doubly hard to provide for her, and she was more than grateful.

Still, she hoped today would be different, for Sunya's sake.

Stepping inside the apartment, Dee hung lovingly over her sleeping firstborn, nestled in her arms so innocently, and sniffed the baby's milky smell. Yesterday, in the hospital bassinet, the baby had cried and squiggled when Prabhu gazed raptly at her. Dee had watched as the nurse swooped down, scooped up the fragile baby, and gave her to Prabhu. He held her close, rocked her, and cooed a few gentle words. Sunya was a bud that represented their married love, the faith they had in their adopted land, and the future they fancied, but Prabhu's face betrayed a shadow of discomfort. Did he need an adjustment period? For a brief moment, Dee considered the possibility that he was disappointed that she had not borne him a son.

No, that couldn't be it. He'd chosen the name Sunya himself. Though Dee had racked her brain compiling a list of stylish Indian names for a girl, such as Anupama, Urmila, Mallika, names with the tonality of a well-crafted bell, and relatives from India had weighed in with additional suggestions, Prabhu had insisted: "We're going to call her Sunya."

"Never heard of such a name," Dee said.

He looked weary, the extra stress of being a father, she assumed. "Her name will be Sunya," he repeated.

Dee had argued, and eventually conceded, albeit reluctantly. She'd hoped that in the weeks to come Sunya, with her tender glances and helpless gestures, would teach him how to ease into the paternal role.

In the bedroom, Dee lowered the infant to her crib, smelling the arrangement of dried yarrow and curled leaves of bird of paradise that sat on the nightstand. A sense of triumph welled in her for the second time in her life. (The first had occurred over a year ago during her marriage ceremony.) Who else but she could have produced this tiny package of delight? Sunya's birth had transformed Dee, with a vibrant person springing from within and taking hold.

Most newborns, wrinkled and reddish, with sparse hair pasted to their heads, don't appear quite human, but Sunya was different. Looking down at those big dark eyes blinking to adjust to the day, the lofty cheekbones glistening in the window light, the hint of a chin already jutting out assertively, Dee was suffused with a gush of pride.

Time to catch up on some neglected household chores. Dee stood up and made a mental note to put red lentils to soak before she started the laundry. Later she'd boil and spice the softened kernels into a textured yellow soup that Prabhu devoured with slurps of appreciation, the only time he abandoned himself to boyish expressions of delight. She loved him more in those moments.

She'd just turned toward the door when her gaze fell on a folded note propped up on the oak vanity, which also housed her hairbrush, hand mirror, and a tea candle. A congratulatory message? Who could have sent it?

As she picked up the note, a faint abstract design in the background filtered through the stark white surface of the paper. Black ink, the familiar tight script darker in some spots than others. Dee glanced at the signature at the bottom and it was then her fingers went numb, her spine rigid. Why would Prabhu write her a note now, when he'd recently forgotten her birthday? Perhaps pressure to finish research meant an unusually late return. She quickly scanned the brief message.

> I can't bear *samsara* anymore. It is not for me. I must
> go in search of deeper truth and won't rest till I find it.
> This has nothing to do with you. Please understand.
> And please forgive me.

It just didn't add up. She felt as though she'd collided with a truck and was struggling to rise from the pavement. She slowed down and studied the note two, three, four times, even spoke the sentences aloud, but still couldn't believe what she was reading. The man she'd

given her love to; the man she'd never been able to understand completely; now a man who'd decided he could no longer deal with the
responsibilities of being the head of the household. Why did he do
this? How would she manage? He'd left her only a meager two-digit
savings account and a charge card. How would she care for the baby?
Her stomach felt acidic; her body still hurt from the delivery. She
dropped the note back to where it was.

He was really, truly, gone.

Almost as if she understood the gravity of the situation, the baby
burst into a fit of crying. Dee picked her up and began to nurse her,
though not with the usual care, stopping when tears started to stream
down her own broad cheeks and drip onto the baby's narrow ones.
Her lungs were ready to erupt into a scream of agony. This must be
what being shipwrecked felt like, or being the last person on earth,
or suddenly being deprived of sight and hearing.

He didn't love her. His devoted gaze in the morning and hard
passionate embrace at night were false and manipulative gestures.

Eventually, Dee wiped her moist eyelids with her fingers. The sun had
retreated beyond the horizon like some pitiless postscript to Prabhu's
note, and a dank chill had crept in through the window to take its place.
Her legs barely carrying her to the phone, she dialed the number of the
chemistry department. It took two tries to get it right. She'd transposed
the digits the first time.

"May I speak with Prabhu Malhotra?"

In her mind, she prepared herself for the usual routine. The high
young voice at the other end, a student part-timer at the reception
desk, would switch her call to either the chemistry laboratory or
Prabhu's cubicle.

"Mr. Malhotra no longer works here," the receptionist informed
her. "He resigned yesterday."

"Resigned?"

"It was all rather sudden."

"Do you know where he went?"

"He said something about going abroad. Are you a student? We're getting so many calls. I can put you through to the department head. She'll be able to give you more information. We all will miss him."

Dee couldn't bear the embarrassment of anyone in the department knowing that it was she who'd called. Think of the gossip it'd generate if they figured out her identity. The genial, well-published chemist and dedicated research scientist, who on numerous occasions slept on a couch in the laboratory at night, had abandoned his wife and baby girl. "Poor thing," they'd muse in patronizing tones over their coffee in the faculty lounge. "Wonder what she was like?"

"Thanks, that won't be necessary." Dee let go of the receiver and with it her last hope for Prabhu.

Stumbling to the kitchen, she fixed herself a cup of fennel tea out of habit, then poured it down the sink where it disappeared with a plaintive gurgling sound. She had no thirst, no appetite, no taste left in her palate. She couldn't hear the traffic sounds from outside the window.

Back in the bedroom, she picked up the baby. During the last few months of her pregnancy, she had quit her part-time job of teaching floral art design—a course called Flowers for Fun—at the trendy School of Flower Therapy situated in the affluent Laurelhurst area. In Calcutta, where she came from, sidewalk flower shops were to be found everywhere but she never had been able to afford such frivolities. Instead, she read up on flower arranging and mastered the essential techniques, employing elements of color, fragrance, depth, texture, form, and space. She came to the States well versed in how to snip the stem ends properly and mix foliage, berries, and flower blossoms to create a seasonal effect, how to select an appropriate container, and how to make even a silk flower bouquet look as though it occurred naturally. The minimum-wage job allowed her only to splurge on a few knickknacks, such as the four wooden picture frames—filled with family photographs—on the wall. But the people she met in her class—wealthy, fashionable, "with it" women—amused her. Their nails painted and hair coiffed, they wore ostentatious long scarves and carried shopping bags that were stuffed with purchases from Nordstrom. (To satisfy their vanity, not out of need.) Their conversation revolved around grilling meat, programs at the Intiman Theater, skiing weekends at Whistler, and occasionally the children who were more a burden than joy. Life, to them, was either ennui, or one continuous celebration. She looked wistfully at them; they descended from another planet.

She'd hoped to give up working altogether and stay home with her blessed baby. Sunya would have a pampered childhood, with dolls, friends, birthday parties, a room of her own (painted in bright orange, Dee's favorite color), and the complete attention of her mother who'd grown up with no luxury at all. Sunya should never have to dirty her fingers mopping floors or selling popcorn after school at a discounted movie theater, never. Dee also longed for some free time of her own—an hour here and there in an easy chair on the roof would do—to dig into a novel, lose herself in flute music, or just contemplate life as one big entity and not merely an endless string of mandatory daily tasks.

Dee walked over to the closet. Most of Prabhu's pants and shirts, in shades of terra cotta and sand—the man had zero color sense—still hung there. His small suitcase was missing. Where had he gone? Certainly not back to India. He'd been glad to escape the stress and congestion of Calcutta with its cacophonous maelstrom of cars, trucks, rickshaws, buffalos, and people, omnipresent teeming throngs of people.

She recalled the morning only a few days before Sunya's birth. On his way out the door, he'd taken her chin in his hand (he always had a thing about her chin) and, in an intimate tone, murmured, "You look especially pretty today." She'd gazed up at him, at her life. His was an easy presence. He filled the living space and her heart. Though he daily sat in meditation for an hour upon arising—in full lotus-position on the living room carpet—he didn't push his religious beliefs or his droll religious witticisms on her. Later the same day, while mopping the tiled kitchen floor, as she reflected on it, his praise seemed out of context. And context might be what he was seeking now. The mundane realities of conjugal life had held little interest for him. He became restless when she complained about how little money she had left in the checking account, how far she had to drive to purchase the best quality *arhar dahl*, wondered if she should renew the lease agreement for the apartment for another year, or seek a more reasonable accommodation elsewhere. It was as though they were living on opposite sides of a partly open window. She could see and hear him through the crack, but not touch him.

Now Dee cooed "Sunya, Sunya," into the baby's ears. Sunya would grow up taller, prettier, more vibrant than her mother, Dee hoped, and would be blessed with her father's intelligence. She would assert herself in a way Dee never had. (Was this not, after all, America?)

To whom should she turn for counseling, for solace? Dee searched her mind in vain, but couldn't come up with any suitable names. Her few Indian acquaintances, degree-worshipers all, were overawed by Prabhu's accomplishments: Bachelor of Science and Master of Science degrees from Calcutta University, first in his class on both. Fellow of the International Union of Pure and Applied Chemistry, a doctoral student at the University of Washington, published in chemistry journals. "He's a good man," they concluded. They would greet the news with skepticism, at least. That overbearing doyenne of the Indian social scene, Mrs. Tewari, who threw a curry potluck every month, would query her, "Have you been nagging him, dear? A man of that caliber doesn't just get up and leave, you know." How could Dee confess that they'd never fought? She wished they had. An occasional spat would have been preferable to this silent, unexplained, deathly desertion.

No, she couldn't return to India and add shame to her aging parents' already heavy emotional load. Somehow, she shivered, she'd have to assemble all her inner resources and make a go of it in this foreign environment.

In the next few blurry days, Dee hung around the apartment, took care of the baby, and fretted about where the rent money would come from. When a neighbor tapped at her door and asked how she was, she hid her chaotic mental state and replied in panic-stricken sweetness, "The baby is a handful, but she's adorable. I'm just fine." The truth was she was worn out and weak from caring for the baby twenty-four hours a day by herself.

One morning, starved for contact with the world "out there" and a doughnut (for which she'd acquired a lusty craving), Dee walked over to the window. The little doughnut shop in the alley across the street would open any minute. The owner, a weary white-haired man in his seventies, made decent powdered-sugar doughnuts, a little too cloying and not enough cinnamon in Dee's opinion, but edible nonetheless. Every morning, upon opening the doors, the man stepped outside and propped a small slate board on the sidewalk. On it was a crudely drawn picture of a doughnut that could just as well have been a bagel or pancake or Indian roti. The squiggly handprinted invitation read:

> *Donuts! Donuts! Donuts!*
> *Hot'n Fresh!*
> *Come'n Get 'em!*

An arrow would point to the alley. Within the hour, dozens of locals would flock to the shop. By seven A.M., a line would spill out onto the sidewalk. Hence, the reason Dee had avoided it over the last few days. Now, in her mind, she sampled a fresh glazed doughnut still warm from the fryer, its round shape and tender feel so appealing. Her teeth penetrated the crunchy outer layer, her palate once again excited by its sugar-dripping yield. Thanks to the proximity of this friendly shop, the fritters, though new to a palate long accustomed to the food of India, had become a habit. She came to fancy them almost as much as *sohan papri*, a fancier, more refined flaky pastry from India, which was truly a king's treat. She delighted in the fact that unlike *sohan papri*, doughnuts were common folk's fare. They didn't demand a particular attitude or special setting to savor; no gratitude need be expressed upon finishing; and they were affordable. She felt totally at ease demolishing several such rounds and walking out into the street, feeling well gratified and right with the world.

Now, in a state of shock, she rubbed her grieving eyes on the sleeves of her flannel nightgown. This morning no slate board was propped on the sidewalk, the shop was dark, and a For Lease sign had been pasted on the window. Obviously, the operation had folded. Barely two weeks ago, she'd wandered into the shop and listened to the owner brag about retiring to Florida to spend his remaining days in a place where "the sun didn't fail to shine." He must have followed through. Change was the only constant in this dynamic land, Prabhu had repeated. To someone like Dee, who'd been raised in a culture where change unfolded at a far more leisurely pace, the concept of constant change was unsettling. She always felt as if she were on a train, looking out the window and yearning for another look at the scenery that had just flashed by.

Quietly, she gave the sign a second look. Black strokes on white background.

```
┌─────────────────────────────────┐
│                                 │
│           FOR LEASE             │
│   MATTHEW McMAHON REALTY        │
│         206–555–9067            │
│                                 │
└─────────────────────────────────┘
```

The telephone number beckoned her. Suddenly out of the rain cloud of confusion swirling around in her head, a daring idea danced.

The baby wailed. Dee drifted away from the window, stopping to look back several times, enchanted.

So that was how Dee's Doughnuts Now got its start. Within a few weeks, the previous owner, who fortunately hadn't left town yet, gave Dee a brief tutorial on how to crank out the fritters. An expert cook, she mastered the process in short order, and soon opened the shop for business as usual. Devotees saw a change of face—from old, white, and complacent to young, dark, wistful-eyed, and nervous to please— and noted the positive changes. The new owner replaced the cooking oil daily and didn't skimp on the glaze. They didn't suspect that she had had to sell all her jewelry and fine saris to pay for the lease. (Her students at the School of Flower Therapy had bought every last item at an auction they'd arranged for her. A neighbor helped negotiate the lease.) She offered exciting variations, such as lime-ginger, double cinnamon, and cashew-cumin-cardamom to perk up their taste buds, but could only afford a meager meal of rice and lentils for herself. As word spread, customers began straying in—nannies, professors, students, visual artists, and ever-hungry runners—in greater numbers every morning. They bit into the thickly frosted rings, glowed in happiness as they chewed, took no notice of the uneven nature of the edges, and ended up ordering more. Some bought a boxful for the office and this always made her smile, though her eyes would remain wistful. She had a bold new signboard made up. Written in toffee color on a shining beige canvas (sunlit, she called it) were the words:

> *Dee's Doughnuts Now*
> *One is Never Enough*

Years later, she'd tell me that I was always by her side. Even as a toddler, I liked to poke my tiny fingers into the dough. For me the sizzle of deep-frying was a comforting lullaby.

We lived in that same Ravenna District apartment, "a doughnut's throw," she joked, from the shop, until I graduated from high school. Money was so tight that we had to keep track of every lowly nickel. When the choices are few, one has the liberty of marveling at the most modest. We'd take walks through the residential district, with its hilly web of streets framed by oak, maple, and chestnut trees. Mother would point out the mammoth sunflowers, bronze-and-green-foliaged lobelia, imperial larkspur, and bee-attracting heliotrope that grace the front yards of the well-kept homes. I wondered: Was she setting a goal for herself to purchase a similar house someday? We'd often end up at Green Lake, where we'd spot a goldfinch stealing a sip of water or a hawk circling overhead in search of the unwary duckling, and these sights would constitute our entertainment. "Thank God," Mother would comment, "the air is free and there's no charge for gawking." During my college years, we moved to a bigger flat in the same locality. When I graduated at the age of twenty-one, I rented a place of my own in Wallingford, not too far away. My heart still trembles when I have occasion to drive through the winding streets of Ravenna District where the air is saturated with our private history.

Mother's shop made a decent profit until doughnuts fell out of fashion and slick bagel outfits began invading the district. Those shiny new emporiums offered free newspapers and comfy chairs to lounge in, endless varieties of coffee, as well as trendy juice concoctions whose ingredients were plucked from the Amazon jungles. The time came when Mother just couldn't compete and had to sell her business. I still remember the desolate expression on her face when she locked the shop's door for the last time. I wondered if it wasn't the same expression that she had worn when Father deserted her.

TWENTY-SEVEN

DRIVING SOUTH TOWARD HOME, AS I REACH THE OUTSKIRTS OF SEATTLE, the freeway traffic grinds to a standstill, some sort of tie-up, and my thoughts turn to the impact Father's abandonment had on me. More than just an aching pain, it has had a debilitating effect. For the first time I come to see how the void within has corroded my ability to form attachments. Like a hermit crab never emerging from its encasing, I've kept parts of myself hidden, protected from emotional risks. I never managed to give myself fully to Roger. I never told him how unloved I'd felt growing up without a father, how I envied classmates whose fathers took them to ball games, never mind that I hated ball games and wouldn't have gone even if I had had the chance.

It occurs to me now that such inhibitions might have been a factor in my breakup with Roger. It just might be possible.

At home again, I make a brief call to Mother to thank her. Then I leaf through the rest of the *News*, skimming an editorial about how our health-care system isn't functioning and that so few people are aware of it. Just as I'm getting ready to fold the newspaper up and drop it into the wastebasket, a "Letter to the Editor" on the Op-Ed page arrests my eyes. A complaint about food rarely appears on this page. I begin to read with great curiosity.

FRUSTRATIONS OF A FOODIE

As a recent transplant to Seattle, I consider myself fortunate to be living in a gourmet's paradise. The Puget Sound area offers fresh produce and seafood of quality that San Franciscans can only dream about and New Yorkers only read about. Of late, with the influx of people from all over the nation, the food scene has gotten even richer. Therefore, I am stupefied that you continue to employ Donald J. Smith as a food columnist.

What century is this clueless ignoramus living in, may I ask? To him half-cooked beef is "grandest theater," and instant potatoes, a "masher's delight." He seems to be way too interested in which chef beds with whom. What does that have to do with selecting one's main course from a menu? And why is it such a big deal that he hates cheesecakes? It destroys his appetite? You don't have to eat a whole cheesecake to appreciate it. Try a sliver at Pastries Café or the Georgian. But cheesecake just might be too sophisticated for Donald J. Smith. As a former San Franciscan, I will also report that a *brûlée* cheesecake is the most elegant dessert you could serve in fashionable circles there. Apparently, Donald J. Smith can only make fun of what he does not get.

Seattle has a just reputation for being polite and tolerant. Perhaps it takes someone like me who's not quite an insider yet to point out this intolerable journalistic buffoonery. It's high time that you put this gossip-mongering, hot-cross-bun-

eating, pompous eighteenth-century food writer out to pas-
ture. The new Seattle deserves better.

Sincerely,

N. S. McEwan

I laugh out loud, the biggest laugh I've had in a month. Another birthday present for me, another triumph for Bob. I cut out the letter and resolve to go over it with my army of bakers at tomorrow's staff meeting. Finally, Donald J. Smith just might have gone too far.

TWENTY-EIGHT

THURSDAY IS ONE OF BOB'S DAYS OFF, SO IT'S MY TURN IN THE BAKERY kitchen. I procrastinate; drink a small cup of coffee, look out at the rainy day outside, and feel worse. In preparation for what we call a nondenominational cheesecake, I set all the requirements on the work surface—eggs, nuts, sugar, lemon juice, graham cracker crumbs, sour cream, and cream cheese—but not my full attention. Now that the grand opening of Cakes Plus is imminent, I've been working extra hard to make sure my cache of customers stay loyal to me. On top of that, I have my lease problem. My two messages to Irene Brown have gone unanswered. I find myself looking out the window when I should be concentrating on my task.

The mayor has ordered four cheesecakes for his wife's birthday party and it's up to me to get them done. Fortunately, Bob's recipe is lucid; despite a few Japanese pictograms interspersed here and there, I find it easy to follow. My hands, however, are another story. Right off the bat, I manage to spill the egg whites that are essential to a rich crust and decide to omit them altogether. Upon tasting the batter, I detect a flat quality: I must have measured the sugar wrong.

A short while later Scott, sensing my frustration, comes over and stands by me in a gesture of support, while I incorporate more sugar, a teaspoon at a time. "Did you add sour cream to the cream cheese?" he asks, licking a finger that has just wiped the mixing spoon. "I don't taste any."

Of course! How could I have forgotten? Shaking my head in disgust, I pour the batter into the stainless steel washbasin; it flows across the smooth metallic surface like a white river of molten lava. I grit my teeth. It's never easy to admit failure in the presence of an employee. "I guess I'll have to start from scratch."

Scott drifts away toward the front, saying as he goes, "Give a holler if you need anything."

I count the number of hours before the mayor's assistant is scheduled to come by, pace up and down the room a few times, then march over to the wall phone and punch in Bob's telephone number. My heart goes hiding as I do so. Asking a favor doesn't come easy to someone who grew up in a household where self-reliance was the only affordable option. Most of all, I don't want Roger to hear how desperate I am, or that I've lost my baking skill.

Bob responds with a guarded hello. Was he expecting my call? Even at this early morning hour a Pearl Jam number is blasting in the background. It's typical of a man who considers sleep time-robbing. I apologize for interrupting his day, then relate the difficulty I'm having with the cheesecakes.

"Wish I could come and take over, Sunya, but I have my aikido class later this morning. I need to practice before I go."

"So it's aikido that gives you the tremendous concentration you have?"

"My aikido teacher tells us to keep our attention 'one-pointed' at all times. Maybe baking is where I actually practice it."

"If you get here right away, you'll be done with your cheese-cakes—your real-life aikido—before your class starts. All the ingredients are recipe-ready. I'll get the cakes out of the oven. And you don't have to do any cleanup afterward."

He considers this for half a second. "Okay, then."

"Take the shortest route to get here, will you?"

"Relax, Sunya." Bob laughs. "It's only a cake. You sound like national security is at risk."

"Baking is my country, Bob. The only territory I have any control over."

In fifteen minutes, Bob's here. I watch as he rearranges the items on the workbench with a deft hand in the order of use, then regards his lineup with calm yet purposeful eyes. His patch of purple hair does not bother me now.

Three quarters of an hour later, I return from the café section, lured by a nutty fragrance. Bob is toasting almond slivers in a dark iron skillet over fire, the heat imparting a flush to his face. He points to the oven from which a sweet breath emanates. "Another forty minutes and the cheesecakes will be done."

"You're my hero. I don't know what has come over me . . ."

"You're driving yourself too hard, Sunya. You need to take some time off."

"How can I? Business isn't good."

"That's what Jill was saying to that director guy yesterday when you went to see your accountant—business could pick up a bit more."

"Jill?"

"Yes. They were having coffee in the rock garden. I happened to be walking by. They seemed pretty thick. Didn't you know that? She was plying him with her flan. He was telling her a story, I think."

I'm grateful that Bob is shelving the flour and sugar packages and not looking in my direction. Andrew was telling Jill a story? Did my absence cause it? Or does he tell stories to all the women he meets?

"Did you see his debut flick, *Storm Country?*" Bob asks.

I shake my head, an embarrassing no.

"It showed in San Francisco last year at a director's festival. It centers on a California village that had been mostly deserted after a major storm and how a man, a former outcast, goes back and tries to rebuild the community. It's a cult film, about ten years old. Those were his drug days, I understand."

"Drug days?"

"Yeah, the story has multiple plotlines that overlap each other. The scenes are all jumbled up, go back and forth in time, and some of it doesn't make any sense. But I was curious to find out if he could bring it all together, and he did. He's talented, that's for sure. From what I hear he's clean now."

I am so devastated that I haul the perfectly clean mixing bowl to the washbasin and start running hot water into it. Just when I think I'm beginning to understand Andrew, this turns up. He's told me about his early life, but never mentioned drugs. What else hasn't he told me?

I must look pretty upset, for Bob says apologetically, "I didn't mean to . . ."

"It's no big deal, just a bit of a surprise . . ." I turn the faucet off and dry my hands on a paper towel.

"By the way," Bob says, "in Kyoto, where I come from, there's a baker whose name is Mori Matsumoto. He has a school called Healing through Baking . . ."

"I've heard of that school. Why do you bring it up?"

"I took his program. I'd recommend it to you, except that you're so shorthanded."

I stare at him. He wrenches his eyes away and starts stacking the measuring cups. "This is a little hard for me to say . . . But I'll have to go back to Japan soon."

My legs have lost all sensation. I counted on his staying here at least till the Cakes Plus crisis was over and hopefully much longer. He's added a quiet grace to the bakery, and I thought I'd given him an opportunity to shine. My frozen mouth forms a reply, though it'd rather issue an SOS signal. "You have to go back?"

He looks down at his feet. "My parents want me to take over their noodle house, although I'd rather convert it into a cake shop."

"A cake shop in Japan?"

His eyes sparkle. "Yes, pastries are the latest rage there."

I forget my immediate problems and listen. He describes in an animated manner how he grew up enjoying *wagashi*, Japanese-style sweets, the jellied bean paste bars that were originally introduced to cut the bitterness of tea. In recent years, *yogashi*, European-style desserts, have swept the country. Before visiting friends and relatives, his mother—who's quite traditional, actually—purchases an assortment of petits fours, chaussons, génoises, and tartes tatin from a nearby bakery, honoring the custom that a guest must not arrive empty-handed. These bakeries have begun to outshine the traditional sweet shops, *kashiya*. Even so, the modern pastries are made in accordance with the ancient ideals of *furyu*—beauty and elegance.

"Most homes don't have large ovens suitable for baking," Bob concludes. "So the bakery shops are always full of customers. And that's where I intend to come in."

"Why didn't Kimiko warn me about this before I hired you?"

"It's not Kimiko's fault."

"So I see." The oven heat makes me feel feverish. It's clear I've been set up. "Could it be a family member of yours who told you to keep this a secret?"

Bob squirms. "I guess, in a way, you could say that, Sunya. Actually, it was Roger who gave me strict orders to keep my mouth shut. You see, he's my elder cousin, so I had to obey him. And he helped me when I first moved here."

I simply can't believe what I'm hearing. Why would Roger pull something like this on me?

"He thought you'd have sold your bakery by now."

That's unforgivable. Roger pitying me. I'll call him with some excuse, get together, and have it out with him.

We spend a few moments in silence. Bob grabs his lumber jacket. The steel coat hanger sways from side to side, making a singing metallic noise. "Sorry . . ." His voice is thicker, as though he understands my feelings. "Got to run. My class starts in fifteen minutes."

He opens the back door, bringing in the musty smell of the rain and a patch of the glum, overcast sky. I thank him for rescuing the cheesecakes and step out of the room with lots more to-dos in mind.

An hour later, I'm womanning the cash register when a pear-shaped man pops up in the doorway. "Thank God, no line." His pendulous belly jiggles as he walks toward me. Breathing hard, he announces he's here to pick up the order for the mayor's office. They always send the heaviest person from that office to fetch the dessert order. I find myself smiling.

"Big bash tonight," the man adds.

"These ought to do it." I reach over to one of the four cake boxes standing on the glass counter and open it to reveal the artistry: a satiny beige round swirled on top with a rich caramel sauce and bejeweled with almonds and tangerines in a flower-burst pattern.

Eyes widened, he licks his lips, showing the pink tip of his tongue. "It's a surprise birthday party for the first lady," he whispers. "Several of us have been working for a couple of days to decorate the place. She's very particular." He puts the charge card back in his billfold. "His Honor will most definitely be pleased. Yes, indeed." Cradling the boxes, he waddles out the door.

I imagine the rented hall, impossibly high and large, subdued by music and flowers, with uniformed caterers circling. Guests assemble; recognizable names. Then the mayor and the first lady, both in formal attire, make their entrance. They move regally through the crowd, beaming in response to the good wishes and pleasantries, eventually stopping before a table draped in soft white linen. With effortless elegance, she nods her appreciation at the candlelit cake, even as she winces at the number of candles. The entire hall fades before her eyes, as the elegance of the cake takes over. Finally, her gaze falls on a small tasteful white card, standing upright beside the cake, with these words engraved in peacock-blue letters:

> PASTRIES CAFÉ
> *We make your moments luscious*

I close the cash register. The tray slides back to its closed position with a sound that cuts my fantasy short. What would I do without Bob, the genius behind this occasion, even if I manage to get repeat business from the mayor's office? The next instant I visualize Bob at the airport, as he hurries down one of the long corridors with over-filled suitcases in each hand to board a flight to Japan. I have the impulse to rush out and grab his arm and drag him back to the café. Selfish motives, perhaps, but I'll have to find a way to keep him here, at least for a little while longer until the crisis with Cakes Plus is over.

I can't lose my prize baker, not for the second time.

I am too much of a fighter.

TWENTY-NINE

JUST BEFORE SIX A.M. I PULL INTO THE BAKERY PARKING LOT, LISTENING TO the KUOW radio station's weather report. The current temperature is thirty-three degrees, going up to forty-five by afternoon. Overcast, no rain is predicted. (I've heard that before. Means it'll rain . . . which also means fewer customers will show up and I'll take in less cash. This line of thought quickly becomes unbearable and I turn the radio off with a flick of my wrist.) Right now, I'm glad for the woolen overcoat and the scarf around my throat. The tip of my nose tingles from the chill, which is causing my breath to rise in a wispy white cloud.

I pull in next to Bob's gray Mustang and climb out. The stars are twinkling, laughing at us mortals as we attempt to make our lives meaningful at this early hour. From the trunk of my car, I retrieve an open cardboard box loaded with deep orange, dead-ripe persimmons. The tender fruits, the size of an apple, shimmer faintly through the velour-rich darkness. Noting with relief they are intact, I remind myself again to handle them carefully. Persimmons in perfect condition are a coveted item and I'm overjoyed at having found them. If times were different, I'd have made a coconut cream pie with a surprise layer of persimmon coulis underneath the meringue, which would have been a smash hit. I guess I'll ask Scott to take over the task. I could use a few more sales. As I walk toward the rear entrance of the kitchen, my mind buzzes with notions of how best to use the leftover coulis—glazed over kulfi, drizzled over a crème brûlée, or in a petite ramekin with a plate of shortbread. Will Scott be able to handle the preparation? I fret.

I unlock the back door and venture inside the kitchen, allowing a nippy breeze to wash in with me. The screen door bangs. My eyes take in the whole room at once. A copper bowl, a marble slab, and a sack of flour are arrayed in perfect harmony on the working table. A swing band quavers from a CD player, a nearly finished pot of drip coffee is filling the room with an earthy Estate Java aroma, while Bob, dressed in denim pants and a flesh-colored ribbed T-shirt, is testing flour by rubbing it between two fingers. He doesn't look up to see who's entering. In fact, I doubt he's even aware of my presence. I'd have to sit in meditation a thousand years to summon that type of concentration.

Calling out a cheery good morning, I haul the box over to the counter. Apparently satisfied that he has the "feel" of the flour, Bob turns the music down and faces me with a dreamy "hi." Just as I try to place the fragile box in a safe spot, one persimmon bumps against another, then against the side of the box and both are bruised. "Oh, no," I mutter. Clumsy me. It proves once again how my baking prowess has deserted me. I can't even be trusted to handle the ingredients carefully.

Bob, now leaning against the counter, not a wrinkle on that forehead, brings me up to date. He's already on his last set of cheesecakes. How can he stand so much stress? Stay so cool and unflustered? Last night, on top of his usual workload, he had to fill a last-minute order from a private dinner party. Despite his efforts at cross-training, neither of my regular bakers is able to craft a cheesecake anywhere near as perfectly as he does, or as quickly. Jill's cookie crumb crust has a bland, out-of-the-box taste. Scott's cheesecake is lumpy from the batter not being spread evenly in the pan.

I pour myself a full cup of coffee, even though I am not a heavy coffee drinker—this just to make the morning seem normal, while Bob plunges back into his routine and starts to crush walnut pieces in a mortar and pestle. The rhythmic grinding sound mesmerizes me; soon a sharp lemony fragrance tickles my nose, while I wonder why I can't work the way he does.

"These are going to be no-bake lemon cheesecakes," Bob announces, boyish enthusiasm sparking his voice. "Double-layered, with maple sugar and walnuts. New variation."

"Sounds awesome. Our customers have gotten spoiled to the point of expecting daily new variations. You know what Caroline Jones said yesterday? 'Eating one of Bob's new cheesecakes is like wearing a brand-new outfit.' How do you stay so relaxed? You never freak out under pressure."

My compliment has the desired effect. As he unwraps cream cheese, Bob grins. "I didn't always have the concentration. As a matter of fact, I was the most distracted teenager you could imagine. I couldn't focus on anything, even for a minute."

"Then how did you . . . ?"

"Let me finish this. Then I'll tell you all about it, if you care to listen."

Forty or so minutes later, Bob and I are sitting in the rock garden, the morning fresh and cool about us, the wooden bench firm. Bob fixes his gaze on the topiary just ahead, though I'm sure his mind is continents away.

"I owe much to Mori Matsumoto," he says, "and his Apsara Bakery."

Immediately the loiterer's calling card flashes before my eyes. A fluke? I keep my tremendous curiosity in check, as I assemble a few more facts. In Kyoto, Matsumoto is highly regarded. Bob's parents sent him to study with Matsumoto when he was going through a rough period as a teenager. Later Bob recommended Matsumoto to his aunt when she had a personal misfortune.

"Her husband and infant son died in a car crash. It happened shortly after I left for the States."

The sad note in Bob's voice tinges my heart with sympathy. While he gathers himself, I contemplate a stately nicotiana plant, whose late-season white blossoms flutter in the breeze like a peace banner. Through the open window drifts a whiff of the buttery Danish twists that are a perennial favorite of the early morning crowd. I've often thought that these flaky pastries, so appealing to the just-awakened palate, are a perfect way to ease into a hectic day at the workplace. I could go even further and say: Such is the nature of the contribution a fine pastry cook makes to society. I probably wouldn't be wrong.

"Matsumoto is esteemed both as a baker," Bob says, "and a spiritual teacher. He's an older man, although no one knows exactly how old. In Japan, we still respect our elders and would never think to ask their age. His talent and techniques are most impressive. He makes génoises, napoleons, éclairs, petits fours, everything. He's studied everywhere—Paris, Vienna, London. He even baked for an exclusive Manhattan bistro for a number of years. And you know, he's the first baker to mix European style with our Japanese flair for the aesthetic to come up with a whole new approach to pastries. If you ever visit Kyoto about this time of year, be sure to taste his Autumn Symphony Tart. He even chose a poetic name for his masterpiece, so it would remind us of nature." A dreamy look steals into his eyes.

"Tell me about that tart."

Bob continues, the brightness in his voice echoing the esteem he obviously feels for the Kyoto baker. Apparently, Matsumoto originated a neotraditional movement by adapting local ingredients to European pastry-making techniques, perhaps best exemplified by his use of chestnuts. He dries fresh chestnuts picked at just the right stage of ripeness and grinds them into a sweet-tasting flour for use in baking. Come late October, people line up at Apsara Bakery to experience his multilayered tart, which has a puff-pastrylike base, an enchanted filling of pureed chestnuts and various fruits, a topping of toasted-hazelnut pastry cream, and, most importantly, Matsumoto's sacred touch.

Bob pauses a second and swallows. I look off at the banked clouds hanging above the eastern horizon, glowing embers above the rising sun. But it's chestnuts that haunt my mind. I'd love to taste Matsumoto's tart. Chestnuts have always been more than a mere edible to me. They're imbued with an emotional significance that goes back to my childhood years when Mother first introduced me to gathering for them.

As an annual rite of autumn, we'd go to a particular street on Queen Anne Hill. Bless the generous residents who planted the trees some fifty years ago for the benefit of the public. On a brisk day, we'd hop out of the car onto a wide avenue columned by colossal chestnut trees. In my impatience, I'd run ahead of Mother. Eyes on the ground, my feet crunching through the fallen leaves, I ran up and down the parking strips searching for plump ripe chestnuts. Mother would throw her arms out, as though ready to gather the world in an embrace. Freed from the demands of the doughnut shop, she seemed almost adolescent. Her eyes sparkling, she would chatter gaily as she stooped to pop the nuts into her basket. The wrought-iron-gated mansions that lined both sides of the street presided over this carefree respite in a detached manner. No questions were ever asked. The street belonged to us. "I got one, I got one," I would crow, as I dropped my find into Mother's basket. It'd take an hour to collect a dozen firm, unblemished chestnuts. "That's enough," Mother would exclaim. "We must not take too many. Let's go." She would stow our loot carefully in the car and herd me into the passenger seat. "Why can't we stay a little longer, Mother? No one else is here." I'd feel frustrated. She didn't understand how much fun I was having. She didn't understand me. Come evening, she'd roast the chestnuts. After cutting each with an incision on one side, she'd pop them in the oven, then light a fire in our concrete-block fireplace. To the accompaniment of logs crackling, the flames leaping up, and the smoky air tickling our nostrils, we would peel off the charred, curled-back skin and nibble on the dense sweet flesh. We took turns throwing logs into the fireplace. We always ran out of chestnuts before my belly was full and, while Mother quietly counted her blessings, I secretly wished she had let me gather a few more.

"You know what else he invented?" Bob resumes. I learn that chestnuts weren't Matsumoto's only stroke of talent. He was also the first chef to fill little pillows of puff pastry with sweet bean paste, an innovation that was a huge hit with Japanese shoppers. (The Japanese have a particular fondness for stuffed edibles of all types, Bob mentions.) But what has garnered Matsumoto national attention is not his baking prowess but, rather, his ability to heal people. "I was a depressed sixteen-year-old."

My serene baker? Depressed? Questions I think, but don't ask.

"My head was so filled with crawly black thoughts that I left my school projects half-finished. Then I stopped going to school and stayed in my room for days. I didn't turn on the lights or speak with anybody. My parents sent me to one counselor after another, even though they couldn't afford the cost. Nothing worked. Finally, I even stopped eating. At that point, they took me to see Mori Matsumoto. The results were pretty dramatic." He watches my face. "Perhaps you have a hard time believing that people can heal themselves by baking?"

"Yes, I'm a little skeptical . . . You have to admit it's not exactly mainstream therapy. How is it done, exactly?"

"To be sure, he makes use of baking, but I'm not really supposed to give it all out. You might consider taking his program. Not everyone who applies gets in. Matsumoto takes in only two or three students at a time, so he can concentrate on them. Those who are crying for help, those who have undergone trauma and need to heal themselves, become his protégés. All I can tell you is I took long walks, and baked, baked, baked. I had no contact with my parents. That helped too. I ended up getting interested in baking for its own sake. And I was able to focus. I finished school and came here to study."

I continue to mull the additional information Bob provides. Detractors say that Matsumoto only gets free labor this way, though both Bob and his aunt, who has recently taken the program, disagree. Now that she's back to a normal quotidian existence, she's overjoyed with the results of her apprenticeship.

"She's so proud of the olive bread she made recently for a charity event. The hours she spent on it calmed her, put a smile on her face when she arrived at the party. She still misses her husband and son and some days she can barely make herself get out of the bed, but mostly she can cope. Isn't that amazing?"

"I guess." Inside I wonder: What do I need this school for? I'm already an expert baker. I don't need to bake bread to feel good. And I dismiss the notion of having no contact with the outside world.

This Matsumoto must be a quack. I put my hands on my lap and begin to get up. "Interesting idea, but probably not for me."

"Wait. Let me tell you what my aunt said in her last E-mail. It's a Japanese proverb—*atette kudakero*. 'If you're not sure, go ahead and take a stab. See what happens.'"

The proverb irritates me. Still, this is the longest Bob and I have talked and I'm getting to understand another facet of his personality. I thank him for taking the time.

He smiles shyly. "Well, Sunya, shall I call the school for you?"

"Not necessary."

"At least let me make a phone call. See if he'll take you. What have you got to lose? Things sure aren't working out for you the way they should in your present frame of mind. At least in my opinion," he adds hastily.

"No rush. If I seemed curious—well, it really was just an idle curiosity, a coincidence that I'm still puzzled by." I spring up, stretch my arms out, and wonder what the loiterer's role might be in all this.

Bob gets to his feet and stifles a yawn—he's been laboring since midnight—and starts to apologize, but I smile knowingly and tell him to go home and get some sleep.

"A Danish twist first," he says. "I've been sitting here smelling them for the last half hour and I just can't take it anymore. Got to have one. It's not a coincidence that they're my favorite at breakfast."

A couple of days later, I arrive home at the end of a workday and unlock the door, fantasizing a good long soak in a hot honeysuckle-scented bath, red-tipped toes wiggling in the thick bubbles. My limbs are heavy and swollen, like foreign appendages attached haphazardly to my body. As I trudge through my home office toward the bathroom, I see that I've received a fax. I shuffle over, pick up the pages, glance at the cover sheet, and forget all about the bath. Surprise. The fax is from Mori Matsumoto, that famous Kyoto baker.

Standing there, I run through his entire letter.

Dear Sunya-san:

As I write this, I can smell apricot brioche baking in the next room. This is a new item I've introduced to Apsara Bakery's menu. My students do all the work these days—better for them, better for this old man. Imagine a surgeon and a former yakuza teaming up to create a winning brioche.

Bob Nomura intimated that you are beset by some personal and professional problems. If I may say so, problems are a sign of being alive. At my age, I don't get excited even when trouble strikes. But then, you are not my age.

I sense a connection with you and will be most happy to offer you the opportunity to study with me at the bakery. But you must accept the fact that even though you are an experienced baker, you'll be treated like any other novice. The mind of a novice is pure. We need to get back to that state of innocence and curiosity from time to time.

*You might think it is a long way for you to come here but then I am reminded of a saying: "*I NO NAKE NO KAWA ZU.*" Do not be content to stay in your little world; go out, explore, live more fully.*

Should you decide to accept, please notify me promptly. We have quite a waiting list and next year we're completely full. Also, please note that you are required to stay here for a minimum of fifteen days. During that period, you must not have any contact with your business, family, or friends. For the healing process to be effective, you must give yourself over completely to the everyday affairs at the bakery. Nothing must come between you and your baking practice.

From what Bob Nomura has said, it appears that your problems are somehow connected to Japan. Perhaps the solution can be found here as well.

Yours sincerely,
Mori Matsumoto

An accompanying page gives details about the school, its fees and hours, and lists nearby accommodations. Attached also is an enrollment form that needs to be filled out and faxed back to him.

The idea of spending fifteen days in Kyoto, the picturesque ancient capital of Japan, in the company of this seasoned baker seems alluring. I walk out of my home office, steeped in thought.

Forget it. My circumstances are such that I can't afford to take that many days off for some dubious "feel good" enterprise in Japan. Who'll oversee the bakery? Cakes Plus will eat me alive in my absence. And I have peeked at the cost of attending that school.

I file the letter, run my bath. Then I indulge myself in the perfumed bath as a small compensation, with a cup of robust rough-textured hojicha and an issue of *Japan Times* that Bob has lent me, as my company. Flipping through the pages, I learn that in Japan, English lessons are more popular than calligraphy, camisoles are the latest fashion for young women, and the expression "breaking the ice" translates into "heart opener."

In an hour, my limbs are so loose that once again they seem part of my body. Water, as a medium, has always seemed like a nurturing presence, giving more than taking. Just for a couple of hours, I float my aches and cares away in this forty-gallon-capacity bathtub.

THIRTY

A S I PULL OUT OF MY DRIVEWAY EARLY THIS MORNING AND ACCELERATE into the benevolent darkness, I spot him just as I am about to make a left turn. Jordan Jorgen, all right; the same blond hair, brown goatskin jacket, and a slouching posture; but this time no sunglasses. He leans against the lamppost across the street and follows my progress like a watchman. When I slow down to get a better look at him, he straightens and inches back into the shadows. Even though I recognize him, my reaction is one of fear. I step on the accelerator and arrive at the bakery in record time. Only in the comforting confines of the kitchen, do I finally shake off the sense of dread.

As my composure returns, it occurs to me that perhaps I am reading the guy wrong. So far, he's caused no damage, certainly not for lack of opportunity. Maybe I should consider what he might be offering rather than focusing on what he might want. Is there a hidden message in his actions and behavior? Something that merits closer attention? Nothing obvious leaps into my mind. Nonetheless, I resolve to give the idea further consideration.

———

A few hours later, I peek through the kitchen door into the retail section of the bakery and spot the staff from George's Cycle Shop, all lean, fit types. Having just wrapped up their morning coffee session, they're vacating their chairs and heading for the door. But Annie, the shop's petite young attractive cashier, is still sitting at the table. Her buttery face is a blank mask of sorrow. Gazing down, she is stirring her coffee. I wait a discreet internal beat, then stroll over with a slice of lemon cheesecake: conversation opener. Maybe Annie knows the whereabouts of Jordan.

"Morning, Annie." I set the plate before her and take a chair. "This one's on the house."

"How nice of you, Sunya." The gloom on Annie's face diminishes as she views the tall ivory wedge, richly beige, and dolled up with lemon slices, coconut shreds, and walnut hunks, "I've heard so much about your new baker but his cheesecake is always sold out. I'll save this for lunch. Thank you. You look nice today."

She reminds me that I am dressed in a yellow-orange cashmere cardigan and a bell-shaped black skirt.

She flips her forearm up and checks her watch. "Oops, I better get back to work."

"Let me get you a box."

"No, I'll just wrap it up." She opens her napkin and folds it loosely around the cheesecake, making sure that the topping doesn't get mashed.

Taking advantage of her momentary distraction, I spring my trap. "I bet Jordan would like a bite of this."

She starts, glances again at her watch. "Too late for that. He's on his way to the airport to catch a plane for Kyoto."

At the table to our left, a server noisily stacks dirty cups and plates. "When will he be back?" I ask over the discordant clatter.

Annie looks up at me, her eyes liquid in their sorrow, then down at her fingers. "I don't know. He didn't say."

For an instant, I consider disclosing Jordan's true identity. Then I realize she might not be ready to hear it, infatuated as she is with him. "You must be terribly lonely, Annie. He sounds like such an interesting person—always on the go, coming and going, a world traveler."

Her pert nose wrinkles. "You're interested in him, aren't you? And you think just because he leaves town all the time that we're having trouble, don't you?"

"Of course not, Annie—"

"Then stop interrogating me about him. You think by bribing me with this cheesecake you can get me to tell you what he's really like, don't you?"

"I have a reason for asking those questions, Annie. Believe me, there's nothing personal in my interest in him—it's all strictly professional."

She shoots me a quizzical look. It's the perfect time for me to make a disclosure. I take a deep breath before I start. "Allow me to explain . . ."

Just then, Kimiko enters the bakery: a pearl-buttoned blue suit displaying a few wrinkles, a sparkle of silver earrings, and a gloomy face. In a flash, I am reminded of the appointment made over the phone.

"Are you ready, Sunya-san?" Kimiko inquires.

"I'll be right with you."

I turn to Annie, who has now stood up and seems to be on her way. "Enjoy the cheesecake. By the way, if you're interested, I'll introduce you to our new baker the next time you're in here. He's a cool guy." I whisper the next set of words: "Just the perfect person to keep you company while Jordan is away."

Annie gives me a bewildered look, but if I am not mistaken, there's a glimmer of interest in her eyes. I derive a tiny satisfaction out of that.

THIRTY-ONE

K IMIKO AND I MEANDER ALONG A LEAFY PAVED PATHWAY WINDING
through the campus of the University of Washington, my alma
mater. She has agreed to search one of the departmental libraries for
me. Already, between long distance calls to her ex-colleagues in Tokyo and surfing the Internet, she's come up with a list of published
articles about "new" Japanese Buddhist movements.

Right now, she's unusually quiet and I am searching hard to find
a reason. Youthful students with straining backpacks pass us as they
rush from class to class. We dodge a jogger who darts from behind
the trees like a mountain goat in flight, only to avoid colliding with
a speedy biker who, without warning, cuts a sharp angular path inches
in front of us.

As we trek past a bank of dwarf azalea plants, their tiny leaves
glistening with the remains of a morning shower, Kimiko, her voice
ever so gentle, informs me that the Japanese use a special verb to
denote the act of "walking pleasantly," *sanposhimas*. My earlier concern about her uncharacteristic silence dissipates as I focus on my
surroundings, a broad gently sloping swath of land defined by Gothic
structures, domed ceilings, grand-column entrances, and groves of

stately trees. My newly heightened senses revel in the cool touch of the breeze, the spicy smell of wet grass, the rhythm of my feet doing *sanposhimas*. Only the rumble of a transit bus mars the effect.

At the East Asian Library, we take over a small study alcove that holds nothing more than a solitary table, a few utilitarian chairs, and a door that shuts on its own. Kimiko tells me she's taken a temporary position at the Japanese consulate where she's in charge of answering questions about Japan. She giggles occasionally as she recounts a few for me: Can you take a pet snake with you to Kobe? What are some popular names for male children these days? How often do you give gifts to your friends? Do you really have to take your shoes off when riding in a private automobile?

And now she's ready to answer some questions of mine. For the next half hour, Kimiko thumbs through newspapers from the archive, adjusts the microfiche, and murmurs occasionally at a news item of interest. I grab today's edition of the *News* from a rack and zoom in on a headline about the global trade conference:

SEATTLE RAISES ONE HAND IN GREETING AND CLENCHES THE OTHER IN PROTEST

November twenty-ninth, the first day of the conference, is only days away. Political tension has gripped the city, even reaching my bakery. The other day, conversing with a customer whose company has downsized, I discussed the issue of whether these trade talks will take us where we want to go. Both of us answered in the negative.

The newspaper article goes on to describe how "objectors to the human cost of globalization," are calling for extensive civil disobedience on the first day. Several demonstration marches and a mass rally are planned. The city government expects to spend $6 million on law enforcement overtime alone. Many Seattle residents are complaining about the chaos the potentially volatile event will breed, but hoteliers and downtown retailers are ecstatic that the event will pump $15 million into the city's economy. "This is our Super Bowl," one shop owner crowed.

My reaction is less enthusiastic. In fact, I am uneasy. My privately owned business, my sense of community, my desire to see individuals retain control over their destiny are at odds with mainstream society's growth-oriented economic philosophy. Being in that position, I am biased in favor of the protesters.

"Look, I found it." Kimiko adopts a lively expression as she points to the screen on the microfiche viewer and explains that it's a compendium of new Buddhist developments in Kyoto, a city where many go in search of a faith. There are sixteen hundred temples there.

Sixteen hundred?

"Does it say anything about the Sunya Tradition?"

She adjusts the viewer to sharpen the screen. "They don't cover it in depth, but here's a short paragraph on the leader of that faith. 'He believes in keeping his teachings simple. He echoes the basic tenets of Buddhism in a contemporary way. Work hard, live well but simply, reflect on life's transience, on nothingness.' He doesn't have a temple. His followers meet in a spare room at the back of Apsara Bakery."

"Aha! Just as I expected all along."

Kimiko dims the microfiche viewer. "Why are you so curious about that particular tradition, Sunya-san? Because it's your namesake?"

"No, I'm not quite that narcissistic. I have a pretty good hunch that the loiterer is connected to the Apsara Bakery and I'm determined to find out what his motives are. Coincidentally, Bob, too, has been telling me about that bakery—"

"It seems quite simple then. You have to go Kyoto."

"Easy for you to say."

"It may be easier than you think, Sunya-san. Japan isn't like the United States. We have a safe society, no guns, and honest people who are kind to foreigners. Someone is bound to make the necessary connections for you. And you'll love the walks through the strolling gardens of Kyoto."

"But I can't take off just like that, not with a bakery to manage. Someday, maybe."

"Spring and autumn are the best seasons to visit Japan."

"I have staffing problems—Bob's going back home. Since we're on the subject, why did you insist that I hire him, Kimiko? His cheesecake has really taken off and it'll be a disaster if he leaves now."

Her serene face transforms into a mask of concern as she touches my hand. "Please don't be angry with me, Sunya-san. I acted on Roger's advice, as Bob has probably told you by now. I've come to regret it very much, because it has caused you some grief. Please accept my apologies. I was raised to please people around me, especially those I love very much."

"I think I understand, Kimiko. The way you grew up, a woman is expected to be accommodating."

Kimiko's eyes glisten. In a tremulous voice she confesses, "Roger and I aren't getting along very well."

Astounded, I fold the News, set it aside, and mentally calculate the length of time they've been living together. Couple of months, maybe? I recall the smug behavior Kimiko exhibited when she first moved in with Roger and, almost immediately, I remember my own smugness. How human we both are beneath our fragile shells.

"I thought life with him would be exciting," Kimiko says, "parties, nightclubs, weekends on a yacht—the life I didn't have in Japan. He always seemed to know what was trendy. Instead, I'm expected to stay in and have dinner ready for him when he gets home late from his meetings. All he says when he comes in the door is, 'It's so nice to see you, Kimiko.' My father used to say something like that to my mother. When we go out he wants me to dress up, really dress up, so he can show me off to his friends, and I don't like that either."

"I didn't cook for Roger every night and I didn't dress up all that often . . ."

"But you're a Western woman. He wouldn't have dared to ask you . . ."

"I thought because you're both Japanese, with similar educational and economic backgrounds, both living in a foreign country, that you'd both go for the familiar . . ."

She slumps back into her chair. "Similarities can actually be quite irritating when you're out of your familiar environment. You see in each other the reasons you left your homeland."

Roger hasn't completely faded from my memory. Every so often events from our four-year life together float before my eyes as naturally as steam rising from a cup of tea. I find myself in the curious position of giving advice to Kimiko, as a sister would. "Perhaps if you gave it a little more time . . ."

Her clasped fingers and her blotchy complexion hint at the conflicting emotions beneath the polished exterior, as she replies in a firm voice, "All that Roger cares about is his cause. Now that the big day is almost here, he's turned into a lunatic. He almost never sleeps and a couple of weeks ago he even quit his job. Can you believe it? His savings will run out soon. He blames me for all the problems between us, and there are so many problems . . . I can't stand it anymore."

I stare at the wall. Until Roger came between us, I considered Kimiko a friend, not a close friend, but someone I liked and respected. Even now, when she has Roger, I hate to see her tormented.

"It won't work, Sunya-san. I could have stayed in Japan if all I'd wanted was a man like Roger. There're plenty like him. Outwardly they're bilingual and wear tailored suits, inwardly they belong to the Taisho era . . . Or maybe I've set my expectations too high. Maybe the New World does that to you."

Words of consolation form on my lips, but upon a moment's reflection, I resolve to stay silent.

"Please don't mention anything to Roger if you happen to run into him." Kimiko gathers her belongings. "He doesn't yet know that I'm moving out. I have found a place of my own."

A dense silence descends over us, making it clear that there's nothing more to talk about. We both rise silently, like strangers, walk out of the building without any further conversation, finally stopping by her car. "I must thank you for all your help, Kimiko."

"It's the least I could do. If you're ever in Kyoto, be sure to visit the Nanzen-ji temple and take a stroll down the Philosopher's Walk just outside it. I know you'll love it."

She smiles—not as brightly as she typically would—and gives me one last wave. Our eyes exchange our affection for each other born of a common hurt. That hurt must be why she came to my aid even at a time when she was under stress. I watch her slim form slide gracefully into a red Volvo and imagine the deep pent-up sigh that must be seeping from her chest now that she's alone.

My Honda is parked a few spaces away. Curiously enough, when I got hold of Roger on the phone about a week ago and he agreed to meet me, he actually sounded cheerful. How clueless he seemed about his status with Kimiko. The date we agreed on was November 29. He said that thousands of demonstrators from all over the planet had poured into the city, just as he'd hoped, and boasted that he and his activist army would have little trouble disrupting the conference. They'd be part of Seattle's history. That evening, after it was all over, he'd meet me to celebrate the victory over a cup of tea. And I could bring up, he magnanimously allowed, whatever topic I might have in mind.

THIRTY-TWO

ON MY WAY BACK TO THE BAKERY, I PASS BY THE CAKES PLUS SITE ON Meridian Avenue and am astounded to find that no construction workers are in evidence. I peer through the window, through the gaps in the white sheets that are hung over them, to see an empty room with paint buckets and a half-finished partition.

I take it as a good omen. Any delay works to my advantage.

A day later, I am at the bakery kitchen, and Bob calls from his apartment. He's done the research on the Culinary Trade Association's food show that I asked for and has all the details at his fingertips. The show will take place in San Francisco early next year. I express my delight that he's taken over a few of my tasks and freed up some time for me.

"I wish I had your business experience, Sunya. When I take over my parents' noodle house in Kyoto, I'll need to know the ins and outs of managing a business. And eventually, I want to open my own bakery. . . ."

"Yes, there's a lot to learn besides baking—let's talk sometime soon."

I make a mental note to explain to him at the very least some basics: cost control, accounting, people management, and customer interaction, but there's something more immediate, a bigger plan that has taken shape in my mind in bits and pieces over the last week or so; like a nimbus gathering force.

"Can I ask you a personal question, Bob?"

"Of course."

"Do you date?"

"I haven't in a while." He barks out a laugh of frustration. "My last one was a blind date."

"Oh?"

"To be honest with you, I'm ultrashy. I haven't told anyone about this, but a month ago, I was introduced to Galina, a tall, no-nonsense, blond Russian high school teacher, five years older than I. A friend fixed us up. He must have hated me, because I felt intimidated by her from the start. I know I look big and muscular, but when it comes to women, those biceps mean nothing. On our first date, she went on and on about the state's deteriorating education system and I couldn't get a word in edgewise. I went to school in Japan and know little about the education system here and quite frankly couldn't care less. I felt like such an idiot. At one point she looked at me and said, 'But how would you understand, you're just a kid yourself.' " There's a brief silence. "I appreciate your interest, Sunya, but I don't want to blind-date ever again, if that's what you're asking."

"Then I guess I won't tell you about a soft-spoken petite redhead, about your age, who says your cheesecake made her practically fall out of her chair the first time she tried it." I pause for effect. "I think she's dying to have coffee with you."

"Petite redhead?" he echoes. "I like all hair colors except black. I don't suppose you'll tell me who she isn't."

"Well," I reply playfully, "she doesn't work at George's Cycle Shop."

"Not the pretty girl at the counter?"

"How did you guess?"

"Oh, I rented a bike from her a month ago. She asked me about Japan. We had a nice chat. Well, if it's only for coffee, I suppose I could do that. But just for your sake, Sunya." He pauses, though not for long. "When will she be free?"

"Let me get back to you on that." I can't resist adding, "Too bad about the culinary trade show in San Francisco. If you stayed here through next year, you could have gone. I'd have paid for it. You have friends there, if I recall correctly."

Bob mumbles a few indistinct words, then we say good-bye and hang up. I walk away from the phone whistling an upbeat little tune.

THIRTY-THREE

THE KITCHEN SMELLS OF MAPLE SYRUP AND RICH SCALDED MILK. YESTER-day, i asked Jill to make bar cookies—pumpkin pie minus the crust—using a flavorful Japanese Kabocha winter squash. This morning I pause in the doorway and watch her lift a large pan out of the oven with hot pads, her diminutive frame struggling a bit. Lately she's been rather cool toward me. She avoids my eyes and gives perfunctory one-sentence answers to my questions. When we discuss her task list, she grumbles more than usual.

Now, she acknowledges me with a flicker of a glance. A glance that makes me step back rather than forward. In the silvery overhead light, her face is pale and her lips are drawn tight in an obstinate line. My gaze trails down hers to the pan. The red-orange surface of the bar cookies crosshatched in a diamond design glistens in the sunlight flooding through the window. I force myself to praise her accomplishment. "I bet some customers will see this as a welcome change from the usual breakfast rolls."

"I bet they will," she replies with a little more enthusiasm.

I decide this is as good a time as any to confront her about the content of the cake box for Pierre. How someone ruined my chance of getting Pierre back, how I still feel sickened when I relive the incident.

"Ah . . . I've been meaning to ask you, Jill . . . Someone switched the almond torte for the cheesecake in the gift box we made up for Pierre . . . Just in case you saw someone do that . . ."

"I really don't recall anything like that," she mumbles and hurriedly walks away to the front, her sandals slapping the cement floor.

The hollowness of our exchanges, her defiance oppresses me. What's behind this? Is she as chummy with Andrew as Bob suggested? If so, I will not concede that battle easily.

This is no way to spend my morning. Perhaps I should concern myself with bigger issues—like how to improve pastry sales, whether I'm really in love with Andrew or this is just a passing phase, the direction the war with Cakes Plus is taking, and the long-range consequences of free trade and the imminent meeting of trade ministers from 134 nations in Seattle.

Just then, the phone buzzes. It's Irene Brown, the health inspector. In the next half hour, we go over her visit to Cakes Plus's original Ballard location, the violations she's uncovered, the threats Cartdale has made to her since, how he's even trying to implicate me. As I listen, I feel as though the roof above my head is tilting.

I hang up and busy myself strategizing the next phase of the war. It looks as though I have no choice but to go see Jim Paradise. Overcoming my reluctance, I place a call to the real estate legend's office and schedule an appointment for Friday.

THIRTY-FOUR

FRIDAY MORNING, AS I ENTER THE BAKERY KITCHEN, I GET A WHIFF OF something fruity and delicate, and I welcome it. My bakery has to stay competitive, innovative. Scott is at the kitchen counter, slicing some plump Comice pears, delicate beads of juice glistening along the edge of his razor-sharp knife. In a new pair of baggy chef's pants patterned with spoons and spatulas, he definitely looks the part, although what I have in mind for him is a most mundane task—cleaning the pastry case.

"I'm preparing a pear clafoutis," he announces. "You don't mind, do you?"

"Of course not. You know I encourage experimentation, as long as I don't have to buy too many expensive ingredients."

As he fusses with a fluted springform pan, he fills me in about his vacation in Palm Beach over a year ago, where he tasted a similar dessert. It made such an impression that he vowed to duplicate it someday. "I met my wife there too. Yesterday when I came across these huge gourmet pears at the Queen Anne Thriftway, I decided it was time to try a clafoutis. But this is just my first attempt. I think I'll serve it with a Chantilly cream topping."

He has come a long way, from slavishly following my recipes down to the last detail, to whipping up his own creations. Bob's blazing success with cheesecake must have put extra heat on him. He's feeling a desperate need to inscribe his signature on an outstanding pastry. I am all for it and more than willing to support such an effort, but with Scott swept up in a creative frenzy, to whom shall I assign the humdrum but necessary task of cleaning the pastry case?

I telephone Bob, apologizing for disturbing him, then ask if he could come back after his aikido session. I expect to hear a litany of excuses.

"I'll be there as quickly as I can." He sounds eager, almost too eager, leaving me wondering what has changed in the last few days.

"Take your time. Scott's in the kitchen—finishing up."

"I need the extra money," Bob says, "to buy some new clothes. And you're right. Management responsibility will help me grow. I can't just be a cheesecake maker for the rest of my life, although it has taken me this far. In the next year or so, I want to move up in the world, take more responsibility."

I am reeling under this unexpected turn of events when he continues. "What's Scott doing?" My silence doesn't hinder Bob. "This might turn out to be what you call a win-win situation. While I am at the bakery, I'll even make an extra cheesecake or two. You'd like that, wouldn't you? By the way, Annie and I went to Nikko last night. The food was awesome."

Now that I've gathered what's going on, I thank my blessed stars. My pairing instincts were right. Bob is, no doubt, a lot better companion for Annie than that loiterer. "Oh, so you'll be seeing her again soon?"

"As a matter of fact, we're going dancing tonight. She's so much fun. She knows all about bicycles. She's even mountain-biked up

Tiger Mountain. She wants to show me one of the trails this week-end."

I can almost see the boyish grin on Bob's face. However, I must not forget the day's agenda. I recite the tasks I have in mind for him: make the prep list and follow up on the deliveries, box some orders. Yes, the pastry case needs to be cleaned and the refrigerator has to be emptied. Oh, and don't forget to check if there's enough ice cream in the freezer.

"Scott *always* forgets to clean the pastry case," Bob says archly.

There's that little rivalry again. Given the importance of the meeting this afternoon, I have to trust that Bob will take good care of the shop in my absence and not get into a verbal fight with Scott.

Within minutes, I select an orange curd tartlet from the refrigerator and hasten out the door. As I drive down Sixty-fifth Street, cruising past a row of symmetrical business offices, I consider the real estate baron I am about to confront. Not only is Jim Paradise renting to Cakes Plus, he also may possibly be trying to evict me. As the traffic degenerates into typical Seattle stop-and-go mode, I fine-tune my plan of getting Jim to listen to my side of the story and act on what I propose.

Whatever vision one may have of real estate agents, Jim Paradise doesn't conform to it. Because of his rugged denims, an outdoorsy air, grimy fingernails, and easy manner, he could pass for a farmer, which is what he is in his spare time. The man hides his multitude of talents rather well. The few times I've met him, I've come away impressed. Paradise is an assumed name. Jim comes from a wealthy Seattle family that has an empire of game and puzzle stores scattered throughout the Pacific Northwest region along with a mansion in Magnolia that commands a multimillion-dollar view of the Olympic Mountains

across Puget Sound. After he graduated from law school, he severed
all contacts with his family, despising them for their slavish devotion
to dollars, and took a job as a public defender. Rumor has it that he
lost his inheritance as a result of this estrangement. Then he got into
real estate, and made it big in short order. Still not satisfied, Jim
started volunteering for Lettuce Link, a local nonprofit organization
that grows organic vegetables for low-income families, and it soon
became the major focus of his life. He quips that his success in real
estate has freed him up to at least put a little romaine "on the tables
of the hungry" if not a roof over their heads. Still, I take a moment
to draw on my business cool as I reach his agency on Roosevelt Plaza.

Jim, trim and wiry even in his fifties, is parked in front of his
computer. He's scrolling down a screen with the headline "Search:
Properties" when I knock on his open office door. He swivels his
chair and waves me in. The gold watch on his wrist flashes as he
gestures toward a chair. The eyes, behind huge light-framed glasses,
are small and dark, and not particularly welcoming.

"What a surprise, Sunya. Not baking this morning?"

Does he have to remind me? I lower myself to a chair, all of a
sudden not trusting the floor below my feet. As we chitchat, I notice
signs of discomfort—he's saying little and looking away frequently.
Deciding it's now or never, I slide the box containing the orange curd
tartlet across the desk toward him.

"For me?"

"Yes, since you haven't been to my bakery in a while . . ."

"I've hardly had any free time lately."

I make a point to look up at the framed certificate of recognition
on the wall, though I can't quite read it from here. "You won't believe
this but I remember you as a lawyer."

His eyes light up. "You do?"

"Yes, you were a mighty good one. I remember when you represented an elderly tenant of a condominium who had an obnoxious neighbor next door. As I remember, she had a nervous breakdown from lack of sleep. You helped her win the case. It made the front page of the Local News section of the paper. They even had your picture with the caption 'Crusader for the common people.' "

"Those were exciting times. Not that my present days are all bad, mind you. But I was young and each day seemed like it'd never end, every tomorrow was like found money. What a difference being fifty makes. My days now come and go like so many sound bites. But, believe it or not, Sunya, I'm still basically the same man I was back then." He stares out the window, then opens the box and gazes at the tartlet. "Do you mind if I taste it? I just finished my usual double loop around the lake, and I'm starving."

"Not at all. You've been running for quite a few years, haven't you?"

"See that map on the wall?" He points to a detailed map of the U.S. on one wall. "Those red flags are the states where I've run races." I begin counting the tiny red flags, but soon give up. "The one in Oregon just last week was a hilly twenty K trail run. I finished third in my age group."

"Not bad."

Smiling, he opens the box and gets the plate out. "Mmm. My normal lunch is a fresh-picked salad from my raised bed, but this, I must say, is a real treat. Citrus is my big weakness. When I remarried, I had my wedding cake decorated with curls of orange zest." Using the plastic fork that I remembered to pack, he digs into the pastry. "I trust your bakery is doing well."

"It's doing splendidly. How many types of lettuce did you grow last summer?"

"Four kinds—cos, romaine, oakleaf, and buttercrunch—but I don't grow just lettuce, you know. I also had a bumper crop of Yellow

Finn potatoes. Don't you just love those buttery yellow spuds? My new wife makes standout mashed potatoes with Parmesan cheese, skim milk, and roasted garlic cloves." Jim pops another forkful of the tart into his mouth and adds, "But she doesn't bake. She says why bother? So many bakeries on the north side."

"With a new one yet to come."

Jim nods, busily munching the last of the crispy crust.

"I don't think it's a smart idea, Jim, to rent out your Meridian location . . ."

He stiffens, puts the fork down. "Why not?"

"For what it's going to do to the district."

"Ah, I get it. It's the Bakery War. Couple of weeks back, Willy Cartdale and I went out for a beer. He talked about you quite a bit. You're in for a bruising tussle, Sunya. He's a real street fighter."

I smile. "I could use a few good soldiers to fight alongside."

"But why should I get involved in someone else's battle?"

"Because it affects the general public. You've made a second career out of feeding disadvantaged families your organic vegetables, so there's no question that you care about the common good."

"I've made a pledge to Lettuce Link," he says after a while. "We're expanding our program. I'm even thinking of adding a floor above your bakery and turning that into a low-income residential unit. Of course, you can move right back once the construction is over in a few months' time—"

"In other words, you're getting ready to evict me."

"I read Donald J. Smith's column."

I place my elbows firmly on his desk. "Have you considered the potential impact on the neighborhood ambience if you close down its main anchoring place? Green Lake Community Council meets there once a month. A book group and a writers' critique group have their evening discussions there. A fair number of students from UW

practically live there. Do you really want to ruin that kind of community spirit? Which is exactly what'll happen if a soulless industrial
bakery moves into Wallingford. It's one of the few real communities
left in the city."

"There's a little more to it than that, Sunya. Cartdale seems to
think that you—"

"That I'm a financial risk. He'd certainly like you to believe that.
Do you think I run the bakery just for money? Would it surprise you
if I told you that I pay my rent and bills to my financial backers at
all costs, even if that means missing a payment to my mother?"

"That's very noble, Sunya—"

"So we're not that different, are we? You with Lettuce Link and
me with my small neighborhood bakery, we're going for the same
ultimate result."

"You have great persuasive powers, Sunya, but it's too late to
change my decision. Cartdale signed his lease a while back. He would
have moved in by now, except that we've run into some difficulties
with the construction work."

"What kind of difficulties?"

Jim pitches the now-empty box into his wastebasket. "The tart's
marvelous, as we have come to expect from Sunya Malhotra. I'll have
to tell my wife to order some for guests we're having this weekend."

I recall taking peeks at the construction site through the windows
and seeing a large room being partitioned. So now, throwing caution
to the northerly wind, I ask, "Is Cartdale remodeling the space in a
way that his lease agreement doesn't allow him to do?"

"You might be right." He shuffles some papers on his desk and
glances at the Day-Timer.

With egotistical Jim and stubborn Cartdale locked in a fight, I
might as well happily step aside. "Then you've got a way out of the
lease. If you really want out, that is. It's your chance to do something

for a great neighborhood. And remember, you're dealing with a guy who's not above bribing public servants and exposing the public to contaminated food."

Eyes narrowing, Jim says, "Bribing? Contaminated food? You seem to be making some serious accusations here."

"Some blackmailing is also involved." I synopsize my telephone conversation with Irene Brown. Jim leans back and thinks for a while. "Let me do some checking on my own," he says eventually. "I can find out anything about anyone. You've brought up some interesting issues. No promises, however."

"Will you let me know?"

"I understand the urgency." Jim checks his watch, stretches his arms out, and rolls his shoulders. "I have to go work on the farm now. It's time to lime some vegetable beds. That's the only kind of work I like to do anymore."

"But I'm sure you'll manage to find time for another public-service challenge like this . . ."

"Sunya, you should have been a lawyer or a private investigator, do you know that?" A hint of a smile.

"No." I stand to go, a soggy blanket of fatigue settling over me. "I'm a baker at heart. But thanks for the compliment . . . I think."

I walk out, feeling like a fraud. I still want to bake, but I haven't gone near an oven in a week, nor have my fingers caressed flour, sugar, or chocolate. Instead, I am up to my pearl-studded ears in that cesspool where business and politics mix.

THIRTY-FIVE

Monday morning. I arise, get myself ready for work, then in a moment of clarity and mental release, trot to my home office, fill out Matsumoto's form, and fax it to him. It seems so easy, so right, as though a new future is gathering momentum on the horizon. Then comes the fax tone. The shrill sound pierces my moment of bliss with a sting of uncertainty.

When I arrive at the bakery kitchen, I find Bob and Jill standing by the oven, chatting. They're about the same age—early twenties—and there is an easy friendliness between them. Bob, in his new button-down denim shirt and grain-colored pants, is telling her a joke. Of late, I've noticed his sense of humor has flourished. Jill, dressed in a flirty pink blouse and polyester skirt, her dense hair piled high, is a bit more dressed up than usual. Does she have a date later in the day? Now she bursts out laughing, her mascara-weighted eyelids squeezing shut, and Bob seems pleased at her reaction. When I was their age, only a few years ago, I, too, was prone to spontaneous jets of laughter that cleansed my insides like a good hot shower. Lately, I haven't found much to ha-ha about. Is this, I wonder, an inevitable part of growing up?

Bob yanks the oven door open and peeks in. As he straightens and turns, he becomes aware of my presence, as does Jill. "Morning, Sunya," they chorus in unison, then Jill hurries to the front section. I have no idea what's going on with her.

Bob extracts a large rectangular pan of white cake with gold bursts, and sets it gently on a cooling rack. Satisfied, he turns to me. "I got another last-minute order yesterday, Sunya, when I answered a phone call for you. This one was from Puget Sound Insurance Company. An executive is retiring."

I peer out the window. A thin morning fog with the consistency of watered-down skim milk is pressing against the building. "I appreciate your filling in for me for the day. How do you like the change of pace?"

He beams. "It's okay."

Now that the iron is red-hot, I decide to strike it. "Suppose you had an opportunity to manage the bakery full-time for a couple of weeks?"

"Why? Are you going away?"

"Yes, I'm happy to say I've accepted Mori Matsumoto's offer. I'd like you to take over for the two weeks I'm gone . . ."

Even as I speak, I realize that from a business standpoint, this is not the best time for me to take off. But then Mother taught me a long time ago that there is no "best" time. Time comes without a label. Take it, do with it what you like, or let it slip off your hand. In the end, it's your own label that counts, mind you, not time's.

"I'm not sure, Sunya . . . I'm new at this. It's an awful lot of responsibility. You always seem to be juggling so many things . . ."

"Why don't you hang out with me the next few days? See for yourself what I have to do."

"But . . . Jill and Scott. Won't they feel they've been passed over? Both of them have been working here much longer than I."

"I don't think Scott is ready to manage and he knows it too. As for Jill, she is young and into chasing boys and having fun. I doubt if she wants the headaches and all the extra hours that go with managing a bakery. You're the only one who's up to the job."

Bob lowers his head. I don't reveal how uncertain I was about hiring him and how delighted I am that it turned out to be one of the best decisions I ever made. Last week Bob stayed three extra hours after his usual graveyard shift when a rush order for a kid's birthday cake came in. The mother, who'd totally forgotten the date, called in a harried, panicky voice, begging for a chocolate cake with peanut butter fudge frosting. Bob cheerfully handled the job with Jill lending a helping hand. He even inscribed the boy's name, Sean, on the cake surface Japanese calligraphy style.

"Why, thank you, Sunya"—he now looks up—"for considering me. The timing seems to be right."

"What do you mean?"

"My parents called me last night. They've found a buyer for their noodle house. Someone made a very generous offer and they've decided to accept it. To tell you the truth, I think they're doing it for my sake. It bothers me, but at least for now, they're financially secure, and I don't have to go back. They want to retire to Miya-jima Island to enjoy the leisurely pace of life and the gorgeous beaches. They've always wanted to spend time there, but haven't been able to afford it until now. Which means I'm no longer under pressure to go back and take over the restaurant. It's just as well. It's an extremely competitive field over there and one must be careful or else one could lose every yen. Eventually, yes, I'll go back and open a bakery, but for now . . ."

"I was so afraid of losing you . . ."

We discuss salary and hours. It all seems to go well. "I have one concern," Bob says jokingly at the end. "In your absence, Donald J.

Smith will have my head on a platter. Jill just told me that he's back from vacation and looking for fresh meat."

"How does Jill know?"

"Beats me. She has a lot of friends."

This sets my mind scurrying through the maze again. Bob's voice interrupts my thoughts. "Last night I also called my aunt and told her about my decision to stay. I was a little surprised she didn't try to talk me out of it. 'It's fate,' she said. 'You are where you're supposed to be.' Do you believe in fate, Sunya? After all, you're going to Japan even though, as I recall, you had some reservations about it."

I'm about to laugh when I look up at Bob. Standing still, he is holding a serious expression and his eyes are lit with conviction.

"Not a chance, Bob. I'm going to Japan of my own free will."

Now he smiles a little.

THIRTY-SIX

THE CLOCK SAYS IT'S JUST BEFORE SIX IN THE MORNING, WHICH MEANS I've overslept. My eyes are still unfocused when I hear two knocks on the front door, someone's knuckles rapping insistently. The sound sends a quake through my body, shooting adrenaline into my system in a way most unwelcome at this hour. I lie there for a few seconds. Who could it be? Loiterers don't knock. What kind of news? How urgent?

The silence that has followed only intensifies the suspense. I stretch my legs out, point with my toes, lurch out of bed, wrap my plush blue robe around me and, still shivering from the first chilly handshake with the morning, shuffle to the door and fumble with the lock.

My neighbor Mrs. Petrocelli, ever the weather lady, is stationed on my porch with her hyperactive dog on a leash. Relief. In the soft light of dawn, her bright coral anorak dazzles my eyes and chases away the last remnant of sleep. I mumble a lethargic good morning. The irrepressible dog trots back and forth on the porch floor, sniffing in the hope of finding a stray tidbit.

"I didn't wake you up, did I? I'm sorry. Usually you leave for work by now." She stares down at the bundle of newspaper lying between us, says with relish, "Donald J. Smith has actually beat today's weather report."

Disturbing thoughts, imaginary situations nag at me. Before I can ask any questions, she has turned away. Her dog pulls on the leash so strongly that she almost loses her balance. She regains a semblance of control, but not for long. A moment later, she is skipping down the front steps in the wake of her manic mutt, flinging a cheery wave and parting admonition over her shoulder as she goes. "Sunny and unseasonably warm all day, get your halter top out, my dear."

I spread the newspaper out on the dining room table, breaking the rubber band in my haste, and pick out the Lifestyle section. Bold printed words and color pictures swim in front of my eyes until I locate Donald's column on page D3.

SAVORING THE LAST PIECE

My dear readers,

I'd like to retract an erroneous assertion that was made in this column several weeks back. It had to do with my insinuation of drug or Mafia connections to a loitering incident at Pastries Café. Detective Jack Colby, who investigated the case and with whom I have spoken several times, insists there's no proof that such a connection ever existed. It's a prank, he has concluded, and I am satisfied with his explanation. The case is, therefore, closed. I must publicly apologize to Sunya Malhotra and take full responsibility for any inconvenience I might have caused her. I was misled by an unreliable source.

There's a bright spot in this whole matter, however. My misgivings about Bob Nomura's cheesecake have only made it more popular. The last one I tasted—a chocolate-orange

variation—had even this hoary traditionalist practically waltz-
ing. And so by way of eating humble pie or, should I say,
cheesecake, I would heartily recommend, dear readers, that
you try a piece of cheesecake at Pastries Café if you haven't
already done so.

In closing, I'd like to inform you that this column is my last.
Sorry to disappoint you. Call it the itch to wander brought
on by advancing age, but I have accepted early retirement
from the newspaper. My management has done its best to
persuade me to stay, but it's high time that I pursue some
lifelong dreams. Soon I'll be sailing through the azure waters
of the Mediterranean, sipping wine, and settling down to my
memoirs, which several New York publishers, I can now reveal, are urging me to finish.

In my thirty-five-year newspaper career, I have had the satisfaction of helping raise the standard of dining in Seattle to
the exalted position it occupies today in the nation's culinary
pantheon.

My replacement will be announced soon. I hope you will
willingly give him (or her) the same enthusiastic support
you've so generously bestowed on me over the years.

Bon appétit
Donald J. Smith

I smile big. Donald was obviously forced to resign. Did the erroneous
information about my café cause it?

And who might have been Donald's unreliable source?

THIRTY-SEVEN

I T'S BEEN SEVERAL WEEKS SINCE ANDREW'S PARTY AND I HAVEN'T SEEN HIM since. So tonight I content myself to recline in my favorite armchair, replaying the party scene in my mind: Andrew and the woman in a violet dress; the undercurrent of attraction that drew us closer as the evening wore on. At the same time, I'm troubled by the rumors of his drug use and his flirting with Jill which came up in that unsettling conversation I had with Bob a few days ago. It is a lot to ask of a woman. If relationships have shapes, then this one isn't a circle or triangle; it's more like a hexagon, one I couldn't put my arms around without being spiked. Given that I leave for Japan in a few days, I would like to sort it all out.

None of this would matter if I didn't have such a strong liking for Andrew. Not only is he smart, he has deep, sacred emotions, which, for some reason, he keeps bottled inside. If on a tough day I hear his voice on the phone or exchange a look with him across the bakery counter, the stresses melt away. And it's a delight for me to enter the private world of his film script, to see creativity of a different nature firsthand. So maybe I should give him a call?

I get off the recliner and pick up the telephone. Andrew's hello, sunny and clear, seems to come from the next room.

"Sunya?" His voice cheers up even more when he recognizes me. "Wow. Downright telepathic. I was just thinking about you. Like to come over for veggie burgers? I know it's presumptuous to try to cook for a professional chef . . ."

Instantly my mood turns giddy. I've never had a man cook for me before. And I like the way it feels.

"Veggie burgers would be just great. And, believe it or not, chefs are flattered to be invited to dinner at people's homes. I'll bring some wine. I think I know just the one to go with veggie burgers."

"Fantastic! I can't wait to see you. I'm getting everything ready right now . . . The only thing missing is you."

"I have a couple of things to do, but I'll be over in half an hour."

As I hang up, I wonder. Why didn't he call me if he's preparing dinner for me? Isn't this a bit lopsided? Me calling him all the time?

In just about half an hour, wearing not-too-fancy knit pants in soft blue and a matching jacket, I am at Andrew's door, a fine white Willamette Valley Riesling peeking out of my tote bag. My hair is loose, falling in curls at my shoulders.

The door opens. It's him: olive polo shirt and canvas pants, one hand carrying an issue of the *Los Angeles Times*. He gives me a kiss on the forehead. There's that scent of his body. In the background, I hear the introspective sounds of Andrés Segovia's guitar—a touch of melancholy. He takes my hand, his gaze so affectionate, and draws me into the living room.

The phone rings from one of the bedrooms. Not again. His fingers are hardening. "I won't answer," he mumbles.

He motions toward the sectional sofa, informing me that his brother Evan is out on a date. We both settle ourselves. The wine soothes my palate, like honey with an overtone of apricot; but my back muscles are edgy from the sound of the telephone. He squeezes my hand, says, "So glad you're here." I take the opportunity to ask him about his day.

"You know, some film students came to talk to me on the set," he says, face displaying a self-satisfied expression. "They're eager to get themselves started and some of them are already making short films. They think it's fun. But wait till they direct a feature film. It becomes your life for months—you lose yourself completely, hopelessly, in it. You fall into bed after a fifteen-hour day . . . Then when you have a free moment, there comes a letdown, a loneliness of disproportionate size . . ."

As he picks up his wineglass, I notice his hand—fine, artistic, an elaborate network of prominent veins, and limp—a telltale sign of his inner turmoil.

"It's so nice having your company, Andrew, knowing how busy you are. It's even better having you just for myself . . . By the way, I've been wanting to ask you . . . and this has been with me the last couple of weeks . . . you don't have to answer if you don't want to . . . but who was that woman at the party?"

There's a silence, impenetrable as a high brick fence. "Katrina is my soon-to-be ex-wife."

He's married! My eyes can't see, my mouth is dehydrated, the air is oxygen-robbing. It takes a few seconds to set my thoughts in order. Well, perhaps it's not the news itself that has crushed me, but rather that he withheld it. Once again, I admit that Mother—bless her intuition, however disconcerting it was at the time—was right. I take a small swallow of the Riesling, which now tastes flat, even stale.

"She's your ex? My guess is"—I stretch my sentence out—"she's still interested in you, Andrew."

"Well, she thinks she is."

"How long were you married?"

"Not even a year. It'll be over in three weeks. The hell of it is Katrina is my costar. She's Emily. She goes back and forth between L.A. and here."

As I look up—his eyes have sunk deeper now—I try my best to grasp the dilemma he's in. The divorce is partly responsible for his rigid posture. Katrina is around him constantly. My mind makes a picture of her snuggling up to him—her bamboo hand on his shoulder—and I flinch.

"I married her for the wrong reasons." He pauses, covers my hand softly with his. "Sunya, Sunya . . . even though we've only known each other for a couple of months you've come to mean a lot to me. I really do want something more with you . . . but I'm scared."

I stare at the puzzled expression, at the features I carry around with me, but the man has so many scars and wounds, and he's not about to ask for help. Caressing his arm, "Do you think you belong to L.A.?"

"No, I'm considering a move. I like it here. Do you know how many films are being shot here? The locations, equipment, studios are all available." A smile—tiny but brightening—brushes his lips. "And the pastries are superior."

Hands in tight grip, we sit, both getting lost in our respective thoughts. My mind goes over the pleasant possibility of his relocation, though I must admit that a vague uneasiness still lingers. It is as though I have opened a box that I will not be able to close.

He stands up. "The veggie burgers should be ready any minute."

I follow him to the open kitchen. A savory smell surrounds me, as I watch him shred the lettuce, chop the tomatoes, select a platter from the upper cabinet, and wash a spoon in the sink. Almost as though he's hiding behind those pragmatic tasks. My gaze falls on a half-eaten pomegranate sitting in the shadow of a tall canister on the counter. Glistening red seeds, sunk inside the fruit's hard, bonelike exterior, stare out like some medieval dragon's glowing eyes, a conversation starter. "Oh, you like pomegranate."

He opens the oven door, lifts a pan out. "I bought this Early Wonderful off-season variety, from California, at Sunrise Produce."

"Don't you lose patience trying to extract the pulp from each seed? I sure do."

"Yes, but I couldn't throw it away. It reminded me of my favorite still life painting by the Dutch artist Abraham van Beyeren. Do you like van Beyeren?"

I only vaguely remember coming across the work of that Baroque era artist at an exhibit in the Seattle Art Museum. Vaguely. Better that way, as I'd rather see the painting through Andrew's eyes. "I'm not that familiar with him."

"To van Beyeren a pomegranate stood for hope. His signature still life had a pomegranate, a chunk of peasant bread, a jug of wine, a fruit bowl, and a pocket watch."

"A pocket watch? In a still life of bread and wine and pomegranate?"

"Yup. I think he was trying to convey the transient nature of life."

"Yet he tried to freeze it at a point in time. Do you think he was just trying to remember how long it took him to eat a pomegranate?"

Andrew chuckles. As I help carry the food to the table, it occurs to me that in the overall scheme of things my personal concerns mean little. About as much, say, as a pomegranate and a watch. Feeling humbled, I decide to forgo asking any more insightful or personal questions.

"I have two mustards," he says. "Would you like orange or Dijon? There's also horseradish and a hot Caribbean dipping sauce."

"There are hard choices in life, but you make this one easy. Orange mustard. It's my favorite with veggie burgers."

His eyes smile as we sit at the table. "I want this to be a good time," he says. "Just you and me . . . It's been a long day. People are bitching, I'm over budget, my actors don't get along with each other, the trade conference starts in two days. We'll have to be out in the streets taking live shots of the drama, aaand . . . I just can't get the death scene to work."

I attack my burger-on-onion-bun, not as voraciously as my hunger would dictate. If the truth be uttered, I am aching to hear more about the final scenes of the script, to re-create the intimacy I've felt in each of our previous storytelling sessions. A raconteur and his listener are bound together in a yin-and-yang way. Something, anything, to erase the itchy reminder in my consciousness that he's married. But I decide to wait. We make small talk throughout the meal, clear the table, and then retreat to the comfort of the sofa, at which point I sense the time is ripe.

"Is that how you want your story to end?" I ask. "With a death. Who dies?"

"Well, I'm still revising as I go, but this is how I think it'll go." He swallows, looks out into space. "Demonstrators have taken over the area near the Convention Center. Werner is in the thick of it. The police are throwing people down on the ground, cuffing them, spraying them with pepper gas, and shoving them into vans. Black-clad anarchists are breaking windows and challenging the police. It's war, chaos. Through the haze of tear gas, Werner sees a riot cop pulling his pistol. Something snaps. He draws his own gun and aims it at the cop. He doesn't see another cop off to one side leveling his gun at him. Then Werner is on the ground, numb with shock, bleeding, barely able to breathe. He figures he's dying."

"So you don't want to kill Werner?"

"That wouldn't be a huge surprise, would it?"

"Why doesn't Emily get shot instead . . . ?"

He ponders an instant, then starts to speak. "Emily's there . . . She watches Werner drawing his gun. She knows what's going to happen. She wants to drag him out of the line of fire. Plausible, so far."

It's delightful the way we're constructing the ending together. My turn now, and I feel emboldened. "She misjudges the distance and lunges in front of Werner just as he pulls the trigger—"

"Wait just a minute. Let me get a tape recorder." Andrew rises, walks toward a shelf, fetches a tape recorder, regains his seat, turns the recorder on, and says, "Keep talking."

"The bullet strikes Emily and knocks her flat. She lies there unconscious, deathly white, badly hurt, her red scarf turning redder. Werner drops the gun with a scream and kneels besides her sobbing. 'Oh, my God, no, no, no, Emily!' He tries to revive her, but it's no use. Her blood is all over his clothes. He takes her to the hospital, and after several hours of agonized waiting, a surgeon comes out and tells him that she'll survive, but that it'll be a long recovery and she'll be partially paralyzed. Werner has to live with that the rest of his life. He'll give up his job as a cop and become an activist."

"Interesting idea, definitely a possibility. But if I do take your idea, I'll let Emily bleed to death on the spot in Werner's arms. Death is so much more effective on film. It's final and graphic. Otherwise, I'll have to do a hospital scene and that gets messy. It'll drag the story out and dilute its impact."

I lean back on the sofa, seeking its cushiony softness. On the one hand, I am pleased that he takes my suggestion seriously and that we've become closer through his film script. On the other hand, I find it disturbing how it doesn't faze him when I suggest killing off Emily. Just like that, a character is expendable. Can he leave that kind of thinking at the movie set, or does it spill over into his personal life?

Barely has the thought blown across my mind than he sets the tape recorder down on an occasional table and snuggles closer. Just as I look up at him to protest—he's technically still married—he kisses me, a more probing kiss this time, as though trying to make up for all that is still unexpressed in him, pouring in some apologies as well. A millisecond of resistance gives way to sweet surrender and, in that moment, I understand why I waited so long, and for this awkward night when I found out about his marriage. Perhaps I was waiting for the time when we'd both know there's no turning back. That such a moment has blossomed through the web of his film script matters not a bit. My fingers trace his strong shoulders. He helps me rise from the sofa and guides me to his bedroom in a slow dreamy walk. We sink as one onto the bed, our bodies finally freed from the chill of isolation, from weeks of silent hunger, meshing, probing, delighting, expanding. It is as though we were designed as adjacent pieces of an erotic puzzle. His lovemaking has a slo-mo, soft-light quality, replete with close-ups and orchestra notes.

Much later, we stretch out on the bed, propped up by pillows with embroidered covers, murmuring and cuddling, satisfied and feeling connected. My eyes take in the details of his living space: an oval mirror on the dresser, its surface dull from a lack of direct lighting, offering each of us a muted reflection of the other. A night table, whose only apparent function is to hold his pen, writing pad, and eyeglasses. Hanging on one wall is a black-and-white poster of his acclaimed film *Storm Country* inviting me to peer out over the shoulder of a man pointing to a storm gathering on the horizon.

I turn to him. In a husky voice, he says, "You're close to my heart, Sunya."

"And I want to be with you."

He traces my forehead with a finger. "I'll make more time for us if I can just get through these next few weeks . . ."

"You have the trade conference to get through, I know that, darling. And I'll be going away for two weeks." Also important, though I don't mention it, is the fact that his divorce would come through.

"You're going away?"

"I have to go to Japan."

"Why?" His voice is glazed with astonishment, anger.

"Among other things, I'll be checking out the Sunya Tradition."

"You don't really believe in that stuff, do you?"

"You're the one who introduced me to the idea, remember?" I laugh. "At this point, I'm somewhat of a skeptic, but . . ."

"Do you just need a vacation?"

"I have been needing a vacation for years but, right now, when just about everything is going wrong with my business, I wouldn't leave just for playtime. I'm a practical person, as bakers have to be. We deal with a set of ingredients and come up with tangible results. I've never done anything quite so impulsive, or pursued anything so illusory . . ."

"I don't want you to leave me, Sunya."

Torn, I push a lock of hair away from my forehead, look down at my hand. The air is musty and the temper of the room has subtly altered. Andrew, lost in a moment of reflection, is in his own biosphere. I don't feel as cozy as I did only minutes ago. If I make this trip to Japan, I'll be risking something I enormously cherish.

As he draws me closer, I hear him breathe out in a sigh—the cry of his heart—and sense that a distance has grown between us, not enough to be alarming, but unsettling nonetheless. Just the postcoital recovery of self, is it? Or something more threatening? Given my exposed emotional condition, I am inclined to chalk it up to the former. Still, a part of me wonders if a shadow from his past has swooped in and reclined hard-won territory. Why does the past hold us so captive? How I wish I could chase its curse away.

THIRTY-EIGHT

THE TRADE CONFERENCE OPENED EARLIER TODAY. IN THE EVENING, THE wind claws at my face with its icy fingers as I cross the Seattle Center grounds and slip inside the doors of the Center House. In downtown, barely a mile away, the day's demonstrations and riots are in full swing. Already I'm anxious, and that shows in my hurried steps.

I pace up and down the aisles of the Center House—a large hall with tables and chairs strewn about the middle and a shopping arcade around the periphery. The blue-violet neon signs hurt my eyes. Where's Roger? I am leaving for Japan the day after tomorrow; hence the urgency for us to get together on this historic evening.

Did he misunderstand that this is where we were supposed to meet? That can't be. When we scheduled our rendezvous over the phone, he agreed that this would be a convenient place for him. The People's Trade Campaign office, where his compatriots will gather later this evening, is only a block away.

There is a loud crashing sound behind me and I jump. Someone dropped a tray, nothing more. Ice cubes skitter across the concrete floor like shards of glass.

My watch says it's just a few minutes before our seven P.M. appointment. Still I can't make myself sit down. I descend the escalator to a dark empty basement and come up again; no sign of Roger.

Throughout the day, I've been hearing snatches of news reports about the riots. My worries have centered on Andrew, who's out there in the middle of things with his crew and camera, capturing live footage of the demonstration—maybe even filming Roger. Sometime around five P.M., Andrew left a short message on my answering machine, indicating he was safe. He ended with a romantic kissing sound. To be truthful, I haven't been concerned about Roger until now.

I walk over to the entrance and stand to one side as a family saunters in with a whimpering child. Stepping outside, I find the grounds deserted, cloaked in a wintry gloom that only intensifies my grave mood.

With a shudder, I retreat inside. Well, Roger's always late. Why should this be an exception? I settle at a table and open the evening edition of the *News*. The bold headlines proclaim:

ATTEMPT TO UNITE RICH AND POOR NATIONS
EXPLODES IN A CLOUD OF TEAR GAS

I can visualize it as it happened. A crowd of 30,000, who had an official permit, marches into downtown near where the trade talks are scheduled to begin. At first, the air is festive. Dance music pours out of sound trucks; festive demonstrators mill about in varied costumes—doves, monarch butterflies, and porpoises. But the jovial atmosphere doesn't last long. Demonstrators attempt to block access to the Convention Center. The police respond with tear gas and pepper spray and pandemonium ensues. Soon fire trucks and medics are called in.

My sympathy for the protesters, Roger and his group among them, grows. Why hasn't he called by now? He has my cell phone number. I am carrying the cell phone for a change.

I examine the photo in the newspaper: police in gas masks and a demonstrator lying on the street, his arms and legs spread out. Not Roger, I tell myself. He's more careful than that. I fold the newspaper, with the picture out of sight, and check my surroundings.

Two tables away the family is having dinner. The child is quiet, but he's making a mess of the noodles. Their blissful chewing and lack of concern about what might be taking place in the rest of the city makes me angry. I open the paper again:

> "Take back our streets," chants the crowd over on Pike Street. Roving bands of anarchists allegedly smash the windows of U.S. Bank, McDonald's, Starbucks, and the Gap. A spokesperson for the conference says that it's becoming increasingly difficult to continue the talks under these conditions.

I recheck my watch. Seven-twenty P.M. Unable to stand the suspense any longer, I riffle through my handbag, retrieve my cell phone, and call the People's Trade Campaign office.

It rings and rings at the other end. Finally, someone answers above a background of agitated voices. "Roger Yahura? Haven't seen him. Let me check around. Please hold on." My grip on the cell phone is cold and stiff. My ears strain to pick up the tiniest sound. A few seconds later, the man comes back on the line. "Are you a relative? No? Are you in town? Okay, I'm told Roger was injured and taken to the hospital. Which hospital? I don't know. I can't hear you very well. Can you call back a little later? I'll try to get you more information . . ."

"Please . . . I'm a friend. I'll hold on. Please get me any information you can right now."

A minute later, the man confirms that Roger is in Harborview Hospital.

"How badly was he hurt?"

"Sorry, ma'am, I couldn't tell you."

I am back out in the autumn chill, but I don't feel it. As I speed toward Harborview, I turn on the radio for the latest news. The police are now shooting at protesters on Capitol Hill with rubber bullets. I switch the radio off.

After walking through endless corridors of the hospital, I locate the right ward. Roger, a bundle of hospital white, his left leg in traction, is lying in the farthest bed, staring at the ceiling. An untouched ham sandwich rests on a side table.

"Sunya . . ." He half rises and extends a hand, which I take into mine. "You're here . . . I wouldn't have expected it. Sorry I stood you up, but . . ." He grimaces and looks down at his leg.

"Don't worry about that. How're you doing?"

"I feel lucky—only a broken shinbone. Not that big a deal. I'll be walking in a matter of weeks."

He looks vulnerable, crestfallen. In an earlier time I'd have kissed him and hugged him, even though there are two other patients in the room, and told him that of course he'd be all right and I'd be by his side to help . . . Right now, I squeeze his hand.

"I literally don't have a leg to stand on, Sunya. I remember how you always warned me . . ."

"Will this change your mind, or—"

"Definitely the 'or.' I'm even more convinced we're doing the right thing. You should have seen what was going on. My work's cut out for me."

I sit beside him. Shocked, angry, helpless, he goes on and on about how he wishes he were still out there fighting the "agents of oppression." Instead, he's cooped up in a hospital room. As he speaks, he grimaces from the pain.

Without any warning, he says, "I'm glad Kimiko moved out."

I allow a short silence. "You're glad?"

"She made me feel like I was still living in Japan, even though I'm a different person now. She was bringing out something in me that I didn't like . . . Between the two of you, I'd have to say—"

"I'd rather that you didn't compare us, Roger."

"I'm so dopey right now. Can we talk sometime, Sunya, after I get out of the hospital? I'd really like to talk with you . . ."

"But . . ." Now is not the time to inform him about my budding relationship with Andrew and how it has led my days in a new direction. Then noticing his eyes are drifting shut, I murmur a good night and leave.

Minutes later, as I drive home, I fight off a tightness in my throat, recalling what friends have often told me. That people come into your life, linger a while, then move on, like rain, like a bad case of flu, like a bottle of fine wine briefly savored but soon no more than a mellow memory. In their view, relationships count no more than the business cards you collect, then toss into the wastebasket. I wonder if I subscribe to that point of view. However wounded I have been by Roger, the answer in my case is no. Sometimes it takes a disaster to prove who or what still matters, if only a molecule. Or perhaps that's just the way I am.

THIRTY-NINE

TWENTY-FOUR HOURS BEFORE I LEAVE FOR JAPAN, I AM IN MY BEDROOM packing, with Mother to keep me company. Though attired in comfortable soft fleece sweats and a pair of slippers, I'm not at ease. We discuss the latest on Roger. While I pack halfheartedly, Mother assures me that she'll look after him in my absence.

She flutters around the room, inspecting the closet and sliding all nine drawers of the vanity open. She's convinced that without her supervision, I'll forget some essential items with calamitous consequences for my trip. She asks me, as she's done many times in the last few days, if I really need to fly that far just to take a vacation.

"Doesn't Whidbey Island have a Zen retreat? Why don't you go there instead? It'll only take you an hour and a half by boat instead of ten hours of flying across the Pacific, crossing the international date line, and losing a day."

"It's not Zen I am seeking, Mother . . ."

"*Tobe ki?*" What is it then?

I fall silent. How to convey the pull I feel toward Japan? It relieves me when she asks, "What's the temperature over there?"

"In the fifties."

"Is the typhoon season still on?"

"No." I shove a copy of *Teach Yourself Japanese* in my suitcase. "It finished in September."

A look of relief crosses her face. For the next few minutes, her voice merry, she fills me in on the preparations for her June wedding, much of it done through wedding-industry Web sites. She's sketched out a preliminary guest list, selected a photographer, hired a DJ to play danceable tunes, booked an extravagant reception site—none other than the Rose Garden in Woodland Park—and ordered finely engraved invitation cards. "I even have a countdown calendar," she announces, "so I won't miss anything. I'm over budget already."

I'd be more excited if Dushan wasn't the man she was marrying. Still, I pay her my complete attention, as I compress the clothing and gifts in the suitcase with both hands to make room for more articles. It's amazing how much a small suitcase can accommodate.

"Dushan was over for dinner last night," Mother mentions quite casually, as she perches on the edge of my high iron bed. "Guess who he brought along?"

"Who?" Warning bells start to chime in my head.

"Willy Cartdale. I made a big Indian dinner for them."

"Cartdale? You must be kidding."

"Yes, 'the Enemy.' He liked my *mangsho* very much. He took three helpings."

"Are you serious? You invited that jerk to your house and fed him your lamb curry? How do you even know him?"

"You can't hide a fish with spinach, as we say in Bengal. I knew that you and Dushan were arguing over Cartdale and his schemes. I pestered Dushan till he told me all. Then I did some thinking and came away with an 'action plan.' I asked Dushan to extend a dinner invitation to Cartdale. It took some arm-twisting on his part before

Cartdale accepted. I figured I had nothing to lose by having him over. He couldn't be too obnoxious to Dushan's fiancée, now could he, my dear, especially one who feeds him a home-cooked meal? I can act charmingly dumb when the occasion calls for it, as you know."

I have stopped packing and am staring dumbly at Mother. "The guy is a creep. I met him. He had the gall to come to my bakery."

"You're letting your personal feelings get the best of you. His mother was a seamstress and she raised him alone, too. His parents had divorced when he was fifteen. Once a week his father would take him to the Woodland Park Zoo and Jack in the Box. But that was the extent of his involvement with Willy."

"It upsets me very much that you intervened in my business affairs. I wouldn't trust a word Cartdale says. A man like him will promise one thing today, then do something entirely the opposite tomorrow."

"My dear, in this life you can only hope to buy *shomoy*." She emphasized the word that meant "time." "Troubles, always, come back sooner or later."

"I can solve my own problems. You don't have to take care of me."

"Believe me, you'll have plenty on your plate when you get back. But now I have Willy on my side. Strange as it may sound, he likes my company. He wants to come back and try some more of my home cooking. He's divorced. He says Indian cuisine is one of the frontiers he'd like to conquer. He's always in a war mode. His mother doesn't cook anymore. The poor guy hasn't had a decent home-cooked meal in years."

"Do you think you can really trust him?"

"No, but it helps to understand what's on his mind."

"What was Dushan's role in this?"

"He was the facilitator. You see, honey, I am learning all the corporate buzzwords. By the way, Dushan is proud of you. You still have your bakery open and the public supports you."

"Why, sure. Some days I can barely balance myself on the edge of the cliff. One false move and—"

"Life is just that, dear, a question of balance. Now, don't look so upset. Ever since you were a child, you wanted to do it all by yourself. Let me do something for you once in a while. Someday you'll be a mother and you'll understand that loving isn't just about sitting and wallowing in kind feelings. Loving sometimes calls for resolute action. It's hard for me to stay put when I see the difficulties ahead of you. I've done so very little, but this makes me feel so much better. You'll be happy to know that my blood pressure was down this morning to a hundred and thirty-six over eighty-four. That's the lowest it's been in a while."

"Keep it that way, will you?" I open my makeup kit and check the level of the Oil of Olay hand lotion. Mother surprises me with her resourcefulness. Who needs a father? However brilliant an academic he might have been, he would never have matched Mother's kindness, humanity, or force of character.

She rises and walks over to the corner of the room, picks up her handbag, and unzips the top. Before I know it, she is holding out two travel-size red and white Colgate toothpastes before me.

"Take these with you," she orders, as she settles down again on the edge of the bed. "Just in case you run out of toothpaste over there. Isn't this the brand your dentist recommends? You might not find this brand or this size in Japan. It might be written in Japanese and you won't be able to read it. What will you do then?"

I accept the tubes and slide them into my toilet kit, stifling the words of protest that well up in my throat. Japan is a modern country and I am a grown adult. I can very well locate a convenience store and get my own toothpaste. Mother, you needn't have bothered. But I decide not to pursue the matter. Now that my suitcase is packed and ready to go, I perch beside her on the edge of the bed and squeeze her hand. The deep, consoling touch of her rough-skinned hands has always kept me from flying off the handle. In a spell, I am back to a real place in real time, with the solid ground beneath my slippered feet. The universe is not a total disaster, after all.

"And don't forget a heavy coat. I'm sure it gets very cold over there at night. You know you don't like to be cold."

We linger a few more minutes and go over my itinerary for the tenth time. No cards or phone calls for fifteen days? Mother doesn't approve of such strict rules, but says she will oblige. She'll count the days and hours and minutes till I come back. Still, as I accompany her to the door, I notice hesitancy in her movement, which means she questions this venture of mine. I wave as she climbs into her car. A call from the unknown has lured me to leave her and my tight little circle of support. The wind that's blowing seems to be sighing to me: Will this trip be worth the risks it entails?

Have I made the right decision? Should I reconsider it? The sky glitters; birds are twittering; there's supposed to be a full moon to-night. Yet, standing on the porch, my elbows on the grillwork of the railing, I'm stung by anxiety.

FORTY

THE MOMENT MY AIRPLANE LANDS IN KANSAI AIRPORT, MY WAVERING IS gone. I feel like a footloose traveler, ready to be reinvigorated by my new surroundings. Upon clearing customs, I claim my luggage and emerge from the terminal onto a pedestrian walkway. A white-gloved traffic officer waves me over to an island where taxis are parked single file. Soon I am inside a spotless cab, cruising down a wide boulevard, lined on either side with tall gleaming steel-and-glass edifices. A sense of compactness, restraint, and discipline prevails. At this late morning hour, the traffic zips along the road, but orderly as the whole scene appears, I still sense the silent pressure of some 130 million people who inhabit a country of islands no bigger than California. Add to that the mysterious Japanese script on banners and billboards everywhere, and my enthusiasm is soon tempered by a feeling of intimidation.

After I check in at a modern hotel in Kyoto, a bellhop shows me to my room. It is only a tiny compartment, but somehow manages to accommodate a bed with a bluish cover, a lacquered chest, and writing desk without seeming claustrophobic. The single window opens onto a large-scale formal garden, creating an illusion of space and proximity to nature. I had planned to take a nap, but find myself wide awake and disoriented after the long flight. I go downstairs and pause at a winding stone pathway leading to the garden. Ahead of me is a pond with a graceful bridge arching over it. To the right I see shrubs, flowering bushes, and black stones arranged beneath a grove of elegant pine trees whispering in the breeze. The overall effect is a subtle sense of geometric order. To the left is a sturdy stone lantern. Somewhere in the distance, a temple bell rings out in deep hollow tones that linger in the air. The garden is so designed that a new view unfolds with each step that I take. Had I not detected a hint of the familiar smell of mushroom pizza drifting on a faint breeze, it'd all seem totally alien albeit in an attractive way.

Afternoon. I venture out of the hotel, wandering through the warren of alleys that lace the hillside, expecting to see traditional tile-roofed houses, but locating only one. Soon I come to a major thoroughfare. A buttery smell permeating the air draws me to a modern shopping complex. The source of the fragrance, I discover, is a croissanterie, the first of several similar establishments that stand on the boulevard. Baked goods, though not traditional here, have caught on, I note approvingly. Passing a yakitori stand and a woman's boutique with a big Mode l'Automne sign, I turn a corner and find myself in front of the gleaming windows of an upscale parlor—Apsara Bakery. I pause and look it over carefully. I have to admit it's much swankier than my humble enterprise.

So, this is where I'll be hanging my toque for the next two weeks. What if I burn the chocolate, forget to add the pineapple extract, overbake the tart crust? Queasiness escalates into a panicky feeling of inadequacy.

With a deep breath, I follow a young couple into the store and browse for a few minutes. Though pricier than the croissanteries I've come across thus far, this shop is crammed with customers waiting in a long line to place their orders. It's easy to understand why. The plate-glass showcase boasts a comprehensive array of classic European pastries—génoise, mille-feuille, and éclair. Had there not been an assortment of Japanese sweets—*mitsumame*—and a few hybrids, such as a green tea cake, I'd have thought I was back in Paris. I am mildly disappointed that there's no Autumn Symphony Tart; perhaps it's already gone. As I watch a barista prepare coffee fresh for an individual order, I overhear an American customer saying that he wants a double order of génoise—apparently he ordered only one the last time and it left him "dying for more." My curiosity heightens, immediately followed by that same queasy feeling.

I lean against the blond wood counter, identify myself to one of the staff, and ask to see Mori Matsumoto. Smart-looking and efficient, she is outfitted in a white uniform and blue apron. "Please have a seat," she replies in almost accent-free English. "I'll tell him you are here."

As I wait at a white-napped table, I listen to the muffled Japanese conversation coming from an adjoining table. It is an eerie sensation to not understand a word being uttered and feel like a complete outsider. Listening to the cadence of the language, I recall a few basic Japanese phrases I learned from Roger but never really used. A car honks raucously just outside the bakery. Through the window, I watch a gaggle of teenagers entering an electronics shop across the street. Wearing tricolored shoes, rhinestone-studded athletic headbands and T-shirts emblazoned with an image of a hot dog with arms and legs, they would not seem out of place in any mall back home.

A man appearing to be in his early sixties emerges from an inside room and walks briskly over to me. Dressed in chef's coat, baggy pants, and a pair of sneakers, he is about average height, with an ebullient oval face, mottled complexion, and deep symmetrical creases in his cheeks. He pulls up a chair and smiles at me with the doting manner of an older relative.

"Welcome to Japan, Sunya-san. I'm Mori Matsumoto."

"It's a special privilege to be here."

"You know I've been waiting for you with great anticipation ever since I talked with Bobu-san on the phone and learned that you're already an accomplished baker." The voice is gravelly; the words seem to come from deep inside him; but it is the receptivity in the untroubled dancing eyes that impresses me the most. "I've been looking forward to having you in the program. You'll be the only new student in these two weeks."

"I know I'm not supposed to start till tomorrow, but I just couldn't wait to come and visit your bakery."

"Never too early to start." He leans forward. "You're from Seattle. I've seen your Mount Rainier, but only in pictures. Have you ever climbed it?"

"No, I haven't. But I have a great view of it from my street on clear days."

"I never visited Seattle, though I lived in Manhattan for a while. Seattle seems less flamboyant, but still makes the news."

It is a relief that Matsumoto hasn't brought up the topic of the recent Seattle trade conference. Instead, he begins to recall his days in Manhattan. "One could really have fun there. I was much younger then, employed as a pastry chef in a restaurant, and making good money. The world was mine for the taking. I'd bake all day then, in the evening, go nightclubbing. I could get by on very little sleep. A foolish young man I was. Still, every so often, I look back fondly on those days."

His reminiscences cause me to consider the struggles of my life, the opportunities for pleasure that I have passed by; but I'm still young. At some point, I'd like to take time off to savor life a little. I feel sheepish that I am thinking like this sitting in a shop where the employees obviously work extra hard. I notice Matsumoto turning his head toward the counter. Immediately a server materializes and takes his order. It is clear Matsumoto completely runs the show here. Could I get used to that?

Soon the server brings each of us a "cake set"—a wedge of génoise accompanied by a bowl of a fragrant green tea called *gyokuro*. I've never imagined such a pairing before, but one tentative sip is enough to convince me that the exquisite brew will be a first-rate complement to the génoise. I find myself without words.

Matsumoto informs me that the tea comes from Shizuoka prefecture, home to Fuji-san—his affectionate way of referring to the country's highest mountain. The leaves are the highest grade and the water in which they are steeped is never brought to a full, harsh boil. He smiles down at his bowl. "The universe comes to you in a bowl of tea, as we say."

His universe intimidates me a bit more when I taste the génoise, by far the best I've ever sampled. The sponge cake has a fine moist uniform texture and a subtle fruity fragrance that I can't quite place. My fears about working here grow.

"Tomorrow morning we'll start off simply, working with basic breads," Matsumoto says. "Later in the week, we'll move on to pastries, like génoise. There is a lot to cover, so our days are long. Perhaps it's time I gave you a little background about what I teach my students."

"Yes, I'd like that. That's what I'm here for."

Matsumoto smiles. "It's not something one can be taught in a day, maybe not even in two weeks."

I set the plate aside. Has he already underestimated me? Immediately I resolve to prove him wrong.

Later that afternoon, seated in the hotel garden, I ponder how much I've already learned from Matsumoto's basic introduction. His healing program takes an experiential approach. He honored me by telling me about his grief, which led him to be the first subject of his experiment. Seven years ago, his only daughter, who was apparently my age at the time, died of pneumonia. For months, the grief was so profound that Matsumoto couldn't bake, or do much of anything else. He'd been raised a Buddhist but, with his attention focused on building a career, he'd ceased practicing. Then he met a monk named Bikkhu Karun, who reminded him about the concepts of *dukkha*, suffering, and *anicca*, the impermanence of things, concepts he'd known but didn't pay attention to. Matsumoto could see that he needed to change his viewpoint to rise out of his desolation, but things were still out of joint for him.

One day, alone in the kitchen, Matsumoto tried to knead the bread dough. Unable to achieve a smooth, pliable consistency, he grew frustrated and was about to give up when it occurred to him that what Bikkhu Karun had taught him was true. He had what he needed to make him happy again, but he was wallowing in his misery, going over the same anxious thoughts, and getting some perverse pleasure out of that. In that instant, he yelled "Stop!"

Matsumoto said this with such comic exaggeration that I broke out laughing.

He went on to tell me that his self-absorption had vanished and this allowed his attention to refocus on the dough. For the next few minutes, kneading was all that mattered to him, as though the cosmos had reduced itself to that lump of dough. He willed himself to complete the remaining steps and, as he did so, his tension and anxieties melted away; he felt refreshed. Eyes clear, Matsumoto looked me full in the face and asked, "Perhaps you are wondering—is it really that simple?"

I responded with a hopeful nod.

Matsumoto resumed speaking, stressing that baking is a simple skill that anyone can learn; it requires nothing more than a few ingredients, an oven, and a willing mind. The object is to nourish people in a pleasing way, which leads to enormous satisfaction—nurturing others, after all, is a basic urge in all of us. Baking also hones your senses. The forms, colors, shapes, and textures lead you to focus on the real world. Matsumoto came to realize that he could touch the lives of other people who had also been traumatized. They can still visit their physicians and therapists if they feel the need, but if they can learn to achieve some inner calm working with him, such visits will not be nearly as frequent. "My mantra became flour, water, yeast, salt, and 'one-pointedness' . . ."

At that instant, he poured more tea into my cup, saying that the last drops in the pot hold the best taste. Though my eyes were dreamily contemplating the aromatic bowl, my mind buzzed with inquiries. I'd been raised in the States to question and double-check everything. "That's all one needs?"

Matsumoto replied that there was one more element—something he referred to as "being present." To bake something successfully you first have to lose yourself in the process, you have to be fully there and giving. The quality of the end result will be proportional to the completeness of your involvement. Eventually the simplicity of the steps, the repetitive motions, the intense focus, and the beautiful results lead you to feel in harmony with your environment, with yourself. He emphasized that he considered baking an expression of his best self. Baking had become his meditation.

As I took a few more sips from my cup (the taste was, indeed, fuller), I considered his teachings. In Paris, I'd been taught baking as a set of techniques, a series of steps leading toward a well-defined goal: the finished pastry. Matsumoto, on the other hand, advocated immersing oneself in the process; the result would follow as a matter of course—an altogether different approach. Fascinating, though I didn't fully grasp it.

Matsumoto then confided that he was often asked why baking succeeds when other, more scientific, therapies and practices do not. Well, once a student gets over his or her initial reluctance—and he assists them with that—they find the kitchen a most comfortable place to be. There's something primordial about the smell of bread and pastries that touches our core. The way we're living our life, whether we're performing with full power and integrity or in a state of disharmony and confusion, shows up in our baking.

Could it really be so? I wondered. People experience failures. I had certainly had more than a few failures in the kitchen recently. But to fault it all on how I live my life is a stretch, or so I mused.

"Baking mirrors your state of mind," Matsumoto said in conclusion. "There's no hiding."

With those words, he gently slapped the tabletop and ended our first visit. Now sitting in the garden and contemplating my day's experience, I reason: if he thinks he can win me over with his fancy theories . . .

It's getting dark. I can no longer see the stone lantern. Andrew's face comes to mind, as it has throughout the day. Seattle's so far away, yet it seems he's all around me. Like I could extend my hand and touch him. Like I could smell his special fragrance. Tucking those remembrances away in a precious little package inside me, I get up, walk back to my room, and draw the window shades down.

Tomorrow, surrounded by mixing bowls and whisks and the aroma of good coffee, I'll put Matsumoto's ideas to the test. I am looking forward to the challenge inherent in it.

In the morning, I take a taxi to Apsara Bakery. I am wearing herringbone coordinates, still uncertain about how to dress and act in my new surroundings. Standing by the counter, Matsumoto greets me with the same bright smile. "Ah, Sunya-san. Maybe we can begin."

I return his greeting. I am not fully awake yet.

At this early hour, the crowd is thin, and together we step closer to the display case. "May I show you what my students have made?" Matsumoto points to a platter of cream puffs. "A young nurse prepared the choux pastry that is used for making the base, a grandmother the coffee-chocolate filling, and together they decorated the tops with toasted coconut. I check their work every day. They're progressing nicely."

"Looks professional," I comment.

"It took a couple of tries. On the first attempt, the nurse put too much butter in the dough, mismeasured the sugar, and forgot to check the oven temperature, while the grandmother underbaked her batch."

I'm eager to hear Matsumoto's explanation and refute it if necessary. Just then, I notice that an elderly man with a cane is shuffling in our direction, his gaze fixed on the pastry case, and I step aside to make room for him. Matsumoto gestures toward an empty table and we take our seats.

"You see, Sunya-san, when they first begin studying with me, students bring their own ways of doing things. My kitchen is a little laboratory, where the results are immediate and clear. During their baking exercises, the students expose attitudes and habits that have been woven into their lives, that have perhaps not worked to their advantage but, instead, have only left them bewildered and frustrated. In this isolated environment, I encourage them to look for the connection between those attitudes and habits and their baking problems. Once they've made that connection, it is not difficult to see how those attitudes and habits affect other areas of their lives. The nurse, for example, came to understand that she was rushing too much in her day-to-day activities. The grandmother realized she was withholding affection from those around her—here it manifested itself in withholding heat from the pastry. They both decided they needed to change their perspective. Such understanding, I must tell you, isn't acquired all at once. After they go home, they'll keep baking and achieve little insights every now and then. It is a lifelong process. We never gain complete mastery over ourselves."

I look away to the flowerpots that line both sides of the entrance, the tender white buds contrasting with the deep green foliage. It'd be hard to quarrel with Matsumoto's philosophy as such, but the question that keeps nagging at me is: Will it work for me?

"In return, my students must take orders from me without question." Matsumoto smiles self-deprecatingly.

"Without question?"

"You must relinquish your ego while you're in this kitchen. As for how much you can learn in a couple of weeks . . . Hopefully these two weeks will set you on the right path. I'm not a scholar, but I've picked up a few jewels of wisdom from Bikkhu Karun, for which I've found practical applications, and which I try to pass on to others. Just a few, but they're so precious. There's a story I like to tell. Once on a dark winter night, my neighborhood had a power failure. I was walking home from work when all of a sudden I found myself in pitch-blackness. I lost my sense of direction, became dizzy, and didn't know which way to go. Then someone lit a candle and put it on a rooftop. I could see the tiny flame shining through the darkness, not enough to totally figure out my way, but enough to quiet my mind. So it is with these teachings."

I have begun to resent Matsumoto's lecturing, the fact that he doesn't allow much questioning.

He gestures to a room in the back. "We have two kitchens. The smaller one is for the students. Would you like to have a look?"

Bread or pastry—I'm not ready to start baking. On top of that, the fragrance of the coffee that a barista is preparing has just hit me. Holding the hope that Matsumoto will offer me a cup, I reply, "The coffee smells terrific . . ."

He apparently doesn't hear me, for he rises and steers me to the compact kitchen, whose walls are a light shade of maroon, and proceeds to show me around. The kitchen is crammed with shiny modern appliances and utensils, clean and tidy except for a gossamer haze of flour hanging in the air. Next to the kitchen scale and flour sifter are some relics of the past—a bamboo whisk, a tea equipage, and a few well-worn pairs of chopsticks that apparently have been used as cooking implements. The distracting aroma of freshly brewed coffee has penetrated even here.

Matsumoto lifts a heavy-duty mixer bowl from a shelf and arranges flour, a frothy yeast starter, water, and salt on the workbench. "Shall we get started?"

I press against the workbench and regard the ingredients with trepidation.

"Perhaps you are feeling some hesitation." Matsumoto places the dry ingredients into the mixing bowl. "We spend half our life resisting. Accept the resistance. See it as your companion in this journey. It'll lose its force, crumble, and reveal a new way for you."

Sure, sure. I lean over the workbench and upon sinking my fingers into the softness of the flour comprehend for the first time that I've come here for far more than recovering my baking skills. I sense that my real lesson, whatever it turns out to be, is just beginning.

"I ask my students to be fully attuned to the task, to become one with the activity. Get rid of the past and the future. Be right here, right now, with whatever you're doing. We're reborn every second of the day."

What a big order. At Matsumoto's instruction, I stir in the yeast mixture and a dollop of melted butter. A heady mélange of scents rises from the mixture. "Do all students eventually learn to bake?"

Matsumoto shakes his head. "Not all. It is enough that they take baking to whatever level they can. Baking can be either a utilitarian skill or an art form. Either way it should be fulfilling."

He grabs a cutting board from the counter, then gives further instructions on how to knead the dough by hand. Let your hands become one with the dough. Let them tell you when more flour is needed. You'll know when to stop adding if you've been truly paying attention, if you've been fully adjusted to your senses. Let time flow around you like a river. Float on its current. Don't be impatient.

I already know the technique of bread making, very well, as a matter of fact. My attitude must have shown on my face.

"The moment we think we've learned a craft, it's the time to start all over again. Life is nothing but a series of new beginnings."

I turn the dough out onto a nonstick kneading mat and knead until it's smooth and elastic. Matsumoto checks the result. "Not quite 'earlobe' consistency," he says, "but close."

He now asks me to prepare another batch of bread dough—a variation that incorporates brown rice flour. First, I want to tell him, I need a break. As I look up at him, he turns his head away.

A few hours later when I have finally finished all the tasks, I find that my legs are about to buckle.

"Enough for one day," Matsumoto says. "You must now go back to the hotel and rest."

Slowly I transfer the mixed dough to a bowl and cover it with a plastic wrap, all the while resenting being ordered around like I was his little child. "But we aren't done. We haven't proofed the dough."

"Tomorrow morning you'll start again at seven with bread. I'm asked all the time, 'You want me to do the same thing again?' Well, we have a saying around here, 'You never bake the same bread twice.' "

Irritated, exhausted, as I walk toward the sink to rinse my hands, it occurs to me that he is imparting some wisdom here: Each of our experiences is unique and deserves our wholehearted concentration, but not a single one is permanent. Viewed in that light, my recent baking catastrophes don't seem half as serious. They were discrete occurrences. One is allowed many such failures. I turn to Matsumoto. "It's been a most interesting day."

"Be your best presence," he says as he sees me to the door.

FORTY-ONE

M Y ROUTINE AT APSARA BAKERY, A NEAR-MONASTIC EXPERIENCE BY MY standards, continues without letup. Each day, under Matsumoto's supervision—I call him sensei, teacher—I bake for several hours, until I'm so exhausted that I stop thinking, then bake some more. I have less need for coffee breaks. If I'm interrupted, I accept that as part of the process, and continue on with my tasks. I'm able to concentrate far better than I used to. It is as though I've broken through a barrier I'd erected in my mind.

As an apprentice, I observe Matsumoto closely. His extraordinary cakes, tarts, breads, and rolls owe much to his delicate touch, but even more to his inner sense of caring and devotion to a greater purpose than just running a business. He inspires me to aim for excellence for its own sake. Slowly I begin to assimilate his innate kitchen wisdom. During these long hours of toil, the four walls of the kitchen circumscribe my world but in a curious way also expand my consciousness. Occasionally my Seattle life—Andrew, Mother, the bakery—shimmers before my eyes in a series of disjointed images. As in a dream, the images quickly evaporate, and I go back to the task at hand: kneading the dough, melting the butter, chopping the nuts, whipping the cream.

The enjoyment of baking has, once again, returned to me. As I crack the eggs, I notice that the yolks have acquired a lustrous glow. When dipping my hand into the flour, I luxuriate in its satin texture. The cinnamon sticks fairly dance out of the jar as I shake it. Their fragrance nourishes my baker's soul. The mid-morning coffee break is not for another hour, but I am oblivious as I grind the sticks to a fine powder, humming softly all the while.

Today we're preparing puff pastry dough, which will form the basis for the opulent dessert called mille-feuille, or "pastry of a thousand leaves." I dice a bar of chilled butter and add it to a measured amount of flour in a food processor. Matsumoto explains to me how the buildup of moisture in the dough will make for flaky layers in the oven. I feel an immediate sense of chagrin at the implication that I don't know this ordinary scientific fact. Almost as quickly, the irritation melts away, restoring an attitude of heedfulness to my work. There's satisfaction in the sameness of the butter pieces. In no time, I am relishing the process again. As Matsumoto assists me in performing the repeated steps of rolling, spreading, folding, and refrigerating the dough, he observes, "A fine pastry is much more than just flour, sugar, and butter. All that I am or have ever been goes into the making."

The dough goes into the oven. As I wait, I pause and reflect on whether I have poured myself into my baking the same way. Was I distracted? Did I hold something back? A short time later, the dough puffs into layer upon layer of flaky "leaves." I pop the pastry out, immersing myself in the heat and the aroma, cut it into serving portions to avoid breaking the crisp golden leaves. I fill each rectangle with chocolate sauce, a bounty of thin apple slices, and whipped cream, thinking about nothing but what I am doing. Me and my pastry. It all comes down to that. I couldn't possibly master philosophical concepts that would take a lifetime of study, but I can do this.

By the time I finish, the long exercise has left me fatigued, but steadied and cleared my mind, and filled my insides with music. To add to that, Matsumoto serves me a wedge of Autumn Symphony Tart, his signature creation, saying, "I'll leave you alone to enjoy it."

For the next fifteen minutes, I sit with the ethereal taste. By now I know that Matsumoto blends three types of chocolates—sweet, semisweet, and bitter—that he orders nuts from Australia and fresh butter from Hokkaido. More than that, what makes the cake a symphony for the palate is the awareness he has put into it. The subtle flavor of chestnut in the butter cream, however, makes me homesick. Quickly I depart from the bakery kitchen through a back door. In an adjoining room, a group of barefooted people are meditating on a tatami-mat in front of a picture, I notice with interest.

A few days later, while preparing an all-purpose génoise batter with cake flour, eggs, butter, and sugar, I wonder what secret techniques and ingredients really make his sponge cake so firm, fragrant, and fine flavored, without ever becoming boring.

As if he has read my mind, Matsumoto, rinsing a pan in the sink, observes, "A sponge cake will be bland, unless you, its creator, give it life."

Now what does he mean by that? With the batter ready, I go over to the shelf and reach for a large rectangular baking sheet.

Matsumoto hands me a deeper round cake pan. "Use this instead," he says, "so the cake won't dry out." His eyes twinkle, as he lifts a pair of bottles from the cabinet. "And a little rum and pear syrup won't hurt either."

I stir the batter, amazed that he discloses his trade secrets so freely. I have never even considered being as forthcoming about my Sunya Cake recipe. "It must have taken you some trial and error before you came up with a perfect recipe like this."

He smiles. "So why don't I keep it a secret, you are thinking? I know most bakers don't like to divulge too much of their craft. For me, it's just the other way around. I find that if I hoard my knowledge, I become fixated on it. I can't move forward to create something new."

I pour the batter into the empty pan. Each moment with Matsumoto is truly a revelation. "I'm grateful to you for letting me into the program, sensei."

"I'm so glad it worked out. To be honest with you, Sunya-san, I had some initial doubts about whether this program would work for an experienced baker like you."

"When I go back, I'll be ready to give Sunya Cake new life. I have a project all planned." I pause and work it out in my mind. I'll ask Bob to continue acting as the manager. I'll confine myself to the kitchen, baking Sunya Cake, just baking. That's where I've gone wrong. Mixing baking with administrative work, thinking I could do it all. I could not and I mislaid my focus by trying. In baking, when you mislay your focus, you drop it all. From now on, I'll also take more time off for enjoyment. "The project will be called Operation Sunya Cake."

Matsumoto smiles again. "The moment you name a project, it begins to take shape."

As I slide the cake pans into the preheated oven, a blast of heat envelops me and with that comes a flash of insight. Cakes Plus hasn't even opened yet and, therefore, the competition hasn't started. By worrying about it, I am living in the future. Besides, Cakes Plus is a competition, an obstacle in my path, only if I believe it to be so. Rather than anguish about how it may take business away from me, I'll just concentrate on running my small bakery. I may have to cut down the hours of operation and the volume of baked goods I produce daily, but as long as I can, I'll hold on to my shop. I am different from Cakes Plus, and in the difference resides my strength. Cakes Plus has actually given me an opportunity to awaken.

A lush fruity aroma seeps from the oven and gives me a sense of exuberance. "I'm beginning to see, sensei, that I can be contented and peaceful regardless of how my bakery is doing financially."

"In other words, you won't cling to your business venture quite so tightly." Matsumoto briskly dries his hands on a towel. "We sometimes use big words like 'nonattachment' and it confuses people. It's a joy to see that you've gotten the essence of that concept."

"Have I really? I mean, my list of attachments goes on and on. Family, boyfriend, pride in my baking, my Sunya Cake recipe . . ."

He smiles knowingly. "To be truthful, I'm still working on 'letting go' myself. For me the ultimate test will be when I retire from the bakery. Already I worry about how much I'll miss this work, how I will fill my hours, and, more importantly, who'll take over this bakery." Matsumoto takes a deep breath. "Oh, well, not for a few more years."

Last night I dreamt a serene pond. Its surface was celestial blue, as if the mighty sky had surrendered its life force to its consort, the earth. A lotus leaf opened, causing the tiniest ripple around it, which then spread out across the entire body of water in ever-widening circles. The leaf remained content merely to float in the center.

In Apsara Bakery's kitchen this morning, I take note of the fact that my sojourn is about to end. Tomorrow will be my last day. Late in the afternoon as I begin wrapping up, Matsumoto appears.

"We have a tradition here," he announces. "On your last day, you don't work, instead you get to make a wish and we do our best to fulfill it."

Last night returns to me, the quiet water surface, the receptive lotus leaf, the ripples in the water. There must be more to that dream.

"If there's any particular sight in the city you'd like to visit," Matsumoto is saying, "I can arrange it for you."

As one of my last cleanup duties, I wipe water stains from the faucet. So far, I haven't seen much of Kyoto except for taking strolls through its streets and gardens and shopping for souvenirs. I've bought a leather-bound address book for Andrew and identical T-shirts for Mother and Dushan. Somehow, I believe I'll return here in the future as a tourist. Then I remember observing a group of meditators in a room at the back of the bakery.

"I'd hoped to learn something about the Sunya Tradition but, so far, no one has mentioned a single word about it," I reply.

"We don't offer any spiritual instruction unless we're approached by someone. But since you've asked . . . Our teacher, Bikkhu Karun, who's a monk, can shed light on the concept of 'emptiness,' and 'infinite possibilities.' For him it is a central tenet. I have taken another aspect of his teaching—the mindfulness, the 'here and now'—and applied it to my personal situation. That's all I can handle. He's very approachable. The word *bikkhu* means 'someone who shares' and he certainly does. Should you want to meet with him, I can arrange that for you."

Joyful anticipation wells up within me. "I'd like that very much, sensei."

FORTY-TWO

I DISMISS THE TAXI IN FRONT OF A MODERN APARTMENT COMPLEX WITH a bank of red-berried nanten bushes flanking its front entrance. There's a moment of trepidation, as I've never met a monk of such high rank. And even though Matsumoto's teachings have helped me, I have in no way bought into a spiritual practice. Standing at the entrance, I smooth my blue linen skirt and push back my hair to ensure that I appear restrained and respectable, like a Japanese career woman. Taking a deep breath of the morning air, I ring the apartment doorbell on the gray wall.

The door swings open, revealing a middle-aged woman with a wrinkled face, her hair bound in a tight ponytail. I introduce myself and greet her formally. *"Ogenki desu ka?"* How are you? Polite Japanese phrases, such as this, are finding a place in my interior. Their hidden deeper meanings both fascinate and elude me.

She bows. *"Okagesama."* I am well, touched by the divine grace.

"Bikkhu Karun is expecting me."

She bows again and ushers me into a corridor carpeted with a rice-paddy motif. We pass by an alcove, which houses an abstract, almost melancholy, parchment-colored ink painting of an injured bird in a pine forest under a darkening sky. I slip off my shoes at the entrance to a small sitting room with exposed wooden beams. It is empty except for several chairs arranged around a low coffee table. The pure cream walls on two sides amplify the natural golden stream of light flooding through the window. The other two walls are *fusuma*, papered screens framed by wood, causing me to wonder how large the room actually is. A brass Buddha gleams on a bracket shelf. Burning sticks of incense set before the carving gives off a thin ribbon of plum-scented smoke. The stark beauty of the uncluttered space is restful to my eyes.

Shortly, a frail shaven-headed man cloaked in a black robe enters the room with halting steps. His serene mahogany-complexioned face is darker than that of most Japanese, with prominent features hinting at South Asian ancestry. I guess him to be in his late fifties. There's a kind of elusive familiarity about him. The moment he sees me he smiles, bows, and clasps his hands together. Leaning forward, I return his gesture.

"It's a pleasure to meet you, Sunya." The voice is deep, the accent slightly British; the words are at once genuine and reassuring. With an outstretched hand, he gestures me to sit, then lowers himself to his own seat with some difficulty. It is clear that he is not in good health.

Somewhat more at ease, I settle into my chair. The monk is every bit as approachable as Matsumoto had suggested. There is such an air of benignity about him that my chest relaxes enough for me to say, "I'm honored to meet you."

The attendant emerges, places a ceramic pot and a pair of cups on the table between us, and pours the tea. He speaks with her in rapid-fire Japanese that I can't follow. She nods respectfully at him, glances at me, then backs out of the room. He waves toward the tea set.

I lift a cup to my lips with both hands. *"Itadakimasu."* The Japanese version of grace. I will receive; I depend on the mercy of the divine. Then with respect and harmony, I take a sip. The brew is light, piping hot, faintly bitter. I raise my eyes to Bikkhu Karun. He hasn't touched his cup.

"I've known Matsumoto for years. We see each other almost every day. He's a remarkable person, so when he mentioned your name . . ."

I begin to fill him in on the details of how I happened to come here. He listens in such an attentive manner that I forget that it is I who want to learn. When I have finished, I pick up my cup and take another sip.

"You want to know the meaning of your name. Am I correct, Sunya?"

I give a nod.

"The word has special significance for me as well. Even before I became a monk, I'd woken up one early morning from my sleep with the word echoing in my ears. Since I was born and raised in India, I knew what it meant. At the time *sunya* was precisely what I'd been feeling inside—a deep void, altogether bereft of meaning—and I'd been questioning my whole existence." He pauses to catch his breath, as though it pains him to speak more than briefly.

"Then, as a young monk, I traveled to this country and took up residence in a temple near Mount Fuji. But I still couldn't find complete peace, or answers to my questions. I had too much noise in my head, you might say. One day, when I was praying in Yakushi-ji in Nara, where I'd gone for a visit, a revelation came to me. I finally understood that I had to let go of the mundane concerns of daily life, attachments I'd formed, self-centered concerns I'd held on to, barriers that I'd erected between myself and others. They'd walled me in, deadened my senses. I came to realize they were just illusions and, from that time on, I stopped seeking and, instead, meditated on the black void. It lost its power, disappeared, and amazingly restored me to bright wholeness, a sort of selflessness. The *sunya* that filled me also liberated and unified me. You see, within the emptiness was love. Love that reached out. I felt connected to others. I wanted to help them in the most compassionate way possible. I knew then I was meant to emphasize this one principle of Buddhism. I still meditate daily on the inner void and, through it, the love within. That's where I ultimately found my truth."

I set the cup down unsteadily, so numb that I can only whisper, "Are you . . . ?"

"Yes, Sunya, I'm your father. In another life, I was known as Prabhu Malhotra, Bikkhu Karun is my adopted Buddhist name."

I turn in my chair and confront a blank wall. My father resurfacing into my life after all these years? Why, I've long since written off ever meeting him face to face. This is absurd. Is he serious, or is this some sort of a cosmic joke? Am I being tested somehow? My thoughts and reactions shift and rearrange themselves as I struggle to formulate a coherent reply.

"My daughter," he says, "you're wondering if I am speaking the truth?" He reels off Mother's maiden name, her age, her parents' names, and our address in Ravenna District in Seattle.

Much to my astonishment, his answers are accurate. I probe my memory further. The photograph that my angry, tearful mother had shown me leaps onto my mind's screen. Yes, it is the same face, only rounder and more lined; the eyes are gentler. The moment dissolves in a maelstrom of distress and confusion, unnerving me. My hands pressed against my knees are devoid of sensation.

"Sunya, my daughter . . ." He wears a sympathetic, if vaguely detached, expression, which stokes in me a jolting surge of rage. He has a lot of nerve repeatedly calling me his daughter, this "holy" man who didn't think twice about bringing me into the world only to desert me when I was an infant. I've never known what it's like to be in the presence of a father, to experience the effect of that simple event on my sense of self. I am having considerable difficulty with the whole idea of "instant" daughterhood.

"It's been a very long time," I murmur as I stand up. "I was a baby when you left." Glancing down at the scar along my right shinbone, I continue. "Where was my 'father' when I fell down the steps on an icy Seattle morning? When the boys picked on me? When I graduated from high school and college? When Mother had her appendix removed and I had to take care of her alone?"

"You have every right to be angry and disappointed, Sunya. But please try to understand that every action has its consequences and I too have suffered to this day, as a result of my decision. I kept moving from place to place in search of peace. I lost my appetite. It wasn't easy for me to leave, but . . . it was necessary . . . And now that I'm nearing the end of this life . . ." His voice cracks and trails off.

I lower myself to the chair again. Mother's rough overworked hands and the wistful eagerness of her eyes checking the mailbox daily in vain materialize in my mind's eye, as though to suppress any nascent feelings of sympathy for him. "What do you want from me?"

His lips are starting to form a reply when the attendant shuffles in, bearing a platter of fruit and sweets in one hand, which she sets on the table. Perhaps she's noticed the agitated expression on my face, for she shoots a stern look at me. This man is our venerable *roshi*, she seems to admonish me as she walks away.

I stare out through the window at the wooden eaves of a pagoda visible above a line of trees. A sneer inside me prompts: all those years of absence and neglect. Wipe them away just like that. Sure.

He draws his robe closer around his gaunt body. "Do you want to know why I left?"

I shrug.

"Ever since I can remember," he begins anyway, "I've wanted to know why I was put on this planet, what was the purpose of my being. This question plagued me even before your birth . . .

"Then you were born. I saw you in that hospital cradle, asleep, so small yet so perfect. I asked the nurse if I could hold you and she let me. That was the most important moment of my life. I'd never felt happier. I slipped my finger into your hand and you opened your eyes and looked up at me. All my loving instincts came pouring out. It was like I had been reborn—there was so much light in the room. Paradoxically that's exactly when I decided to leave. The conflict between my search for enlightenment and the way of the householder was illuminated for me. The time to respond came when I was most attached, when I had the most to lose, when I loved the deepest. With a feeling of profound sadness that I carry even today, I gave you back to the nurse and walked away."

The confession contorts his serene composure. For just a moment, his eyes belie a struggle. Then his expression becomes placid once more. I struggle with a jumble of questions in my head. This unexpected meeting has shaken up my universe even more.

"How did I end up in Japan, you probably are asking yourself?" He seeks my eyes for affirmation, then smiles. It must have hurt him—the smile fades as quickly as it came. Then, as he recounts his journey from the States to Tibet and eventually on to Thailand, I see a young man of robust health and searching heart, his meager worldly possessions in the rucksack on his back, knocking on the doors of Buddhist monasteries. In return for his studies, he cleans the courtyard and does odd jobs in the kitchen. Every morning he goes begging for his food. Whatever devotees donate makes his single meal of the day. That was the life he left Mother and me for? The stuttering roar of a motorcycle outside provides a welcome distraction.

My gaze eventually turns back to Bikkhu Karun, who's waiting for

me to regain my balance. In the quietness that once again ensues, I
decide that I'll try to maintain an open mind and hear him out. Then
I'll decide whether to accept or reject what he's saying.

"But does one necessarily have to make such long treks in time
and space to find one's truth?" I ask.

"Not at all. I'm speaking only about my personal experience. Truth
is like the sky above. Wherever you are, it extends over you and you
can claim a part of it. Your truth is yours alone. When you finally
understand it, it resonates inside you. You understand it better than
anything you've ever been aware of."

"I doubt if this explanation would have satisfied Mother. She had
to struggle to put food on the table, balance the checkbook, take care
of an infant, and cope with the question, Why did her husband leave
her? Finding her personal truth would have been a frivolous luxury.
And I suspect she would have wondered why, if the truth is wherever
you are, you couldn't have found it in Seattle?"

"You're my daughter. You question everything, do you not? Well,
here's how I'd like to answer your question. We're born for our
family's sake and most of us are quite content to live that way. But
there are a few like me who respond to a different calling. We abandon those we love and reach out to a larger family. We don't fulfill
our destiny until we've made the biggest sacrifice we can make. Once
I came to understand my true nature and purpose, I saw that I belonged to this country, where Buddhism has had a strong influence.
Many of the ancient teachings have been incorporated into the basic
beliefs of the Japanese society. Here I could live and teach in harmony. I don't mean any of this in a grandiose sense. All I've done
in my life is to guide a few people. We've sat in the empty space
together. I feel far more humble now than when I first started. But
there has been a great price to pay . . . In following my path I've
brought grief to those who meant the most to me . . . Could you find

it in your heart to ask Dee to forgive me or, at least, to understand why I left?"

"No," I answer firmly, even though his obvious remorse echoes in my ears. "I'm not going to tell Mother anything about our meeting. I'd rather that she doesn't even suspect that you're alive. She is about to remarry and start a new life. I don't want to spoil her happiness."

"I see . . . Yes, perhaps it is for the best."

I rearrange myself in the chair. I am not buying his explanations, though I grudgingly accept the fact that he's an unusual person. "But I'd like to come back and visit you again . . ."

"Nothing would make me happier, Sunya, but . . ."

"I guess that means 'no' . . . ?"

"I fear it is too late for that. You see, my health is failing." He shifts his gaze to the floor and a brief sigh escapes him. "I make very few appearances in public anymore . . ."

I straighten up. There he goes, rejecting me again, but I won't allow it this time. "I'm not exactly the public. You can't dismiss me that easily. Perhaps I can see about arranging better medical care for you."

"I've done what I was destined to do in this life. I already have a fine doctor taking care of me, Sunya. There's not much more he can do . . ."

"You're still young, and we have so much to talk about. To be honest, all this is happening too fast for me. I need time to absorb—"

"By all means, come back again and study the Sunya Tradition further. Or, maybe what you've gained during this visit—"

"It's not sufficient . . ."

"That's all I can give you, Sunya. You'll discover more on your own along the way."

He makes a feeble attempt to rise. Simultaneously, from outside the door, there comes a movement. The attendant hustles in—she must have been waiting—and offers him a hand.

I spring up. "We've barely gotten started . . ."

"I wish this meeting had come sooner, Sunya, but—"

"Maybe we could meet again . . ."

He grabs the attendant's wrist as he stands unsteadily, takes a long look at me, his beatific gaze offering a blessing, and shuffles toward an inner chamber, as though he hadn't heard a word I said.

And then the room is empty. The silence only amplifies my desolation. I am standing alone, numbed, with an aching hollowness echoing inside me.

The attendant returns and inquires in a stiff manner whether there is anything further she can do for me.

"I'm leaving for the States tomorrow afternoon, but I'll have time in the morning. I'd like to come back and say good-bye if I may. Would you ask him? *Onegai shimasu.*" Please.

Sadness etched around her eyes, she stares through me and beyond, as though my further presence is an intrusion.

"*Sumi-masen,*" I murmur. Sorry. "Please call a taxi for me."

In my tiny room, the bed is tidied up, a fresh robe hangs on the bathroom door, and the house slippers are set just so by the door. In this world of order and perfection, I find it difficult to give vent to my surging emotions. As I hang my street clothes in the closet, I imagine Mother's face. There will be times during our talks when I'll turn my gaze away. She'll not have the slightest inkling that I'm thinking about my father, a man who isn't nearly as despicable as she imagines. This secret, locked securely in my core, will both burden and sustain me. Would I risk Mother's love if she found out all that had transpired today?

I feel a sudden urge to take a stroll through the garden. Soon the lush passivity of the green surroundings evens out my emotions. The constantly changing vista as I walk makes me aware of the transitory nature of life. For familiarity, there's the solemn hollow resonance of the temple bell, and that mushroom pizza smell.

Much later, as evening shadows enshroud the surroundings, I return to my room in a better frame of mind and start packing. My suitcase is not the only thing fuller than when I arrived.

I awaken to a brilliant morning. As I climb out of bed, Bikkhu Karun's face shimmers before me, a face etched with soft lines of wisdom. I realize as I watch a bird fluttering about in the bluish-white vastness of the sky that I have a similar struggle inside me.

Today is my final day in Kyoto. I slip into a black wrinkle-resistant shirtdress perfect for travel, then decide to make one last trip to Apsara Bakery to seek Matsumoto's advice concerning Bikkhu Karun.

At the bakery entrance, luggage in hand, I pause and take note. Something has changed. Gone is the usual bustle, inviting smell of fresh-pressed coffee, welcoming greetings of *irasshaimase* and parting thanks of *domo*. Instead, there is an undercurrent of confusion. Customers are standing around in clusters instead of lining up and conversing in subdued tones. The solicitous baristas have abandoned their posts behind the counter and are wandering about. What's going on? A server signals to catch my attention, utters a "*Konnichiwa*," and guides me to the kitchen, with the assurance that Matsumoto will join me shortly. There is no sign of anyone having baked here this morning. Without the noise of the food processor and sounds of nuts and spices being ground, the kitchen is uncomfortably quiet.

Matsumoto walks in as briskly as usual. His eyes are red and his face is drawn, as he drags up a chair opposite me. He takes a few seconds to compose himself.

"Sensei . . . ," I address him.

"It is most difficult for me to break this news to you, Sunya-san." We sit facing each other, our eyes to the floor. It is as though we've already communicated on a deeper level. Words are a mere formality. Eyes conveying a message of sorrow and sympathy, Matsumoto adds, "Bikkhu Karun left his earthly body last night."

Outwardly calm, I take in the news. Then as the initial shock subsides to be replaced by sad acceptance of that which cannot be changed, an image of the monk's patient face reappears and the blessing of his presence envelops me. Only yesterday, he seemed so happy to meet me, happiness that became a gift. Why did I have to be so obstinate? Fighting back pangs of remorse and futility, I find myself wishing we had reconciled.

"He has been ill for about a year."

Head low, as I sit there aching, my eyes turn damp—no way to hide it. Matsumoto leans forward protectively and offers me a handkerchief. I press its cottony softness over my eyelids.

"It may seem ironic, coming from a man whose life was dedicated to the renunciation of desire," Matsumoto continues after a short silence, "but Bikkhu Karun suffered much because he still loved his wife. He never totally came to terms with that. He tried to put her away from his mind, but every so often memories would flare up. He believed that kept him away from attaining true enlightenment. He told me that a man who hadn't gotten rid of his desires didn't deserve to be a priest. In his own opinion he was, at best, a flawed Buddhist."

Should I stir up Mother's sentiment by telling her about her husband's unexpressed devotion? She who has felt so unpretty and unloved after he left and for years afterward? Or should I let the incident slip and not ruin her current genial frame of mind?

"More than anything else, Bikkhu Karun wanted to see you before he died. Once he told me that he'd hoped to leave this life, seeing your lovely face once again, talking with you, knowing you've forgiven him. He believed the moment your love and forgiveness touched his life he'd feel incredibly light and he'd be set free."

"I wasn't prepared . . . I regret that I wasn't able to . . ."

Matsumoto nods in warm understanding. "Perhaps that is his parting gift to you. After the pain and grief has diminished you'll be able to perceive that if you truly want to be *sunya,* there mustn't be any place in your heart for anger and grudges."

"I just so wish I knew him better . . ."

"In death, Bikkhu Karun will receive buddhahood. We call a dead person *hotoke-san,* or respected Buddha. He was an extraordinary monk who taught selflessly for twenty-five years. He never refused help to anybody. He donated all his money to the needy. But he was particularly good with children, especially troubled youngsters. They seemed to sense that he was truly a holy man. They listened to him."

"He brought me here, didn't he?" I venture.

"You could say he had a hand in it." A hint of a grin crosses Matsumoto's face. "Bikkhu Karun told me the whole story. He had a most devout follower, an American, who assisted him in this matter. His name is Jordan Jorgen."

I gasp in disbelief. "Jordan Jorgen, the loiterer?"

"Loitering wasn't his motive. He just didn't know how to approach you. He's been in Tokyo for the last three weeks to take care of some urgent business for Bikkhu Karun; otherwise, he'd have been here to meet you."

"Surely that would've been interesting. If he didn't have ulterior motives, kindly tell me why he hung around my bakery and house? If he was my father's emissary, why didn't he just introduce himself?"

"Let me tell you the whole story."

By the time Matsumoto has finished, I gather that Bikkhu Karun had once mentioned to Jordan that he left his wife and a newborn child in Seattle decades ago and had never completely come to terms with the guilt he carried within him. He meant that as a lesson on giving up worldly things and the suffering it can entail. Jordan, however, took it in another way. He loved and respected his teacher so much that he wanted to make him happy. Coincidentally he had been born and raised in Seattle and his parents still lived in the area. He asked, "Do you want me to look your family up the next time I visit there?" Bikkhu Karun replied, "No, no. My wife would probably throw you out and my daughter doesn't know me at all . . . But I'd like very much to see her before I die. Otherwise, how will she ever know how dear she was to me?" Bikkhu Karun forgot all about the conversation. And Jordan didn't let his master in on his plans, fearing he'd be stopped. Six months later, Jordan dropped by Bikkhu Karun's quarters. He'd just returned from Seattle and wanted to tell him about his trip. "By the way, I found out that Sunya Malhotra is a well-known baker in Seattle," he said. He had more things to relate: How he'd dropped off a business card from Apsara Bakery on the front porch of her house. How protective he felt toward her after reading in the newspaper about the Bakery War. How he hung around to make sure no one harmed her.

Bikkhu Karun was so overwhelmed that he just sat there, then asked if those were the right things to do. "Didn't you teach us that our intentions count as much as our actions?" Jordan replied. "My intentions are beyond reproach."

"Actually," Matsumoto now adds, "this whole episode shouldn't be that much of a surprise. Once Jordan sets his mind to do something, he follows through. He just uses, how do you say it, 'unconventional methods.' "

"How strange," I muse out loud. "All along I had the feeling I was being led here."

"We have a saying—*ushi ni hikarate Zenkō-ji mairi*. 'Come to the temple to pray, even if a mad ox has led you there.' What it really means is that a chance encounter, apparently threatening, can bring beneficial results. However, on your father's behalf, I must apologize for any distress Jordan's loitering may have caused you."

"No need to apologize. I wouldn't have missed this experience. But I didn't make the connection to your bakery with his card alone. It was Bob Nomura, currently my head baker, who convinced me to come here."

Matsumoto smiles. "Bob Nomura was one of those wayward kids Bikkhu Karun turned around, and he did so without any expectation. See how it benefited him. Bob brought him his fondest wish—a visit from his daughter."

"I'm amazed. These events seem to run in circles."

"I must make a confession here. I, of course, knew who you were when you came. Many times, I thought about taking you to Bikkhu Karun, but that would have violated the teachings. It was a bit of a struggle for me to keep quiet."

Still trying to digest all that has happened, I barely notice it when Matsumoto reaches over to the counter, picks up a cardboard box, and offers it to me. I accept it with both hands and open it. A rosewood-framed portrait rests inside. It's a recent headshot of Bikkhu Karun. Clad in a black robe, his gaze benevolent, he generates hope and confidence, even in a black-and-white photo.

"He wanted you to have that picture, Sunya-san."

I turn to Matsumoto with subdued words of thanks, and a guilt-laden heart.

He continues to chat amiably for a little while longer until it's time for me to head out to the airport. A staff member bustles in to inform us that a taxi has arrived.

The time has come to say good-bye to Matsumoto. It is difficult to express my tangled sentiments in words. In a short time, I've become close to this fatherly man, philosopher, and mentor. Though I have only skimmed the surface of a vast body of learning, my life has undergone a major transformation. My gaze sweeps the room. It is as though I have earned the right to be in a bakery kitchen again.

"I'm happy that I met you, sensei."

Matsumoto closes his eyes for an instant; his eyelids are full. "You've been like a daughter to me. I didn't realize how much grief I was still holding inside. Your presence has soothed the bruises on my soul. I've learned from you just as much."

That note of humbleness only serves to magnify my gratitude. I thank him warmly and promise to return. In my head, I'm already planning a longer trip.

Matsumoto walks me to the door. We stand quietly for an instant. One last fond look at Apsara Bakery and I turn.

"Shine radiantly like the sun," Matsumoto says with folded palms, "and softly like the moon."

I walk out into the glowing sunlight, the roar of traffic slicing through me. A taxi is waiting. As I approach, the white-capped driver gives me a welcoming wave through the window. The moment I climb into the back seat, he revs up the engine.

A couple of tormenting hours later, my plane takes off, soaring up through wisps of white cloud. As I pull down the window shade to cut the glare, I suddenly feel lost and weepy, as though I've been abandoned once again. A deep emptiness, *sunya*, claims my emotional center. It spreads itself silently, a dense massive darkness that I neither fight nor deny. The theory behind it all escapes me. I can only sit with this emptiness, feel its silent weight. And as I do so, it shatters. The fragments fall away to reveal a point of bright light within that swiftly expands to overflow inside me, to release the pent-up love within.

In that instant, I realize that this is what Father intended all along. He wanted me to put aside the emphasis on the daily realities, and practice compassion, understanding, and love. He wished for me to live up to my name.

I extract his photo from my duffel bag and view it. It is as though he's sitting with me, touching me with his grace and kindness, and reassuring me that there's nothing more to forgive. Slowly my feelings of guilt seep away. All that has troubled me, all that I have considered important, now seems so trivial. The clear space around me is bubbling with light and joy. There's a source of strength inside me, a hidden wellspring that has been there all along, I just needed to be shown the way to find it. Father was there for me when I needed him the most. When I return home I will hang this picture in my bedroom, next to the one of Mother. I'll take comfort from finally being able to look at both my parents proudly. Just as quickly, I discard the idea, realizing that Mother will be certain to come across it there.

For nine long hours, I sit awake, ignoring the in-flight feature film and lamenting that I am going farther and farther away from Apsara Bakery. And the place where Father spoke his last words to me and where his spirit abides. The pilot announces the final approach to the Sea-Tac Airport. Through the plane window, I look down on the Emerald City, its familiarity like a banner of welcome unfurled for me. I feel a smile coming to my lips.

Soon my plane will touch down. Soon I'll alight and make a new start.

FORTY-THREE

OF COURSE, I WON'T TELL MOTHER THAT I'VE VISITED FATHER. NOW that I've stepped into the arrival gate of the airport, the only thought in my mind is to embrace her. Face framed by the straight lines of her gray-streaked hair, body shrouded in an ankle-length raincoat, she smells faintly of sandalwood, her favorite fragrance. As we hike toward baggage retrieval, she fills me in on the high point in her life. She and Dushan are on the verge of signing the papers to purchase a one-bedroom condominium in Seattle's Fremont District, which will be their second home.

I'm glad she's doing all the talking.

"It happened all of a sudden," she adds. "We were driving by, I saw the For Sale sign and just wanted to have a look. the next thing I know we're talking with the real estate agent. Dushan says he wants to make me the happiest bride on earth. That's his way. He does something wonderful when it's least expected of him. He's paying for the condo, even though it puts him quite a bit in debt. As you know, I don't have any money. He'll cut down his commute time and we'll be closer to you during the week. On weekends we'll drive back to Mount Vernon for some peace and quiet." As she talks about ceiling fans, a breakfast nook, and overhead skylights, features she'd always wanted in a house and will now finally have, her eyes become tender and luminous.

I think kindly about Dushan. It's obvious he loves her. His commitment to her runs deep.

"You're very quiet, Sunya, but you look well. *Bolo, bolo*." Tell me, tell me. "What happened in Japan?"

I'm about to speak when a woman with a pet pig—a cute, clean, tiny, and unexpected passenger—bounces past us. I wonder with amusement if the pair will board a flight. Years ago, Mother would have shaken her head in disgust at the woman and her pig, now she just smiles and watches.

I feed her a brief summary of my trip—Matsumoto's lessons, nature walks, Japanese phrases I've picked up. "It was like a year's worth of experience compressed into fifteen days." I look away as Father's blessings, his compassionate presence, steal into my mind and I can't continue.

Mother's laugh pierces my trance. "That's why I don't travel. I can't live so much at one time." As we pass by a concession stand with a showcase bursting with candies in various colors, she asks, "Would it be okay for you to stay with me in Mount Vernon tonight? Dushan is cooking dinner for us. Tomorrow morning we can drive you back to Seattle."

"Dushan cooking?"

"He can make three dishes—spaghetti, spaetzle, and boiled dinner. His signature dish is boiled dinner and he's making it in your honor."

Boiled dinner! I feel my gorge rising at the prospect. With an effort, I will it away. Oh, well, I will approach Dushan's cooking with an open heart. I will not deny him a chance to exhibit his culinary prowess for Mother's sake and, yes, for his.

We reach the luggage carousel. As I listen for the telltale drone of the conveyor belt starting up, Mother says, "Roger's cast comes off in a couple of weeks. He's thinking about moving to D.C. He's been offered a staff position with some liberal politician. Just like that, he's going to throw away all those years of fashion school. Why, after the next election, he may not even have a job." She clucks. "Do you think you could talk to him? He's been asking about you."

I let my eyes roam around the vast hall, with its changing configuration of passengers and luggage. "We'll see, Mother. He's had a comfortable life. He needs to test himself, and this cause gives him an opportunity that a regular job never could. And, with two relationships not working out, he probably needs a change of scenery as well."

I imagine the man, now in his early thirties, who's suffered some painful setbacks and added a few pounds to his frame. Paradoxically, failure has compensated him with a more solid appearance. His fashionable clothes no longer fit him and the old sleek veneer is gone but, at last, he's willing to sit down with me and rehash the time we spent together. Maybe, just maybe, we might become friends now.

"Pierre called last week."

It takes a moment to digest the news. "Pierre?"

"Apparently he's been trying to get hold of you. He left a message on your home phone. When you didn't return his call in a couple of days, he rang me to find out where you were. No, he didn't tell me what he wanted. He sounded a little hyper. His French accent is charming when he's upset."

Poor fellow. The job with Cakes Plus must not have worked out. Perhaps he wants reconciliation, maybe even his old job at my bakery. A delicious irony strikes me: If things go as planned and Bob takes over the management of my shop on a permanent basis, will Pierre be able to deal with it? Will he find the extra heat in the kitchen tolerable? Can French and Japanese influences coexist in my bakery?

FORTY-FOUR

IN THE MORNING, WITH MOTHER OUT SHOPPING, I AM SITTING IN HER LIVING room and browsing the *News* when I hear Dushan's urgent voice calling from across the coffee table, "Good morning, Sunya." I put the newspaper down and face him. We talk about the weather, housing prices, the difficulty of hiring tellers at the bank, and I know we're warming up to something.

"I'd like to bring up a matter that's been on my mind a long time," he says, "if I may."

"Of course." Even without focusing on him, I detect a hint of embarrassment in his expression, as though he has given the issue, whatever it might be, considerable thought and now finds himself backsliding at the actual instant of truth.

He clears his throat twice, the second one patently forced. "We have had our share of disagreements in the past, but . . . it's important that you understand me better."

In other words, he's asking for acceptance. I preserve a neutral attentive expression, and listen, really listen.

"I know I'm not terribly diplomatic . . . It's hard to break old habits that I acquired growing up in a country where you couldn't trust anybody. Not a soul. You had to be mean and nasty-mouthed, or else people walked all over you and beat you up. This was not my basic nature, not at all, but after being pushed around enough I learned . . ."

Daylight accentuates Dushan's puffy eyes with a shade of pink around the iris. I can sense the turmoil bubbling within him. I can sense how in his childhood he'd gone through the same emotions.

"I have, no doubt, hurt your feelings many times, Sunya. You see, I grew up hearing yelling and squabbles all the time. My parents never spoke to me gently. They screamed or sneered and they called me names—ugly, stupid, boorish, glutton—a long list. My brother did the same. I never heard one loving word from any of them. I could never do anything right. I always had to protect myself."

In his vulnerability, in the sweaty sheen that veils his face, he looks more human than ever before. "I'm as much at a fault, Dushan—"

"But when I came to this country in my forties and met your mother, it was like I'd landed on a beautiful shore. Never have I met anyone so sweet and gentle. Never has anyone given me so much peace. And people here are different. I don't have to act the way I did back there to succeed. Now I consider life worth living, every second of it. Crude and ugly that I am, she accepts me. No matter what, she loves me. And you're her daughter, Sunya. Believe me, I'd like nothing better than to be friends with you. I'm on your side. In my own clumsy way what I'm trying to tell you is—" He starts coughing so hard that his forehead first turns pink, then a darkish red. He stands up and rushes to the kitchen.

A morsel of truth has a way of hushing even the crudest noise, like that long truck whizzing past the window. I let my eyes rest on the December green of Mother's lawn. Plenty of rain has fallen recently. I can't guarantee that Dushan and I will never again argue.

We're vastly different people, I'm far more assertive than my mother, and I doubt Dushan will ever entirely smooth out his jagged edges. As I watch him walk back into the room, I can't help but notice the warmth and helpfulness on his face, what Mother must have seen in him. His goodness, which lies way deep inside him, just needs the right circumstances to sprout. As he reclaims his seat, his head drooping a little, I observe what it must have cost him to reveal this much. He's done so because he cares.

"Well, I haven't exactly made it easy for you either, Dushan."

Barely have I spoken some extra words of apology than an expression of release spreads across Dushan's face. He lifts his head. "Ah, that's wonderful. I hoped it'd turn out this way . . . I'd have felt very foolish if you still . . . if you still despised me when I have taken the liberty of establishing a line of credit for you at the bank."

"You what?"

"Yes." He grins. "I've seen how hard you're trying . . . I wouldn't have been able to stand that kind of pressure myself . . . It's the least I can do . . . And I'll make sure Jim Paradise knows. It'll make him feel more secure about your rent, I trust . . ."

"But, Dushan . . ." My armpits feel sweaty in the pullover. Oh, no, not one more time, him butting into my affairs. My finances are my business. Leave it alone, will you? Then I catch that fervent look on his face. He's doing this for both Mother and me, and for his own reasons. This can bring us closer together, or spoil it for us. I take several moments.

"Why . . . why . . . I don't know what to say. Oh, thank you, Dushan, this—"

Footsteps on the carpet. I turn to see Mother approaching with a brilliant toothy smile. "I was checking out the smoked salmon at the market. *Bhalo kichu na.*" Nothing special. "I'll probably end up shopping at Pike Place. Got to have the best for our housewarming."

Dushan beams at her. "Yes, dear, the very best."

A light of happiness glows in Mother's eyes. Her embroidered mango-colored blouse peeks out from under her dark coat. It strikes me that the once-stranded woman has finally reached her distant shore too. What an odd pair. As I reflect on their future together, I feel nothing but happiness for them.

Dushan excuses himself and goes toward the kitchen. Mother drops down into the couch next to me and picks up an ivory greeting card from the coffee table. "It's from Willy Cartdale. He was gracious enough to send me a thank-you note after his dinner here."

I peek at the card: a standard Hallmark thank-you note. Illegible handwriting. "You know, I'm not as upset now as I was when you first told me about the dinner."

"But you're not sure just how long we'll be able to keep Willy at bay? Well, my dear, Willy keeps Dushan posted on all his activities. And whatever Dushan knows, I know too. Between the two of us, we have him covered. Willy will not pull any big surprises on you without my knowledge, that you can be sure of."

"You always look out for me, Mother."

She turns toward me, that patient face with its characteristic shine of protectiveness, eyes so steady in their devotion. Her deep beauty, through all the furrows and imperfections, through all that she has suffered, illuminates the room. Ignoring my command to remain un-sentimental, my eyes turn moist. I blink.

In the last few months, when the world has dimmed its lights for me, Mother has been there, a petite but awesome force, never wavering in her determination to assist me. "I'm so very fortunate . . ."

She waves a hand in dismissal. "Are you ready to go home, Sunya?"

I fetch my luggage from the bedroom. Dushan has just joined Mother. They're standing close, chatting and smiling, two loving people secure in the knowledge that they can count on each other. In that, they are indomitable; they're an inspiration to me. I really mean it when I smile at both of them. Then suddenly, memory of Father bounces to me, and the joy of the moment floats away.

After arriving at my house, Mother and I proceed to the bedroom. Over my protests, she insists on helping me unpack and plops herself on a corner of the bed to do so. I continue filling her in about my Japan trip as I empty my suitcase, setting aside for the time being the duffel bag that contains Father's photograph. She delights in every detail, peppering me with numerous questions. "They still have cobblestone streets? Do they really smoke that much? Sushi isn't as big a deal over there?" I sense that she suspects I haven't told her about all that has happened.

Mostly, though, she's fascinated with Matsumoto and wants to hear more about him. As I bustle to the bathroom to put my travel toilet kit away, I mention how Matsumoto helped me rediscover a quiet spot inside myself and how he taught me to be present in the instant.

"He seems so mature, yet so enthusiastic," Mother is saying. Peeking through the door into the bedroom, I observe that she has just opened my duffel bag. "Was he always that way?" she asks.

"No." I reenter the bedroom. "You won't believe this, but he told me about his time in Manhattan as a wild youth . . ."

I stop speaking the moment I notice that the contents of the duffel bag are neatly arranged on my bed. Mother has uncovered the rosewood-framed photo, carefully wrapped in tissue paper and my bulky sweatshirt, and is examining it, a frown furrowing her well-shaped eyebrows. "Who is this?" she asks.

Oh, no! I take a moment to breathe deeply, work to control my voice. "A very wise man, a Buddhist monk, who taught the Sunya philosophy."

"What's his name?" The voice is panicky.

My knees soften. Standing there, I make an attempt to return to a deeper, unperturbed, lighted center. "He's called Bikkhu Karun."

"Somehow, I get the feeling I've seen him before. Is that his real name, or just a title?" As Mother regards the photo, the frown is transformed into a scowl. The skin of her powdered cheeks doesn't appear as unwrinkled now.

Unable to maintain the façade any longer, I whisper, "Yes, Mother, it's him."

A suffocating silence enshrouds us. She stands up and slaps the photo facedown on the bed. "So, this is what has become of my brilliant husband . . . How did you get his picture?" I swallow and search in vain for an answer, worrying at the same time about her blood pressure rising. She picks up the photo again, turns it over, and studies it with eyes of both curiosity and disbelief. "You weren't going to tell me about it? Sunya . . ."

"Let's sit down, Mother."

We perch on the edge of the bed. Despite the softness of the quilted comforter, Mother sits achingly, her eyes narrowing at the corners in accusation. "This man was the center of my universe. I haven't seen or heard from him in thirty years, and you weren't going to tell me . . ."

"I think there are some things you need to know, Mother." I take her silence for acquiescence and relate the circumstances of my meeting with Father and his subsequent death. As I speak, I pause many times to regain my voice. When I finish, we sit without a sound a while. "And so you see," I point out in conclusion, "even though we didn't have any contact with him, he didn't forget us. He never stopped loving us, and though he had his reasons for leaving, it had nothing to do with you."

"So you say."

"Look how strong you've become. How well you took care of me . . ."

As I recall those years, Mother's expression changes from anger and disbelief to sorrow. I wish we could hug each other this very moment in honor of Father's memory. Throw a beam of light on the ancient miseries. But she, still distraught, stares vacantly out the window, then abruptly lurches to her feet. "Got to meet the real estate agent at ten. We'll talk another time."

"Let's have dinner together . . ."

She gathers up her purse and jacket and races for the door, barely turning to wave good-bye to me.

Overcome with remorse and a sense of futility, I pick up Father's photo and gaze lovingly at it. As I do so, a calm peacefulness settles over me. Father left his love for me. Self-sufficient that I am, that is all I ever needed.

FORTY-FIVE

ON THE MORNING OF MY FIRST DAY BACK AT THE BAKERY, MY STAFF greets me with a large white cake bordered with rosettes and garnished with thin rounds of lemongrass. A surprise. I call Andrew right away to see if he can join us, but he's not there. Standing around the kitchen table, we celebrate with slices of cake, glasses of eggnog, and anecdotes about Japan, my eyes falling on the door often. It astonishes me even more, given our history of intermittent antagonism, when Jill gives me several friendly glances, then sidles up, and whispers, "Glad you're back, Sunya. This place isn't the same without you."

I give her an affectionate smile, which springs spontaneously from an inner sense of forgiveness. I am about to reply when Scott pulls out pictures of his new baby, obviously eager to share them. "Dylan's so intelligent already," he says. "He looks a little like me, don't you think?"

It is good to get back into the soothing comfort of a routine. With Bob assuming management responsibilities, I am devoting all my time to baking in this, the busiest season of the year. Bob is far more organized than I, as far as administrative tasks are concerned, and things have gone much smoother since he took over. This morning, I concentrate on filling a large order of champagne truffles for an office Christmas party. As I open the upper cabinet for the bottle of hazelnut syrup, I notice that Bob has posted a printout of the weekly cleaning schedule on the door. Previously I used to enlist staff members to specific cleaning tasks on an ad hoc basis.

Within minutes, newspaper under his arm, Bob walks in. In a crewneck sweater, heavyweight cotton pants, and new loafers, he's far better dressed than he once was. He has redyed his purple strand of hair to its original black. There's a certain confidence to his movements, like he knows what he'll do next. We greet each other and, before I can compliment him on his organizational ability, he blurts out, "Well, they finally announced Donald J. Smith's replacement."

"Who is it?"

"Some restaurant critic from Washington, D.C. What I can't figure out is how an outsider would be expected to understand the Seattle food scene. Although, I must say, it's been a relief not to have Donald sniping at our bakery."

"It's funny, but I actually miss old Donald."

"You can't be serious, Sunya."

"I'm serious. And I regret that I may have had a hand in his dismissal from the paper."

"He'd have been fired anyway. There were so many negative reactions to his column."

"He had a right to be the way he was."

"Maybe, but the newspaper still has to pay attention to readers' comments, and he was getting to be a laughingstock. Anyway, I hear he's staying home these days. He never did take that trip. Apparently, his health isn't good."

Bob sets the newspaper down on the counter, washes his hands, and starts sectioning some mandarin oranges. Silently I send Donald my warmest wishes for recovery. Someday we may run into each other; and I hope to make my peace with him then. But for the present, I continue melting chocolate, a small batch at a time.

An hour later, taking a breather, I walk over to the retail area. It's about half full. I am startled to find Jim Paradise at a table. The windbreaker he wears reminds me that a storm has been forecast. He has a book at his elbow, though it's not open. As I approach him, he straightens up from the remnants of an orange-pecan muffin.

"Ah, Sunya, you're back. Did you make this?"

I nod happily.

"So fresh and light. It's still warm. Must have just come out of the oven. And this homemade cranberry-orange marmalade is incredible. I'd forgotten how habit-forming your bakery is. I brought my wife here a couple of weeks ago and I've been back three times already. By the way, I've been meaning to get in touch with you."

"Anything in particular . . . ?"

"Have a seat."

As I grab the arm of a chair, Jim's voice turns low and serious. "I know about your line of credit at Home Street Bank. That helps. My assistant is preparing a new three-year lease agreement for you."

Mutely I thank Dushan. A smile, I feel, is coming to my lips. The moment of celebration fades, as Jim adds, "But . . . Cartdale is suing me over a clause in the lease agreement."

"What are you going to do?" I ask, once the shock subsides.

"I'm countersuing him. If only I'd known in advance what kind of a . . ." Jim pauses, stabs his fork at the last piece of muffin. "You'll be pleased to hear that the grand opening of his Wallingford branch has been scrapped."

"Truly? Why, that's a relief. The best Christmas present anyone could give me. Oh, these last few months . . ." I notice a dark gloom falling over Jim's face.

"Your problems are far from over, Sunya. Even though Cartdale won't be opening his bakery on my Meridian Street property, he's already scouting for alternative sites in the vicinity. It's only a temporary delay for his plan. Apparently, he's of the opinion that Wallingford is a choice area for what he calls 'big business penetration.' It's been a sleepy residential neighborhood for too long. He'd like to wake it up."

"I'll be prepared if and when he 'wakes us up.' Meanwhile I'll serve my customers as best I can."

"I wish I could be as Zen about it as you are." He sighs, glances at his empty plate, makes a motion to rise. "I think I'll have one more muffin. I'm running a race this weekend, so I'll burn up the extra calories. At least that's what I tell myself."

I rush to the kitchen to brief my staff. Survival, in our fragrant little nook, is a chancy, day-by-day proposition. Like relishing a wild strawberry patch on the hillside before the bear makes its appearance, I remind them and myself.

The yellow of butter still smeared on my hand, I am loading the pastry case with a tray full of daisy buns—golden puff pastry nestled beneath a sugar-frosted bumpy top—when I hear a cherished voice ringing out gently, "Sunya!"

"Andrew!" My comfort, the tendermost spot in my heart, so huggable in his white Irish cable knit sweater. He must have got the second message I left for him. In this instant of pure bliss, I edge around the pastry case. Weeks of miserable separation melt into a tight embrace, a secure feeling. Secretly I hope he's divorced by now. We let go of each other only because it is a public place and we don't want to put on a show.

The eyes from behind the glasses are eloquent. "You're back. How was the trip?"

"Fabulous."

"The healing program . . . ?"

"I got a lot out of it."

"I almost didn't recognize you. A new Sunya."

Even as I accept his compliment, I am eager to find out which ending he finally chose for his script, the final title of the film, and its release date. More than that, with every atom of my being, I am dying to be with him, to rest my face fondly against his chest, to take comfort in his touch and kiss.

"You missed our wrap party," he says.

"We must get together soon."

"Save tomorrow evening for me."

"I will."

Tomorrow seems like a faraway harbor. Bringing my attention back to the pastry case, I offer him a daisy bun that I've just baked and whose aroma is perfuming the air. A short, impatient line has formed behind him.

His gaze burrows into mine. "Sunya . . . I want to stay . . . but I'm late for a meeting. I'll just get a coffee to go."

Cup in hand, he walks away. Such a brief visit. I stare after him, taking in every last detail of his even-paced walk. At the door, he turns, smiles with reserve, and waves. A few seconds transpire before I can fall back in step with the task at hand.

FORTY-SIX

Buried in the stack of mail waiting for me at home, I find an envelope from Kimiko. It is addressed in her familiar neat script, but the stationery is plain white, rather than the usual warm peach. I take a seat at my desk and scan the contents of the letter.

Dear Sunya-san,

By the time this reaches your mailbox, you will have returned from Japan. I am happy that you were able to visit my country. It makes me feel closer to you in a way I can't explain.

Though we discussed Roger briefly a few weeks ago, I didn't confide in you completely. So, now, I feel compelled to offer you a confession. I was smitten by Roger the first time I met him at your house, and hated it that you, a non-Japanese, were living with him. I convinced myself that you had no right to such an attractive Japanese man. Not only did I deserve him more as my birthright, but I could take care of him and understand him in ways that were beyond a gaikokujinn josei.

I was taught from childhood how to please a man, espe-

cially one who is Japanese. Shamelessly I followed him to his global trade meetings and kept inviting him to my place afterward. At first, he refused, but then on a rainy night, he relented. He was vulnerable at the time, because your bakery had become well-known, you were the public's darling, and he was feeling more than a little threatened. In my apartment, he was torn by feelings of guilt and betrayal, but I massaged his body until he felt completely free and loose and willing.

Had I not tried so hard, he would have stayed with you, I'm sure.

How awful of me. I betrayed not only a sister, but also myself. And all for a relationship — no, an affair — that lasted only a few months.

I regret that I ruined your love. You trusted me as a friend and I proved unworthy. I presented a pleasant face to you, but inside I burned, burned, burned. I am filled with remorse and will remain so till the end of my days.

I am hoping for your forgiveness, but if that is not possible, I will understand.

Yours,

Kimiko

I sit with the letter, as the past washes over me, bringing with it the tears and insecurities of a severed relationship. Instead of banishing those thoughts, I allow them to sink in. It's finally okay to feel this low, to go back and reexperience events that I wish had never happened, to see how long the dark sensations last. Eventually, the reminiscences lose their hold over me—they dissipate in the glow of a newfound sense of inner energy, then fade away.

Now is the time to reach deep within for the compassion that could ease Kimiko's sufferings. As I slip into the deepness of silence, slowly, gently, I sense a weight being lifted from two souls.

I open a desk drawer, pull out some pretty stationery and a ball-point, and soon my sure steady hand moves across the paper.

> *Dear Kimiko,*
>
> *My trip to Japan was extraordinary. And it has helped in responding to your letter. I might have reacted differently in the past and we both would have been the worse for it. At best, I might never have answered.*
>
> *Thank you for being so open and honest and sharing with me an episode that must have been difficult to tell. I am in awe of your courage and integrity. Both our situations have so changed that any further discussions would be pointless. It just feels good to draw the heavy dark curtain on that episode of my life and, hopefully, yours.*
>
> *What is there to forgive? You're on a new road, doubtless with trials and tribulations along the way, and so am I. Please don't be too hard on yourself. I stopped holding any anger toward you by the time I finished reading your letter. Then as I sat with thoughts about you, it came to me that only a forgiving attitude would wipe out our mutual misery.*
>
> *Yours,*
> *Sunya*

With care, I seal the envelope. Kimiko's face shimmers before me, no longer coldly perfect but somehow easier to carve in my memory. I doubt I'll hear from her again soon, although one day we just might find ourselves sharing a *sanposhimas* through the gardens of Kyoto's Nanzen-ji temple. We'll stop to greet each other and chat under the shade of a camellia tree. Then she might suggest taking tea and I would hesitate at first, then eventually agree. It might take some time for us to get back to the warm closeness of the time when fuchsias were the only topic between us. But then, when it comes to friendships, one can always hope for a fresh new start.

FORTY-SEVEN

IT IS EVENING AND MOTHER HAS JUST ARRIVED AFTER A DAY OF SHOPPING downtown. I've invited her over for dinner, with some trepidation, I must admit. We're sitting in the living room, where Mother, wearing a celadon sweater-and-slacks set, is cradling a glass of cherry juice and chatting about her fruitless daylong search for a dining set.

"I decided not to make a purchase today. There wasn't much out there and, besides, I wasn't in the mood."

She must be referring to my father, how his memory must have spoiled her day. That puts me even more on edge. Then I notice the change. Mother's expression is one of quiet acceptance. Her posture is straight but relaxed. Her feet are firmly placed on the carpet.

"I had a long talk with Dushan," she says. "He helped me come to terms with the whole thing when he said 'Had your husband not left, Dee, I'd never have met you.' He hugged me tight like he couldn't bear the thought. Then I realized everything had worked out for the best. You know, Sunya, your father never once held me like that. Yes, there were several gifts in this situation for me . . ." Her voice coagulates. "And I'm glad you finally met your father. You really needed that."

Once again, I see Father walking, sitting, and talking. I hear the serenity of his voice and feel his spirit expanding into the room. Meeting him has helped soften a corner of my heart, validated who I am as a person, and made me feel whole. "From time to time, I'll be traveling back to Japan to see what he found there."

Mother drains the last of her cherry juice, making sure not a drop is left, and gives out a reddish-purple smile. *"Tumi koro."* You might do that.

Now, with her looking suitably content, I can accomplish another mission. I rise from my chair. "Come, I have something to show you."

We go over to the south wall of my bedroom where two photos hang. Mother takes a long look at the one with the rosewood frame. "Why, you've made a little shrine, haven't you?" Then she steps back. "Now that I've put it all behind, I still feel terribly sad, but I have no more regrets. *Ek dom na.*" None at all.

"He asked for your forgiveness, Mother . . ."

"I see that he was a man bigger than the life I could have made for him. If his family in India had known about his accomplishments, not just academic either, they'd have been proud. *Maha manush,* they'd have called him." A man of great integrity. "He really lived up to the high ideals, impractical in my opinion if you ask me, that India instilled in him."

Eyelids heavy, her face swollen, she seems lost in her reverie as she perhaps recalls her early years in India. How much she left behind. How that pushed her to a new life. In a few seconds, she casts off her thoughts, pushes a forelock back, and faces me.

"Well, are you going to feed me, Sunya? I'm famished."

"Dinner's ready. Pasta and curry primavera."

"That'll be perfect."

I smile into her moist eyes as we adjourn to the kitchen.

FORTY-EIGHT

IT'S JUST ABOUT DUSK WHEN I ARRIVE AT ANDREW'S PLACE, WEARING A SILK blouse with billowy sleeves, an A-line skirt, and mid-calf boots. I've put my hair up in a chignon, something I rarely do. As I tap the doorbell lightly, its gentle airy chiming complements my mood. I take a moment to visualize Andrew's pleasure, the delight in his eyes as they alight on the gifts in my tote bag. From the condominium across the hallway, quarreling voices strike a discordant note.

On the third ring, Andrew's brother Evan opens the door, his autumn-brown hair a shade darker than usual, obviously damp. He bears more than a passing resemblance to Andrew around the eyebrows and lips.

"Sorry, Sunya, didn't hear you. I was in the shower. Come on in. I don't know when Andrew will be back, but you're certainly welcome to wait."

The wait I didn't expect.

Evan motions toward the seating area, then hurries off toward his bedroom, pausing halfway there long enough to say, "Andrew's leaving very early tomorrow, but you probably know that already. This'll be the last chance to catch him."

I hear the closing of a door.

The last soft light of the day fades before my eyes. The air in the room is dense as in a dust storm. I wander into the open kitchen. The refrigerator hums annoyingly. The fruit basket is empty except for a twig with a shriveled leaf attached to it. I remove the cake box from my bag and slide it onto the tiled kitchen counter. On a whim, I open the top flap and inhale the fresh fragrance of the tiered cake cloaked with chocolate icing and studded with Bosc pear slices. It is as perfect as any I've ever assembled. I picture Andrew taking a bite, losing himself in the sensations of taste and texture for a few moments, then raising his face with the expression of ecstasy that goes back to the beginning of our relationship.

Evan emerges, jangling a set of car keys, his gaze fixed on the cake. "Sunya Cake?"

I manage a facsimile of a smile.

"Never seen a whole one before. It sure is a beaut and it smells great. I'll have to try it later. I've got to run off now, though. Good to see you again, Sunya."

I mumble a listless farewell to his back, then stroll over to the window and part the jacquard-woven curtains. Blue-purple shadows are creeping across Green Lake. Here and there, building lights are flashing on to fight off the long enervating hours of December darkness, a darkness that already presses down on me. As I watch, cars snarl by down on the street below in a mechanical world that seems hectic and noise-prone. Here in Andrew's living room, I am only aware of the vague passage of time, second by second, quietly, gradually, ineluctably.

How long have I been standing like this? My fingers have turned cold and stiff. What is on the far side of the lofty peak called anticipation? With a start, I spin and walk over to Andrew's bedroom.

I stare at the disarray. This is where we made love, our first and only time. The room was neat and orderly then, the bed inviting. The dresser mirror reflected each of us to the other in the soft light. I rotate away from the mirror's taunting stare now.

How different the space appears, how remote it feels. The bed, bereft of its sheets, seems somber and cold; the feather pillows, stripped of their embroidered covers, look flabby and sallow. Two half-packed suitcases clutter the floor: shirts, pants, sunglasses, and underwear, a Frisbee too. Open suitcases are not only ugly, but also malevolent obstacles that trip you no matter which way you turn.

A man on the move. A man who does what he wants, yesterday's promises forgotten.

It is then my eyes focus on a note propped up on the dressing table—plain white paper and blue ink, a familiar script—addressed to me. My fingers hesitate to pick it up; they recoil from grasping the still-burning embers of a dying fire.

> *Dear Sunya,*
>
> *A postproduction crisis has come up and, as usual, I'm the one who has to put everything back together. Please forgive this note. I wanted to spend my last evening in your lovely company, holding your hand and looking deep into your eyes. I tried calling you but, by then, you'd already left your house. I'm just sorry that I wasn't able to be there to explain all of this in person.*
>
> *Wish you could come with me to L.A. I have to go back, you know. I just can't handle the gloomy weather and mellowness of Seattle. I need the chaotic energy and intense sunshine of L.A. to function.*
>
> *You've indicated that your life is here with your bakery and I have to respect that. I have no doubt you'll do well. I don't*

suppose I could persuade you to open a bakery in L.A.?
Sunya Cake would be a huge hit there. The enclosed card
has my address and home phone numbers.

In the future, if you can manage some free time, I'd like
very much for you to come visit me. I'll show you my town
and all that makes life worth living for me. Who knows,
maybe I could even change your mind.

Meanwhile, I'll certainly miss you. The taste of Sunya
Cake and the memories of our times together will remain
with me. You are a rare person. You've brought out feelings
in me that I thought I'd lost forever.

Do catch my film, whose final title is A Season of Love,
when it's released next year. I chose the ending you sug-
gested. It's really the most logical one, and I can never thank
you enough. I'm dedicating the film to my parents and an
unnamed friend who inspired me. That friend is you.

I hope you'll forgive me, if not now, someday.

> *With deepest love,*
> *Andrew*

I read the note a few more times and still the meaning doesn't sink
in. Sadness and a sense of loss have slowed my comprehension. Why
did the season have to end so prematurely? With weary fingers, I put
the note back where it lay before.

Should I compose an answer? What could it possibly say? The end
of a script is an exhausting moment.

Through stinging eyes, I grope in my tote bag and retrieve an
index card inscribed with my most cherished possession. Years of baking have culminated in this recipe for Sunya Cake he loved so much.
Last night I had to overcome a fanatical inner resistance to writing

out the step-by-step instructions, the precise measurements for each ingredient, and notations indicating the best brands to use. After I had signed my name at the bottom and put the pen to rest, I felt serene.

Now, as I hold the recipe card, its gilt edges glistening, an episode from childhood sparkles in my mind. It was the day I went to the Puyallup Fair, carrying in my pants pocket a meager allowance saved over several months. I took rides till I was nauseated, laughed till my belly cramped, and agonized, as the setting sun bathed the merry crowd in its honey glow, that I'd blown my last cent. Upon returning home, when I emptied my pants pockets, I found that a few coins were stuck at the bottom. What a thrill. Even when you think you've spent it all, you probably still have a secret reserve to go on. The trick is to have faith, to keep looking until you find it. That's the great secret of life I stumbled on that day.

The words on the recipe card blur. I place it on a pillow and stare at it fondly for a moment. With affection, I whisper, "Dear Andrew," and blow a kiss gently into the air.

A moment later, I walk out of his condominium surefooted, with shoulders back, breathing in the night's soothing breeze.

READING GROUP GUIDE

PASTRIES

1. Lately there has been an explosion of literature by Indian authors. Is *Pastries* a departure from these works?

2. Talk about the structure of the novel, the many plotlines, the story-within-a-story methods used to bring a full cast of characters from the bakery onto the stage.

3. Discuss the sensuous writing—colors, smells, shapes, and tastes. Comment on the significance of food and the symbols it represents.

4. How would you describe the relationship between Sunya and her mother? How does Sunya's mother contribute to the story?

5. Discuss the betrayals that change the lives of the characters, such as Sunya's father leaving his family and Kimiko stealing Roger from Sunya.

6. The story takes place during the historic 1999 World Trade Conference in Seattle. Comment on the globalization issues we face today and those that this novel brings out.

7. Talk about the lessons in mindfulness Sunya learns in Japan? Do you see yourself needing this type of teaching? If so, how would you apply these principles to your life?

8. Seattle and Japan form the backdrops for the story. How well does the author evoke these settings?

9. How does Sunya evolve over the span of the story? Will she be able to make a life for herself despite her losses?

For more reading group suggestions visit
www.stmartins.com

Get a
Griffin St. Martin's Griffin